STORIES OF PEOPLE & CIVILIZATION
SLAVIC
ANCIENT ORIGINS

FLAME TREE PUBLISHING
6 Melbray Mews, Fulham,
London SW6 3NS, United Kingdom
www.flametreepublishing.com

First published and copyright © 2024
Flame Tree Publishing Ltd

24 26 28 27 25
1 3 5 7 9 10 8 6 4 2

ISBN: 978-1-80417-618-4

All rights reserved. No part of this publication may be reproduced, stored in a retrieval system, or transmitted in any form or by any means, electronic, mechanical, photocopying, recording or otherwise, without the prior written permission of the publisher.

Cover and pattern art was created by Flame Tree Studio, with elements courtesy of Shutterstock.com/svekloid/RedKoala/Lawkeeper. Additional interior decoration courtesy of Shutterstock.com/Dreambook.

Judith John (lists of Ancient Kings & Leaders) is a writer and editor specializing in literature and history. A former secondary school English Language and Literature teacher, she has subsequently worked as an editor on major educational projects, including *English A: Literature* for the Pearson International Baccalaureate series. Judith's major research interests include Romantic and Gothic literature, and Renaissance drama.

A copy of the CIP data for this book is available
from the British Library.

Designed and created in the UK | Printed and bound in China

COLLECTOR'S EDITIONS

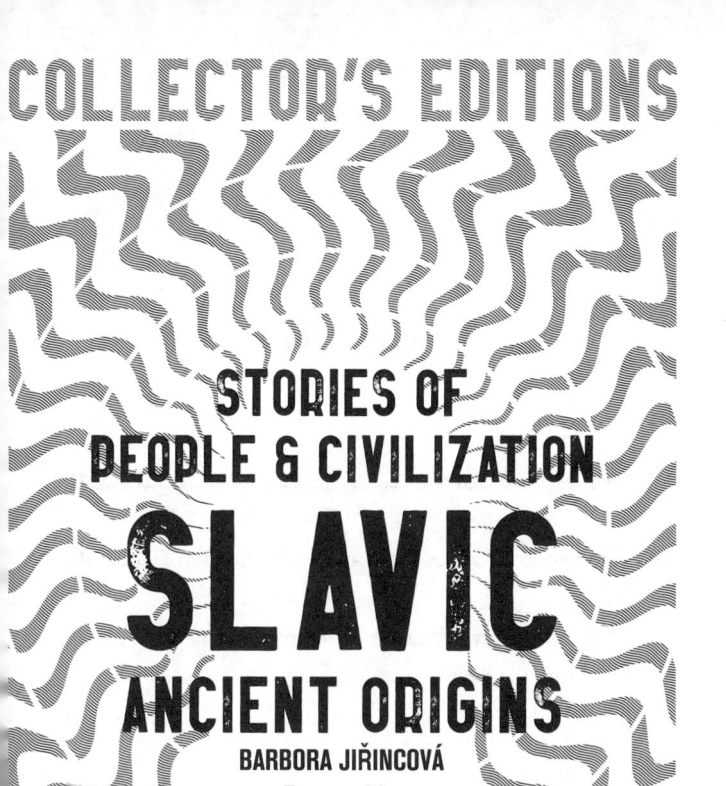

STORIES OF PEOPLE & CIVILIZATION
SLAVIC
ANCIENT ORIGINS

BARBORA JIŘINCOVÁ

Foreword by
DR. ALEXANDRA VUKOVICH

Further Reading and
Lists of Ancient Kings & Leaders

FLAME TREE PUBLISHING

CONTENTS

Series Foreword 12

Foreword by Dr. Alexandra Vukovich 15

Introduction to Slavic Ancient Origins 22
Who are the Slavs? 23
The Structure of this Book 25

Further Reading 30

The Dark Ages 34
How the First Slavs Lived 35
The Sources of Our Knowledge in the Dark Ages 38
Let Us Visit the Land 41
The Most Ancient Origins of the Slavs 43
The Ancient Slavs' Ordinary Lives 48
How the Slavs Lived and Did They Trade? 52
What Did the Ancient Slavs Believe in? 55

CONTENTS

The Origin of the Word 63
The Slavs Finally Set out on the Journey 65

The Migration Period 67
Migration or Invasion? 67
The Migration Begins 72
The Byzantium and the Slavs 76
The First Slavic Invasion 79
The Slavs and the Avars 80
Francia and the Franks 86

The First Slavic States 89
New Political Reality of the Seventh Century 89
Slavic Myths of Origin 92
Samo's Empire: An Unlikely Alliance of a Frank and
    Slavs Against the Avars 101
Pannonian Plain and the End of the Avars 107

Great Moravia 113
Pribina and Mojmir 113
Mojmir and His Moravia 118
Rastislav: On the Way to Great Moravia 122
The Mission of Constantine and Methodius 128
Svatopluk the Great 140
The Hungarian Invasion 142
The Legacy of Great Moravia 143

The First Bulgarian Empire 145
Who were the Bulgars? 145
The First Bulgarian State Is Created 146
Justinian II and Tervel 148
Bulgarians Stop the Arabian Invasion 149
Krum the Great 150
Bulgaria Becomes a European Power 155
Boris I, the Bulgarian 157
Finally: The Baptism of Boris I 162
Boris, Vladimir and Symeon 165
The Decline of the First Bulgarian Empire 166
How the Bulgars Lived 167
The Legacy of the First Bulgarian Empire 169

The Serbian State 172
Vlastimirović Dynasty and the Serbian Beginnings 172
The Lifestyle in the Serbian Principality 180
The Legacy of the Serbian State 182
The Conclusion to the First Chapter 183

The Slavs Enter the Middle Ages 185
The Europe of the Ninth Century 185
The Slavs Enter the Middle Ages 188

The Kyivan Rus 190
The Slavs Found Kyiv 191
The Slavs of Kyivan Rus 192

CONTENTS

The Vikings Enter the Scene 193
Kyivan Rus: An Introduction 200
Oleg and the Magician 203
Igor Ascends the Throne.. 204
Olga: The Mother Ruler 205
Sviatoslav Rules Independently... 209
Vladimir the Great: The Last Pagan................................... 210
Yaroslav the Wise... 219
The Fall and Decline of Kyivan Rus................................... 224
The Legacy of Kyivan Rus 227

Bohemia: The Slavs in the Heart of Europe.....230
The Dark Ages in Bohemia.. 231
The Eighth Century 233
The Přemyslid Dynasty Emerges from the Darkness 239
Spytihněv I: The Provider of Stability and Prosperity ... 240
Vratislav I and Drahomíra... 243
Saint Wenceslaus and the Beginning of His Reign 252
Boleslav I: the Builder of the Czech State........................ 263
Boleslav II the Pious (c. 932–999) 267
Adalbert of Prague: The Third Bohemian Saint............. 269
The First Dynastic Crisis 275
Oldřich and Břetislav: The Father and Son..................... 276
The Legacy of Bohemian State 286

The Shooting Star of Poland..289
The Founding Myth of the Polish Dynasty..................... 289
Mieszko I: Poland Emerges.. 291

Boleslav I the Brave 297
The Legacy of the First Kingdom of Poland 304

The Kingdom of Croatia 307
The Duchy of Croatia 308
Vladislav and Mislav 308
The Tripimirovic Dynasty 309
The Legacy of the Tripimic Dynasty: Croatia under
    Hungarian Rule 314

Ancient Slavic Origins: The Story Goes On 317
The Story of Slavic States 317
The Spectre of Nationalism 319
The Slavs of Today and Their Origins 321

Ancient Kings & Leaders 323

STORIES OF PEOPLE & CIVILIZATION

SLAVIC ANCIENT ORIGINS

STORIES OF PEOPLE & CIVILIZATION
SLAVIC
ANCIENT ORIGINS

SERIES FOREWORD

Stretching back to the oral traditions of thousands of years ago, tales of heroes and disaster, creation and conquest have been told by many different civilizations, in ways unique to their landscape and language. Their impact sits deep within our own culture even though the details in the stories themselves are a loose mix of historical record, the latest archaeological evidence, transformed narrative and the unwitting distortions of generations of storytellers.

Today the language of mythology lives around us: our mood is jovial, our countenance is saturnine, we are narcissistic and our modern life is hermetically sealed from others. The nuances of the ancient world form part of our daily routines and help us navigate the information overload of our interconnected lives.

The nature of a myth is that its stories are already known by most of those who hear or read them. Every era brings a new emphasis, but the fundamentals remain the same: a desire to understand and describe the events and relationships of the world. Many of the great stories are archetypes that help us find our own place, equipping us with tools for self-understanding, both individually and as part of a broader culture.

For Western societies it is Greek mythology that speaks to us most clearly. It greatly influenced the mythological heritage of the ancient Roman civilization and is the lens through which we still see the Celts, the Norse and many of the other great peoples and religions. The Greeks themselves inherited much from their neighbours, the Egyptians, an older culture that became weary with the mantle of civilization.

Of course, what we perceive now as mythology had its own origins in perceptions of the divine and the rituals of the sacred. The earliest civilizations, in the crucible of the Middle East, in the Sumer of the third millennium BCE, are the source to which many of the mythical archetypes can be traced. Over five thousand years ago, as humankind collected together in cities for the first time, developed writing and industrial-scale agriculture, started to irrigate the rivers and attempted to control rather than be at the mercy of its environment, humanity began to write down its tentative explanations of natural events, of floods and plagues, of disease.

Early stories tell of gods or god-like animals who are crafty and use their wits to survive, and it is not unreasonable to suggest that these were the first rulers of the gathering peoples of the earth, later elevated to god-like status with the distance of time. Such tales became more political as cities vied with each other for supremacy, creating new gods, new hierarchies for their pantheons. The older gods took on primordial roles and became the preserve of creation and destruction, leaving the new gods to deal with more current, everyday affairs. Empires rose and fell, with Babylon assuming the mantle from Sumeria in the 1800s BCE, in turn to be swept away by the Assyrians of the 1200s BCE; then the Assyrians and the Egyptians were subjugated by the Greeks, the Greeks by the Romans and so on, leading to the spread and assimilation of common themes, ideas and stories throughout the world.

The survival of history is dependent on the telling of good tales, but each one must have the 'feeling' of truth, otherwise it will be ignored. Around firesides, or embedded in a book or a computer, the myths and legends of the past are still the living materials of retold myth, not restricted to an exploration of historical origins. Now we have devices and global communications that give us unparalleled access to a diversity of traditions. We can find out about Indigenous American, Indian, Chinese and tribal African mythology in a way that was denied to our ancestors, we can find connections, plot the archaeology, religion and the mythologies of the world to build a comprehensive image of the human experience that is both humbling and fascinating.

The books in this series introduce the many cultures of ancient humankind to the modern reader. From the earliest migrations across the globe to settlements along rivers, from mountainous landscapes to vast steppes, from woodlands to deserts, humanity has adapted to its environments, nurturing languages and observations and expressing itself through records, mythmaking stories and living traditions. There is still so much to explore, but this is a great place to start.

Jake Jackson
General Editor

FOREWORD

Slavic history, just like the Slavic people, is a historiographic, literary and political construct. It is an idea born of nineteenth- and twentieth-century aesthetic, literary and political movements, such as pan-Slavism, a nineteenth-century Romantic nationalist movement that sought to unite the so-called Slavic peoples under a political banner. Often this political banner was associated with repressed cultural groups (or nations) under Austro-Hungarian or Ottoman suzerainty, but it was also a method for powerful 'Slavic' nations, like the Russian Empire, to present themselves as the emancipatory leaders of the Slavs. Of course, pan-Slavism was neither the only, nor was it the most compelling, ethno-supremacist movement of the nineteenth century. Turanism (a Shamano-Turkic Eurasianist movement) and Aryanism (the Germano-Nordic ethnoracist movement embraced by the Nazis) bore great resemblance to and shared the same pseudo-scientific basis with pan-Slavism. This is key in understanding both the development of the field of Slavic history, as well as the author's, Barbora Jiřincová, repeated emphasis that Slavic represents a linguistic and loose cultural group, connected by language, custom and history-writing. So, what is Slavic history and who are the Slavs? As Jiřincová emphasizes, they are neither a circumscribed territory (like a single nation or state) nor are they a group of people linked through genetics. In summary, neither blood nor soil define the Slavs.

In her eminently readable assessment, Jiřincová points out that the Slavs are, in effect, speakers of a language known as Slavic (or Slavonic), a language with a writing system that first appeared in the Balkans in the early medieval period, first written down by the saintly monks, Cyril and Methodius in the ninth century. The earliest alphabet, known as Glagolitic, would be foreign to the modern eastern Slavic reader, who would be much more likely to recognize its uncial cousin, the Cyrillic script. Many of the letters that exist in modern Cyrillic alphabets today, derive from this script. Of course, all Slavic languages do not employ the Cyrillic script, nor are all languages employing the Cyrillic script Slavic languages. As Jiřincová shows us, it is language that determines a certain unity for the Slavic world. The historical cohesiveness of Old Church Slavonic determined the trajectory of Slavic culture, coupling it with Eastern Christianity (also Latin Christianity) and its literature, but also its icons and iconography.

In the case of Slavic, religion determined writing. The first Slavic texts were mainly translations of the Bible, Byzantine saints' lives (hagiography) and numerous other Eastern Christian religious texts useful for monastic study and for leading the congregation. Besides translations from Greek, native writing in Slavic most often focussed on the deeds and misdeeds of the various Slavic-speaking dynasties that arose east of the Elbe: whether the Nemanjids in medieval Serbia or the Riurikids of early Rus, medieval Slavic texts recounted vibrant tales of emergent dynasties. It is these tales that inform Jiřincová's vivid storytelling, such as the travels and travails of

FOREWORD

Princess Olga of medieval Kyiv who, by the same token, adopted Christianity and was baptised by the Byzantine emperor's own hand, and who avenged her husband by inventing various lethal torments for his murderers. This stock of princely characters was depicted in various medieval texts, including princely biographies (for the Serbian Nemanjid princes) or princely chronicles (for the Rus) or even saints' lives (like the holy king Wenceslaus). As Jiřincová relates, so much of what we know about Slavic history and the Slavic peoples is filtered through a distinctly elite and highly stylized group of sources. These texts, usually produced either by the official Church (or monastic milieu) or at the courts of local dynasts, relate an exciting and biased story about the Slavs, from a distinctly religious and kingly perspective.

Nevertheless, Jiřincová's book brings to life both the princely characters of medieval Slavic books and manuscripts, while exploring Slavic folklore through custom, material culture and oral culture. This is a book that weaves formal historiography with an engaging narrative style, it retells old tales in an engaging manner, while making salient important points of historiography; namely, that the story of the Slavs is neither the story of a nation nor of a single people, rather it is the story of a language and its speakers and writers.

Dr. Alexandra Vukovich

STORIES OF PEOPLE & CIVILIZATION
SLAVIC
ANCIENT ORIGINS

SLAVIC ANCIENT ORIGINS

INTRODUCTION
& FURTHER READING

INTRODUCTION TO SLAVIC ANCIENT ORIGINS

Everything possible to be believed is an image of truth.
Willian Blake, 'Proverbs of Hell', *The Marriage of Heaven and Hell,* **1790-93**

Imagine the scene if you will:

It is midnight, and František Palacký (1798–1876) is sitting at his table and finishing the first part of his masterpiece. He is writing the history of the mighty Slavic nation. Palacký fills his book with accounts of valiant warriors who fight only when need be; they go to war only to protect their diligent wives and beloved children. These warriors take advice from wise elders, who know how to live in perfect harmony with nature and keep to rituals that ensure the land will yield fruit year after year. They do not fight for power among each other and respect their neighbours as equals, as there is no ruler above them. Palacký is a historian; he consults the sources, yet he knows very well that the sources are scarce. He realizes that his imagination has to amend for what they do not reveal.

Yet he does not feel uncomfortable about the liberty he takes when filling the blanks in the historical knowledge. Palacký's nation needs to know how great it used to be in order to fulfil its historical role. His compatriots need to realize what made Slavs different from Germans, what made them better than Germans. After all, the Germans did the same with their history. How he sometimes envied the German historians who had plenty of sources from ancient times. He and his Slavic colleagues had to make do with so little. Now the work is nearly finished, however, and he is content. Little does he know that centuries after him historians will work hard to uproot all the myths he and his like have created.

Yet he would not care, for at the time his nation demanded it. Those who come after will have their own battles to fight, their own questions to answer.

Today, we are ready to admit how little we know about the ancient origins of the Slavs. Arguably, it is possibility, not certainty, that makes history fascinating. The fewer sources we have, the less we know with certainty. We must be humble enough to admit this and to honour the secrets that history will keep from us for ever.

WHO ARE THE SLAVS?

We are in a hut in a small village near the forest, somewhere in the centre of Eastern Europe. A woman toils to make lunch for the family. With the grinding mill an invention of the distant future, she must bend low and grind the grain manually with a heavy stone. It is summer, and summers are warm in this country. Her simple clothes stick to her back as sweat breaks on her skin. But she does not stop, nor does she complain.

Life is good as long as there is grain for the bread, and maybe her husband will bring some game from the forest. She stops and thinks for a moment. Her husband. His shirt was torn beyond repair, and she had not yet finished the new one. It is her job to make clothes for the family. Unlike ladies in the Byzantine cities (places that she knows nothing about), she cannot buy clothes from the market; there is no market nearby. Still she does not complain. Life is good, there is grain today and there will be grain next year, for the priests will make sure of that.

Slavs lived relatively primitively, even in the sixth century. Their homeland was too far from the main trade routes and the cultural influence of the Mediterranean world. They even took longer to learn the skill of sword making, as there was very little ore in their homeland. Later, they came into contact with the Roman world, and later still the more prosperous Vikings. Even the Slavs' painful relationship with the Avars helped to elevate their lifestyle. The Avars plundered and did not build – but in their plunder they travelled far and brought novelties even to their subjects, the Slavs.

As soon as the Slavs set on a journey to settle in new places, however, they learned quickly. Unlike their ancestors in the homeland between the Vistula and the Dnieper River, each branch faced different challenges. Soon their ways and culture began to differ.

The Western Slavs in Central Europe met with the Holy Roman Empire, a German-speaking federation of states and free cities. Later on, the Hungarian element came into play. The Eastern Slavs had to face a Mongolian invasion – an encounter that proved fatal for Kyivan Rus and formative for the future state of Russia. The Slavic nations fought for their statehood against and within the Byzantine Empire on the Balkan Peninsula. Much later, they fell under the dominion of the Ottoman Turks.

The Colourful World of the Slavs

The Slavs are the most numerous ethnic group in Europe, but we know relatively little about their ancient past. Historians, and sometimes even politicians, have filled thousands and thousands of pages in discussing this subject. It is thus essential to understand this colourful and diverse part of European history.

The Slavs were the youngest of nations to enter European history and to create their states. With them, the shaping of Europe as we know it culminated around 1000 CE. Apart from similar languages, the Slavs share some traditions, mythology and rituals originating in pagan times. We can be certain that even as late as the eighth century the Slavs of all Europe understood one another and spoke a proto-Slavic language common to them all. The differentiation came later when states originated, each facing different political realities.

THE STRUCTURE OF THIS BOOK

This book follows both a chronological and geographical structure. We start in the possible Slavic homeland between the Vistula and the Dnieper River. Then we travel with the Slavs, first to the west to avoid the oppression of the violent Avars. We watch them struggle against the Franks over their place on the European political map and see them emerge victorious around 1000 CE.

Some of the Slavic tribes travel a little to the north. There they will give rise to Kyiv and create the marvel of Eastern Europe, the state of Kyivan Rus. Here these tribes live in perfect harmony with the Scandinavian Vikings, a rare example of Slavic and German elements working together to create something unique.

Last but not least, we see how Slavs populate the Balkan Peninsula. They begin to co-operate and compete with the colourful Mediterranean world, represented by the city of Venice, and to struggle against the glory of the Byzantine Empire for an enduring place on the map.

Geography Matters

We divide our narration into two main parts, one ending in the ninth century and the second in the tenth. Some Slavic states will spring up in each section and others will perish, leaving the historical records for a while. The first section focuses on the very first Slavic state-like formations: Samo's Empire, the Great Moravia, the first Bulgarian Empire and the first Serbian state. In these cases, we leave the Slavs defeated and trampled under their enemies' heavy feet. It was too early, but their history still brings thrilling stories.

Here we read of the mysterious Frank, Samo, whom the Slavic leaders persuaded to lead them in their rebellion against their Avar masters; in the end, they fought against the mighty Franks themselves. We learn how the Moravian Rastislav engaged in diplomatic games and brought Byzantine teachers to Moravia. One of them, a linguistic genius, created a new language and a script that people in Eastern Europe still use today. Their stories will continue to be told far into in the future.

The second section ends on a more optimistic note. At least half of the protagonists, the Czechs and the Poles, secure a homeland to make their own. And they will hold these places for a thousand years, withstanding perils and disasters beyond the scope of this book. However, this section also tells of the bitter end of the two remaining heroes of our story, the Kyivan Rus and the Croatian kingdom. In Kyiv, the literate scholars and ladies dressed in silk shivered, realizing that the walls of the splendid city would not save them from the Mongol hordes outside. We may spare readers a description of the massacres that followed, in which only 2,000 of the city's 50,000 inhabitants survived.

And so Kyivan Rus fell. But states do come and go, and people still remember. The remembrance can create a lot of good and a lot of evil, as the present conflict in the east of Europe shows. For the war that started in Ukraine in 2022 is all about the question of to whom the Kyivan Rus belongs. The destruction of Kyiv by the Mongols some 800 years ago may horrify us, but we must save our tears for the living.

The Ethnicity in the Early Middle Ages

Each section tells the story of Slavic states created in a particular place on the map. It is important, however, not to mistake the people living in that country for a nation in the modern sense. Nations as we understand them today did not exist until the nineteenth century. In the ninth and the tenth centuries people felt loyalty to their family, blood, tribe, village, leader and, later, to their state. They did not feel any allegiance to a nation, nor to an individual language. At that time common language was merely practical and apolitical. It mattered as a means of communication; you simply learned the tongue most people spoke when you came to a particular place. In the late ninth century most Slavs understood each other very well. Newcomers from different tribes, be they Germans, Avars or Bulgars, simply learned the language and adjusted to the lifestyle and culture; the majority accepted them. Ethnicity did not matter; what mattered was what tribe you came from. Later, when the tribal structure melted into the cauldron of the first Christian states, even tribal loyalty ceased to be a concern.

This happened because Christianity worked like a solvent to the old structures and loyalties, creating an entirely new society. The rulers of the first Slavic states, such as Kyivan Rus, Great Moravia, Poland or Bohemia, usually offered a replacement for the tribal loyalties. They gave their people a new identity.

We read in the oldest chronicles how Mieszko I, the first Polish duke, married a Czech princess and promised her to honour her Christian God. Even before that, he had unified all the Polish tribes under his rule and the chronicles called his subjects Polonians. But who were these Polonians? Did Mieszko himself come from the Polonian tribe? Historians have spent centuries trying to unravel the mystery, only to agree (relatively recently) that the Polonian tribe never actually existed. It was an artificial identity, created to bring all the rivalrous tribes under one rule, the Piast rule.

And then there are the cases of Kyiv and Bulgaria. Pure Scandinavians ruled Kyivan Rus and chose to mingle with their Slavic subjects, becoming like them in every way. The Bulgar Khans ruled the oldest Bulgaria with their belligerent tribe that spoke the Turkic language, yet most of their people were of Slavic origin. For years they lived together, learned from each other, mingled and married as members of one state. Today Bulgarian is a Slavic language and Bulgars see themselves as Slavs. They look with joy to their glorious past. So it is that we tell the story of Slavs in general, of the states they created, but not of Slavic ethnicity.

Contrary to national historians' belief, nationality has nothing to do with genetics, while ethnicity is far from given. To be part of a nation is a result of choice. Luckily for us, the very choice is usually visible in the historical records. It was the will of the people, or rather their elites, to be a part of something bigger that created the nation. The human will has made the first Slavic national states, not genes or blood.

FURTHER READING

Bursche, Aleksander, *The Migration Period Between the Oder and the Vistula* (Brill, 2020)

Charvát, Petr, *The Emergence of the Bohemian State* (Brill, 2010)

Čornej, Petr, *Great Stories in Czech History* (Práh 2005)

Crampton, R.J., *A Concise History of Bulgaria* (Cambridge University Press, 2006)

Cvetkovičm, Stephan, *Slavic Traditions & Mythology* (independently published, 2001)

Davies, Norman, *Heart of Europe: A Short History of Poland* (Oxford University Press, 1986)

Davies, Norman, *God's Playground: A History of Poland, Vol. 1: The Origins to 1795* (Columbia University Press, 2005)

Dawson, Christopher, *The Making of Europe: An Introduction to the History of European Unity* (The Catholic University of America Press, 2003)

Forbes, Nevill, *The Balkans: A History of Bulgaria and Serbia* (Pyrrhus Press, 2007)

Grudziński, Tadeusz, *Boleslav the Bold, Called Also the Bountiful, and Bishop Stanislaus: The Story of a Conflict* (Interpress Publishers, 1986)

Has, Petr, *Serbia and Montenegro History, and Separation: Europeanization, Ethnic Relations Ancient time, War time, People and Environment* (Createspace Independent Publishing Platform, 2016)

Hichens, Robert Smythe, *The Near East: Dalmatia, Greece and Constantinople* (1913; modern reprint: CreateSpace, 2015)

Hilmarova, Kytka, *Saint Wenceslaus: A Saintly King and Patron of the Czech People* (Czech Revival Publishing, 2023)

Kalhous, David, *Anatomy of a Duchy: The Political and Ecclesiastical Structures of Early Přemyslid Bohemia* (Brill, 2012)

Korolyshyn, Dan, *The Primary Chronicle of the Kyivan Rus* (Xulon Press, 2020)

Máchal, Jan and Gray L. Herbert, *Slavic Mythology* (Mythology eBooks, 2010)

Norwich, John Julius, *A Short History of Byzantium* (Vintage, 1998)

Pac, Grzegorz, *Women in the Piast Dynasty: A Comparative Study of Piast Wives and Daughters* (Brill, 2022)

Plokhy, Serhii, *The Gates of Europe: A History of Ukraine* (Basic Books, 2015)

Pohl, Walter, *The Avars: A Steppe Empire in Central Europe, 567–822* (Cornell University Press, 2018)

River, Charles (ed.), *The Slavs and the Slave Trade: The History of Enslaved Slavs across Eastern Europe and the Islamic World* (Charles River Editors, 2021)

Runciman, Stephen, *A History of the First Bulgarian Empire* (Lulu.com, 2018)

Snyder, Timothy, *The Reconstruction of Nations: Poland, Ukraine, Lithuania, Belarus 1569–1999* (Yale University Press, 2013)

Stepanov, Tsvetelin, *The Bulgars and the Steppe Empire in the Early Middle Ages: The Problem of the Others* (Brill, 2005)

Tachiaos, Anthony-Emil N., *Cyril and Methodius of Thessalonica: The Acculturation of the Slavs* (St Vladimir's Seminary, 2001)

Wilhoda, Marin and Jan Machacek, *The Fall of Great Moravia* (Brill, 2019)

Wilkin, Stanley, *Kyivan-Rus and Russia: Two Separate Roads Taken* (independently published, 2024)

Barbora Jiřincová (author) is a historian who loves taking different perspectives when studying history. She always remembers that even when history was written, the people suffering, celebrating or simply living in those moments were real. She specializes in the history of women and Central Europe; in 2020, she finished her PhD in History at Charles University in Prague. Now, she writes for TheCollector and Culture Frontier sites, and has her history blog therebelhistory.com.

Dr. Alexandra Vukovich (Foreword) is an assistant professor at King's College London in late medieval history, focusing on early Rus and medieval northern Eurasia. Following her work on early Rus chronicles, at the University of Cambridge, Alexandra has been exploring the development and politics of Slavonic historiography, as well as cross-cultural contacts in the Black Sea region through material culture.

STORIES OF PEOPLE & CIVILIZATION

THE DARK AGES

Before we move to the first Slavic states that sources reveal more about, we will dive into the so-called Dark Ages. We call the times from the fourth to the sixth centuries in Slavic history 'dark', but not because the people of those times would live in darkness. Their lives for sure were full of colour. They loved, bore children, played with them if time and worries permitted, fought and died. Basically, they desired what people of all times have wanted: to lead happy lives, have meaning and leave a legacy. We call these ages dark because we, as historians, stumble in ignorance.

The first Slavs left no written records. Instead we rely on written sources mainly from the Roman Empire, records that are full of misinterpretations. Their authors considered the Slavs primitive barbarians and described them as such. Sometimes they discuss them with a scientific curiosity – on other occasions with fear and disgust. Significantly, of the time when the Slavs lived in peace at the borders of the more evolved civilization, we know almost nothing. The Romans wrote about the Slavs only when conflicts arose or were imminent; their sources are thus scarce and far from objective. The information they provide must be combined with archaeological findings and linguistic research to create a more accurate picture of how people really lived and died.

HOW THE FIRST SLAVS LIVED

Here we focus on these Dark Ages and what we know and believe about the early Slavs' culture, mythology and lifestyle. We try to distinguish what historians believe to be valid from what they wish to be true for the sake of their nation's glory, like the writer seated at his desk in the opening section of this chapter.

It is certainly a challenging task. Modern historical science evolved from the late nineteenth century under the influence of romanticism and nationalism. At that time the Slavs in Europe competed in the political arena with the German element, with some of them favouring pan-Slavism. In the hope of securing protection from the biggest Slavic country, Russia, they sought evidence that Slavic tribes of the past shared as much in common as possible. European politicians have used Slavic history, for good or bad, for over two centuries. We will try to find the core under the confusion.

The truth about the first Slavs is more complex than it may appear, not least because the Slavs in the south, west and east soon acquired very different characteristics. Their culture, mentality and even their version of Christian religion varied as early as the tenth century. In the east, many generations worked hard to pay tribute to fearsome Mongol hordes. In the Balkans, they prospered under the formal dominion of the civilized Byzantine Empire. These influences shaped them in a myriad of ways: geography matters.

Slavic history is colourful, yet there was once one people and one language. Let us dive into their magical world.

The Slavs in the Dark Ages

In history, we search for answers to basic questions about our identity. Who we are, where we come from and where we should direct our steps. However, mystery shrouds the origins of the Slavs for many reasons.

First, historians are not entirely sure where to look for the motherland of the ancient Slavs.

We place it somewhere in Eastern Europe; the more precise location is a matter of dispute and many theories. The Slavs did not write, so they left no written records. Similar is the case of the oldest German, Turkic, Greek or Latin nations. The problem with the Slavs is that this absence of written sources lasted for a very long time. In Western Europe the Franks were already using Latin and writing books about their past and present when the Slavs first came to Europe and began to write down their chronicles.

Distance Matters

The disputed Slavic homeland lay too far from the Roman world. We know about the lifestyle of Germans in the first century CE, or that of the Huns two centuries later, because the Romans encountered them, fought them and traded with them. The mentality of explorers today, who travel deep into remote places to write about the people and animals living there, driven by a thirst for knowledge, is very different from the perspective of late antiquity and the early Middle Ages. The Romans and other literate nations of antiquity did not learn and write about other countries out of curiosity. Only their imminent neighbours, enemies in war or trading partners earned their interest. The rest were considered to be barbarians, illiterate and uninteresting.

The Slavs lived far from the Roman borders and, with few exceptions, gained the interest of Roman or later Byzantine writers only when their paths crossed. In contrast to the Avars or Huns, who travelled far and constantly threatened the empires, the Slavs had permanently settled in one place. They travelled only when they had to.

Second, the reason why few sources inform us about the ancient Slavs is their paganism. In keeping to their pagan religion for so long, they were excluded from the interest zone of the Christian Church that represented education and literature in the early Middle Ages. No churches and no monasteries meant no people of scripture, nor any reason for the Church as an institution to care for the pagans in the far lands. Some missionaries did come to preach to the pagans, their written records forming our primary source of knowledge about many barbarian nations in the first centuries CE. However, the image of a brave missionary coming to the pagan village alone and preaching to them because of the love of Christ is usually incorrect. The missionaries knew very well the danger and poor results of such an action.

Christianity and the Tribal Society

Christianity was considered dangerous by tribal pagan societies. A priest who taught that there was One God, and declaring all others to be false messengers of the devil, was not a mere nuisance. He was an insult to their existing gods, who would surely punish them if they did not dispose of him. Isolated missions did not run well and were a reliable means to fill the Christian pantheon of saints with martyrs. As a result, missionaries usually came to pagan lands only when invited by the elites of that particular land. Their missions were nearly always linked to politics. The Church sent their missionaries only to lands that promised something, such as political allegiance or the possibility of establishing new monasteries and new churches.

The Slavs in the fourth century probably lived in a simple tribal society that had no elites or political aspirations. There was no individual leader who could ask for a missionary to convert his subjects, nor any elites able to provide protection for the missionaries and promise something in return. The Christian rulers and Church took no interest in the Slavic pagans of Eastern Europe. The pagans knew little or nothing about Christianity. No Christian missionary wrote about them, nor did any bishop in the Roman Empire send envoys to learn about them – not until the pagans crossed swords with the empire and so gained its interest.

THE SOURCES OF OUR KNOWLEDGE IN THE DARK AGES

To start with, we have archaeological evidence, although this is not as rich as later findings or those findings in parts of Western Europe inhabited by the Germans. The Slavs did not build cities fortified with thick walls in their original homeland. They also traded very little. Our knowledge of the relationships between ancient nations usually derives from the objects that have survived for centuries in the ground. Those are usually luxurious goods such as jewels and weaponry. The Slavs had little iron ore and usually employed natural resources to make weapons. They had no elites who would buy luxurious goods and only began to make swords in any numbers in later centuries.

In addition, there is an absence of coins. Those coins found in the remains of ancient settlements explain the international relations of those settlers, confirming who people of that country traded with or into whose army they entered. We can therefore say confidently that the Slavs in the fourth century rarely joined the Roman military, as the Germans did, nor did they trade with the Roman Empire.

The Archaeological Sources

We can study graves and remains of their settlements, which provide evidence about the Slavs' lifestyle and religion. Even here we are unlucky, however, because the Slavs cremated their dead. Scarce written sources are also a challenge. Mostly we rely on the language as a source of information, especially the names people give to things around them. As these names changed little, we can track the origin of these terms. The language is still here, and the names people gave to landmarks in ancient times have often endured until today.

People give names to mountains, forests, rocks and fields – but the river was the most crucial element in every premodern society's life. Historians thus consult the linguists and search for the oldest names of every river and stream. On the banks of rivers and streams, people build their settlements.

We must combine these pieces to compile knowledge about the Slavs and their societies. But let us start at the beginning. Where did the Slavs come from?

The Search for the Slavic Motherland

The search for the Slavic motherland has filled thousands of pages. Some theories are more plausible than others; some sounded more logical, while others were simply convenient for the nation that came up with them. Nowadays, however, historians believe they have reached a consensus. The early homeland of the first Slavs lay somewhere in the centre of Eastern Europe. Most historians place the proto-Slavic homeland between the Vistula and the Dnieper Rivers. They believe this because of the names of the rivers and streams in the region. We can trace the oldest Slavic names for rivers north-east of the Carpathian Mountains, somewhere in modern Belarus.

Some historians or linguists, most famously Oleg Nikolayevich Trubachyov (1930–2002), place the origins of the Slavic peoples further south, next to the Danube River. He relies on classical sources that describe nations in these regions that may be considered Slavic.

The language helps us to find the proto-Slavic homeland in yet another way. We may not have written records, but we do have the language we speak today. The linguists know how the language evolved; they can compare the languages and tell which words are Slavic or foreign. Linguists are able to reconstruct accurately the proto-Slavic language according to sources from the eighth century and the names people gave to landmarks around them. They can therefore tell that the oldest Slavic tongue contained words not only from Baltic languages (today's Latvian and Lithuanian), but also from the Celtic and Germanic (mainly Gothic) languages.

In addition, the tracks of the languages spoken by Iranian nomadic tribes living in the steppes between the Black Sea region and Mongolia and China are significant. The language thus implies which nations our Slavs met and had contact with. The Iranian influence is prominent in the Slavs' culture and religion as well as in their language.

THE DARK AGES

LET US VISIT THE LAND

Imagine you are a child living in this area around 350 CE:

You leave your hut with a piece of warm bread your mother put in your hand. You look over your shoulder at the little house with a straw roof and wood walls. You shudder as you remember the night chill. And smile as you remember how your mother cuddled you under her blanket to chase away the cold. You chew your bread, walk on the grass and consider your next steps. You earned your bread helping your mother harvest the vegetables and tending the geese on the pasture beside the river.

Now you will finish your last errand and take carrots to your uncle in exchange for fresh cherries. He lives at the other end of the village, but you do not mind that. Your mother certainly knows that you will help yourself to some cherries on the way home, before they reach the safety of her hands. No wonder this is your favourite errand!

When you have finished, you will go to the forest to wait for your father to return from his hunt. The forest fascinates you: it is dark and deep, tempting and enormous. You can barely see the end, but you can test your courage at its edges and play at being a hunter. The forest lies across the plain; when you turn your head to the right you can see the plain itself. It stretches away like an endless sea of green grass (or how you imagine the sea to be, as you have never seen it). One day you will get a horse and cross the plain to see what lies on the other side. Or you will follow your father deep into the forest, hunting for fresh meat.

Meanwhile your mother is calling, reminding you to pick up the basket and run for your errand. You smile; there are cherries ahead.

How the Slavic Homeland Appeared

The homeland of the first Slavs was thus fertile, green and flat. Forests provided wood and game – as well as material for scary fairy tales about the creatures living in its dark, impregnable corners. The climate was mild; there were warm summers and cold winters, but no extremes in either season. The natural habitat matters as land shapes its people first, before they learn to shape the land.

Today we believe in our pride that the environment around us does not matter, but it still does. Advanced modern armies learned that technology would get them nowhere in mountainous Afghanistan. No one in modern history has been foolish enough to try invading Switzerland, for the same reason. The people in ancient times, in contrast, realized the limits that nature had set for them on a daily basis, and learned to respect them very well.

Across the plains, to the east of these green, fertile lands full of forests, were the waste steppes. The nomadic peoples who inhabited them revered their horses and moved quickly; they did not indulge in agriculture and did not settle. The Slavs knew these nomads and feared their attacks. Their lifestyles differed, but only because their habitat shaped the characters and cultures of both.

The Settlers versus the Nomads

It is true that nomadic peoples, such the Huns, Avars, Bulgars and later the Hungarians, came to love the freedom of these vast plains. Yet the life was hard. When the Bulgars, or later the Hungarians, came to fertile lands suitable for settlement, they chose to learn how to cultivate the soil and enjoy its fruits.

The Slavs, by contrast, had always been agricultural; they built settlements and hunted in the nearby forests. Unlike the nomadic peoples, for whom the horse was everything, playing an essential role in both culture and religion, the Slavs revered the trees.

THE MOST ANCIENT ORIGINS OF THE SLAVS

Slavic languages are a part of the Indo-European family. They separated from the rest of this large language group around the second and third millennia BCE. However, we cannot say much about their history before some ancient authors noticed them as they were only in oral form; the Slavs did not write themselves.

The Greek historian Herodotus (c. 484–425 BCE) first mentioned some peoples that may have been the ancestors of Slavs. He named them Neuri, a nation living north of the Scythians:

The Neuri follow Scythian customs, but one generation before the advent of Darius' army, they happened to be driven from their country by snakes, for their land produced great numbers of these, and still more came down on them out of the desolation on the north, until at last the Neuri were so afflicted that they left their own country and lived among the Budini. It may be that these people are wizards; for the Scythians, and the Greeks settled in Scythia, say that once a year every one of the Neuri becomes a wolf for a few days and changes back again to his former shape. Those who tell

this tale do not convince me, but they tell it nonetheless and swear to its truth.
Herodotus, translated by A.D. Godley, 1920.

Historians are keen to draw upon any source that can enlighten us about ancient times. Herodotus does not help us much here as his narrative seems pure fiction, especially the tale about the snakes. He does mention werewolves, however – mythical creatures that were a feature of Slavic folklore.

A more precise description comes from the historian Procopius of Caesarea (c. 500–566 CE). He wrote about the wars with barbarians following a direct order from the Byzantine emperor Justinian the Great (500–565) and his military leader Belisarius (c. 500–565). These records are precious because Procopius accompanied the armies on their campaigns and personally visited the Slavic lands.

In his *History of the Wars* he describes two nations, the Sclaveni and the Antae, with the same customs, language and institutions. According to Procopius, their Slavic language is utterly barbaric. Their system involves a sort of democracy – the people discuss every decision they make.

He further explains their religion. Supposedly, they believe in one god, the lightning maker, a supreme deity. They sacrifice cattle and even human victims to him. But according to Procopius, the Sclaveni do not think much about worship, not until they are in imminent danger of death. When death approaches, either because of an illness or in war, they promise to sacrifice to the deity, and once saved, they do as they had promised. Consequently, they believe that the promise of sacrifice saved them from danger.

Procopius points out that the maker of lightning is not the only supernatural being they revere. They also worship rivers, nymphs and other spirits, offer sacrifices to them daily, and perform ancient rituals for them.

As for their lifestyle, they supposedly live in pitiful hovels, which they build close to one another, but do not settle in one place for a long time. In war, they do not ride horses; most go to battle on foot with shields, spears and no armour. Some of them do not even wear a shirt or a cloak and only wear some kind of trousers to protect their private parts.

Procopius did see the Slavs in person, but his evaluation was far from fair. First, we should appreciate the cliché. Much of the description fits a typical pattern of how an educated Roman would describe barbarians.

The Slavs and Their Democracy

We should not overrate the mention of democracy among the early Slavs. The Slavs lived in a traditional tribal society; it had no feudal ties, rulers or elites. Procopius's description fits the archaeological findings. To call it democracy in a modern sense of the word would be far-fetched, however, as we will explain in a section dedicated to the social order within ancient Slavic settlements (page 51).

On the other hand, the paragraph concerning Slavic religion is more interesting. It seems probable that the Slavs would practise both animal and human sacrifice to the gods they revered, and we have no reason to doubt Procopius's remark regarding that. However, let us not be too hasty with the 'one god ... alone lord of all things'.

The Religion of the Early Slavs

The first implication would be to connect this deity with Perun, a god of thunder and lightning whom we know the Slavs worshipped in later years. Yet the image of Perun from later days was clearly influenced by the Scandinavian god Thor, a consequence of the Slavs' contact with the Vikings. Procopius's god of thunderstorms might indeed have been called Perun, or to have gone by any other name. Various tribes might have called him differently and revered him as a particular form of primary deity.

Nevertheless, it is very unlikely that the early Slavs would have been monotheistic. This is more likely the conviction of a Christian writer striving to understand the pagan world. The Slavic deities would not be creators who had made the Earth and then moved away. Such an idea of creation would be incomprehensible to Slavic pagans, who saw their gods in natural phenomena and believed they were always around. In contrast to the Christian God who had created the world but was not of it, pagan gods were always present in the world of those who worshipped them.

There is also the comment from Procopius concerning the Slavs not minding their religion, remembering only to worship when death approached. A pious Christian writer who prayed every morning for the forgiveness of his sins, visited church regularly and accepted the clergy as messengers of his God might indeed interpret their faith in this way. To him, the daily acts of worship would be pure superstitions. In contrast pagans were always conscious of their gods' presence; they might not pray or look above for their salvation, but they would honour the trees and rocks. They displayed their reverence in different words and actions than Christians or Jews. It is also worth remembering that Procopius despised paganism and would use every opportunity to diminish its significance.

However, his observation that the Slavs worshipped rivers, nymphs and spirits is probably accurate.

Strong, Light-Haired and Ruddy-Faced

What did the first Slavs look like? Procopius described them in vivid detail. To him, they looked similar to each other. They all seemed very tall and muscular, with neither fair nor dark hair and complexions, being instead rather 'ruddy'. As they lived a hard life, they did not bother with hygiene very much and were constantly filthy. But Procopius gave the Slavs credit for their character. He saw them as simple but not evil, rather honest. He compared them to the Huns in their simplicity.

When we read such a description, we must realize that Procopius compared the Slavs to men and women from Byzantine, his homeland. We can therefore dismiss the mention of rugged clothes and dirt covering their bodies, recognizing that they must have seemed dirty to a man used to a luxurious life in the city with developed hygiene.

More interesting is that Procopius, in accord with other descriptions (like those of other writers), says they were unusually tall and strong. This characteristic was widespread in Europe. Slavic slaves were highly valued in slave markets across the civilized world, primarily because of their hardiness, strength and height.

As for skin colour, Procopius and later sources mention that they had neither dark nor pale complexion and that their hair was usually light, reddish or blond. This description also fits the popularity of Slavic women on the slave markets of the early Middle Ages; their exclusive looks were exotic and would not be surpassed by any other race.

THE ANCIENT SLAVS' ORDINARY LIVES

Just imagine you find yourself on the bank of the Dnieper River around 350 CE:

It is late morning, the air is humid from yesterday's rain, a soft breeze ruffles your hair and you can smell baked meat in the distance. The place is buzzing with life. Dogs are barking, ducks are quacking; you move aside as a goose hisses and snaps at your leg because you stand in her way. A flock of geese is passing by, and a boy walks behind them and urges them, swinging energetically with a twig. On your right is a field where a group of young, muscular men clothed in dirty linen breeches work with a mouldboard plough. Immediately in front of you a woman is sitting on the ground before a wooden hut with a straw-covered roof. She is grinding barley with a stone quern. Her neighbour is doing the same with her cereal, yet she is watching the other woman with envy. She has no quern and has to manage with two stones, which is very difficult.

Between them, an old woman with no teeth is peeling onions and carrots and chewing something. You turn around and watch a group of older children led by a tall, slender girl. She is carrying a basket full of herbs that they had all collected. They walk by a yard with farm animals where another girl is milking a cow tied to a pole. Suddenly you hear a victorious cry. It comes from the river. You turn around and see a tall young boy with a dead beaver in his hand. He is happy; he will bring the beaver home and they will use it for fur.

The lifestyle of the early Slavs did not differ very much from that of other people living in the settlements of the early Middle Ages and late antiquity. They settled in villages and became skilled farmers and hunters, eating European plants and breeding familiar animals.

Agriculture and Craftsmanship of the Ancient Slavs

The Slavs were skilled farmers. They used a mouldboard plough that could break up the soil and help to make it more fertile. Millet was their primary crop, but they were also familiar with wheat and barley. They used both, not only to bake bread but also to make beer (along with hops). They harvested the crops with sickles twice a year and added herbs such as garlic or parsley to their meals. Grinding cereal was a laborious task, one primarily done by women. The quern was a tool made of two circular stones, one of which remained still while the other turned around. However, not every housewife possessed such a device, or their querns were at least less efficient. Some had to make do with just two stones.

The nutrition of the early Slavs was rich enough. They knew many traditional species of fruits and vegetables. They grew carrots, onions, radishes, cabbage, pumpkin or peas. In Slavic villages you would also find orchards full of fruit trees; the trees would grow cherries, apples and pears, even peaches in warmer climates. Nutritious walnuts, as the traditional Slavic recipes reveal, also belonged on the Slavic table.

As for animals, they bred cows and occasionally sheep, as well as goats or pigs. They would use these animals as sources of meat and milk, and to help with soil cultivation. The manure of farm animals was highly valued and the animals grazed the fields. In the winter herdsmen would chase their animals into the lowlands; later in the spring the animals were driven higher up to graze the fresh grass after snow and ice had left the fields. Geese and ducks were the most popular forms of fowl, as the Slavs usually lived close to a river. Dogs were important domestic animals, a companion for guarding the houses and accompanying the hunters. The oldest Slavs knew how to breed the best lines selectively. They rode horses less frequently in ancient times. Only after encountering the cavalry of more developed nations did the Slavs start to breed horses in larger numbers and to use them in warfare.

Until their encounter with the Romans, however, the Slavs had to get by without the help of cats when guarding their cereal from mice.

Hunting and Crafts

Wild nature complemented the ancient Slavs' diet, providing both fresh meat and wild fruits. Skilled in fishing and hunting, they hunted both river and forest animals. Beavers or martens were trapped to provide winter clothing with their valuable fur. Forest animals that could be baked and eaten included hares, deer and elk. The forests were dangerous, populated as they were with wolves and bears, so the hunters had to protect themselves. They knew how to use the bow and sometimes caught a boar or a bear.

When you visited the Slavic village at the beginning of this chapter, you might have noticed the buzzing of bees. Slavs were skilled beekeepers who used honey as a valuable source of sugar in winter. They also learned how to ferment the honey to make mead. Before they met the Mediterranean culture, the Slavs had never tasted wine made of grapes. Even when wine reached the tables of Slavic elites as a result of their encounter with the Romans, they still preferred beer. Interestingly the Slavs grew hops much earlier than other nations, meaning that their beer tasted better and remained fresh for longer.

Wheat was a favourite crop when brewing beer until very late in Europe. Barley replaced wheat as the primary beer ingredient for the brewing of beer in the sixteenth century.

The oldest beer was thick and gruel-like; it served as a drink for celebration and a highly nutritious beverage.

As for craftsmanship, the Slavs drew upon all essential materials. When they came to Central Europe, they already knew how to work with various kinds of metal. However, iron ore was scarce and expensive in the Slavic homeland; so were other metals such as gold. They therefore mainly used bog ore, which did not produce the best material. When in ancient times the Slavs went to war they had to employ sticks and bows; expensive iron swords could be used only occasionally. But after a series of encounters with the rich Mediterranean world they acquired proper swords. Later, after migrating to regions richer in iron ore, they became skilled in metallurgy. Often whole villages specialized in this industry.

Wood was omnipresent. The Slavs built structures, created furniture to equip their houses and used wood for tools, dishes or toys. It was abundant as the habitat was filled with forests and the Slavs revered their trees. For them trees represented sacred objects, for the source of their most valued material. They used leather to make more durable clothing, such as jackets and boots; it also served them in making ritual objects. The oldest Slavic word for the devil ('črt') comes from the word for a particular mask, probably made of leather, that dancers representing supernatural beings wore during certain rituals.

Textile and Clothes

Clothes production was laborious work, traditionally undertaken by women. They would manually spin threads of raw tow, wool or hemp, taking their time, ignoring the pain in their fingers and stopping only when these started to bleed. Then the women would patiently wind these threads and use the weaving loom, sighing with visible relief when the textile took the shape of the essential pieces of fabric. Mothers would distribute these pieces to their families as underwear, scarves or head coverings, or to sew into shirts, breeches, skirts or other clothing. However, the second part was not so hard.

The Slavs also knew about ceramics, a source of satisfaction to archaeologists today. Even broken pieces are helpful to them. Unlike wood, ceramics endure longer in the ground, and so represent an essential source of information when differentiating one subculture from another or identifying foreign influence.

HOW THE SLAVS LIVED AND DID THEY TRADE?

Slavs lived in villages or settlements consisting of between 50 and 70 people. Each village would be separated into two parts: the area where people lived and slept and that where food and tools were produced. They built houses of wood, sometimes strengthening the walls with clay; their wooden roofs were covered with straw. Typical of Eastern Europeans was the stove, made of clay or stone, that featured in every building. The houses were large enough to house one family consisting of a father, mother and children. Sometimes grandparents would live with them, but only when necessary. The early Slavs did not fortify their villages as they usually settled in places that offered natural protection. The settlements usually had a river on one side and a deep forest on the other, with a mountain or a lake probably providing further protection.

Commerce was limited, as the early Slavs did not trade with anybody very much. They did not use money in any form. All they needed they made themselves, trading only in the village and between neighbours. While the Slavs lived in a relatively egalitarian society with no leaders, they had no need for jewellery or ornamented silks. The need for foreign trade only arose much later, when elites emerged and a demand for luxurious goods grew. The elite men and women wanted to be seen in clothing that represented their status, distinguishing them from the rest of society at first sight. In the simple tribal structure of the ancient Slavs, luxurious items would be a waste of time and resources.

Social Order of the Ancient Slavs

At the beginning of the book, we mentioned how nationalist historians in the nineteenth century desired to see the heroes of their Slavic history. Their Slavs were supposed to be wise and peaceful, fighting only when the need arose. This image was in direct opposition to the image of belligerent Germanic tribes, who sought expansion at every opportunity.

Yet the real-life Slavs were belligerent and wild enough, as the Byzantine sources tell us with a certain fearful respect. It is only logical that for a tribe or nation to be successful in late antiquity and early Middle Ages, it had to conquer or enslave, to avoid suffering that fate themselves. There was no place for peaceful humanity and goodwill; danger and death waited at every corner, be it a hungry bear or a lustful neighbouring villager who desired your daughter.

However, the historians still agree on one point. Unlike nomadic peoples, the Slavs seem to have lived in a particular form of 'democratic' order. Procopius explained that they lived under some form of democracy and discussed all decisions amongst themselves.

Archaeologists uncovered villages where there was no visible distinction between the houses. They thus concluded that Procopius was right. There was no military caste and no leaders; decisions were taken after thorough discussion among the members of society. However, we cannot say at what age men were allowed to join in the debate, nor whether women played a role in decision-making. As every society of ancient times was patriarchal, it is probable that women played little role in these village meetings. Nor can we say for sure if everybody in the clan had their say or if only certain members of the family did. Was there a time-honoured system of debate, or did only the strongest and loudest press their will?

We should, therefore, not overrate the 'democracy' of the first Slavs. Today's conception of the word implies some order in which the majority makes decisions in a firmly defined process. The early Slavs most probably consulted one another. They made decisions together, but that does not mean everybody had their say. It also may imply that the most muscular men in the clan would decide a course of action and the rest would agree, as they needed their protection and lacked the means to protest.

The Traditional Tribal Society

However, there is one thing we can be sure of. In the ancient Slavic society, you would not care to protest too loudly and risk falling out of favour with your neighbours. Your tribe, your clan, was everything. Out of your clan, on your own, you would not survive. The tribe took care of you not only in a material way, but also in a metaphysical sense. Religion was not perceived as an individual act of devotion; people relied on priests performing rituals and the whole clan participating in them. The dead were always with you, too – helping or harming if you did not follow the given order of life.

The priests probably enjoyed a more elevated status in society because the agricultural culture depended on nature in every way; they were needed to perform the seasonal rituals. But they did not possess any particular access to the divine, in contrast to priests in the monotheistic religions or even those of ancient Greece and Rome. The gods were always present for Slavs in the form of natural phenomena. You met them regularly, yet still needed the rituals to retain their favour.

WHAT DID THE ANCIENT SLAVS BELIEVE IN?

Pre-Christian Slavic mythology is a complicated matter. We must distinguish between what historians believe to be accurate and what modern widespread interest in Slavic paganism has created. Today, especially in Eastern Europe, neo-paganism presents the Slavic religion as a complete set of dogmas and rituals similar to Scandinavian mythology. However, unlike the pre-Christian Viking religion, in the case of the ancient Slavs we lack the sources to be so concrete. Not only are written resources missing, but so too are objects of worship that archaeologists could study. The Slavs did not build statues or paint their gods in the early days. They only did so later under the influence of Christianity.

Most of our records about the Slavic religion and mythology thus come from later sources. Such records may not reflect the reality of the ancient Slavic religion. The religion of the Slavs living in twelfth-century Central Europe would be influenced by the Christian faith, as was the paganism of the Kyivan Rus. We read about the pantheon that Vladimir the Great (c. 956–1015) revered before his conversion to Christianity and have archaeological evidence of the statues he erected. But Vladimir was of Scandinavian origin, and the Norse mythology must have significantly influenced the religion of the Kyivan Rus. It is no coincidence that the Slavic Perun of Vladimir's time resembles the Norse Thor. There is no reason to believe that the old Slavic supreme god (if any such existed) bore the same characteristics.

We do know that the religion of ancient Slavs was polytheistic and that there was no codified religious text. The tribes did not meet regularly to celebrate festivals as one nation, as the Greeks did. Rather, their beliefs were passed down orally from one generation to another.

The old Slavic religion revered deities that lived in this world, seeing them in nature and natural phenomena. Procopius refers to one supreme god, the creator of all things, as the god of lightning and thunder. We can identify this deity with Perun, whom we know from popular folklore and later sources. Archaeologists have found statues of Perun in various places inhabited by the later Slavs. Procopius also mentions a belief in demons and nymphs. From much younger sources, we know about other gods of the pantheon. Nestor the Chronicler (c. 1056–1114) describes the gods that the ruler of Kyivan

Rus, Vladimir the Great, worshipped before his conversion to Christianity.

The Slavic Pantheon

These were Perun, Hors, Dažbog, Stribog, Simargl and Mokosh. *The Tale of Igor's Campaign*, an epic dating from the twelfth century, adds Veles to their number, although the authenticity of this work is disputed today. Other records also exist that describe Slavic paganism; they were written by missionaries who came to Western Slavs in the twelfth century.

These sources include Radegast, Svarog or Chernobog, a deity that the missionaries compared to the Christian devil.

The early Slavs' religion relied on sacrifice, a concept that presents a simple mechanism. We give something to the gods; they provide us with something in return. We have evidence that the Slavs practised human sacrifice. Procopius vividly described the cruel ways in which the Slavs sacrificed captured enemies to their gods.

He wrote about the rituals in which they murdered the prisoners of war, not by sword or a spear, which would be usual. They rammed stakes into the ground, sharpened them and then sat the victims on top of the stakes, pushed them down so that the stake entered the buttock of the victim and tore through their entrails. For the Sclaveni, this was a proper way to execute the prisoners.

Other gruesome practices of disposing of the victims, which Procopius outlined, included tying the hands and feet of the poor prisoners to four thick pieces of wood in the ground and then striking them on the temples with maces as they would do to dogs or vicious beasts. When the Sclaveni entered a village, they often locked up the inhabitants with their cattle (those that could not be taken with them) in their huts and burned them alive.

Because their gods liked these practices and the rituals of killing the prisoners of war was a popular public display to celebrate the victory, they took care not to kill their enemies in battle but to capture them alive and drag them home in great numbers.

Modern historians believe that those descriptions in part fit a familiar pattern. They are a cliché, used to show how primitive and vulgar the barbarians are. Despite this, their work helps to uproot the myth of the peaceful and wise Slavs favoured by Slavic nationalist historians. Such texts rather suggest that the Slavs of the sixth century were as savage as any other nation that had to survive in hard and brutal times. The vivid descriptions of the executions of victims may be a little exaggerated. However, in the Middle Ages in Central Europe, we know these practices as corporal punishment. Impaling the criminal on a stake was a punishment reserved for the most severe transgressions, and it prevailed for a long time.

The Slavs and the Sacrifice

Procopius's text also mentions sacrifice. We can be confident that the sacrifice of fruits, crops, animals and humans played an essential role in Slavic culture. These rituals ensured the favour of the gods, represented above all in the weather and crops that the soil would yield every year.

An invaluable source from the twelfth century describes the rituals that took place on an island called Rügan. In his *Deeds of the Danes* a Danish historian, Saxo Grammaticus (c.

1150–1220), wrote about the worship of Sventovit, a Slavish deity. The cult at Rügan was well organized. Sventovit might not have been known to our Slavs in ancient times but the rituals, including the sacrifice of the yearly harvest, may have looked very similar to this.

> *The solemn worship of this idol was organized according to the following rules: Once a year, after the harvest, with the indiscriminate attendance of the entire island before the idol's temple, after offering a sacrifice of livestock, they celebrated a solemn feast in the name of their religion. Their priest, who could be easily distinguished by his long beard and hair against the common style in his homeland, on the day before the rites were to be completed, would carefully clean the sancta sanctorum, which only he was allowed to enter, using even a broom, and taking much care that his breath did not enter the building; to do so, whenever he needed to inhale or exhale, he would run to the door, so as to prevent, evidently, the presence of the deity from being tarnished by contact with a mortal spirit.*
>
> *The next day, while the town looked on attentively in front of the doors, the priest, taking the vessel from the hand of the idol, would observe it very carefully, and if the amount of liquor in said vessel had decreased, he thought that the next year there would be scarcity. And taking note of this, he would order that some of this year's harvest be saved for the times to come. If he did not see that the liquor had decreased at all from its usual height, he would announce that times of agricultural abundance would come. According to this omen, he would sometimes recommend that the current year's provisions be used more sparingly, and other times with greater generosity.*

Then, after pouring the old wine at the feet of the idol as a libation, he filled the empty vessel with new wine and, representing the role of cup bearer, he would worship the statue and would make petitions for himself, for the homeland and for the citizens, with invocations of solemn words, for the deity to increase their wealth and victories. Having done this, bringing the vessel to his mouth, he would empty it in one single swig, drinking very quickly, then, once again filled with wine, he would return it to the statue's right hand.

The sacrifice also included a cake made with wine and honey, round in shape, and so large that it was almost the size of a man. The priest, positioning it between himself and the people, would usually ask if he could be seen by the Rani. And if they responded that he could be seen, he would request that the next year he not be able to be seen by them. With this type of petition, he was not asking for his destiny or that of his people, but rather to increase future harvests.

Then he would greet the crowd present in the name of the idol, and he urged them to continue to pay tribute to this deity with a sacrificial ritual that was carefully executed, and he promised them victory on land and sea as a sure reward for their worship. Once this had all been done in this way, and spending the rest of the day at feasts full of extravagances, they transformed the sacrificial festivals into the practice of the feast, and into food for their gluttony, making the victims consecrated to the deity serve their immoderation. At this feast, it was considered pious to transgress sobriety and bad luck to maintain it.

Saxo Grammaticus, *Deeds of the Danes*, Book XIV, translated by Oliver Elton, 1905

Saxo was a skilful writer who filled his description with vivid details. However, as no pious Christian historian would, he did not avoid judgment and disdain. The festivals in which the whole island's population participated, involving eating, drinking and probably sexually uninhibited behaviour, must have seemed rather barbarous in the twelfth century. For us, it confirms what we believe about Slavic paganism. For the rituals to be valid, the whole community had to join in.

The Priests in the Slavic Society

We can notice more details in the text. First, the priests differed in appearance from the rest of society. That might have been true for the first Slavs, or it might have changed under the influence of Christianity. Second, the Slavs sacrificed their harvest and livestock. But most important of all, the rituals on Rügen illustrate the role that pagan festivities played in the lives of premodern society. As people's survival depended on nature, they did not like leaving the harvest to chance. The sacrifice and the ritual were an inevitable (even a rather desperate) deed that should ensure that the next harvest would suffice to sustain them. These practices continued in the folklore and customs of Slavic people long after they converted to Christianity. We can still trace their remains in our traditions, such as Easter festivities.

The Christian Church worked hard to uproot the pagan practices but it repeatedly failed. In the end Christianity accepted people's need to bring a sense of security into their lives and tied the festivals to the new faith, offering a pantheon of saints. From the point of Christian faith, the rituals were wrong; there is no place in Christianity for such a relationship with God. Pagans wanted to give and get in return; Christianity maintained that there was nothing they could offer God but their faith. No ritual would ensure a plentiful harvest; instead you needed to have faith that God would provide.

Pagan Rituals

For pagan people used to rituals that brought safety into their lives, and even Christian people living in pre-industrial society, faith was not always enough. They believed and prayed, but desired to keep to their practices just in case.

In Slavic culture special treatment was given to the dead. We know this from the trouble that Christian missionaries encountered in seeking to promote Christian burial practices. For the early Slavs, the dead stayed with you. They would not depart for some afterlife and not bother you any more. Your ancestors would help you and protect you – but they would haunt you if you made them angry. First of all, the Slavs cremated their dead, believing this was the proper way to deal with the dead body. If you did not cremate the body, the dead could become unquiet and return to haunt you. The male restless dead came back as vampires and the females in the form of water nymphs called Rusalki; these nymphs would lure you into the water and drown you there. Not only improper cremation may have resulted in problems with the dead. Certain ways of death were also considered improper, such as drowning, hanging or dying on your wedding day.

We know these beliefs from the records of the Christian missionaries, although we cannot be sure these tales are true for early Slavs, living in Eastern Europe during the fourth to sixth centuries. However, their relationship with the dead can be traced from the archaeological findings.

THE ORIGIN OF THE WORD

Before we finally let our Slavs move in the western, southern and northern directions, let us consider the term 'Slav' itself. A common mistake in the English language is to believe that the word Slav is derived from the word 'slave,' as the Slavs were often enslaved in the early Middle Ages. It seems that it works the other way round.

The Slavs called themselves the people of the word: those who could speak and be understood. In most Slavic languages the word for 'word' is '*slovo*' or some similar form. Slavs used this technique to describe other nations as well. The Slavic translation of German, for example, means one who is dumb, one who cannot speak. The Slavic word for 'dumb' was '*němý*' or similar. This name for the German prevailed in many contemporary languages, for instance '*Němec*' (Czech) or '*Nijemac*' (Croatian). But what about the slaves?

Slavs and Slaves

The Slavs were often enslaved. Many people around the world first came to know Slavs on the slave markets rather than as a nation to fight against or to trade with. The Arabic word for Slavs was '*Saqaliba*', and Arabic slave traders found many uses for these strong and beautiful people. But why were they slaves rather than others? Why were the Slavs enslaved in such numbers that their names would become a synonym for someone whose freedom was taken from them?

There are two reasons why Slavs were so often enslaved. The word first appeared around the seventh century, the time that saw the globalization of the slave trade. Arabic expansion had created new wealthy states; Vikings raided and enjoyed the money they got through spoils of war and other forms of trade. Prosperous kingdoms existed in the west, and there still remained the classical world, with its longstanding tradition of slavery. People were sold and bought; they were used for labour or war, as servants or concubines, in all these places. The society of the early Middle Ages accepted – and depended upon – slavery.

The one reason why people accepted a ruler above them and learned to respect the state and pay their taxes was that the state would not enslave them; it would only tax them. Such a state had an economic interest to protect them from being captured and taken away, as part of its income would be lost. However, the Slavs did not have such a state until very late.

More importantly, they remained pagans for a long time. The enslaving of fellow believers was prohibited by both monotheistic religions. Christians were thus not allowed to enslave other Christians and Muslims were not allowed to enslave other Muslims. Pagans, however, could be enslaved by Muslims, Christians and other pagans. Both Muslims and Christians could buy them on the market without remorse.

Slave traders thus raided the Slavic lands. Prisoners of war were captured and sold, and most of the people on the global slave market were the Slavs. This word entered Romanic and Germanic languages and acquired a new meaning. This was a later development, however. In the beginning, there was a word, the Slav, which meant a person who understood the word and could speak.

THE SLAVS FINALLY SET OUT ON THE JOURNEY

Let us now consider the movement of the Slavs, with some relief. For as they leave their homeland, we also leave the darkness. As soon as the Slavs clashed swords with the Roman Empire, as soon as they moved into the Balkans and Central Europe, or themselves learned to write in the Kyivan Rus, we begin to have written sources, names and dates. Finally, we can tell the stories of the Slavs and describe their colourful world in more vivid detail.

THE MIGRATION PERIOD

The migration period is a historical phenomenon that started sometime around 375 CE. This was the time when the Slavs started travelling from their original homeland and populating Europe. Historians believe that the migration period ended around 568 CE. However, in the case of the Slavs, we cannot stop there because they also moved in various directions during the seventh and even the eighth centuries.

MIGRATION OR INVASION?

Let us now put the migration period into context. First, let us discuss the terminology. You might have heard about the Barbarian Invasion, as this is what English or French historians used to call this era in the past. In other languages, notably Slavic, we call it 'migration' (of the nations or tribes). Words matter. Some call it invasion because it certainly looked like it from the point of view of the settled people in the Western and Eastern Roman civilizations. Hordes of unwashed, wild barbarians speaking various languages came to their land with their families and demanded a place to settle. And were ready to fight for their demands with formidable force.

However, from the point of view of the barbarians, their movement was inevitable. They did not travel on a whim – mostly their land was taken by some other tribe, whose land had again been taken by some other tribe. They travelled to move their families to safety. Yet they destroyed and burned in the process, because they took their own customs with them wherever they went. And, of course, because the land they wanted to move on to was already taken.

Furthermore, their ways of life were incompatible with those of the Romans. However, in a few generations the barbarians learned Latin well enough, became more civilized and created a fusion of the Roman and barbaric world. In the meantime, the Roman world changed as well. Western Rome lost its political importance, and Christianity, the most notable of Roman institutions, adjusted to barbarians.

The migration period thus also covers a time when the barbarians became Christians – while Christianity acquired some barbaric features that it did not have before.

The Migration Period: Like a Game of Billiards

Imagine you are playing a game of billiards. You strike a red ball, which touches the green and the blue. These two then strike another three each, and one ends up in a hole. That is what happened in the migration period.

The red ball represents the Huns. A nomadic nation that rode short-legged horses and came from Asia. The Huns stormed the area between the mouth of the Rhine and the Danube Rivers, conquering various territories on the way. They forced the Germanic tribes who had settled there to move further south. So the process began. The unlucky ball that

THE MIGRATION PERIOD

ended up in a dark hole was the Western Roman Empire, which disintegrated in the process.

This metaphor explains the process from a long-term perspective, but for the people involved it was certainly no game.

Imagine you are a German man, perhaps a Goth, living next to the Rhine with your wife and children:

As the Huns came, you were not surprised or scared at first. You are used to worrying constantly about attacks from your neighbours. You understand that living in peace is impossible: constantly fighting for land is the way of life. It is the only way you know, and you teach your sons to be successful in this game.

Yet when the Huns came, the attack was beyond your imagination. It was unlike anything you have seen so far. They moved so fast; they shot countless arrows without stopping their fast, tiny horses. They never even slowed down, and their manoeuvres as they stormed the village would have been almost beautiful if not so terrible. Every moment they turned their galloping ponies, you thought the pony must surely break its short legs, slide or stumble, but it did not. It kept running, changing directions abruptly and perhaps listening to the very thoughts of its diabolical master because the rider did not even hold reins in his hands. The rider's hands were busy shooting arrow after arrow into the bodies of your fellows, who fell one by one.

Those horses would appear funny, small and short-legged as they were. But they were so fast, and the men riding them so formidable, that jokes vanished the moment you thought of them.

The Huns came, burned, killed and left. Once, twice, three times. You were lucky enough. Your family survived, and your wife hid your children in the forest, as your hut is close to the trees. But next time you might not be so lucky. You got shot with an arrow in the leg, but the shot resulted in a mere scratch and you lived through all three attacks. Yet most men fell, and only a few remained. There is no time to lose; you must go, take all you can carry and leave this place. There is the Roman Empire; you will be safer there. You might even find a job in the Roman army and some brother Goths living beyond the borders might accept you in their ranks. Let us go.

So the migration period is presented to schoolchildren as a neutral term, but it nevertheless contains a lot of suffering and death. Suffering and death of not only men but children and women as well. The term 'barbarian invasion' is misleading because the Germanic tribes moving beyond the Roman borders looked only for safety for their families. On the other hand, some of the barbarians did invade the empire. Archaeological sources show that in some cases only elite warriors attacked the wealthy cities and villages in the Roman Empire. They probably hoped to find bounty and treasure, earning a valued place in society when they returned home.

Huns Start the Migration Period

Historians are unsure why the Huns mounted their sturdy horses and moved westward. One reason is seen in the Alans, or another Iranian tribe, that took their place. But why the Iranians moved, we do not know. Climate change may be a reason, but we mostly blame demographic development. Some nomadic nations changed their way of life, settled and started to use agriculture. This new way of life ensured that more people survived every winter. Children were better fed and more of them reached adulthood. The population grew. Yet the primitive way of cultivating fields did not produce enough crops to sustain the growing population, so the soil was soon exhausted. Tribes therefore had to move to look for another land in which to settle down and grow their crops.

However, it was not only settled nations who profited from agriculture. The nomadic tribes did not settle nor grow their own crops. Yet they could steal more and subdue other tribes that did grow crops, so even the number of nomadic people grew. They also had to go and look for more land – and for more bounty.

The nomadic nations, such as the Huns, lived only from war. A man could only earn a place in society through fighting. The only way a leader could keep his place was by gaining victories over his people's enemies and by providing spoils for his companions. He could not lose, and he definitely could not stop and settle. When the number of ambitious young nomads with their own companies among the Huns grew, the pressure to invade new lands and earn new victories increased.

The other reason the migration started at precisely this point in time is that the nations invaded by the Huns suddenly had somewhere to go. The Roman Empire was in a deep crisis and unable to stop them as they crossed its borders. And since the beginning of the third century, barbaric tribes were allowed to settle officially within the safety of their borders. They entered the Roman army, creating separate units consisting solely of barbarians. These units could not be entirely relied on as their brotherly tribes attacked.

THE MIGRATION BEGINS

The Huns invaded the mouth of the Rhine and settled there, staying until the second half of the fifth century. They attacked the Roman Empire from this area, which promised rich spoils and prestige. Under the rule of the legendary Attila, they founded a short-lived Hunnic empire. As the Huns attacked the area inhabited by the Goths, most Ostrogoths fell under their dominion (providing the crops the nomadic tribes did not produce). The Visigoths moved into the Roman Empire and settled there. However, inside the Roman Empire they caused problems. The ensuing chaos startled other Germanic nations inside and beyond the Roman borders, resulting in the destruction of central power in the Western Roman Empire. The Eastern Roman Empire survived until 1453, however, and played an essential part in our story.

The Slavs Enter the Story

The Slavs enter the story very late. They are the latest ethnic group to take part in forming Europe, together with other nomads, the Avars.

The Slavs joined the process of migration in the sixth century. For various reasons, probably the same as those mentioned above, they moved from their homeland to settle along the rivers of Eastern and Central Europe. The second wave of the Slavic movement is related to the Avars, as some Slavic tribes moved out of reach of the belligerent nomads. They moved westward and inhabited mainly Central Europe.

Let us stop now for a moment and try to understand why people move, why they settle and how they choose where to stay. One apparent reason is described above. People move because somebody attacked them; they escape to safety. They move because they exhaust the soil, which stops yielding crops. They cannot cultivate it with their primitive agricultural methods. Then they pack up their family, cattle and possessions. But where do they settle down?

A prominent place to find a settlement would be a riverbank. Early settlements always stood next to a river. The river provided water for cattle as well as fertile soil, but it also proved convenient for trade. The Kyivan Rus was prosperous mainly because the Dnieper River was the primary trade route. The people living on its banks prospered.

Not only rivers worked as trade routes. Merchants also travelled with their valuable goods on land. And anywhere the trade route went through a settlement, that settlement prospered. The more influential the settlers became, the happier the traders. Not only would they buy more expensive goods, but they would also prove more effective protectors. The wealthier the trade made the settlers, the more motivation they had to invest money and people into protecting them. People therefore settled along riverbanks and trade routes.

Rivers rarely change their courses, however, so why did states come and go?

The Role of Trade Routes

The answer is because the trade routes changed according to the political situation, so the settlers living along the trade route might have little to do with the politics. Great Moravia, for example, thus prospered from a trade route going through their land. This trade route was one of the reasons the state first came into being.

For centuries, the merchants crossed the Adriatic Sea with their goods. However, the arrival of new Slavic tribes in the Balkans brought chaos in the eighth century. As a result pirates seized their opportunity to attack trading ships, and Slavic pirates joined them. The traders started to look for safer ways to travel with their goods. They chose to go across the future Great Moravian state. So we can see that sometimes an event from hundreds of miles away can prove crucial to the life – and death – of a state.

The Main Directions of the Slavic Migration

In our story, we will delineate the three directions in which the Slavic settlers moved. Initially they inhabited the Balkan Peninsula. Here, they lived in a more or less symbiotic relationship with the Avars from the sixth century and threatened the Byzantine borders. In the seventh century at the latest, they crossed the borders, settled in the eastern Roman provinces of Moesia, Trakya and Macedonia, and penetrated the Peloponnese Peninsula. In the second part of the sixth century, the Slavs appeared to arrive in Dalmatia and Istria; the Byzantines were unable to stop their ascent.

The Slavs and the Avars ruled the Balkan Peninsula, and it is there they broke the power of the Byzantine Empire. In the early Middle Ages the following states began to emerge in this area: the Serbian state, the Bulgarian Empire and the Croatian Kingdom. Some Slavs would move as far as the Alps to Carinthia (modern Slovenia) and Bavaria.

Those who travelled in the northern direction settled on the banks of the Dnieper River and founded Kyiv. This would be a founding moment for contemporary Ukraine, Russia and Belarus.

In the western direction, the Slavs clashed arms with the Franks and founded the Samo Empire, Great Moravia and the Czech and Polish states. Here they probably met Celtic ethnics and some Germanic nations, but they assimilated with them. Some Slavic tribes went as far as modern Germany, with the Serbians in Lusatia providing just one example. Most of them assimilated with the Germanic inhabitants like the Slavs in Bavaria, however, and we do not hear of them in later years. In this book we will deal simply with the early Slavic inhabitants who did form their states – otherwise 10 books would not be sufficient.

Because history consists of the past that is clearly connected with the present, today's people decide which tribe's history will get into our story. We are the ones who label one state as a success and the other one as a failure. For the Slavic people establishing themselves in Bavaria, there was no reason why their settlements should be less critical than those settling down on the banks of the Moravia River. Yet the latter created a prosperous state that fits the national story of Slavic history in Central Europe. The former learned German, adjusted to the Alpine lifestyle and forgot their Slavic past; the present Slavs do not remember them. It is from a modern perspective that we decide which nation's history will be considered here, and which will be mentioned as a marginal ethnic group.

Now we finally turn to explore how the Slavs entered European history.

THE BYZANTIUM AND THE SLAVS

The **Byzantine Empire** had been the major player in Eastern European politics since the fourth century when Constantinople was founded. Byzantium, and the Eastern Roman Empire, defined the classical world for the first Slavs.

First, let us establish one fact. Byzantium is Rome. In the Western historiographical tradition, it sometimes seems that in 476 Rome fell and was no more. Then the Franks came, renewed the empire and created the medieval Holy Roman Empire. Yet from the point of view of Byzantine emperors, there was never any need for renewal. The empire's capital had been Constantinople since 330 CE; Rome became just a provincial city in Italy.

The barbarian conquest of Italy and Rome in 476 was watched with apprehension in Constantinople. However, Odoacer (c. 433–493), the conqueror of Rome, sent the emperor's insignia to Constantinople and swore allegiance to Zeno (c. 425–491), the Eastern Roman emperor. From now on, Odoacer would rule Italy only as the vicar (representative) of the emperor.

Nevertheless, this did not satisfy the emperor. No barbarian was allowed to depose emperors on a whim, no matter that they swore allegiance after the deed was done. Zeno thus sent another barbarian, the Ostrogoth Theodoric (454–526), to depose Odoacer and rule Italy in Constantinople's name. Justinian the Great would re-conquer nearly all of Italy only a hundred years later. The Eastern Roman Empire did not stop calling itself Rome. In the early Middle Ages, within the scope of this book and in the regions where our Slavs lived, Byzantium represented the classical world more visibly than the empire that Franks and Charlemagne (748–814) created.

The Eastern and the Western Empires and their Barbarians

The reason why the eastern part of the empire prevailed and the western part declined and fell lay in geography, and the different way in which they dealt with barbarian tribes. The administration of the west, seated in Ravenna, managed the flood of barbarian tribes poorly in the migration period. They lost control over most of their territory, resulting in a terrible economic situation. However, the Eastern Empire in Constantinople retained control over the transformative processes that the migration period brought for most of the time. Byzantium cleverly used the barbarians. They eliminated a dangerous group within their territory when they sent Theodoric with his Ostrogoths to conquer Italy. Byzantine rulers used the barbarian tribes in their politics without scruples and to their advantage. They used bribes and threats to set the tribes against each other.

But geography matters – and regardless of how innovative the eastern leaders were, they had an advantage. The most populous and economically important regions lay in Asia and Egypt, in parts not influenced by the barbarian invasions.

The Slavs Threaten the Byzantine Empire

The Slavs evolved from the very beginning as neighbours to the Byzantine Empire. The first recorded contacts came in 518 when a sizeable barbarian group invaded Byzantine territory. The leaders of this invasion were probably the Antes, a large Slavic group. The Antes allied themselves with the ancestors of Bulgarians. Together they would repeatedly attack Byzantine provinces, attracted by spoils and prisoners of war. They would become a nightmare for the Byzantine administration.

Let us listen to Jordanes, who introduced Antes and the neighbouring Sclaveni to the Byzantine public:

In the land of Scythia to the westward dwells, first of all, the race of the Gepidae, surrounded by great and famous rivers. The Tisia flows through it on the north and northwest, and on the southwest is the great Danube. On the east it is cut by the Flutausis, a swiftly eddying stream that sweeps whirling into the Ister's waters. Within these rivers lies Dacia, encircled by the lofty Alps as by a crown.

Near their left ridge, which inclines toward the north, and beginning at the source of the Vistula, the populous race of the Venethi dwell, occupying a great expanse of land. Though their names are now dispersed amid various clans and places, they are chiefly called Sclaveni and Antes. The abode of the Sclaveni extends from the city of Noviodunum and the lake called Mursianus to the Danaster, and northward as far as the Vistula.

They have swamps and forests for their cities. The Antes, who are the bravest of these peoples dwelling in the curve of the sea of Pontus, spread from the Danaster to the Danaper, rivers that are many days' journey apart. But on the shore of Ocean, where the floods of the river Vistula empty from three mouths, the Vidivarii dwell, a people gathered out of various tribes. Beyond them the Aesti, a subject race, likewise hold the shore of Ocean. To the south dwell the Acatziri, a very brave tribe ignorant of agriculture, who subsist on their flocks and by hunting. Farther away and above the Sea of Pontus are the abodes of the Bulgares, well known from the wrongs done to them by reason of our oppression. From this region the Huns, like a fruitful root of bravest races, sprouted into two hordes of people

These people, as we started to say at the beginning of our account or catalogue of nations, though off-shoots from one stock, have now three names, that is, Venethi, Antes and Sclaveni. Though they now rage in war far and wide, in punishment for our sins, yet at that time they were all obedient to Hermanaric's commands. This ruler also subdued by his wisdom and might the race of the Aesti, who dwell on the farthest shore of the German Ocean and ruled all the nations of Scythia and Germany by his own prowess alone.

Jordanes, *The Origin and Deeds of the Goths*, translated by Charles Christopher Mierow, 1905

THE FIRST SLAVIC INVASION

The invasion in 518 ended in a catastrophe for the Antes. Germanus, a valiant general and nephew to the Byzantine emperor, defeated them and destroyed the hordes almost completely. The same fate awaited another invasion in 530 under the leadership of Bulgarian tribes. After their defeat, the Byzantines penetrated the Slavic regions and took many of the people captive. From now on the relationship between the Byzantine Empire and the Slavs will be complicated, balancing the thin line of armed neutrality and open hostility.

The Slavs Enter the Balkan Peninsula

The worst times came for the inhabitants of the Byzantine provinces on the Balkan Peninsula. These people, usually of

Thracian and Illyrian origin, spoke perfect Latin and kept to the Roman way of life. They comprised one-quarter of the population of the empire and were thus very important in preserving its Latin character. At the same time the rest of the empire felt the prevailing Greek and Asiatic influences. Their meeting with the Slavs was excruciating. Barbarians had troubled them in the past, but the Slavs were unlike anything they had seen before.

Goths, the previous barbarians they had encountered, were Christians and at least knew some civilized manners. The Slavs seemed incredibly primitive, with their pagan religion, human sacrifice, primitive weapons and clothes, and savagery. Until 600 CE the old population of the north of the Balkan Peninsula (modern Serbia and Bulgaria) was nearly exterminated; it was also significantly cut down in the south in the Macedonian and Thracian provinces. The villagers had no protection, enabling the Slavs and their allies, the Avars, to sweep bare the open fields. The people prevailed in the cities, however, because the Slavs and Avars had initially no experience in siege operations.

Now let us shed light on the more or less complicated relationship between Slavs and Avars.

THE SLAVS AND THE AVARS

Slavs knew the Avars well. They knew the nauseous feeling in their guts, the gripping, paralysing fear that took them when they realized that the Avars were coming.

First, you notice the ground trembling. Just slightly, but distinctly. Then you hear the distant rumbling; you see the line of riders on the far horizon coming in your direction. And the moment you recognize the sound of hooves drumming on the ground, you know it is too late. Too late to run, too late to hide. Yet even then you may be lucky and escape the arrows. To conceal your family.

The Avars were a nomadic tribe, and the nomadic tribes had always brought fear into the settlers' hearts, descending on the villages with such speed and so unexpectedly. They were swift to kill, happy to steal and challenging to negotiate. Because they did not build, they needed little. There was little they could be bribed with, and spoils of war were more important to them than success gained by politics. Even later, when they built their empire that prevailed until the end of the eighth century, they retained the nomadic way of life. The khagan, the leader, was an ultimate ruler, a deputy of heaven charged with the khaganate. He was an absolute ruler, to whom his subjects were no more than slaves. However, he had constantly to prove his authority and manifest it through his military exploits, subjecting new tribes under his rule, gathering spoils and performing symbolic rituals.

The Avars saw themselves as an elite. They were proud people who believed themselves destined to rule; all other races were meant to become their slaves. Yet the Avars did not make war mindlessly. They were aware of how fragile their positions were; an unsuccessful campaign could break the illusion of their invincibility, leading to rebellions and bringing terrible personal consequences for the ruler and his followers. In the beginning, the khaganate lived on the spoils of war; the Avars gained food by traditional pasturage or took crops from the subdued settlers. Because waging wars was so risky, the khagans later learned the art of armed diplomacy. They invaded a prosperous country and negotiated a regular payment for peace.

The Avars came from Asia; they were similar to Huns in manner and lifestyle. They invaded Europe on their escape from the Turks, who began to build their empire in Central Asia. As they came, they wrought havoc in the Byzantine Empire. Yet, on their way, they met the Slavs.

The Relationship Between the Slavs and the Avars

The historians are not completely sure what the relationship between the Slavs and the Avars was like. It seems probable that it changed over time. The Slavs provided Avars with harvest from their agriculture while the Avars provided military protection. The Slavs did join the Avar military on their campaigns, however, but always as special units. Archaeological sources reveal that in the sixth century the region of Pannonia (a part of today's Hungary, Slovakia and Moravia) was inhabited by Slavs who came to the area relatively suddenly. This coincides with the point at which Avars conquered this region. When they came here, Pannonia was fertile yet bare. Avars did not know how to cultivate land, nor did they wish to learn. They resettled Slavs scattered around the khaganate and settled their prisoners of war, as well as possibly some volunteers enticed by the promise of protection. The Slavs then cultivated the land for them.

According to the Chronicle of Fredegar, the Avars treated Slavs terribly. They made them pay brutally high tributes and in winter they lived in their houses, using the Slavic wives as concubines. Supposedly the Avars put Slavs at the front of their army in combat, so that they suffered the most severe blows. Today historians are cautious in interpreting these sources. It seems probable that the Slavs served as a regular unit next to their Avar allies in the military. However, Avars valued their own soldiers higher than the Slavs. Slavs were viewed by the Avars as a lower race. At least in Pannonia, they used the settlements of their subjects as a comfortable place to endure winter and treated their subjects harshly.

The relationship between the Slavs and Avars was complicated, however – sufficient to prevent Byzantine diplomacy from engaging in its usual tactic of playing one against each other. Some Slavs fought in the Avar military; others ran from the khaganate, wishing to escape the Avar yoke and settle down beyond the Roman borders. They were desperate enough to prove nearly unstoppable.

The Allies Plunder the Empire

The Avars and the Slavs plundered the empire for many years. Of the two ethnic groups, the Slavs were the more dangerous. The Avars came, attacked and left, or could be bribed into leaving. The Slavs, on the other hand, sometimes searched for land on which to remain and settle, which proved devastating for the inhabitants of affected regions.

The problem culminated in the second half of the sixth century, a time when the Eastern Roman Empire was waging war on many fronts. In the west, the Teutonic barbarians raided Italy. They threatened to lay waste to everything Justinian the Great had re-conquered at high costs. In the east, peace with the Persian Empire that lasted for many generations was broken; an expensive and exhausting war broke out. There were still the Slavs and Avars.

The central crisis came under the rule of the emperor Maurice (539–602), for whom the Slavic attacks proved fatal. The Balkan Peninsula suffered for generations under Slavic plunder, but the cities endured due to solid fortification. Priscus, the emperor's valiant general, used the towns as starting points for his campaigns against the Slavs, with much success. He even crossed the Danube River and caused severe damage to the Slavs and Avars in their own homes. Yet the fortune of war then turned around, and the Slavs fought back. The emperor Maurice was not very popular at that time, but it was the failure in the Avar and Slavonic wars that finally broke his back.

The last straw was an unfortunate order to the discontented army to spend the winter beyond the Danube in 602. Here the soldiers would spend the winter in the immediate neighbourhood of the hostile Slavs or retreat into marshes. The army rebelled and marched on Constantinople; they deposed Maurice and brought their own emperor, a simple brute called Phocas (547–610). This pretender proved so incompetent that his rule was a disaster for the empire. For the Slavs, this allowed a time of undisturbed plundering on the Balkan Peninsula.

The Slavs Attack Constantinople

In the last years of the sixth and the beginning of the seventh century, the Slavs and Avars presented a constant danger for Byzantium. They raided the Balkans so intensively that the Byzantine military was helpless and could not stop them. In addition, the Slavs tried to settle in the Byzantine territories and rather than returning with the army. This proved confusing

THE MIGRATION PERIOD

for the administration. Their attempts to escape the Avar khaganate were often met with displeasure by the Avar masters, who desperately needed their Slavic subjects to provide food.

Worse was yet to come, however. The allied Slavic and Avar armies twice laid siege to Thessaloniki, the second-largest city in Byzantium. The town was protected by solid fortifications, but the Slavs and the Avars learned how to lay siege. The attacks came in 614–616 and then in 674–677, with the Avars attacking from the land and the Slavs from the sea.

As Slavs proved skilled sailors, they attacked Crete in 623 and later attacked the capital itself – Constantinople.

In July 622 an army of 80,000 men appeared under the walls of the mighty city. Slavs and Avars brought their siege equipment with them and intended to break the power of the flailing empire. The threat was worse because the Avars dealt with the Persians. After the Byzantines had pushed the Avars and Slavs back, the khagan tried to transport the Persians across on rafts. This also resulted in failure, and the whole enterprise ended as a glorious victory for the Byzantine army and a catastrophe for the Avar khaganate. The khagan blamed the Slavs, who fought loyally till the very last moment. He executed their captains.

After the khagan returned home, he tried to present the battle as a victory, but nobody was fooled. It proved a turning point in the history of the Avar khaganate, breaking the myth of their invincibility and providing the last straw for the fragile loyalty of their Slavic subjects. Some of them left, which was catastrophic for the parasitic lifestyle of the Avars, and even more so for their pride. The rest of them rebelled, a story that we will tell in another chapter.

Before we do that, however, we have to introduce another player on the political map of Europe of the seventh and eighth centuries: the Franks and the renewed Roman Empire.

FRANCIA AND THE FRANKS

he Franks were Germans and Christians who ruled most of Central Europe. Later, in 800, one of them, Charlemagne (748–814), would become the West's first emperor; he renewed the Western Roman Empire and founded the Holy Roman Empire. All the Slavs who came to Central Europe had to deal with the Franks and their political culture, distinct from what they had learned in the Byzantine Empire.

Unlike Byzantium, where the administration was entirely used to dealing with other religious systems (such as the Persian or later Islam) as equal political adversaries, it was either Christianity or paganism for the Franks. Paganism was inferior; pagans could be enslaved and pagans would not be dealt with.

Christianity has played a crucial role since the beginning of Western political culture. To convert to Christianity meant that the ruler became worthy of diplomacy and a potential partner for marriage matches; above all, he entered a family of European rulers. As the Slavs remained pagans when all other barbarian nations converted to Christianity, they had difficulty adjusting to this political reality.

We must remember that there were thus two versions of Christianity. The patriarch in Constantinople represented the Eastern, and the Western was under the pope's rule in Rome. The Church was united, yet they competed for power and differed in liturgy, language and political practice. And the Slavs, newcomers to European politics, would become the battleground for these two versions of Christianity.

The Eastern and the Western Political Traditions

More differences remained between the Eastern and the Western political traditions. The relationship between the secular and spiritual powers differed significantly. In Constantinople the patriarch was subject to the emperor; both secular and spiritual power lay in the hands of the emperor as such. In the Western Christian Church, on the other hand, the pope and the emperor were two distinct entities, one wielding spiritual and the other secular power. They constantly competed against each other. This relationship of State and Church helped to create the unique relationship between the secular and spiritual that formed Western society.

Last but not least, the West and the East both lay their claims to Roman inheritance. The Byzantines felt that there was no end to the Roman Empire because they *were* the Roman Empire. However, their dominion over the Western part of the empire fell and the former provinces were ruled by various barbarian tribes. When the Franks united the disintegrated Roman heritage under their rule, they made a deal with the pope in Rome. They claimed the Western Roman Empire, proclaiming it had fallen and risen again. In the eyes of Byzantium, this was initially preposterous. Yet in the end they had no choice but to respect the reality.

In the following chapter, we will watch the Slavs enter the political arena of early medieval Europe. Eventually they manage to form their own states and establish a new social order, but first they must shake off the Avar yoke.

THE FIRST SLAVIC STATES

We have reached the late seventh century in Europe. In the west, the feisty Germanic tribe, the Franks, rule their empire Francia – an empire that would be called the Holy Roman Empire a century later and claim the Western Roman inheritance. However, in the seventh century, the Latin world bows to no one. Germanic tribes of various origins, usually Goths, rule Italy and wage wars, while the pope is in Rome.

NEW POLITICAL REALITY OF THE SEVENTH CENTURY

Nominally, the pope is only one of the bishops who should, in all things, obey the patriarch and emperor in Constantinople. However, the popes of the early Middle Ages soon learned to exploit the fact that the patriarch was far away. Meanwhile the barbarian, yet Christian, kings lived close enough to listen to their preachings. They could instruct the Germanic elites and gain influence in regions where the patriarch in Constantinople was powerless. The popes thus mingle in Italian politics, teaching the rulers to know right from wrong. They are set on a path that will one day enable them to depose and install emperors on a whim.

In the north, the Vikings remain peacefully in snow-covered Scandinavia. A century later, they will learn to use rivers for trade and invasion, and so start the Viking era. In the east is the Byzantine Empire. It calls itself Rome: the only Rome there was and ever will be. Yet the empire has lost its Balkan provinces to the Slavs. It is constantly bothered by the Slavs and Avars, wages war on the Persian Empire and is about to face the most dangerous enemy of all its history – the successors of Mohamed.

This is the Europe that serves as a background for the stories in this chapter, the setting from which we watch the first Slavic state-like formations emerge. For the first time the Slavs will express their will to be part of something bigger than a family or a tribe. For the first time they say yes to a central authority, prompted by various incentives, for multiple ends. However, state-building is a process that usually follows a significant pattern.

History is not given. It is a chain of choices made by human beings of flesh and blood. People naturally tend to do what works, what seems good for them. The oldest Slavs did not build a state, therefore, and fostered no elites – they had no need for any of it.

During the migration period, the Slavs' situation changed. The calm, peaceful times of ploughing the fields were over. Now they had Avar masters ruling them, and some of them had to make war their daily life, experiencing a system where some enjoyed more rights and more luxury. The constant wars they had to go into made some of them learn the craft and become professional warriors, while others stayed at home to provide for them. So it was that elites were born. They saw the Avar leaders display their authority with luxury goods, rituals of obedience and expensive clothes and jewellery. The desire to have more was born. But still, under the rule of the oppressive

Avars, they needed no ruler above them. They only recognized that they needed one leader to rule them all when they wanted to shake off the Avar yoke.

The Model of the Origin of the Early Medieval States

The states in the early Middle Ages did not come about through chance. They came to be because people needed a ruler to help them succeed in ongoing power struggles. It was either get a leader of their own and obey him or be ruled by some other tribe. The pattern was always similar.

Once there was a king, or a duke, or a leader. The title did not matter. Power did and so did respect. A leader was ready to take control once he got the respect of enough strong men to form his company. He had to be strong and charismatic and he must have been really clever, thinking strategically enough to see around every corner and to avoid every ruse. But he had to possess something more, something no one else in the tribe could offer. Experience from the outside.

The Germanic rulers who rose above the rest of their brothers and became kings in the fourth century served in the Roman army. They learned Latin and, more importantly, the military skill that awed their subjects at home. The Slavic rulers usually offered experience from a Western army or culture as well. Samo (c. 600–658) was a Frank. The Bohemi elites founding the Bohemian state probably served in the Italian army because they spoke Latin. Rastislav (r. 848–870), the founder of Great Moravia, arrived as an ally of Francia. Authority from the outside was as crucial as a solid company inside.

Once the leader had a strong company, he could defeat other tribes and unite them under one rule. Yet that was still not enough to ensure the longevity of the state. The leader's authority was bound to him personally. If he could offer no more, the state would disintegrate with his death. He needed an idea. A myth of origin or a new religion. Or both.

SLAVIC MYTHS OF ORIGIN

The surface of this land was then occupied by vast forest wastes without human inhabitants, but it was loud with the buzzing of swarms of bees and the singing of various birds. The animals were as numerous as the grains of sand in the sea or the stars in the sky and wandered undaunted through the wilderness; the flocks of cattle were scarce. In summer, the number of locusts could scarcely equal the amount of cattle that leapt over the fields. The waters were clear and healthy for humans, and the fish were tasty and nutritious. It is a strange thing, and one may see from it how high the country rises: no foreign river flows into it, but all the streams, small and significant, are a part of the larger river, which is called the Elbe and flows down to the North Sea.

When man, whoever he may have been, entered these wastes with an unknown number of people, looking for suitable places for human dwellings, he overlooked with keen eyes the mountains and mines, the plains and hillsides. Passing around Mount Říp between the two rivers, the Ohře and the Vltava, he arranged settlements, founded dwellings, and joyfully set up on the ground the idols which he brought with him on his shoulder.

Then the mayor, who was accompanied by the others as a lord, among other things, spoke thus to his entourage: 'Friends,

THE FIRST SLAVIC STATES

who have more than once endured with me the hardships of the journey through the impassable forests, pause and offer a sacrifice pleasing to your idols, by whose miraculous help you have at last come to this country, once destined for you by fate. As I remember, this land I have often promised you is a land subject to no one, full of beasts and birds, moist with sweet honey and milk, and, as you observe, pleasant in climate to inhabit. The waters are everywhere abundant and more than usually full of fish. Here, you will not be in want of anything, for no one will harm you. But when such a beautiful and great land is in your hands, consider what would be a fitting name for the land.'

They immediately, as if by divine inspiration, exclaimed, 'Since you, father, are called Bohemus, where shall we find a better or more fitting name than that the land should also be called Bohemia?'

Then the mayor, moved by this prediction of his companions, began to kiss the earth for joy, rejoicing that it should bear his name. He arose and, lifting both his palms to the stars of heaven, began to speak thus: 'Hail to me, promised land, sought of us by a thousand desires, once in the time of the flood deprived of a people, preserve us without calamity, and multiply our offspring from generation to generation.'

But he would fall into gross disfavour who should attempt to relate in detail to our present people, who delight in the very opposite, what were their manners, how upright, how simple, and strangely noble were the people of those days, how faithful and merciful they were to one another, how gentle and temperate they were. Therefore, we do not mention this; we want to tell you only a little about what that first age was like. They were happy, contented with modest expenditure and not swelling with pride.

They did not know the gifts of Ceres and Bacchus, for these did not exist. They ate acorns or venison for supper. Unclouded springs provided a wholesome drink. Like sunshine or water, meadows and groves, yes, even women belonged to everybody. After the manner of cattle, they sought new relations every night, and then the rising of the morning broke the bond of the three Graces and the iron bonds of love. Wherever the night found them, they lay in the grass and slept sweetly in the shade of a gnarled tree. They knew not to use wool, flax, or clothing; in winter, they used wild beasts' furs or sheep skins.

Nor did anyone know the word 'mine', but in the manner of the monks, they declared all that they had to be 'ours' by mouth, heart and deed. There were no bars at the stables, nor did they shut the doors against the poor walker, for there were neither thieves nor robbers nor the poor. No crime was more grievous to them than theft and robbery. They knew no weapons, only arrows, for shooting game.

What more need I say? Alas! The beneficial turned to the opposite; the common turned into the private; secure poverty, once pleasant, they avoided like a muddy wheel and fled from it, for the desire for wealth burned in all of them, fiercer than the fires of Etna. When these and similar vices grew worse and worse day by day, the injustice, which no one knew how to do before, was patiently suffered by one from another, having neither judge nor prince to whom to complain.

Then, he who was acknowledged in his tribe or clan as a person more honourable for his manners or more honourable for his wealth, to him they came together in goodwill, without a bier, without a seal, and discussed their quarrels and the wrongs which anyone had suffered, without injury to liberty.

Among them, a man named Krok arose; by his name, a castle already overgrown with trees was in the woods near the village of Zbeczna. He was a man of his age, perfect, rich in earthly goods, and prudent and rational in his judgments. And like bees to a hive, men flocked to him, not only from his own family but from all the land, to be judged by him. This excellent man had no male offspring, but he begat three daughters, to whom nature has bestowed no fewer treasures of wisdom than she gives to men.

The Chronicle of the Czechs, Cosmas of Prague, 1125; translated by the author

What the Czech Myth of Origin Says

The Czech myth of origin contains important features. It describes how the Bohemian tribe arrived in the land to find it fair and fertile yet empty. That is definitely not how it was. Archaeological sources testify that both Celtic and Germanic tribes were inhabiting Bohemia when the first Slavs came here. We may be certain that the Slavs came in many waves before the ruling dynasty could start the unification process. But the myth of origin needs not to bother itself with reality. Its only aim is to justify the claim of the dynasty already seated firmly on the throne.

When you read the myth, you notice one necessary pattern. The Bohemian tribe came to the land and settled there. They lived happily, as if in paradise. But that is not enough. The author needs to present the need for a ruler. He therefore introduces discord in their lines. Some other myths of origin (the Polish one, for example) contain an enemy to deal with. In the Czech myth, it is the discord among the people that means they no longer deserve their freedom. They need a leader. And the chronicler provides a leader. A goddess and a duke.

The third, the youngest in age but the oldest in wisdom, was called Libuše; she also built the most powerful castle at that time by the forest that stretches to the village of Zbečn, and she called it Libušín after her name. She was a unique woman among women, clear-sighted in judgment, vigorous in speech, chaste in body, noble in manners, equal to no one in judgment; with the people, kind, or rather affectionate, to everyone, an ornament and glory of the female sex, giving orders as clear-sighted as if she were a man. But since no one is wholly blissful, a woman so excellent and worthy of praise – oh, unhappy human fate! – was a prophetess. And because she had indeed foretold many things to come to the people, the whole tribe, after her father's death, assembled in council and made her their judge.

At that time, a considerable dispute arose between two inhabitants, who were distinguished by wealth and birth and were neighbours. And they got into such a quarrel with each other that one drove his nails into the other's thick beard, and, calling themselves shamefully indiscriminate names and snapping their fingers under their noses, they thundered into the court, and with a great noise came before their mistress, and importunately demanded that she should decide the dispute between them in law and justice.

Meanwhile, the lady did as dissolutely capricious women do when they have no man to fear, lying softly on high embroidered cushions and leaning on her elbows as in childbirth. Then, going in the way of justice and not looking at the men, she rightly decided the whole dispute between them. However, he who had not won the dispute in the court shook his head two or three times in anger and, according to his custom, struck his staff three times on the ground and, spitting spittle from his mouth, exclaimed:

'This is an injustice unbearable to men! For we know that a woman, whether she stands or sits on a table, has little sense; how much less when she lies on cushions? Then, indeed, she is better suited to get married than to give orders to warriors, for it is a certain thing that all women have long hair but short minds. It would be better for men to die than to suffer it. We alone have been abandoned by nature, to the shame of all nations and tribes, that we have no administrators or male government, and that women's rule is upon us.'

And the lady, concealing her reproach and hiding the pain in her heart with a woman's shame, smiled and said:

'It is as you say; I am a woman, and as a woman I live, but perhaps you think that I have little sense because I do not judge you with a rod of iron and because you live without fear, you do not rightly heed me. For where there is fear, there is discipline. And now you must have a ruler more cruel than a woman. So also the pigeons despised the white-headed moon, whom they chose to be king, as you despise me, and made a hawk, much more cruel, to be their prince, who, devising iniquities, began to kill the guilty and the innocent; and from that time to this day the hawk hath devoured the pigeons. Go home now, and whoever ye choose for your master tomorrow, I will take to be my husband.'

On the second day, as it was ordered, without delay, they called an assembly and gathered the people together, and they all met together. The woman sitting on the high table said to the rude men:

'How exceedingly worthy of pity, O people, who know not how to live freely, a freedom which no good man loses except with life, which you not unwittingly abhor, and willingly submit your necks to unusual bondage. Alas, you will regret it in vain, as the frogs regretted it when the water snake, which they made king, began to kill them. If you do not know the rights of princes, I will only try to tell you a few words on the subject.

First, it is easy to set up a prince but not easy to depose one who is set up. For at this moment, the man is under your power, whether you make him a prince or not, but as soon as he is made a prince, you and all you give him will be in his power. Your knees shall tremble like a fever before his face, and your tongue shall cleave to the dry palate.

You will only answer his voice in great fear, 'Yes, sir; yes, sir,' until he shall, by his mere command, without your knowledge, condemn this man, put that man to death, and order one to be put in prison, another to be hanged on the gallows. He will make you, and you whom he pleases, some servants, some peasants, some taxpayers, some tax collectors, some executioners, some beaters, some cooks, bakers, or grinders. He shall also appoint colonels, centurions, sappers, husbandmen, vinedressers, and husbandmen of the fields, as well as reapers, smiths of weapons, tanners, and shoemakers. He shall set your sons and daughters in his service and take the best he pleases of your cattle, horses and mares, or your beasts. All that you have that is better in the fields, meadows, and vineyards, he will take and turn to his advantage. But why have I detained you long? Or why do I speak as if I were trying to frighten you? If you persist in your resolution and are not mistaken in your wish, I will tell you the name of the prince and the place where he is.'

At this, the vulgar people shout in confusion; they all demand with one voice that the prince be given to them.

'Behold,' *says she,* 'behold, beyond the mountains,' *and she points her finger to the mountains,* 'there is a small river called Bielina, and on its banks is a village called Stadice. There is an estuary within its circumference, and from it a field of twelve crofts, which, strange to say, though it lies among so many fields, does not belong to any field. Your prince ploughs with two speckled oxen; one has a white belt around the front and a white head; the other is white from forehead to back, and his hind legs are white. Now, if it please you, take my sash and cloak and coverings, such as are fit for a prince, and go and give the man a message from me and the people, and bring the prince to you, and my husband to me. The man's name is Přemysl. His seed shall reign in all this land for ever and ever.'

Meanwhile, messengers were appointed to deliver the man's message to his mistress and the people. When the lady saw that they were hesitating, as it were, not knowing the way, she said:

'Why do you hesitate? Go on your way; follow my horse, and he will lead you in the right way and bring you back again, for he has trodden the way more than once.'

A false rumour and an incorrect opinion spread that the lady herself always made that fabulous journey on horseback in the silence of the night and returned before dawn.

What next? The messengers walked wisely, unlearned, wandering wilfully ignorant, keeping to the horse's tracks. They had already crossed the mountains and were nearing the village where they were supposed to arrive. Then a boy came running to meet them, and they asked him, saying:

'Hear, good boy, is this village called Stadice? And if so, is there a man named Přemysl in it?'

'Yes,' he answered, *'it is the village which you seek, and behold, a man named Přemysl is in the field not far off, driving oxen to finish the work he is about to do.'*

And the messengers came to him, saying:

'Blessed man and prince, thou art born to us of the gods.'

And as peasants who repeat everything twice, they spoke again:

'Hail, prince, hail, thou art worthy to be celebrated above all others; change your garments and mount your horse.'

And they showed him his garments and the stallion, which neighed.

'Our Lady Libuše and all the people bid thee come soon and take the dominion destined for thee and thy descendants. All we are in thy hands; thee for the prince, thee for judge, thee for the steward, thee for the defender, thee alone we choose to be our lord.'

At this speech, the wise man, as if foreseeing the future, paused, thrusting the staff he held in his hand into the ground and, letting go of the oxen, cried out to them: 'Go whence ye came!'

The Chronicle of the Czechs, Cosmas of Prague, 1125; translated by the author

The author of the text was Cosmas the Chronicler, a court historian of the Přemyslid dynasty who lived in the twelfth century. However, he recorded the myth that lived in the collective memory of the Bohemian people long before then. We can probably ignore the features Cosmas took from the Bible, although some of them are important because they appear in the mythology of many nations. Přemysl, ploughing the field in Stadice, is a mythical founder of a dynasty that would rule Bohemia until 1306. But his claim comes through a woman with supernatural powers, a near goddess. A marriage or any other intimate relationship with a goddess was a common way for rulers to get legitimacy, something that we recognize in Indo-European mythology, be it of the classical world or Scandinavia.

Now comes the time to establish the first Slavic state. It was one that lacked a myth of origin or any other foundational idea and thus failed.

SAMO'S EMPIRE: AN UNLIKELY ALLIANCE OF A FRANK AND SLAVS AGAINST THE AVARS

His name was Samo. He was a Frank and came to Central Europe as a merchant around 623. Yet that is all we know about him. We cannot even tell for sure what the subject of his trade may have been. Historians believe that he might have bought luxury goods from the Slavs and the Avars or garnets – unique, blood-red gems from Bohemia. Nevertheless, Samo was an authoritative figure skilled in trade and obviously in warfare because the Slavs chose him as their leader.

The Slavs, at this moment, found themselves in a challenging situation. They felt harshly oppressed by the Avars and, after the battle under the walls of Constantinople, they lost faith in the Avars' invincibility and saw no reason to obey the leaders, who rewarded loyalty with execution. The most discontent of them all were the half-Avars. These were the sons of Avar fathers and Slavic mothers. The Avars treated Slavs as lower people; if they took a Slavic woman for a concubine, any children would still be treated like Slavs. Only Avars of pure blood could earn their place in the Avar society. And so these sons could not stand it any more and rebelled. Other Slavs joined their revolt, and Samo came into the land at that precise moment.

We will probably never understand why the rebels chose Samo to lead them against the terrifying Avars. The first purpose of the revolt was for the half-Avars to get the rights they believed were theirs. However, after several victories, they began to hope to achieve more far-reaching goals.

What if they could free themselves from the Avars once and for all?

The time was ripe. The Avar khaganate suffered defeat under Constantinople, their Slavic subjects were running away and their political structures were shaken to the core. Nomadic states rely on success; if defeats come, the wheel of power has to turn. And as it is turning, someone else may profit. This happened to the Slavs under Samo's leadership.

After the series of battles, the Slavs won their freedom.

Just imagine a dining hall as Samo informs the warriors that the Avars will not threaten them again. That they are free after centuries of oppression. This land, this beautiful, fertile land, is theirs.

Victorious cheers erupt in the hall, mugs of beer clink and men pat themselves on the back. Amidst the emotions, someone calls:

'Let's make Samo our king!'

For a split second, there is silence. A king? Are we to have a king above us? But then, why not? It has served us well so far when Samo was the leader. And there are other dangers to face. Let's have a king!

'Yeah!' the crowd shouts their obvious acclamation, and the surprised Samo smiles nervously.

THE FIRST SLAVIC STATES

Me? A king? I came here as a merchant buying gems. Things are happening a little too fast, aren't they? And to rule these unruly people? The Franks will not like it. There will be another war. But, then, why not? It has been fun so far...

Samo: The King of the Slavs

Historians have no idea whether these words ran through Samo's head as he accepted their crown. But he was clever enough to realize that Francia and the king of the Franks would not like the idea of a Slavic just right beyond their borders. Up until now, the Franks barely noticed the Slavs. They were the property of the Avars and nobody wanted trouble with them. And with the Avars expelled, the empire might swallow the Slavs one day. Because the kings of the Franks never considered their borders to be final as they were. The Slavic lands in Central Europe might be theirs for the taking. Now there was a king to be reckoned with. That is something the mighty Franks could not tolerate.

We are standing at a turning point in Slavic history. So far, it has been the Slavs against the Avars or the Byzantines. From now on, in Central Europe at least, it will be the Slavs against the Germans.

Samo and the Franks

The king of Francia, Dagobert (r. 603–639), certainly did not like the idea of a king in former Avar territory. He wished to destroy the young state as soon as possible. As a pretext for a military campaign, he chose an unlucky incident. A group of merchants from Francia was assaulted, robbed and murdered on Samo's territory. Dagobert sent an envoy to Samo, demanding compensation for the damage and Samo's acceptance of Dagobert as his suzerain. To the envoy's surprise, Samo agreed.

Yet he proclaimed that he wished to live in friendship with his mighty neighbour. The envoy revealed poor diplomatic skills, replying with obvious disdain:

'You are a pagan dog; a Christian king does not make friends with pagan dogs. The only way to treat a pagan dog is to beat him into obedience.'

Samo supposedly smiled and answered: 'The Slavs might be just dogs in your god's eyes. Yet dogs can bite.'

Thus the military preparations began.

In 631 King Dagobert stands in front of a large wooden fortification. This is Vogastisburg.

The king desperately searches his thoughts for a solution to this situation.

He promised his soldiers a straightforward campaign. The Slavs were supposed to be primitive savages, armed with sticks and stones. The campaign has not brought any severe challenges so far. His men were thrilled with the wagons of spoils and slaves they loaded and sent home when they looted villages and little merchant towns. Yet King Dagobert did not share his soldiers' enthusiasm. The Slavs were supposed to be primitive savages, easy to defeat. But if they were so primitive, where did all this wealth come from?

He swore to execute the envoys who persuaded him to underestimate this Samo. And every evening, as his suspicion grew, he added more and more torture to their punishment. Now, as he stood before the strong fortifications and faced the armed Slavs ready to defend them, he swore to burn the envoys alive.

THE FIRST SLAVIC STATES

'Dogs can bite,' this Samo supposedly said. And as Dagobert watched the defenders of Vogastisburg, he did not doubt for a second that their teeth could do much damage.

He looked over his shoulder at his captains and saw his own doubts mirrored in their eyes. He had promised an easy victory. Most of them had already got their loot; now they desired to go home and enjoy it. None of them wanted to die in this pagan land or, worse, serve as a sacrifice to their strange pagan gods.

This would not be an easy victory if they could win at all. And if they won, then what? Dagobert never planned so far ahead. He counted on the Slavic Empire to fall apart once he had given it one gentle nudge. Now he was not so sure. He might win today, and other battles will follow. His army is not equipped to withstand such a war. His position in Francia might not be solid enough to withstand such a war. This was madness. He would burn the envoys alive, he swore.

With that thought in mind he turned his steed and, without uttering a word, he walked through the ranks with his back straight.

The captains did not hesitate once they understood what it meant and followed him.

And Dagobert, ushering the horse to a trot, tried to close his ears and not hear the victorious cries of the pagan dogs once they realized that they had won.

From then on, an armed peace reigned between the Samo Empire and Dagobert. After this memorable moment Samo ruled his empire for the next 35 years. He supposedly had 12 wives, 25 sons and 15 daughters. After his death, the empire disintegrated.

Samo's empire is essential to the Central European national memory because of the conflict with the Germanic tribe. The

Germans (Franks) wanted to subdue the Slavs, but the Slavs resisted and won. The mighty Francia had to admit their power. So children in primary schools in Bohemia and Slovakia learn about Samo and his empire. The only problem is that we do not know where the empire was precisely. First, we cannot locate Vogastisburg; current historians have placed it somewhere on the banks of the Thaya River in South Moravia. The centre of Samo's empire must have been somewhere on the borders with the Avar khaganate, in modern southern Slovakia or northeastern Austria.

What Happened Next?

Samo himself died peacefully between 655 and 660. His empire did not fall in some dramatic crash: it was nothing more than a loose confederation of tribes, created for one purpose: protect the tribes from Avars on one side and Francia on the other. In the second half of the seventh century the Avar khaganate shook with civil war and was no danger to anybody. Francia had its own problems and did not bother the Slavs. Samo's empire served as a protective umbrella that allowed the tribes to settle and peacefully evolve in the area. Now that both sides, the Avars and the Franks, came to respect that the Slavs lived in Central Europe, the tribes could quietly go their own way.

Samo's empire was not a state per se. We lack written sources from the seventh century to tell us more than the barest facts. So it is with relief that we turn the page and move into the ninth century. So long do we have to wait for the Slavic tribes, whom Samo helped free from the Avars, to create their first state. As with later years, the number of written sources grew – and thus, finally, we have more to say.

THE FIRST SLAVIC STATES

PANNONIAN PLAIN AND THE END OF THE AVARS

Pannonian Plain is a large, fertile lowland region in Central Europe. The Czech Republic (Moravia), Lower Austria, Slovakia and Poland (Silesia) share this territory today. No traces of Latin culture of the old Roman province of Pannonia remained in the ninth century. The climate here is hot compared to the rest of Central Europe; it is said that the soil here could feed the whole of Europe. Today the land suffers from summer droughts, not a problem in the ninth century. Then the scarcity of rain favoured Pannonian farmers. Pannonia is relatively poor in natural resources such as metal. Yet trade routes came through here, and what the settlers could not make themselves they could buy.

Pannonian Geography

Before the Slavs and before Samo, many nations settled in this fertile region. First, the Huns made this part of their short-lived Hunnic Empire. Next, Pannonia was part of the Kingdom of Lombards and later the Ostrogoths. Most recently, from our point of view, the Avars made Pannonia part of their khaganate – but not all of it. Geography matters, and in this case even biology matters a lot. Nomadic nations never came to the very heart of Moravia; they stopped on the line marked by the Palava mountain range. The steppe named Pouzdřany, which lies down this mountain range, is the last place where specific plants grow – *stipa capillata* and its family of grasses. The nomadic nations travelled across wild plains because it suited their way of war, and because the plain could feed their sturdy horses.

The nomadic nations in the Eurasian Steppes ride small, hairy ponies. Incredibly fast and very good at surviving, they can find grass in frozen land and go very long without water. Yet they do not do well on hay or on traditional Central European grass. They love *stippa* and other plants that grow on the vast steppes. That is why Huns or Avars never went as far as Palava. Beyond this mountain range the first Slavic inhabitants of the region lived, protected by the climate.

The archaeological sources reveal that the first Slavs arrived here before the year 535. When they came, the region was scarcely settled by Germanic people, who politically did not belong anywhere. Thus they lived together, and in time the Slavic element prevailed.

These Slavs lived here like the old Slavs did; we do not hear of any state-like formations and they did not wage wars. However, when war came to their land, they were a force to be reckoned with. But they remained hidden from the attention of written sources. Of course, their leaders joined the rebellion of their neighbours against the Avars. They celebrated with their brethren and their leader, Samo. They fought with him against the Franks and lived happily after Samo's empire disintegrated – until we meet them again in the ninth century.

The Charlemangne's campaign in 796 resulted in the final end of the Avar threat to the world. It all began with a seemingly unrelated event. Charlemagne, trying to unify as many independent lands as possible under one rule, merged the Bavarian dukedom with his empire. The Avars who lived east of Bavaria grew restless. Gone were the days when they could dictate to the empires. The khaganate was weak, and with apprehension they watched the mighty Franks coming closer

THE FIRST SLAVIC STATES

and closer to their own borders. Bavarian dukes had not been Avar allies, yet their rule helped to create a balance of power, which was now gone.

Thus the Avars decided to act before it was too late. They invaded the Bavarian lands, trying to usurp as much land as possible. Then they engaged in diplomacy. The envoys from the Avar Khan came to Charlemagne, meeting in Worms on the Rhine to negotiate new borders. Yet the emperor did not fear the pagans and had no real interest in negotiating with them. He only wanted to buy time to prepare for the mighty campaign that started in the autumn of 791.

Charlemagne's War Against the Avars

Charlemagne intended to amaze all the chroniclers writing about this war. Avars still held a terrifying reputation, and the glorious army of the Christian emperor – who set out to exterminate the pagan dogs once and for all – was designed to impress not only the Avars themselves but the whole of Europe, the Byzantine Empire included.

Charlemagne had no idea that victory would be so easy. He himself fell prey to the reputation of magnificence and strength the Avars spread. He thus assembled an army of 12,000 warriors, including Franks, Bavarians, Saxons and even Slavs in his ranks. The terrible army crossed the Danube and met in the old Roman *Lauriacum* (Upper Austria). Here the host prayed for three days for a happy outcome of the campaign.

As they moved on, they suffered terrible losses. Yet no glorious battle caused this disaster. First, they did not face the giant, mighty Avar warriors. The fiercest enemy for the Franks proved to be a tiny, unseen adversary in the form of a virus or bacteria that befell the greatest allies of medieval knights: their horses.

The medieval army relied heavily on its cavalry. Yet the vast plains proved deadly to the mighty steeds, used to green grass and supplies of oats and hay. The beautiful animals strong enough to carry a knight in full armour grew thin in these conditions. Worse, an epidemic in their ranks broke out in the autumn of 791. Some illness that the sturdy ponies probably withstood without trouble decimated the cavalry of Charlemagne, and he had to turn back. His son with the second host fared better and his army gained some spoils. However, he still had to go home without winning any significant victory because the Saxons rebelled in the empire. Yet this campaign revealed one surprising fact – the Avars were far from invincible, and not as threatening as everybody thought.

The Second Campaign

And so it was that, four years later, the emperor returned to Pannonia. Luckily they found the Avar khaganate in the turmoil of a civil war. There was no big, glorious battle that would destroy the Avars, simply infrequent fighting and a lot of plundering. The Franks brought home Avar treasure that awed the whole of Europe. The very same year, in the autumn of 795, Avars sent their envoys to Charlemagne to accept the truce on the Franks' terms – they would convert to Christianity and accept the emperor as their sovereign. This practically meant the end of the khaganate, because the khan who agrees with the rule of others and foreign faith ceases to be a khan.

The Franks and the Slavs living on the borders of the former Avar khaganate thus travelled to Pannonia without much trouble. There they gained land and treasure, while missionaries also came to Pannonia to baptize those inhabitants who were still alive. After the campaigns, the Avars themselves were no more. Now the story of Slavs in Pannonia could begin.

The political and cultural climate of the ninth century differed significantly from the times of Samo's empire. First, there were no Avars who could threaten the Slavs. The vast plains of Pannonia were free for their taking. Second, the Carolingian Empire was a brand-new element. The Slavic elites met the Christian knights and their attractive culture, and wanted a chance to build something similar. They also wanted to join high European politics, to be kings.

GREAT MORAVIA

The Great Moravian story begins in sources of Germanic origin. We have no idea where the two heroes came from. Still, they competed for the favour of the Holy Roman Emperor and tried to enter the family of European princes by converting to Christianity. Their names are Mojmir and Pribina, yet only the first succeeded and founded a dynasty to create the first flourishing Slavic medieval state.

PRIBINA AND MOJMIR

The chronicler tells us of the events around 838 when a Moravian duke named Pribina (r. 825–840) loses a power struggle with a Mojmir in Moravia. Pribina accepts Christianity and the sovereignty of Louis the Pious (r. 814–840), a successor of Charlemagne, and is given a new dukedom in Pannonia. Thus the Duke of the Slavs accepted Christianity and became a part of the European family of rulers. Historians believe that he had decided to become a Christian before he came before Louis the Pious; he had already been married to a Bavarian noblewoman, and such a lady would not marry a pagan. Thus he probably promised to convert sometime before 838, fulfilled his promise to build a church in Nitra to prove his intentions and married the lady. Before he could convert in reality, he was expelled from his land by his adversary Mojmir and was baptized in exile in Louis' court.

Before we move on to his more successful opponent, let us emphasize the importance of this moment. What did conversion to Christianity mean to the rulers of the early Middle Ages?

Pribina knelt before Louis the Pious. Behind him, his 12 most loyal men knelt as well. They were simply dressed in linen robes. Then Pribina spoke:

'I see now that I have been living in mortal sin. All the gods I had hitherto bowed to were no gods. They were just an invention of the Devil, who made us bow to the inventions of our hands like the Israelites of the old days. I see now the terrible sin of the human sacrifice, and the blood of sacrificed men and animals that my people and I gave to the bloody idols calls to Almighty God for revenge. I see now that only through the washing of baptism can I wash away the blood, the sin.

I see now that there is only one God, the God who came on earth as Jesus Christ, and there is no salvation but through him. The salvation comes through the one Church I wish to be part of. I swear to spread the faith in the one God and to bring it into the land of my fathers. I swear that my subjects will become Christians, so help me God. I swear to do this task with the help of the mighty Church.'

Then Pribina and his men would enter the bath of baptism, and the bishop would make them anew. So the Moravian duke became a member of the Almighty Christian Church.

What Did Pribina Mean by His Confession?

This is how it might have happened, and these are the words Pribina may have used. However, we have no idea how sincere he was. Probably not very. The conversion of elites in the early Middle Ages usually had little to do with personal faith and desire for salvation (however they understood the term). With few exceptions, the elites accepted baptism out of political calculation. If they became Christians in heart, they did so only later, once they had learned enough about the religion. But for the Church of the early Middle Ages, this sufficed. The inner thoughts of the ruler mattered little; more important were his actions.

What Pribina really meant with these words and how the listeners would interpret it would go something like this:

'Almighty king, Louis, I accept your way of life and your culture. I desire to be like you, your equal, and to enter the world you rule. I recognize that there is no place for pagans in the future; paganism is doomed to become extinct and all will be Christians. I wish to be part of the future. To build the future and to join the future as a ruler of an independent state that recognizes a higher authority, the emperor's authority. And I accept that you are the emperor, not the one sitting in Constantinople; that emperor has no jurisdiction here.

From now on, I recognize that the Church that bows to the pope in Rome has authority in my land. I wish that you appoint teachers and, one day, I want to have a bishop of my own, a leader of the Church from my own land. I will destroy the pagan idols and I will suppress the pagan religion because from now on the pagans are a threat to my new chosen path. My men accept this because they are loyal and will help me in this endeavour.

Because now we are of one mind, I can negotiate treaties on an equal basis; I might have a bride for me and my sons in Christian ruling families and further elevate my house. And because I am a Christian ruler, I will wage wars on pagan rulers. And I will take their land and their pagan subjects as slaves. Because I can. Because pagans have no future place; I am one of the first to realize that. I will use the opportunity as best I can, because now I have the support of the emperor and the Church. And I am very sorry that Mojmir, my mortal enemy, accepted Christianity before me. I cannot call him a pagan dog any more.'

Thus Pribina became Christian, one of the first Slavs to do so, and a line of rulers followed in his footsteps to build Christian Europe. The sources tell us that his adversary Mojmir I was the first of the two to convert. Only after that did Pribina recognize the pressing need to follow him.

Yet it is one thing to convert yourself and bring your most loyal company or family to conversion. The promises considering your subjects are necessary, but it will take generations before the whole country becomes Christian. The point is that Christianity must have been tempting for the elites. Unlike paganism, it opened doors to an attractive Western culture; more importantly, it brought contacts with Christian ruling families around Europe. It even provided acceptable career paths for young, ambitious men (in the early Middle Ages, priests or monks did not live in celibacy, and had families). Christianity brought education; those who thirsted for it must have been awed by the knowledge they found in the libraries of educated monks. They learned to read, they learned of faraway lands and they learned all that classical knowledge, dating back many centuries. And some of them, if not most, realized then that Christianity offered more to an individual than paganism.

Christianity and the Traditional Tribal Society

Unlike the pagan gods, who had to be appeased through magic and ritual, the Christian God cared for the believer. The believers were encouraged to pray and to entrust their God or the pantheon of saints with their daily struggles. One section of society found this incredibly tempting: women. It is no wonder that in many early medieval royal families, women were the first, as wives or mothers, to convert. For the women bore children, then watched them suffer and die, and the pagan idols would not listen to their worries. They would not care. In the Virgin Mary, Mother of Christ, women found a mediator who understood their fears. It is no small thing to be able to pray to someone who gave birth, cared for a child and had to watch him die on the cross.

Furthermore, Christianity is an individualistic religion. The believers were suddenly responsible themselves for their salvation and for their actions. The price they had to pay seemed small.

However, believers usually learned this after they converted nominally; most of them knew very little, if anything, about the religion before their conversion. But the situation is very different for the broader masses, the peasants over whom they ruled.

For the traditional pagan society, Christianity initially offered very little. Life for them was a struggle against nature and pagan gods helped in that struggle. The paganism was bound to the tribal structures. What would happen if you converted and your ancestors got angry? Moreover, what would the pagan gods do to the whole community if one person converted and got them angry? It was one thing to let the priest talk and not to kill him on the spot, but another to do as he said, bathe in the river and let him baptize them.

Another, entirely different matter came when the priest asked his converts to stop performing the rituals they relied upon. One of the essential rituals was the burial. People were terrified that if they did not cremate their dead, they would come back and haunt them. Unlike the elites who relished the idea of individual religion, the community would not have it. So some fought hard against Christianization, while others somehow converted and kept to their rituals.

Yet, precisely because paganism relied upon the traditional tribal society, the ruling elites had to uproot it. The tribal structures threatened the state that began forming in the early Middle Ages. The new rulers did not want people to be loyal to their tribe; they wanted people to be loyal to them, to join their companies and to respect one ruler sitting in the centre. Christianity helped them in this because the Church taught that all Christians were brothers and tribal loyalties no longer mattered.

Thus the building of a state and the change of social order went hand in hand with the slow victory of Christianity over paganism. Unlike the conversion of elites, however, which usually happened overnight, the conversion of the rest of their subjects was a slow and often painful process.

MOJMIR AND HIS MORAVIA

Now we have our first Slavic Christian rulers. One, Mojmir, rules Moravia and Nitra, and the other, Pribina, sits in

Pannonia. Pribina disappears from our sources. He failed in building his own domain and our eyes must now turn to Mojmir, who will establish a new ruling house.

The Moravian land of Mojmir differed from the one Charlemagne marched through on his campaign against the Avars. First, there were churches built by Moravian aristocrats. Second, society had changed; some elites built fortified castles for themselves and lived lavish lifestyles. After the Avar khaganate fell, these Moravian warriors grew rich with the spoils they looted in its remains. Then, around 830, the Roman Empire was weakening. Nobles revolted against their emperor, leaving the Moravian duke free to build a power base without looking over his shoulder and asking for the emperor's approval.

How the Moravians Lived

It was a time of prosperity for the Moravian people. The land was fertile, and there were enough farmers to provide for people's nutritional needs. Higher lands with forests served as pastures for cattle, and miners searched the land for minerals. Trade prospered. As the elites grew rich, merchants came in larger numbers into these unknown lands with their expensive goods.

Elites in the Middle Ages wore colourful and expensive robes; men and women also wore jewellery. The aristocracy wanted to differ as much as possible from the ordinary people in order to defend their elite place in society. Everyone meeting a nobleman in the field had to recognize from the very look of the animal he rode that a lord was passing by, so that they could greet and treat him accordingly. Archaeological sources reveal items coming to Moravia from afar, from Italy, Byzantium and even as far as Persia. Pious founders installed relics in their churches, and the churches were filled with gold and jewels far beyond the skill of local jewellers. The wealth of the Moravian aristocracy implies another luxury item found in the ground – silk. This expensive textile must have come to Central Europe from the southeast, probably from Byzantium through the Adriatic Sea or Italy.

What goods could the Moravians offer in exchange? Let us not forget that in the ninth century they still lived in a slaver society. Moravian elites were, at this time, primarily Christian. Still, enough pagans resisted conversion, and those could be sold into slavery. Those living at the borders of the former Avar khaganate could travel and catch many slaves. These they sold on to Italian buyers, who brought the unhappy captives to the Caliph and to Arabian slave markets. Here Slavs were sold for premium prices.

Mojmir I: the First Moravian Duke

So what do we know about Mojmir I? He recognized the need to become Christian in 822 when he travelled to Passau with his loyal aristocracy to accept baptism from the hands of the bishop. Unlike the baptism of Pribina in exile described earlier, this was an initiative of the ruler and his closest company. Nobody made them do it. For the Moravian central power, it would be typical to always consult the nobles and abide by their will. Moravian dukes never acted like authoritarians. They kept to an oligarchical way of rule. The baptism of Mojmir and his most loyal men included a promise to convert the whole land of Moravia. After Mojmir I returned, he stabilized power and sent his competitor Pribina into exile.

He acted in concord with the emperor in Frankfurt, who called for a general assembly. All important noblemen were invited, and Louis specifically asked for the presence of the Eastern European princes. Emissaries came from the Obodrites, the Serbs, the Wilzi, the Bohemians, the Moravians, and the remaining Avars in Pannonia. But also Western princes, for example, ambassadors from Normandia, were present.

At the assembly in Frankfurt, Mojmir I accepted the emperor's sovereignty and agreed to pay tribute. However, in later years he cleverly used the mayhem in the empire to lead an independent policy of his own. Louis the Pious was not a very competent ruler. Soon after the events of 822, his own sons and his nobility rebelled against him, and the empire threatened to disintegrate completely. It fell to his successor, Louis the German, to stabilize power. This left Moravian nobility and Mojmir I more than 10 years to prosper. Yet, when the empire was strong enough again, Louis the German set out to put an end to it.

Louis the German and Mojmir I

Louis decided it was against the empire's wishes to have an independent Slavic ruler just beyond its borders and deposed Mojmir. The first Moravian duke was killed in battle or may have fled; either way, nothing is heard of him again. It proved not to be a difficult campaign as the German army met little resistance. Moravian nobles did not show any particular loyalty to their duke, a common thing at this time. The idea of one state and one ruler was still too young. Moreover, the leader of the invasion came from the ruling house itself. He was called Rastislav of Moravia, a charismatic and ambitious young man who inspired greater loyalty than his predecessor.

Rastislav came to Moravia with a German army behind him. Yet, if Louis the German counted on him as a loyal subject of the empire, he could not have made a worse choice, because it would be Rastislav who would tear Moravia from the German grasp. He would lead a series of merciless battles with Louis. It was to be Rastislav who would genuinely make Moravia 'Great'.

RASTISLAV: ON THE WAY TO GREAT MORAVIA

Rastislav was Mojmir's nephew. We have little record of his youth, yet we can probably say he spent considerable time at Louis the German's court in Frankfurt. As Mojmir had no male offspring but a nephew, Rastislav probably played the role of a noble hostage, ensuring that Mojmir upheld his part of the agreement.

East Francia never forgot its claim on the Moravian land. It could not; it was an empire. There is a reason why the word 'imperialism' derives from the term 'empire'. The moment the Franks named themselves emperors, they also promised that the borders of their empire would never be final.

Because an empire's mission is to grow constantly; a good emperor enlarges it. Therefore East Francia would not tolerate an independent ruler just beyond its borders, especially one who was Christian. You might tolerate pagan tribes who performed their uncivilized rituals because they did not threaten you. You could invade them from time to time to gain sufficient slaves and loot. But a Christian ruler is a different matter. A Christian ruler should, by all right, accept you as his sovereign.

Let him rule his little empire as your vicar and liege under your command. That is what the emperor would be thinking.

Yet the Moravian dukes were of a different opinion. They would respect the emperor as their equal, but not bow to him. And they would always try to get more independence, disrupt the empire and use every opportunity to shake off the yoke.

Consequently when Mojmir accepted the truce with the empire, he would have provided insurance in the form of noble hostages – one of whom was Rastislav.

Rastislav: The Hope of the Emperor

We cannot tell when Rastislav became Christian, but it could have happened here in Louis' court. Rastislav was a clever young man. Thus he probably used all the opportunities this environment offered to learn to read and write, to learn about religion and, most importantly, to learn the arts of diplomacy and war. Louis may have had a warm relationship with this Slavic duke, or they may not have met very often. We cannot tell. But one meeting had to take place and it could, with a bit of poetic licence, go something like this:

Louis was sitting on a throne, and Rastislav knelt. They often met on more equal terms, but Louis wanted to emphasize their relationship this time. It was necessary for what he had to say. He let the young man kneel for a split second longer than necessary, a little psychological trick that he knew Rastislav would not fail to notice. Then he gestured for the young man to stand up and stood himself. The two nobles started walking, pacing the room slowly.

'Your uncle, Mojmir, has grown too proud,' Louis started and waited.

Rastislav was quick to answer: 'I understand, my lord.'

When Louis was sure that the Moravian would say no more, he continued.

'I thought we were agreed with Mojmir. I thought he understood his position. Yet he has plotted against us and believed we were weak enough not to answer. But I am strong now and I cannot tolerate this. Moravia is to become a reliable part of the empire. The eastern mark. And I need a duke to rule the Moravians, somebody I can rely upon.'

Rastislav was silent longer before he spoke, though Louis did not doubt his answer was carefully prepared. That the boy had perfected his speech for days in advance:

'My lord,' Rastislav started. 'My uncle is a fool, yet he cares about his people. He is not an evil man and he proved his loyalty to the Christian faith. I do not doubt this. Yet he is a fool to think he can compete with the empire's glory. As there is a universal Church we all bow to, there is an emperor all Christians must kneel before. My uncle is a man of the past, so he does not see the future.'

'And what about you, Rastislav?' asked Louis mildly. 'Are you a man of the future?'

'I learned a lot at your court, my lord,' answered Rastislav carefully.

Yet Louis was not fooled by the art of diplomacy. The boy was clever, far too clever. The emperor saw the sparks of ambition flicker in his brown eyes. He knew Rastislav would say anything to grab the opportunity that awaited him.

Louis had known Rastislav for years. He was sure of his firm character; he studied him closely and enquired with the teachers often about him. Yet character is one thing and loyalty is another. He might be loyal to the emperor, or he might be loyal to his people and his noblemen. Loyalties change even with the best of character.

Men are not dogs. If you take your most loyal dog and make him a pack's leader, you have a loyal pack. Do this with a man and you might lose his loyalty once he discovers his power. Then you lose the whole pack. Men cannot be trusted. And no, Rastislav could not be trusted.

But what choice did Louis have? Mojmir was out of control; he plotted against the empire and forsook the emperor's authority openly, which had to be punished. Yet Louis had only recently stabilized his power; he could not afford a long and demanding campaign.

And the Moravians might fight back.

Yet give them one of their own, a member of the ruling house, a man of the future; give them Rastislav and they might yield before the battle begins.

And if Rastislav turns around to bite the hand that used to feed him? Well, that could be dealt with later...

He turned to face the young duke: 'Rastislav, I will invade Moravia and depose Mojmir. I want you to lead the invasion.'

The young man did not even try to look surprised; he had long expected this. He only bowed respectfully: 'I will not fail you, my lord.'

Louis sighed: 'Oh, I hope you will not, son. I like you. It would sadden me if I had to do with you as I do with your uncle. But you are clever not to betray me, are you not, Rastislav?'

'My lord, I understand that you are an emperor, and we are all your subjects,' Rastislav said and raised his head.

Louis smiled with relief. The answer came too quickly; the boy was too eager. That was a good sign. Perhaps he was not that clever after all.

So it was that Rastislav came to Moravia with a German army behind him. Louis' calculations were correct. Moravian nobles did not move a finger for Mojmir and swore allegiance to Rastislav. Mojmir had to flee, cursing his nephew. It was 846, and Rastislav of Moravia had started his rule as a Moravian duke.

Louis the German had little reason to doubt his decision during the first eight years of Rastislav's rule. If he watched with apprehension how the young duke stabilized power in his country, worked to set up the social order in his favour and gained new territories, we cannot tell. But the new lands merged with Moravia were in the east of the country, far from the empire's borders. Rastislav fought with a Bulgarian khan who plotted with the emperor of West Francia. He worked hard to convert the Moravians to Christianity and accepted the help of Bavarian priests who came from the bishop of Passau. All he did was for the glory of the empire – until 855.

Rastislav Against the Empire

Then, apparently, Rastislav felt strong enough to threaten his old benefactor. He attacked the empire together with the Bulgarians and allied with Louis' enemies.

We can only imagine how Louis the German reacted when he heard the news. He might have expected it long before. He might have even been surprised that Rastislav remained loyal for so long. Nevertheless, he prepared a military campaign to invade Moravia and teach the young duke a lesson.

As we read in the chronicles, the lesson failed. Louis took an army to punish Rastislav but had to return without victory, as the enemy proved too strong and too heavily fortified, and he could not afford to risk an open invasion. His army, however, plundered and burned as they left Moravia, annihilating a considerable military force assembled by Rastislav. Rastislav retaliated by following Louis beyond the borders and devastating the area across the Danube.

The German army shattered like a giant wave against a cliff at the walls of Rastislav's fortified settlement Mikulčice. There was a battle and a small victory, but in the end the Moravians chased the Germans out and plundered their own homes, bringing rich bounty back. Worse was to come for Louis. He sent his son Carloman (*c.* 830–880) to deal with the defiant duke. We know nothing about the relationship between these two men of similar age. They may have been friends from when Rastislav lived as a hostage in Louis' court, or they may have been enemies, competing for acknowledgment in the emperor's eyes.

Anything is possible. But what we do know for sure is that Carloman allied with Rastislav and defected from his father. Together, they usurped a considerable part of Louis' domain, as far as the Inn River.

Rebellious Carloman and Rastislav

Rebellions of sons against fathers were a common way to deal with family business in the early Middle Ages. Young princes with loyal and ambitious companies did not wish to wait for a chance to rule. The fathers usually forgave the betrayals. If you raise a tiger, you expect it to bite once you give it a chance. And no lesser animal than a tiger could survive once the father's protection was gone. Thus Carloman sided with Rastislav against his father.

Louis allied with his old rival, the Bulgarian khan. He attacked Carloman and kept him in custody for 10 years. Then the young prince escaped and rebelled again, but father and son were reconciled and worked together from then on. Carloman's rebellion was vital for Great Moravia because it weakened the empire and gave Rastislav the time he needed to gather his strength and use his diplomatic mastery.

Now he was free of the empire's yoke. He chased the Germans away, and Louis had enough on his hands not to try another campaign for some time. Everybody knew another war was inevitable, but the stronger Moravia grew the firmer Rastislav's position became; the greater the chance for a better outcome. Complete independence was maybe still a dream, yet there is a huge difference between the direct rule of the emperor and an independent empire of one's own. To have as much leverage as possible, Rastislav turned against the mightiest allies of the Franks, against the Bavarian priests that operated within Moravia.

But he needed Christianity and priests to teach Moravians the way of Christ. The Bavarian priests were the only possible clergy, as Moravia belonged to the bishop of Passau. Rastislav then sent envoys to Rome to ask for priests independent of Passau. As this mission proved fruitless, he turned to the other Rome; he sent envoys to Constantinople. This proved to be a turning point in Moravian and Eastern European history.

THE MISSION OF CONSTANTINE AND METHODIUS

And it came to pass in those days, that Rastislav, the prince of the Slavs, and Svatopluk, sent a message from Moravia to Michael the emperor, saying: 'We thank God, we are well. Many Christian teachers came to us from Wallachia, from Greece and from Germany, and they taught us in various ways. But we Slavs are a simple people, and have no one to lead us into the truth and to explain its meaning. Well, my noble lord, send such a man, who will give us all righteousness.'

> Then Michael the emperor said to Constantine the philosopher: 'Hear, philosopher, what he says? No other can do it but you. Behold, you have abundant gifts, take your brother Methodius and go. You are both Thessalonians, and the Thessalonians all speak pure Slavonic.'
>
> **Life of Methodius, translated by the author**

There once lived two brothers, both extraordinary men. Their father was an influential Byzantine citizen. Their uncle was Theoktitos (?–850), a minister, adviser and courtier of the Empress Theodora (c. 815–867), who ruled as a regent for her son Michael III (r. 840–867). Before the brothers came to Moravia, they had splendid careers behind them.

The older of the two brothers, Methodius, had led military campaigns against the Slavs in the Balkans; he retired to the monastery only to avoid political displeasure.

> He was of a family, not of small birth, but a perfect and noble one, known primarily to God, Caesar, and all the region of Thessalonica. Hence, the jurists liked him from his childhood and talked about him with praise until, at last, the emperor also learned of his abilities and entrusted him with the administration of the Slavonic principality. I should say as if he foresaw that he would want to send him to the Slavs as a teacher and first archbishop so that he might learn in advance all the Slavonic customs and slowly acquire them.
>
> Having spent many years in this princely rank and having witnessed many unmanaged confusions in this life, he exchanged his fondness for earthly darkness for heavenly thoughts, not wishing to disturb his precious soul with things that would not

last for ever. As soon as he found an opportune moment, he freed himself of the monarchy and went to Olympus, where the holy fathers live, took the tonsure, put on the black robe, and humbly submitted to and fully observed all monastic order, and diligently devoted himself to study.

Then, such an opportunity arose that the emperor sent his philosopher brother to go to the Khazars, and he took him with him to help him. There were then Jews there very much ashamed of the Christian faith. Then he said:

'I am ready to die for the Christian faith,' and he did not hurry but went and served his younger brother as a slave and obeyed him. He overcame them by prayer and the philosopher by his words.
Life of Methodius, translated by the author

That was Methodius. Now to his younger brother.

Constantine was a linguistic genius, able to master any language in months and a university teacher of philosophy. He was called a philosopher and won great renown for his education and skill with words. It was said that Constantine could win any argument with his reasoning. He was consequently sent on many missions to defend and spread the Christian faith. The mission to the khazars mentioned in the quoted text was one of his greatest successes; he argued with Muslim and Jewish supreme scholars, and won.

Unlike Methodius, a skilled leader and a charismatic figure who inspired awe in women and respect in men, Constantine was a unique child from the beginning. A sickly child physically, he thirsted for knowledge above all else. His biographer in the legend informs us of his childhood and the early sense of vocation the young man felt.

GREAT MORAVIA

In the city of Thessalonica, there was a noble and rich man named Leo, who held the office of drungarius under the strategos. He was pious and kept all the commandments of God, as Job did of old. He lived with his wife and begat seven children, of whom the youngest, the seventh, was Constantine the philosopher, our tutor and teacher.

When his mother gave birth to him, he was given to a nurse to nurse him, but the child would not accept any other breast but his mother's until he was nursed. Thus, it was God's direction that the excellent branch from the good root should be suckled with milk and left undefiled. Then the good parents, out of respect for each other, agreed to have no more intercourse with each other, and for fourteen years, they did not break this resolution but lived in the Lord as brother and sister until death parted them.

At the age of seven, the child had a dream and told it to his father and mother, saying:

'The chief gathered together all the girls of our town and said to me, "Choose from among them whom you want for a wife and helpmate, equal in age." And I looked at them all, and looked at them, and I saw one more beautiful than all the rest. Her face was glorious, and she was adorned with gold jewels and pearls and all manner of splendour. Her name was Sophia, that is, Wisdom.'

Life of Constantine, translated by the author

Envoys from Rastislav in Constantinople

In 862 Rastislav sent envoys to the Byzantine emperor. He asked for teachers to preach to the Moravians in their tongue. What he truly asked for was ecclesiastical independence. To have a diocese of his own, to be fully independent from the bishop in Passau. That the Byzantine emperor refused, for the time being.

First, make your country Christian. Uproot paganism, build churches, prove that you are a true Christian ruler. Then we will see about the bishop.

Constantine, whose uncle Theoktitos still enjoyed the favour of the young emperor Michael III (soon to be named Michael the Drunkard), was an obvious choice. First, both the brothers came from Thessalonica, where the Slavic language was still spoken, and Constantine knew the language well. In the ninth century, all Slavs understood each other; their languages did not differ. Second, this task required a linguistic genius. No script was suitable for Slavic tongues, and the liturgic and biblical texts needed to be translated.

Yet it is said that Constantine lingered before accepting the task. First, he was sick. For all we know he might have inherited his mother's tuberculosis (or got infected from her early in childhood), and the illness took its toll on him. Moravia was far away; it was a cold country and Constantine knew the task might prove too much for his frail constitution. Second, he feared the accusation of heresy and needed promises and assurances before he set out.

The emperor assembled a council and summoned Constantine, the philosopher, and told him the matter, saying:

'I know, philosopher, that you are tired, but you must go there, for no one can do this as well as you.'

The philosopher replied: 'Though I am tired and physically sick, I will go there with pleasure if they have a scripture for my tongue.'

The emperor said to him, 'My grandfather, my father and many others have sought it and have not found it; how can I find it?'

The philosopher said: 'Who can write a speech on water and earn the name of heretic?'

Again, the emperor answered him with his uncle: 'If thou wilt, God can reveal it to thee, who gives to all who ask for something without doubt, and opens to those who knock.'

So the philosopher went and, as was his ancient custom, gave himself up to prayer with other helpers. Soon afterwards, God, who hears the prayers of His servants, revealed them to him, and immediately he composed letters and began to write the words of the Gospel: in the beginning was the Word, and the Word was with God, and God was the Word, and so on.

The emperor rejoiced and praised God with his counsellors. And he sent him away with many gifts, writing to Rastislav a letter like this:

'God, who desires that everyone should come to the knowledge of the truth and strive for a higher degree of perfection, saw your faith and effort, revealing the writing to your nation. Thus, He has done now in our years what was not given in the first years: you may also be numbered among the great nations that glorify God with their tongues. And we have sent you one to whom God has revealed it, a man of honour and piety, a very learned man and a philosopher.

Accept therefore a gift greater and more precious than all gold and silver and precious stones and perishable riches, and seek with him to establish the cause speedily, and seek God with all your heart, and do not neglect the salvation of all, but urge all not to be slothful, but to put themselves in the way of truth, so that you also may be, when thou hast brought them by thy *efforts to the knowledge of the true God, receive for it the reward in this age and the age to come for all those souls who shall believe in Christ our God from now until the end, and that thou mayest leave behind thee a memorial for posterity like the great Emperor Constantine.'*

When they came to Moravia, Rostislav received him with great reverence.

Life of Constantine, translated by the author

And so Constantine and Methodius came to Moravia to teach the Moravians about Christianity. The brothers lived at Rastislav's court for five years and accomplished a magnificent task.

First, they raised priests from the Moravian folk. For the first time, the Moravians had teachers of their own, not Bavarians loyal to the Germans but somebody who understood them. That did much to help the spreading of Christianity.

We know that many pagan rituals prevailed in the society, and Constantine and Methodius tried to educate people with empathy and mildness unknown to the Bavarian clergy. But their masterpiece was the linguistic work.

Old Church Slavonic and the New Slavic Script

Constantine invented a new language, Old Church Slavonic, and a scripture, the Glagolitic alphabet. Thus, for the first time, the Slavs had words and letters of their own. The brothers translated the Gospels and liturgic texts into the new language and started teaching in Moravia. They even wrote the first Civil Code of Great Moravia in the new language. From the beginning the mission was not merely cultural but also political, its success entirely dependent on Rastislav and his position against the empire. Because the Bavarian priests would not give up their rights as missionaries, this was their ground, their rightful diocese, and they had the empire's support. Thus the brothers were accused of heresy and invited to Rome to acquit themselves of the accusations.

As they travelled to Rome, they continued their mission on the way; not only the bishop of Passau but also the archbishop of Salzburg got angry at them for doing this in his jurisdiction. The brothers had started their mission as envoys of the Byzantine Empire but, as the political situation in Constantinople changed and the young emperor sat firmly on his throne, they lost the support of their old masters. Rastislav could not protect them any longer. He saw that the empire would strike again. The only chance for Old Church Slavonic and Moravian independence thus lay in the brothers' success as they came to Rome. If the pope permitted them to teach in Old Church Slavonic, if the pope acknowledged the new liturgy, there still might be a chance.

The Brothers in Rome

All looked fine in the beginning because the brothers discovered a powerful relic during their journeys, the body of Saint Clement. They presented this treasure to the pope as a gift to Rome and gained support of the pope, and Methodius was named an archbishop of Sirmium, with the whole of Pannonia and Moravia as his jurisdiction. The pope consecrated Methodius's disciples and sent the brothers to Moravia again. However, only one of them left Rome. Constantine fell prey to the tuberculosis that had bothered him for years. He took the name of Cyrill, retired to the monastery and died in Rome in

869. Before he died, he perfected his Glagolitic script to suit the Slavic languages better.

And when the philosopher was going away after many days to the judgment of God, he said to his brother Methodius:

'Behold, brother, we two were a team, and we were pulling one furrow. I have finished my day and am going to the other bank.'

Emissaries came from Moravia asking for Methodius.

And the Pope said: 'Not to thee only, but to all the Slavonic regions, I send him as a teacher from God and the holy Apostle Peter, the first deputy and key-bearer of the kingdom of heaven."

And when he had sent him, he wrote this letter:

'Hadrian, bishop and servant of God, to Rastislav, Svatopluk and Kocel. Glory to God in the highest, and on earth, peace, and goodwill in men.

Now we have heard of your spiritual endeavours, to which we have wished your salvation with longing and prayer, for the Lord has awakened your hearts to seek Him and has shown you that not only by faith but also by good works you must serve God: for faith without works is dead, and those fall away who think they know God but renounce Him by works.

Not only did you ask for teachers with this High Priestly See, but also with the blessed Emperor Michael, so he sent you the blessed Philosopher Constantine and his brother when we were not yet able to send anyone. They two, when they perceived that your country belonged to the Apostolic See, did nothing against the canon but came to us, bringing the relics of Saint Clement. We, filled with threefold joy, having examined and ordained Methodius and his disciples, resolved to send him, our son, a man of sovereign wisdom and truth, to your lands, to teach you as you requested, to translate the books into your language in the full extent of the Church's order, with the holy Mass, that is, the service, and with baptism, as the Philosopher Constantine began, and by the grace of God and the intercession of Saint Clement.

Further, suppose anyone else can worthily and orthodoxly interpret the Scriptures so that you may quickly learn the commandments of God. In that case, it will be holy and blessed by God, us, and the general Apostolic Church. But preserve the one custom, that the Apostle and the Gospel be read first in Latin at Mass. Then, in Slavonic, the word of the books may be fulfilled. All nations shall praise the Lord, and elsewhere, they shall all speak of the great works of God in diverse tongues, as the Holy Ghost hath given them to interpret.

If any of the teachers assembled among you, who flatter the ears and turn away from the truth to error, shall presume and begin to divide you by slandering the books of your nation, let him be excommunicated, not only from communion but also from the Church, until he is reformed. They are wolves and not sheep; they are to be known by their fruits. But you, little children, be obedient to the doctrine of God and do not reject the ordinances of the Church, that you may be true worshippers of God our Father in heaven with all the saints. Amen.'

Life of Methodius, translated by the author

The battle was not yet won. Methodius travelled through Pannonia to Moravia, where the situation changed in the meantime. Rastislav met the same fate as his uncle of old and was deposed by his nephew Svatopluk (c. 840–894), who worked with the empire. The papal authority in the Middle Ages was not as strong as in later years. The appointment of the archbishop that Methodius got from the pope himself did not help him against the archbishop of Salzburg, who had him imprisoned on the way. Yet after two years the pope ensured his release and reinstatement as an archbishop.

However, it was to prove a bitter victory. The Slavonic liturgy would be forbidden from then on. The dream of an independent Slavic Church seemed to be crushed – or was it?

Old Church Slavonic in the Eastern Church

Methodius had to watch as the new Moravian ruler, Svatopluk the Great, chased away his disciples and invited in the Bavarian priests again. His life's work was shattered, and he suffered more losses and had to defend himself in Rome once more. Yet, from the ashes, something new began to grow.

Methodius died in Rome in 885.

Methodius pointed to one of his trustworthy disciples, called Gorazd, and said:

'He is a free man and of your country, well versed in the Latin books and devout. This be God's will and your love, as well as mine!'

When all the people were assembled on Palm Sunday, Methodius entered the temple, and being sick, he pronounced a blessing on the emperor and the prince and the clergy and the people and said:

'Take care of me, little children, until the third day.'

And so it was done. When it dawned on the third day, he said for the last time: 'In thy hand, O Lord, I commend my soul.'

He passed away in the hands of the priests on April 6 in the third indication of the year 6399 from the world's creation (i.e., April 6, 885).

The disciples wrapped him in a shroud and made him worthy tributes, performed the funeral rites in Latin, Greek and Slavonic, and buried him in the cathedral church.

Life of Methodius, translated by the author

Gorazd and the Pope

The pope had not accepted Gorazd, as mentioned above, and another successor to the archbishopric of Smirnium was named. Yet Gorazd, with his followers, would not give up. They withstood persecution and fled to the First Bulgarian Empire, and the khan accepted them warmly. Because the Bulgarian emperor feared the influence of Byzantine priests who taught in Greek, a new liturgic language came in handy.

Thus the disciples of the Old Church Slavonic Moravian priests established two academies to teach theology in Old Church Slavonic. Unlike the Moravian example, this enterprise did not meet a bitter end. From Bulgaria, Old Church Slavonic spread around Eastern Europe and still remains an official language of the Orthodox Church today.

For the Eastern Slavs, this meant a chance for independence from the Byzantine Empire and the opportunity to spread Christianity without learning difficult Greek. The church and state also adopted Cyrillic script and Bulgarian is, to the present day, written in Cyrillic. Many Eastern European nations – the Russians, the Ukrainians, the Serbians and the Macedonians – still use Cyrillic in a slightly adjusted form.

Thus the mission Rastislav called for to gain independence from the German emperor brought freedom to other nations and helped spread Christianity in the far eastern lands. None of this would have happened without Rastislav's choice, or without the linguistic genius of Constantine and the political expertise of Methodius. As we have said, history is not given; it is a chain of choices that can have unpredictable outcomes.

SVATOPLUK THE GREAT

If we cannot tell whether the 846 betrayal by Rastislav hurt his uncle Mojmir, we can be pretty sure that Rastislav was hurt when his nephew Svatopluk betrayed him in 869. The two had shared rule for a long time; Svatopluk was raised to be a successor and Rastislav made him great. Yet Svatopluk did not want to wait.

So it was that in 869 Svatopluk plotted with the invading army of Carloman as they came to punish Rastislav for his audacity. The plot had been discovered by Rastislav, who decided to do the only reasonable thing a duke in the Middle Ages could do. He invited his nephew to a feast to murder him, intending to strangle him there. Svatopluk learned about the ruse and escaped before his uncle's soldiers could capture him. Thus the former friendship of the two men was ruined without a chance for repair and Rastislav lost the most valuable ally he had had for years.

Open war broke out, but this time Svatopluk had a powerful ally on his side. Carolman, the German king and son of the emperor, continued in the traditional dealings with the Moravian dukes, so one could be used against another. Svatopluk helped to capture his uncle, who was brought in chains before the emperor, blinded and thrown into prison. Yet the reward was less than Svatopluk expected.

Carloman let him remain a ruler of a small part of Moravia and appointed two German stewards to govern the rest. That was a grave mistake. Moravians had by now become proud people and would not suffer foreign rule.

Moravian Nobles Defy the Empire

They rebelled, chased the stewards away and chose one from their midst, Slavomír, to lead them. Carloman had no other option than to appoint a loyal Moravian duke to stop the rebellion and he had Svatopluk, who proved to be loyal enough so far.

We cannot say whether Carloman truly believed that this time it would work, that this Moravian duke sent with a German army behind him would prove a loyal subject. If he did, he would be wrong again. Maybe his father, Louis the German, would have been wiser by now. But perhaps Carloman did not seek his father's advice when dealing with Moravians.

As Svatopluk entered his old uncle's castle, he renounced all loyalty to the empire and joined the Moravians. Their army went on to slay the complete Bavarian force in one strike. This moment is crucial; only now can we speak of a state. We know that the Moravians accepted their ruler and were willing to fight for their state. Yet a decisive battle awaited them still. Louis and Carloman assembled a large force and wanted to crush the Moravians once and for all. They failed.

After a series of battles, a stalemate was reached. Svatopluk sent envoys to the emperor, asking for peace. He did get peace, with the emperor conceding that Moravia was not to become a part of the empire. Svatopluk promised to pay a yearly tribute, recognizing the strength of his adversaries, yet he would keep the title of an independent duke and be free to run politics his own way. So it was that Great Moravia became a free empire.

Svatopluk and his followers started territorial expansion that brought them as far as the Vistula River. Yet the empire proved short-lived because yet another fearsome barbaric tribe invaded Central Europe at the end of the tenth century – the Hungarians.

THE HUNGARIAN INVASION

This was the last Hungarian invasion that Europe would face. After the Hungarians were defeated, they would settle and create a state, completing a political map of Europe. Yet before they did that, they would destroy Moravia. Svatopluk's sons lacked their father's political prowess; they fought against one another and plotted with the empire, thus destroying the work of their father and his uncle before him. Soon the Bavarians discovered the weakness of their old enemy and Moravia lost its first territory. It may not have mattered much, however, because the Hungarian invasion was so terrible that nothing was left once the hordes had passed.

THE LEGACY OF GREAT MORAVIA

Great Moravia was short-lived empire. The story now continues in Bulgaria, and in Bohemia, as Great Moravia provided a shield for the Bohemian tribes living in its western regions. These tribes had remained protected by the mountains from the plundering Hungarians; when the Moravian dukes left, they started to build a state of their own. Yet that is a story for another chapter. For the moment we will return to the Balkan Peninsula and consider the strange case of the Bulgars.

SLAVIC ANCIENT ORIGINS

THE FIRST BULGARIAN EMPIRE

Historians have their own way of naming empires. We usually label them in hindsight, with the luxury of knowing their future. Because their future is our present, we may decide to call the state ours and hail its inhabitants as our ancestors. Today the Bulgarians proudly look back to the First Bulgarian Empire that stood for years against the mighty Byzantium, the aggressive politics of East and West Francia and even the terrifying Arabian expansion. However, let us start with a question.

WHO WERE THE BULGARS?

One of the first Slavic states was not founded by the Slavs, which is a mystery. However, the Bulgars today are clearly a Slavic nation. Bulgarian is a Slavic language and they use a script devised by Constantine for his Slavs in Moravia. Slavs were excellent at spreading their influence and assimilating even the proudest of their conquerors. These usually acquired Slavic names in a century at most. So it worked in Bulgaria or Kyivan Rus; only the Avars kept their distance. There must have been something attractive about the Slavic culture, particularly alluring to nomads and raiders who wished to settle down.

The Bulgarians came to Bulgaria from Central Asia as a loose federation of tribes. They entered the Balkan Peninsula around the fifth century, when they raided the province of Thrakya. Historians believe they moved from their homeland under the pressure of Huns. Even before they arrived they had divided the tribe into two branches, while Byzantium cleverly used one against the other. Later, however, the Avars were to subdue them all. Yet unlike the Slavs, the Bulgars in the Avar khaganate enjoyed an elite position. When the crisis struck the khaganate in 631, the Bulgars fought against the native Avars for leadership of this empire. Yet the Bulgars lost, left the khaganate and were massacred by the Bavarians.

However, the first Bulgarian state originated after the Avar threat stopped menacing Europe.

THE FIRST BULGARIAN STATE IS CREATED

The first state followed the usual model. There was an able warrior who lived in Byzantium for a particular time. His name was Kubrat (?–668) and he learned Greek, accepted baptism and became an educated man. With the help of his Byzantine allies, he rid his brethren of Avar rule and established the first state. He died in 651 and the structure followed a similar fate to Samo's empire, disintegrating into the old tribal loyalties without serious battles.

But Kubrat's followers managed to unite the tribes again. By 681 we can talk about a loose federation of tribes, united under one rule. This federation would later evolve and form a firm empire. The tribes in this conglomerate had reason to remain together, unlike the tribes under Samo's leadership. They had powerful enemies. In contrast to the Slavs in Central Europe, the Bulgars struggled with the Avars and also had to wage war against the Byzantine Empire.

Yet the Byzantines had a new enemy, which might be the only reason they allowed Bulgarians to exist.

From the Arabian Peninsula, the followers of Mohammed began their expansion. Unlike the Bulgars, who could be tolerated, the Arabs were relentless. Thus Byzantium dealt with the Bulgars only in interludes when the Arabian pressure eased.

The Social Order of the Bulgarian Empire

The First Bulgarian State was where the Bulgars and the Slavs lived together. Bulgars were the rulers, but Slavs did not suffer in a lower position as they did under Avar rule. The settlers created a symbiosis with the feisty raiders who protected them. Marriages between people of different ethnic origin were not uncommon. Bulgars were a minority in their state; most people were of either Slavic origin or old Romanized Thracian ancestry.

The top caste of the state was made of Bulgars. The ruler named himself khan and surrounded himself with his company of the best Bulgar warriors. The khan's court was positioned in Pliska, a former Slavic village. Over time the Slavic population formed its own elites. These came slowly but surely to the khan's court in more significant numbers, and mingled here with the Bulgarian elites. The Bulgarians who settled and learned agriculture assimilated with the more established Slavs. The process of creating the state was working against the Bulgarian elitism.

The khans had to choose. Either they might hold on to elitist principles like the Avars – and face the same fate – or they had to offer the Slavic people something greater. So it was that the khans began centralizing the power. In doing so, the Slavs and the Bulgars became indistinguishable.

Warriors kept a prominent place in Bulgarian society for a long time. The military was everything, skill with weapons essential and emphasis on physical prowess distinct. The discipline was strict and military style permeated the civil administration. The land was divided into 'comiti', with each 'comit' being subordinate to the khan in person.

It is difficult to say more about the First Bulgarian State before it accepted Christianity. Byzantine sources remained silent when there was no open conflict between the two empires and the Bulgars themselves were not literate. From the seventh to the ninth centuries, Byzantium was the mortal enemy of the Bulgars. This relationship did not play out only on the battlefield; Bulgars even got involved in the politics of the empire.

JUSTINIAN II AND TERVEL

In 695 the emperor Justinian II (r. 668–711) was deposed by his general Leontius. The latter slit Justinian's nose and sent him to Crimea. The exiled emperor escaped from his captivity and was accepted by the Bulgarian khan Tervel (r. 701–718), who offered the deposed emperor his protection and an army. The two became allies and Justinian conquered Constantinople with a mighty ally – a Bulgarian khan with a splendid army consisting of Bulgars and Slavs.

As Justinian II sat back on his throne, he issued the title of Caesar on the Bulgarian khan. That meant they would rule together and Tervel might one day succeed the emperor. He also rewarded the Bulgarian khan with the land of Zagore, which reached as far as the Black Sea and would be merged with the Bulgarian Empire. In addition, a large tribute would in future be paid to the Bulgarians.

The friendship did not last long, however. First, Justinian II proved to be a monster, unfit to rule. He took a terrible revenge on his old enemies, burning them alive and drowning them in bags. He also proved to be an ungrateful traitor; as early as 708 he invaded Trakya, trying to reclaim Zagore. The Bulgarians won the battle and chased the Byzantines away. When Justinian II got into trouble again, however, he asked Tervel for help. This time the khan was more wary, providing only 5,000 soldiers.

BULGARIANS STOP THE ARABIAN INVASION

When Justinian lost the campaign and was killed, battles between Bulgaria and Byzantium continued. The peace treaty signed in 716 was advantageous for the Bulgarians because Byzantium desperately needed an ally against the Arabs, who laid siege to Constantinople in 717.

What followed was an event of historical importance. The Arabian Empire spread from Iran to the Pyrenean peninsula. The whole of Europe was shaking in fear. When the Arabs attacked Constantinople, the Bulgars attacked them in Thrakya. A terrible battle followed, in which more than 30,000 Arabs were killed. Constantinople broke the siege and the Arabs left for home. This victory saved Europe from the Arabian invasion that could have come from the south. The allied victory ensured friendship between Bulgars and Byzantium, which means we lacked written records about the following years, because the Byzantine only kept records on the Bulgars when there was a conflict with them. Some 50 years later, however, the wars broke out again.

KRUM THE GREAT

The history of the Bulgarian Empire is a history of war with Byzantium that seems to have no end. For the Bulgarians, the need was acute: they must either win or perish. They could not stop; Byzantium was too strong to be left alone, and it only responded to power. The Bulgars attacked repeatedly, the Byzantines came back in response, and so it went on and on. Bulgars wanted to instil as much fear in the Greeks as possible. And there was one man who made them tremble in Constantinople.

In 803 a new khan sat on the Bulgarian throne. His name was Krum (r. 803–814) and he founded a new dynasty. He lived in a new political reality. In 800 Charlemagne was crowned emperor of the Western Roman Empire. Byzantium was no longer the only heir to the mighty Roman Empire; it had no universal claim as a secular or spiritual power. And Charlemagne destroyed the Avars. Both events proved crucial for Bulgaria's situation.

Krum Starts His Invasion

First, Krum attacked the remains of the Avar khaganate and his invasion reached as far as Pannonia. Suddenly the Bulgars stood on the borders of the Carolingian Empire. No longer merely a local power, they had now become a force to be reckoned with in European politics.

More importantly, however, Krum was very successful in the war with Byzantium that broke out under the emperor Nicephorus I (r. 750–811). Krum invaded Byzantine and defeated the empire in two significant battles. That provoked Nicephorus to lead a massive military force and try to chase the Bulgars back. He was ready to eradicate Bulgaria, even though Krum sued for peace as soon as Byzantine forces started plundering. Twice Nicephorus refused the negotiations. Instead, the Greek army conquered the capital, burning it nearly to the ground, and the Byzantines began to massacre the population. The emperor also stole magnificent treasures in Pliska.

Krum Strikes Back

The response of the khan was swift and terrible. As the emperor's army had been busy burning, looting and pillaging, Krum gathered a great army of his own. He distributed weapons among the peasants; supposedly even women fought in the host. This was a moment of national crisis: the Greeks had to be defeated at all costs. They succeeded and eradicated the Byzantine army, killing Nicephorus on the battlefield. As Krum found the emperor's body, he had his skull carefully cleaned and subsequently used it as a cup in feasts. We have no idea what wine tastes like when you drink it from a skull, yet the psychological significance of the act was huge.

Krum cut off the emperor's head and hung it on a pole to exhibit it. Various tribes and people came to witness it. As many people lost their relatives not only fighting the Byzantine enemy but also due to the massacres in the capital, this proved a consolation. They saw the emperor dishonoured and thus humiliated, which helped soothe the country.

Then Khan bared the skull, decorated it with silver and gems on the outside, and gave it to the chieftains of the Slavs to drink from. He also used this gruesome cup on many occasions during feasts.

Using the enemy's skull as a cup was not unusual for the nomadic warlords, yet, it shocked the Mediterranean civilization.

After this incident, Krum did not sue for peace with the empire again. He invaded Thrakya and evicted the region's population, leaving them to flee to Constantinople in great fear. From this position, the Bulgarians offered to return to a previously signed peace treaty from 716. This was a generous gesture, but one that they probably knew the Byzantines would not accept. And they did not: the war went on and Krum stood again under Constantinople's gates in no more than a year.

There, he performed a gruesome spectacle: the pagan rituals that shocked the population of the ancient city. Krum gave sacrifices to his gods right at the gates of the Christian metropole, and he sacrificed not only animals but also humans in great numbers. Then he asked the emperor to leave the city and face him in a single combat. It should not surprise us that the emperor refused. Krum simply could not conquer the walls of Constantinople; this was a mere demonstration of power.

Krum returned to his tent, ready to start negotiations. Yet, the emperor had a nasty plan. His emissaries entered the talks

THE FIRST BULGARIAN EMPIRE

not to sue for peace but to assassinate Krum instead. Krum, wounded, survived, yet his most trusted advisor was killed in the plot. So he left the city and took revenge on the people and buildings that he encountered as he went back to Bulgaria.

Krum Sees the Downfall of Yet Another Emperor

We are unsure whether Krum's religion resembled Slavic paganism or the shamanism of the nomadic peoples native to Bulgaria. He definitely made an impression on Byzantine inhabitants, watching the gruesome spectacle of both human and animal sacrifice helplessly from the walls. Yet nobody until 1453 would break the walls of mighty Constantinople, so Krum had to leave the city.

The Bulgarian campaign's failure discredited the emperor Michael (770–811), who had to flee. The third emperor tried to defeat the Bulgarian khan, and he lost the throne because he failed. For the Byzantines, Krum had turned into a nightmare.

The fourth emperor, Leo V the Armenian (775–813), was a military expert and did not start his rule with any foolish invasion. He entered peace negotiations with the Bulgars, yet his intentions were far from honest. The emperor prepared an ambush in which the khan should have been assassinated. Krum escaped, yet his son-in-law and a nephew were captured and his most trusted advisor was killed. The khan's revenge was terrible. He plundered and pillaged the Christian churches within his reach, destroyed the city of Adrianople and prepared a second siege of Constantinople – this time to be an actual siege, not a mere demonstration of power.

Yet the Greeks were saved. Amid the preparation, the great khan died as a result of either a head injury or a stroke.

Krum's Reforms

Besides his military campaigns, Krum is remembered for his social reforms and law codification. On his orders, the first laws of the Bulgars were written down. His code was progressive in its dealing with the poorest. All beggars were ensured subsidies, and the state was bound to protect the poorest inhabitants. It also contained severe punishment for excessive drinking, robbery or slander.

Legislation in a young state means one thing: that the central rule feels strong enough to dictate norms to the people. Legislation usually does not mean the laws would always be kept; there is a long way to go before the whole population or even its elites accept them. However, the mere fact that a ruler dares to present his elites with a moral code to which they should adhere means that he has strong authority because the families were usually happy with the common law, which they could enforce themselves. They might have even resisted the central authority that required their obedience in legal matters. As we do not hear of any resistance to Krum's legal reforms, we believe that the Bulgarian state was stable enough at that point.

These same Bulgarians destroyed the Avars. Krum asked the avar prisoners: 'What do you think caused the death of your leader and all your peoples?'

And they answered: 'For the reason that mutual accusations multiplied, the ones who were braver and smarter perished; also because those who were unjust and the thieves became accomplices to the judges; also, due to drinking, because as wine became more abundant, everyone became a drunkard; also - due to bribery; also - due to trade, because as everyone became a merchant, they cheated one another. And in truth, doom followed from all this.'

And when Krum heard this, he summoned all the Bulgarians and ordered them, and he decreed by law:

1. If someone accuses someone else, he should not be heard beforehand; instead, he must be tied up and questioned. And if found that he has slandered and lied, he is to be slain.
2. It is not permitted to give food to a thief. And if someone dares do so, his property will be seized. And the thief's shins are to be broken.
3. All vineyards are to be rooted out - he ordered.
4. And to anyone who begs, do not simply give at random, but give according to his need, so that he may not again be driven to begging. If one does not do this, his property will be seized.

Laws of Khan Krum, author's translation based on 1834 Oxford edition of *Suidae Lexicon* (edited by Thomas Gaisford)

BULGARIA BECOMES A EUROPEAN POWER

In the early Middle Ages the states usually originated on the border of an empire. It makes sense that the cultural influence of the empire, be it Francia or Byzantine, was attractive and brought life to the cultural spheres of the barbarian states. However, an empire does not like powerful neighbours. We watched the Moravians struggle against Francia, while the Bulgarians battled against the Byzantine Empire all the time the state existed.

Krum could not enjoy his victories; it fell to his son and successor Omurtag (r. 814–831) to reap the harvest. He signed a peace treaty with Byzantium to confirm their borders, and the bloody conflict was finally over. In the west, the Bulgarian Empire bordered on the Frankish Empire. In the northeast, the state reached as far as the Dnieper River.

Omurtag the Khan

Omurtag set out to rebuild the capital and finally live peacefully with the Byzantines. It seemed that the emperor Michael II (r. 820–829) would be wiser than his predecessors, remain true to his word and be loyal to his new Bulgarian ally. Omurtag was then free to get involved in European politics.

His Slavic subjects in Pannonia rebelled and Omurtag approached the Frankish emperor, asking for an alliance. However, he was surprised to receive complete animosity. Unlike the Byzantines, who dealt with different religions daily, the Franks would not negotiate with pagans. This was something new for the Bulgars; until now, their paganism had not mattered, only the strength of their arms. It would take another generation before the new reality struck the Bulgar khans, however, and they also came to accept Christianity.

Omurtag started the last Christian persecutions in the empire when he became khan. He attacked monasteries and Christian settlements within his reach and promoted pagans into leading positions. Many accounts of the martyr deaths of Christians were recorded by the missionaries from these times.

BORIS I, THE BULGARIAN

Boris was the first Bulgarian ruler who clearly recognized the allure of Christianity. He used the position of Bulgaria, set between two competing empires, to his advantage. One story says that Boris felt a terrible premonition when he looked at a holy icon depicting Judgment Day. The other legend places the conversion in the hands of a typical agent, a woman – namely his sister. According to the legend, the Byzantines captured the sister of the Bulgarian khan, Boris, and kept her in Constantinople. In the palace, she learned about Christianity and converted. This action earned her a higher status in the court, and when her brother asked for her, the emperor let her go. She returned to her brother and started instructing him in Christianity. He became interested because she struck some chord in him that his previous Christian instructors had not.

But then, as the story goes, a tragedy came: an epidemic of leprosy. The khan was still a pagan, but his sister persisted in teaching him, and once he himself accepted Christ, the illness went away. This impressed the Bulgarian khan so much that he asked the emperor in Constantinople to send clerics to baptize him. However, the Bulgarian nobles did not agree with his newly chosen course and rebelled. He defeated them, bearing a cross in front of the army, and Christianity was victorious after that. As a member of the Christian family, Bulgaria became an ally of Byzantium for a while.

Both stories are undoubtedly false, however. The incentive for Boris to accept Christianity would be political. As he desired to participate in European politics, he had to become Christian. Moravian dukes had done so before, and so did the Polish and Bohemian elites; there was no time to waste. The fact that the conversion had nothing to do with faith is confirmed by written sources. We know that Boris asked both Constantinople and Rome for teachers to instruct him and his family in the Christian faith.

Patriarch Photios (810–893) sent him a letter with specific advice on how a Christian monarch should live and rule. Boris obviously did not understand (or would not understand) the commands and sent a list of 113 questions to Rome.

The Many Religions of the Bulgarian Empire

Yet not only the Western and Eastern Churches competed for the soul of the ambitious khan. Many sects of both Christian and Oriental origin wanted to take part in the process of creating a state, and missionaries from the Caliph desired to convert the khan to Islam. Boris had a choice and many options, so he chose the one that benefited him the most.

What if he did not choose? What do we know about the religion of Bulgars before the Christianization of the country?

Paganism had firm roots in this country, unlike Moravia, Bohemia or Poland; here, the Christianization did not go so fast. It is the only Slavic land where an open armed rebellion in defence of paganism arose.

The religion of Bulgarians was different in many ways.

Paganism also enjoyed a longer tradition and firmer position. Unlike other Slavic states where the ruler accepted Christianity as soon as they started building a proper state, Bulgaria remained pagan for much longer.

We have little evidence about the Slavic religion in Bulgaria. It may have been similar to what we have already said about their mythology.

The religion of the Bulgars was different, however, and the two traditions seemed not to compete but rather to complement one another.

Tengrism as an Integral Part of the Bulgarian State

Bulgars revered Tengri or a sky god under some other name. Like many nomadic tribes of Eurasian steppes (such as Huns and Avars), they were polytheistic. Yet their pantheon followed a given hierarchy with a sky god on top. Later, as they met with Christian and Muslim influence, they would highlight the position of the one sky god.

Their religious tradition included features of shamanism and animism. Every tribe or village had a shaman who enjoyed special access to the spiritual world through altered states of consciousness involving trance and dances. This practice was not as common among the Slavs. However, the second, animism, was a common way of seeing the world with many pagan religions. The animist worldview sees living souls everywhere in nature; every animal, rock or plant has a spirit, either good or evil, and people believe these spirits are involved in their daily lives.

Tengrism, the belief in the almighty sky god, was firmly connected to the states of the nomadic tribes. The ruler was for them the chosen one, a representative of the sky god, one destined to rule in the god's name. The cult thus helped build the state and could have worked even as the khan wished, uniting the tribes under one rule. Unlike Christianity, the religious system of the ruling caste did not compete with the traditional beliefs of the Slavic settlers. Bulgaria could thus have the best of both worlds: a state cult that bound the tribes together and a religion that made the masses happy. Yet none of it worked on the field of the international politics in the early Middle Ages. At that point, when the khan wished to enter the family of Christian rulers, he had to choose his family and his new religion.

Boris and His Religious Gamble

Boris I started his rule in 852. When he sat on the throne, Bulgaria bordered on both Roman Empires – the Western and the Eastern. Both had to respect the khan as a political and military force. To be entirely accepted, baptism was required. Yet Boris could choose. Both churches courted him, and he manoeuvred with a fantastic diplomatic tact. It was not an easy choice. Those who accepted Christianity from Constantinople would have to listen to the emperor enthroned there and accept cultural and political Greek influence.

On the other hand, those who let the Latin bishop baptize them would have to cooperate with the Germans, accept priests speaking German and Latin and let the influence of the Carolingian Empire permeate the country.

Boris, as Rastislav of Moravia, desired none of these things. As we will see, he would watch Rastislav and the struggle of the Old Slavonic Church with interest. Yet at that moment he, like Rastislav, had to choose which basin with baptizing water would be more convenient for him and his country.

First, the khan sent to the court of Louis the German in 864 and asked for missionaries. They came and started their work. Yet, to their dismay, they soon met Greek-speaking preachers because Boris sent the same plea to Constantinople the very same year.

The Risks of Accepting Christianity

Boris I had reason to tread carefully. Most of the Bulgarian elites were against the newly chosen course, which would not help with the conversion of the people. We must therefore realize that the political reality of Bulgaria was unique. When Kyivan Rus, Poland or Bohemia converted to Christianity, the state was at relative peace with most of its neighbours. Great Moravian dukes converted before they even began the state-building process. Yet the Bulgarian khan chose to convert at the moment of armed neutrality on both sides of his empire.

Without the support of his elites, the conversion was a risky business. Let us remember that it looked different from the viewpoint of a ninth-century ruler than it looks today. He probably would have already seen that Christianity was the way to go for the larger empires in Europe. Yet Bulgaria stood on the borders with Asia, and Islam was on a march in Asia. And an impressive march it was. Was the trouble with conversion and suppressing opposition worth it? The khan knew about the animosity of the elites towards the new religion; he risked the open revolt of not only the subjects but the nobility as well.

What Boris I desired most was not to be seen as weak. He had to retain as much control as possible, even though the conversion to Christianity meant that he would have to accept some influence from the Christian empire he chose. In this context his political manoeuvring makes sense. It was vital for the khan to choose wisely.

We know that Boris faced a rebellion right immediately he converted. He suppressed the revolt and repented for his revenge on the plotters. Later Boris asked for absolution from the pope.

FINALLY: THE BAPTISM OF BORIS I

ventually, in 864, Boris was baptized by a Greek bishop. He had the blessing of Constantinople and the emperor acted as his godfather – thus, from now on, he would be called Boris-Michael. The khan did not want to close the doors in Frankfurt or Rome and kept the baptism secret. Only he and the most loyal men in his company who joined him and accepted Christianity knew about it.

The patriarch in Constantinople, Photios, used this opportunity to gain more influence in Bulgaria and sent the newly converted khan a note. He explained Christianity to him and instructed how the Christian ruler should execute his power. Boris had expected some instructions, but he felt the patriarch went too far. He therefore turned to Rome and to Frankfurt. First, he asked for German priests and sent envoys to Pope Nicolas II (800–861) to instruct him in the faith. The request consisted of more than a hundred questions that should be answered.

Moreover, Boris wanted a patriarch for Bulgaria; he wanted his church to be independent. That decision the pope postponed for later.

You ask if we can ordain a patriarch among you. We cannot say anything definitive about this issue until our envoys, whom we sent to you, have returned and reported to us how many Christians there are among you.

In the meantime, you can have a bishop, and when Christianity has spread there with an increase in divine grace and bishops have been ordained in each church, then one among you should be elected, who should be called, if not patriarch, then indeed archbishop; to him all shall come and ask his advice in the serious matters.

Pope Nicholas I's answers to the questions of the Bulgarians, translated by the author

However, the pope tried to answer the questions as favourably as possible. He rightly understood that the Bulgarian khan wanted as little change in his country's law and moral code as possible.

Christianity prescribed mercy towards all members of society. However, the popes and archbishops throughout history had to be careful and adjust their instructions to the customs of various peoples. The Bulgars, being first and foremost warlords, had stringent laws.

Thus, the pope had to be lenient in his emphasis on mercy and only instructed the khan to always abide by the law, never take personal revenge, and avoid barbarous customs that would not be codified in legislation.

Furthermore, he pleaded for the deserters to be treated with less severity because the Bulgarian law prescribed harsh punishments. Then he asked that the wives should not be cast away by their husbands in any other case than adultery.

The most problematic part of the pope's letter thus provides his prohibition from praying for relatives who died non-believers.

Bulgaria as the Pretext for the First Schism

Thus Boris I started to Christianize Bulgaria properly, declaring the Roman version of Christianity to be the only correct one. Yet he never forgot the dream of an independent Bulgarian Church. The loss of Bulgaria proved consequential for the Church in Constantinople. In May 867 a synod was called to decide how to deal with the apostate khan. The priests on this council decided to name all the Roman priests and their followers heretics and put an anathema on the pope's head. There had been disputes between Rome and Constantinople before, but this was different. Bulgaria served as a pretext for the start of the process that would, less than 200 years later, result in the Great Schism – the final division of Eastern and Western Christianity.

Boris did not remain a loyal Roman for long. He asked the new pope, Hadrian II (r. 967–972), to name an archbishop of the Bulgarian's choice. After the pope refused three candidates, the khan lost patience with Rome and tried to reconcile with Constantinople. The new emperor and a new patriarch wanted to be as benevolent as possible; they called for a council to solve the Bulgarian question, and in 870 Boris was once again a loyal member of the Eastern Church. Yet he still did not get what he wanted. He wanted an independent church, and neither Rome nor Constantinople would grant him a patriarch of Bulgaria.

Boris watched what Rastislav did in Moravia with excitement. Before he could try something like that, the opportunity was already knocking on his door. The disciples of

Methodius were exiled from Moravia and Boris accepted them. They could not have been more welcome.

BORIS, VLADIMIR AND SYMEON

Boris wanted to spend the rest of his life in a monastery and retired in 888. His eldest son Vladimir (r. 889–893) was to become a ruling prince (as the title of khan stopped being used after the conversion) after him. Yet Vladimir proved to be an impotent ruler who renounced Christianity and resumed the persecution of Christians. Boris therefore had to leave the monastery and depose his son. In 893 he named his other son, Symeon, the next ruler.

Symeon I (r. 893–927) became one of the most successful rulers of Bulgaria. He inherited his father's diplomatic talent and enjoyed all the results of his predecessors' accomplishments.

Symeon grew up in Constantinople; he received a Greek education and decided to elevate Bulgaria to make it equal to Byzantium. At first, however, he had to handle a war with Byzantium and face a Hungarian invasion. Under his rule, Bulgarian culture reached its apex. The language and script they used was Old Church Slavonic and people acquired a new Slavic identity. Academies founded by Methodius's pupils flourished and literacy rose. Symeon even started using the title of tzar, the Slavic word for an emperor. Slavs in the Balkans used it for a long time and named Constantinople 'Tzargrad'. When Symeon acquired this title, he was indicating that he considered Bulgaria equal to Byzantium.

THE DECLINE OF THE FIRST BULGARIAN EMPIRE

Symeon reached the apex of Bulgarian power – but new powers then rose in the Balkan Peninsula: Croatia and Serbia. As usual, Byzantium used the new Christian princes in their favour in the power struggle against Bulgaria. Symeon's son Petr I (927–970) married the Byzantine Emperor's granddaughter, and Byzantium accepted the title of the 'tzar of the Bulgars'. Yet, the decline had begun, and Bulgaria became increasingly dependent on Byzantium. The noblemen recognized the weakness of their ruler and plotted against him. Magyars continuously plundered the regions behind the borders, and both Byzantium and Bulgaria had to pay tribute to the feisty raiders. The Magyars were a threat to the whole of Europe before they settled down in today's Hungary.

A new state, Kyivan Rus, competed with Byzantium. Every attack on the empire proved to bring the most difficulties to its ally, Bulgaria. The Bulgars lost territories and the tzar lost authority with his people. Under the pressure of his nobles, the tzar changed his relationship with Byzantium, instead signing a peace treaty with the Magyars. In the treaty, the tzar promised neutrality in case the Magyars invaded Byzantium. At that point Constantinople's friendship was gone. From now on, Bulgaria would have to defend itself from Byzantium, the Magyars and Kyivan Rus, all at once.

After the Kyivan prince conquered Bulgaria, the Byzantine Emperor came triumphantly to save his ally from the Rus. He dragged the tzar and his brother to Constantinople, removed his crown and turned him into a Byzantine noble. At that point Bulgaria lost independence and became a mere Byzantine province. The Bulgars had to wait 200 years to get back their own state.

HOW THE BULGARS LIVED

The Bulgars, like all Slavic nations, lived on agriculture. The archaeological findings prove that they were familiar with all basic types of grain and grew mainly wheat and barley. They also cultivated fruit trees and had vineries. Of course, they bred farm animals and used horses as working and riding animals. In the cities skilled craftsmen worked with all primary materials. Bulgaria had its own coins, although only a few have been found. The country was poor in mineral sources, so they generally used Byzantine coins rather than minting their own. However, trading was primarily done through an exchange of natural resources.

As for the social order, the tzar owned all the land, at least formally. He gave or lent the land to church institutions (bishoprics and monasteries) and to the nobility. The peasants paid taxes in natural resources to the nobles and the state. The payment would very often be replaced by free work for the nobles or the tzar. Unlike the early Slavs, who lived freely, peasants in this feudal society were entirely dependent on their masters. They were not allowed to leave the land and would be punished if they tried.

Bogomils

Bulgarian cultural life led to a phenomenon that remained influential through the Middle Ages. Bogomilism was a sect founded by a certain Bogomil under the rule of Tzar Peter I. The sect's teachings would be part of heresies around the Middle Ages.

However, Peter I was unhappy with this phenomenon that sprang up during his rule. He called for a general council, at which he let the Bogomils present their teaching and invited orthodox priests to judge and condemn it.

Yet, at this council, he did not condemn the Bogomils themselves. They were released to repent and live in peace. The persecution did not start yet.

The Teachings of Bogomil

The Bogomils formed a traditional heretical sect in their social order. They rejected church hierarchy and, moreover, defied the social order. It is no coincidence that the spread of Bogomilism corresponds with the rise of the feudal system that made the once-free inhabitants dependent on their masters. This social aspect of the heresy made it alluring for the Slavs around the Balkans and helped it to spread quickly.

As for theology, Bogomilism relied on Oriental sources and saw the world as a constant battlefield of two principles. They accepted Christ as the good principle and declared the world to be a place created by the Devil, the evil principle. They used ascetic rituals such as fasting and did not frequent churches. Nor did they accept many dogmas about the Holy Communion and other sacraments, about the saints or salvation through faith. Bogomilism was very dangerous to the Orthodox Church because it spread in the freshly converted countries. The heresy was considered hazardous to the secular authorities because it encouraged peasants to defy the social order.

Thus both church and state united to persecute the Bogomils harshly. They did not crush the sect completely, however. Some heretical texts remained and went on to influence medieval heresies in later centuries.

THE LEGACY OF THE FIRST BULGARIAN EMPIRE

Present-day Bulgarians remember their glorious past. They remember Krum, who instilled fear in the lavish Byzantine Empire, made emperors come and go and drank wine from the emperor's skull. However gruesome this myth might be, it serves as a powerful reminder to Bulgaria's enemies, and they would not fail to be reminded of it. Bulgarians saw themselves as heirs of the past, confident that Bulgaria would rise again, shake off first the Byzantine and subsequently the Ottoman yoke and become an independent national state, as they are today. The First Bulgarian Empire was their story of origin – and they remember.

The Bulgarians remember Boris I and his clever diplomacy that made all the empires of the world court him. They remember Symeon I, who named himself the 'tzar of the Bulgars and the Greeks'. Yet they also remember the fate of Bulgaria after his death, how the nobles acted against their leader and how the leader courted foreign powers and forgot his people. There are various interpretations as to why the first Bulgarian state failed. Modern historians believe that geography was simply against it. A combination of the Kyivan Rus, the pressure of the Magyars and Pechenegs from the south, the spread of Islam and the rise of both

Eastern and Western empires meant that Bulgaria was destined to lose.

Nevertheless, under the rule of Byzantium, Bulgarian culture in the Slavic language and Slavic script quietly evolved. The Old Church Slavonic language and the Cyrillic alphabet remain the First Bulgarian Empire's most important legacy. It originated in Central Europe in Moravia but was preserved in Bulgaria. Centuries later, after Constantinople had lost one region after another, Old Church Slavonic resonates in the Orthodox Churches of Ukraine, Russia and Belarus. Today, millions of people use the script that the exiled disciples of a defeated archbishop brought to an ambitious prince, seeking to elevate his country.

One of the first countries to adopt the new script and culture was the young state of Serbia, which now enters our story.

THE FIRST BULGARIAN EMPIRE

THE SERBIAN STATE

The Serbs are the last Slavic ethnic group to enter the Balkan Peninsula. The trouble with the Serbs in the early Middle Ages is that it is hard to distinguish them from the Croats. Even today, the languages are very similar. We have seen how the Bulgarian state struggled for its place on the map against the Byzantium Empire. Now the Serbian state would engage in mortal battles with both Bulgaria and Byzantium.

VLASTIMIROVIĆ DYNASTY AND THE SERBIAN BEGINNINGS

The first house to rule Serbia was Vlastimirović. Around 780, we know of the existence of a ruler named Višeslav and the Serbian Principality. The princes ruled in the surroundings of the capital, Raška. The tribes who wished not to be conquered by the expansive Bulgarian Empire united under the leadership of 'župan'. Then the 'župans' accepted the leadership of a prince in Raška. Thus Raška resisted Bulgarian expansion, and in 839 the pressure resulted in open war.

Prince Vlastimír (r. 836–852) stabilized power in Raška and assembled a large army of local župans. He used the political situation cleverly. The Bulgars were on hostile terms with the Byzantines and had reached Constantinople. Seeing that this prince in Raška might be able to intervene and stop the Bulgarian invasion, the emperor in Constantinople accepted his title of a prince (under Byzantine sovereignty). He encouraged Vlastimír as an ally to stand firm against the Bulgarians. The Serbian army exploited the land's natural terrain; they fought in forests and gorges, then chased the Bulgarian army from their territory. This was a huge victory that proved formative for the young state. The prince gained both the nobility's respect and the people's loyalty.

Fighting continued under the successors of both the Serbian prince and the Bulgarian khan. Boris I acknowledged that the Serbs would not be defeated, however, and a peace treaty was signed in 854.

The Serbian Duke Converts to Christianity

Vlastimír's visionary leadership manifested in his strategic decision to embrace Christianity. Like his neighbour, the Bulgarian khan, he had a choice. He could have chosen either Byzantine or Western influence. Everything we have said above about the Bulgarian dilemma also applied to Serbia. Greek or Latin, the East or the West, the patriarch or the pope, Frankfurt or Constantinople. However, Serbia did not then share Bulgaria's desire to mingle in Central European politics. The choice was much more about surviving the mortal struggle against the Bulgarians and the Byzantines. The Western emperor did not have long enough fingers to help, so the choice was simpler for Vlastimir. He decided on Constantinople.

Adopting Christianity, as in the cases of Bulgaria and Great Moravia, was not merely a political manoeuvre. It served to usher in a cultural renaissance that transformed the Serbian lands.

The Crisis of the Early Serbian State

After Vlastimir's death, a dynastic crisis ensued. The weak central rule weakened the Serbian position further. During the ninth century and the beginning of the tenth century, Serbia became a plaything in the hands of two competing powers: Bulgaria and Byzantine.

In the annals of Serbian history, Časlav Klonimirović (r. 896–960) stands as a remarkable figure. He came to Serbia with the Bulgarian armies; they practically forced Časlav on the Serbian nobles and hoped he would remain a loyal puppet. Časlav's fate demonstrates the complexity of Serbian history.

He came to Serbia as a proponent of Bulgarian power, supported by the Bulgarian tzar. However, after the Bulgarian tzar lost a decisive battle to a Croatian king, he could no longer support Časlav, who had to flee to Croatia. There he engaged in diplomacy and gained Byzantine support. After the death of the Bulgarian tzar Symeon, the Byzantine Empire, already strong enough to wield its influence on the Balkan Peninsula, backed Časlav up. He became ruler of the Serbian principality in 890, ending the dynastic crisis that threatened to destroy the young Serbian state.

Then, together with Bulgaria, he faced the Hungarian invasion confronting the young states in the Balkans and Byzantium. Under the rule of Časlav and his followers, Serbia had to manoeuvre delicately in the diplomatic arena, supporting one power against the other and at constant risk of complete destruction.

Časlav's reign came to a tragic end despite his resilience and diplomatic prowess. In the year 960 he fell in a battle against the Bulgars. However, his legacy endured, providing a testament to the resilience and fortitude required to navigate the complex geopolitical currents of the age.

John Vladimir: Byzantine and the Enduring Struggle for Independence

The Byzantine Empire, under the emperor Basil II (958–1025), sought to exert control over the Slavic territories, posing a challenge to the autonomy of the Serbian state. John Vladimir proved to be a competent diplomat, however, and used the situation to his advantage.

He allied with Byzantium to hold positions against the Bulgarian expansion policy. Bulgaria at this time was too strong, however, and Byzantine support did not help the Serbian ruler. John Vladimir lost much of his territory when the Bulgarian tzar attacked Serbia in 1009. He had to flee to a fortress on a hill named Oblik where a supposed miracle happened. John Vladimir later became the first Serbian saint.

He returned and climbed back up the Black Mountain with his men.

When the emperor arrived, he saw that the king would not fight. So he left part of his army at the bottom of the mountain and attacked the city of Ulcinj with the rest. Meanwhile, the venomous snakes that inhabited the Black Mountain hurt them. They began to strike immediately, and whoever they bit died without delay, be it man or beast.

King Vladimir cried and prayed to the Lord, begging him to save his people from the tragedy. Almighty God heard his servant's prayer, and the snakes stopped attacking them from that day.

Until today, if a man or beast is bitten by a snake on that mountain, he survives. From the day that St. Vladimir prayed until today, it has been as if the snakes on that mountain have no venom. The emperor sent messengers to King Vladimir, asking him to descend from the hill with his men. But the king remained where he was.

**Chronicle of the Priest of Duklja,
translated by the author**

John Vladimir and the Bulgarian Princess

The battle between the Bulgarian tzar and the Serbian prince continued. In the end, Vladimir surrendered and was sent to prison, while the Bulgarian tzar plundered Serbia, eventually asserting complete control over the principality. In the Bulgarian prison Vladimir met the princess Theodora Cossara, daughter of the tzar himself. The chronicles describe the events in a very romantic way, but the union was probably a calculated political move. The tzar realized that he could only hold Serbia by drawing on support from within. He thus married his daughter to Vladimir, in order to have his own blood on the throne. However, the story told in the legends describe John Vladimir, Theodora Cossara and their rule in the most poetic way:

Vladimir was held in chains in a Bulgarian prison, fasting and praying. He had a vision, a premonition from God by an angelic messenger. The angel told Vladimir that he would leave the prison to become a saint and a martyr. Vladimir was happy with this message and continued praying with an even greater resolution.

The tzar Samuel's daughter Cossara was a gentle and merciful woman. She took pity on the prisoners held in dungeons in chains and begged her father to let her help them relieve their pain and misery. The Bulgarian tzar gave her permission to enter the dungeons and wash their feet and heads.

Cossara fell in love with King Vladimir. She was impressed not only by his handsome appearance; it was not lust but a heavenly spirit that led her heart. She fell in love with the king's humility and gentleness and even more so with his wisdom and knowledge of the way of God. She returned to the dungeons often and earned his affection, as she was a charming young woman thirsting for spiritual things.

Cossara knew that Vladimir was a king and thus asked his father for permission to marry into the Serbian royal family. The tzar was happy with the news, and they got married. Vladimir earned back the tzar's favour now that he had become his son-in-law, and the couple got the whole territory of Dyrrachium as a wedding gift.

Cossara and Vladimir lived happily, worshipping God and being a perfect Christian royal couple. Yet, after Samuel died, his son, Cossara's brother Radomir, ascended the throne. He was a warrior of remarkable ambition and waged war against the Byzantine Empire where the scheming Emperor Basil ruled. Basil feared Radomir and used his cousin, Vladislav, as a tool in his political game. Because Vladislav's father and brother had been previously murdered by Samuel, Basil provided money and military force for his revenge.

Thus Vladislav murdered Cossara's brother Radomir. Now was Cossara's time, and Serbia was in danger. First, the treacherous Vladislav summoned King Vladimir. His noble wife implored him not to go and offered to visit her traitor of a cousin herself.

Vladislav welcomed his cousin Cossara and invited King Vladimir to the court, saying:

'What are you waiting for? Your wife is safe and well-treated. Come and join us.'

The messenger brought this letter and gifts. Amongst these gifts lay a splendid golden cross ornamented with gems of great value.

King Vladimir replied with a famous sentence: 'We believe that our Lord Jesus Christ, who died for us, was suspended not on a golden cross, but on a wooden one.'

And he asked for a wooden cross to be brought by godly men. Only then would he come and visit Bulgaria.

Thus Vladislav summoned godly men, not revealing his terrible intentions to them. He gave them a wooden cross to give to King Vladimir.

Seeing them, King Vladimir kissed the cross and set out on a journey.

Vladimir arrived in the capital, miraculously surviving an ambush set for him on a journey. He first went to give thanks and pray to God.

Vladislav was furious because his plan failed. Had Vladimir been murdered en route, Vladislav would be blameless. He would be seen as an oath-breaker if he were to assassinate Vladimir now.

Still, the decision was made; King Vladimir had to die. Thus the tzar sent soldiers to kill him while he was at prayer.

The soldiers allowed him to make his confession and struck him dead.

> *Cossara wept, and when the tzar learned of all the miracles that took place around Vladimir's dead body, he got scared and allowed her to take her husband's body and bury him.*
>
> *While she and her dead husband travelled from Prespa to Krajina, the tzar set out with an army to finally conquer Dyrrachium. He desired this region, which was given to his cousin and Vladimir as a wedding gift. This was the reward the Byzantine emperor offered for his treason. But, while resting in a camp, Vladislav saw a vision of Saint Vladimir as an armed soldier. He cried out:*
>
> *'Help, Vladimir is here to murder me!'*
>
> *As he tried to flee, God's angel struck him with a sword, and he was dead. Thus, Saint Vladimir, the greatest and most noble Serbian king, was avenged.*
>
> **Chronicle of the Priest of Duklja, translated by the author from the Serbo-Croatian edition from 1926 (edited by Šišic Ferdo)**

Most of the story in the chronicle is a legendary cliché: Vladimir is presented as a customary saint, the saint-ruler type of saint. However, the historical account in the story is valid. The Byzantine Empire did use Bulgaria and Serbia against each other, gain influence in Bulgaria and subdue the country entirely.

After Vladimir's assassination, Serbia suffered a dynastic crisis that eventually led to the Byzantine Empire's direct rule over Serbia. The principality would gain independence in the eleventh century, which is a story for another book. Above, we introduced the ancient origins of the state. Serbia became a kingdom in the Middle Ages; it struggled and emerged victorious in the turbulent twentieth century. It played a crucial role in the international politics of the late nineteenth century as a pawn, then a more active role at the beginning of the First World War – when Serbian assassins provided a pretext for the superpowers who sought to destroy one another.

In all these cases, Serbians remembered their first principality, John Vladimir and Cossara, their battles against the mighty Byzantine Empire and the glory it brought. Sadly, they remembered their ancient history later, in the 1990s, when the war in the Balkans shocked the whole world with its mindless brutality. Yet even that was the legacy of the ancient Slavic origins on the Balkan Peninsula, because then the ethnicities evolved and acquired their names and identities.

THE LIFESTYLE IN THE SERBIAN PRINCIPALITY

In contrast to all the early Slavic states introduced so far, the Serbian state lay in the Mediterranean region. This means that the state's economy relied less on agriculture, specifically on grain production. Serbians had to import most of its grain; they grew little themselves. They mainly focused on cattle and exchanged meat for wheat to obtain proper nutrition.

The villages of the Serbians differed little from other Slavic settlements. The houses were primarily built of wood and, because of the difficult security situation in a region constantly plagued by war, most of the settlements gathered together. The settlers fortified them with a wooden palisade. There had been wealthy cities on the Adriatic Sea coast in Dalmatia, mostly built on old Roman foundations. The Venetians, who exercised economic and political influence over Dalmatia throughout the region's history, influenced the cultures of these cities.

Serbian traders exported wood, meat and olives. They brought back Byzantine and Oriental silks, other textiles, luxurious clothes, cosmetics, jewellery, weapons and spices. Dalmatia has always been exceptional: like the Dalmatian towns in the wealthier Croatia, they looked more like Venice than the towns and villages on the remaining Serbian territory. It seemed as if time had stopped here and people remembered their Roman heritage. The buildings from ancient times still stood and the merchants spoke many languages. Unlike the inner regions of Serbia, life here was full of colours and foreign influences. These proud cities enjoyed a particular form of autonomy under the central rule. They cared little where they sent the taxes: to Raška, Duklja, Pliska or Byzantium. Although their wealth and trade contributed highly to the economy of every state that ruled these cities, the merchants enjoyed a life of their own. In the inner parts of Serbia, close to the power centre Raška, we find villages and castles rather than cities.

The Christianization of Serbia

The area of Serbia had been under the influence of Byzantine missionaries since the ninth century. However, over the sea from Venice came Latin-speaking priests. Until Serbia had a central rule, however, they had to meet and compete on equal terms. The church organization of Serbia reflected this reality. Some priests preaching in local churches regularly changed their loyalties from the pope to the Constantinople patriarch and back again. This was possible as the Church was formally one body, with both branches proclaiming the unity of Christianity.

The varying influence of Eastern and Western Christianity gave the Serbian Church a unique character that would prevail into the Middle Ages.

Another influence arrived in the late ninth century: the language of Old Church Slavonic. The disciples of Methodius and Gorazd, who helped to spread Christianity in Bulgaria, came to Serbia and preached in Slavic. On the banks of the beautiful romantic Lake Orchid (in present-day Macedonia) a monastery was founded by Saint Naum. Here, monks wrote in Glagolitic script, creating many written sources in Old Church Slavonic. This unique harmony of Greek, Latin and Slavonic features is typical of Serbian culture and literature. In the tenth century Glagolitic was replaced by the Cyrillic alphabet still used by Serbians today.

THE LEGACY OF THE SERBIAN STATE

The Serbian culture is a legacy belonging to the Serbians, to other Balkan nations and to European history as a whole. The Old Slavonic literacy that created its masterpieces in the tenth century belongs to the best that the Slavic literature of the early Middle Ages created. Together with the Bulgarian tradition, this branch of Christianity provides something new and fresh. This synthesis of Latin, Greek and Slavic bound together the best of these traditions and was understandable to the masses of Slavic inhabitants. The Old Church Slavonic tradition formed the Eastern Orthodox Church to which millions of believers belong today, in Eastern Europe and worldwide.

THE CONCLUSION TO THE FIRST CHAPTER

In this chapter, all the states that the Slavs founded failed. Samo's Empire disintegrated without even trying to build something more enduring. Great Moravia fought against the Franks for its independence, only to be destroyed beyond repair by the hordes of Magyar raiders. Bulgaria tried desperately to provide an alternative to the mighty Byzantine Empire but failed. Serbia struggled in an impossible war between all possible enemies and lost.

Yet light emerges from the ashes of losses, tears and blood, and Samo provided the basis for all of them. Without Samo's Empire, there would have been no Slavic states at all. The German element would have swallowed them up, or they would never have freed themselves from the Avars. Great Moravia provided safety for the Bohemian tribes on the other side of the Palava Hills, bringing Christianity and higher culture into these barbaric lands. From the Moravian nobles, the bohemian nobles learned that the state with a central rule is stronger, better able to withstand the enemy outside. Bulgarian and Serbian independent states emerged in the Middle Ages on the foundations that their ancestors had built, finally to establish national states that are a part of all European institutions today.

But the most enduring legacy of Moravia, Bulgaria and Serbia is the Orthodox Church. Whenever you are standing in an Orthodox church in Russia, Ukraine or anywhere else, you appreciate this synthesis of Byzantine (Greek) culture and pure Slavic heritage. Every time you read a Russian or a Serbian text, frustrated that you cannot decipher the script, you can remember Constantine and Methodius, and a brave Moravian duke's desperate struggle for independence in the ninth century.

SLAVIC ANCIENT ORIGINS

THE SLAVS ENTER THE MIDDLE AGES

The Europe we are exploring here has changed. The states featured in the previous chapter had emerged in the seventh century, or the ninth century at the latest. Now we move forward in time. What does Europe look like now? How does it differ from the Europe that Samo entered in the chapter above?

THE EUROPE OF THE NINTH CENTURY

First, this is the Viking era. The Vikings came from the north and soon became Europe's new nightmare. They raided the coasts, but managed to navigate their fast ships on the rivers to reach inner lands too. They also dominated trade. For a long time Vikings kept to their pagan religion and thus became a terror for Christians. But some of them settled and built states that would later become great. Such was the case with Normandy, England and Kyivan Rus.

Next, this was the time when the first Slavic states already existed and had converted to Christianity. In this era, every state that wanted to become successful knew that Christianity was the way to go. One of the incentives for conversion was the slave trade. We are still living in a society of slavers. Pagans could be enslaved by anybody; Christians could not be enslaved by other Christians. Yet nobody could defend the Christians from Vikings, who did not care what religion their slaves were. They cared only for their own.

Finally, we enter the century in which two versions of Christianity compete. The popes in Rome already knew their power and wielded it. They became allies of the Frankish emperor, who proclaimed himself emperor of the renewed empire. Every state originating in Central or Western Europe had to take the Western empire's presence into their calculations. Byzantium still existed and called itself Rome, refuting the Western emperor's claim. The pope in Rome and the patriarch in Constantinople were slowly becoming mortal enemies. The breach in the universal Church was not yet formally complete. Nominally, there was only one church, but in practice they started to differ in many ways.

Two different versions of Christianity

First, in Rome, they spoke Latin; in Constantinople, they spoke Greek. After the Slavs conquered Trakya, the Balkan Peninsula and parts of Dalmatia, Latin-speaking inhabitants of Byzantium ceased to exist: the whole empire fell under the dominance of the Greek element. Some Eastern Christians in Bulgaria and Serbia would use Old Church Slavonic in their liturgy. In contrast, the official language of the Eastern Church remained Greek. The liturgy was different, and the churches looked different too. For a long time they had evolved separately, and the differences were palpable every time you entered a church. In dogma, however, they did not differ yet. Eastern and Western priests did not agree on some details, and sometimes on more significant issues too, yet they could still discuss them. Men of the Church did not

THE SLAVS ENTER THE MIDDLE AGES

excommunicate one another over dogma, although they might sometimes do so because of political issues, such as control over newly converted states.

The difference between the East and the West was also reflected in two versions of secular power. There were two emperors, both of whom claimed universal rule over all of Christianity. Unlike the classical Roman Empire, they did not claim that they, in reality, ruled everybody. Rather, the emperors desired to exert their power over independent states. Not only direct parts of their empire that fell prey to the expansion should obey them. Instead they claimed that all Christian rulers should listen to the emperor because he wielded authority over all Christendom. The problem for those who had to decide was which emperor to choose.

In the West, however, matters were more complicated. In Constantinople the patriarch remained under the direct control of the emperor. The emperor deposed and appointed the patriarch, the head of the Church, as he wished. On the other hand, the Western emperor was equal to, or even subordinate to, the pope in Rome. The pope was elected by a conclave of cardinals and appointed his subordinates. It was the pope who crowned the emperor, not the other way around. The emperor had to come to the pope, to Rome, to let him place the crown on his head. He thus had to fight his way through the rebellious Italian cities on his way.

However, the emperors did not give up easily. They would fight many battles with the papacy. The dual claims of universal rule over the souls of the Christians in the West would prove typical for Western history. Both the secular and the spiritual power had constantly to defend their authority.

THE SLAVS ENTER THE MIDDLE AGES

Sources are abundant for the Slavic states featured in this chapter, in contrast to the previous one. We now focus on the Kyivan Rus in the east, the Croatian kingdom in the Balkans, and Poland and Czechia in Central Europe. These states were established according to a pattern, and it is no coincidence that this pattern repeats itself. It does not mean that this is how all states become states, or that this is the only way to create a state. It rather means that clever and ambitious noblemen looked around and applied a tactic that had worked well for somebody else.

For our states, this means that Moravia and Bulgaria, however hard their beginnings, provided models for Kyivan Rus, Croatia and Bohemia. The people of these countries respected the central rule, in part because they heard from traders coming to their lands how their neighbours had prospered under a central authority. It enabled the state to protect them from raiders and the slavers – it was better to pay taxes than to be enslaved. The road had thus already been paved for Kyivan Rus or Bohemia, so creating a state became a much more straightforward business.

All these states have their dark beginnings – periods in which only legends and myths of origin can enlighten us. As time passes, however, we have more and more sources and can reconstruct history much more accurately. Let us start in the east with Kyivan Rus.

THE SLAVS ENTER THE MIDDLE AGES

THE KYIVAN RUS

When **Andrew was teaching** in Shinopia, he came to Kherson. He thought to go to Rome, and thus travelled to the mouth of Dnieper.

As he went up the river, suddenly, he stood under the mountains on the bank. And he arose in the morning and said to the disciples who were with him: 'Behold these mountains, the grace of God will shine upon these mountains, and there shall be a great city, and many temples shall be raised to the glory of God.'

He went up into the mountains, blessed them, erected a cross, prayed to God, and came down from the mountain where Kyiv was later built and went down the Dnieper.

Then he came to Slavonia, where Novgorod now is, and saw the people dwelling there washing themselves and scrubbing themselves with brooms. He marvelled at their customs. He arrived in Rome and told me how much he had learned and how much he had seen.

'I saw strange things in the land of the Slavs when I went up hither; I saw a bath of wood, and it was heated.

And they strip themselves naked and pour leaven upon themselves, and take young wicker, and beat themselves, and they shall be so drunk that they shall scarcely come up alive.

And this they do all the day long, not being tormented, but tormenting themselves, and this they do to themselves, not to discipline themselves.' And they, hearing that, were astonished.

**The Primary Chronicle, Nestor,
translated by the author**

THE SLAVS FOUND KYIV

The region where Kyivan Rus lay is positioned on the most fertile soil in Europe. The black soil of Kyivan Rus could feed whole nations, and the inhabitants of these lands suffered for it throughout history. Every superpower wanted to rule the land to feed the world. The river was the most crucial element of the first Slavic settlements in this region – specifically the Dnieper River. The Slavs who came into the area of the future Rus settled along this river, their settlements creating a relatively long stretch of land from the middle stream of the Dnieper to its mouth. The Dnieper was a part of all major trade routes in this region; in antiquity it was part of the famous amber route.

Traditionally Kyiv was founded in CE 480, but historians dispute this. Archaeological findings help us to date the founding of this city to the sixth, seventh or even the ninth century. The legends quoted above mention Saint Andrew and the legendary founding of Kyiv.

Another myth tells of the Polonian tribe who travelled along the Dnieper, and the brothers Kyi, Shchec and Khoryv who, together with their sister Lybid, founded Kyiv. As an honour to Kyi, the eldest, the city was named Kyiv. However, there is no archaeological evidence to support these accounts. We have, in fact, no idea how Kyiv was founded.

The first inhabitants of Kyiv paid tribute to Khazars, whom we met in the story of Constantin and Methodius. The brothers went on a mission to the Khazar khan and tried to convert him to Christianity. Khazars were a mighty empire until the tenth century but are still something of a mystery for historians. However, Kyiv probably had some connections to their mighty neighbour. It may be even possible that the Khazars founded the city as a trading point on the banks of Dnieper.

THE SLAVS OF KYIVAN RUS

The most prominent Slavic tribe in the Kyiv region were the Polonians. We should also remember the Slavians, who had built a fortress named Novgorod on Lake Ilmen. These Slavs lived in the same way as the Slavs in their homeland. They discussed all crucial matters in assemblies where competent men (probably every man who could wield a sword) had a vote. The executive power lay in the hands of venerable elders and their religion was Slavic paganism. The inhabitants' lives were framed by repeated rituals and everything depended on nature.

They practised agriculture, grew crops and bred cattle. Land and cattle belonged to everybody; the villagers lived in a community made up of relatives of one tribe. They also indulged in hunting, fishing and beekeeping. Honey was an essential commodity for these Slavs, not only as a sweetener but also as a valuable source of mead, the popular alcoholic drink of Eastern Slavs. These commodities were also valued by the traders. Merchants would buy wax, honey and furs of animals living in the deep forests. The Slavs bought weapons, textiles and jewellery for their elites. The villages along the Dnieper River soon grew very rich through trade, inevitably creating elites in the once egalitarian society.

The Slavs would also sell slaves. We cannot be entirely sure of their origin, but they may have been enslaved as a result of debts or crime. However, the large numbers indicate prisoners of war. The Slavic warriors may have raided raid neighbouring regions where Baltic and Turkic tribes lived and brought slaves home. These would then be sold to merchants and shipped mainly to Arabia.

THE VIKINGS ENTER THE SCENE

The **ninth century** is often described as the Viking Age. The Vikings left Scandinavia and discovered that they wielded unmatched military power. More importantly, nobody came even close to the strength of their naval force. However, there is one crucial thing to remember among the plundering and pillaging that we have learned to associate with Vikings and their culture. First and foremost, Vikings were traders. Once they learned that there was Byzantium – an empire of unprecedented wealth and Arabian silver, which was also unprecedented – they were determined to get there. Not to plunder, but to trade.

The Vikings thus tried to navigate the coast and get to the south of Europe, to the Mediterranean. However, that is an awfully long way to go. When they discovered the great rivers of Europe, they realized that they could use these to find new trading routes, plunder helpless villagers who built their settlements mainly along the big rivers and eventually reach the south. So it was that, on their way from Scandinavia to Byzantium, along the Dnieper River, they encountered Kyiv.

The Varjags, Rurik, Novgorod and Kyiv

Nestor the Chronicler tells a tale that probably is pure fiction: he describes the lawlessness of various Slavic tribes in the area around Kyiv and Novgorod, and how when some of the nobles grew tired of constant fighting, they decided to look for a ruler abroad. Thus, they went to the Vikings and told them: 'Our land is great and rich, but it has no order. Come to rule and reign over us.' One of these men answered the call. Rurik took his brothers, Sineus and Truvor, and set up his court in Novgorod. He gave cities to his followers and assumed authority over all the land. On his deathbed, he bequeathed the realm to his relative Oleg because his own son, Igor, was yet too young.

This explains how the Varjags, Vikings from Scandinavia, came to rule Kyivan Rus. However, the accounts of Nestor the Chronicler cannot be trusted in this because nobody needed to ask the Vikings to come. They came as they pleased; nobody could stop them. Before we move on, let us discuss the names because names matter.

Rus is a name associated with Kyivan Rus, with Russia or Belarus. We know Kyivan is so-named because the capital lies in Kyiv. But what does the word Rus mean? By the tenth century everybody understood the term 'Rus' to mean the inhabitants or at least the elites of the Kyivan region. But it seems they brought the name from a Finnish or Old Scandinavian word for 'rower'. Thus, among the Slavs along the Dnieper, this might be a word used for Vikings who rowed down the river on their terrifying longboats.

The Varjags Rule over Rus

Nestor might be wrong in his comments about direct invitation. However, that does not mean that at least some of the people around Novgorod would not be pleased with Rurik's intentions as he came to conquer the land. If he was not entirely mythical, Rurik was a man of vision. And this vision meant one thing: there would be no more pillaging and plundering. Just imagine:

You find yourself in a village near Novgorod on the bank of the Volkov River. It is a peaceful afternoon; the farmers harvest the crops, children play as they watch the geese on the pasture and women scrape honey from the honeycombs. The children watch their mothers eagerly. When the honey is in the jars, their mother might call them to lick what remains on her tools or to chew on some of the honeycombs. That would be lovely.

Then, all of a sudden, a cry of horror pierces the silence.

'Ships are coming! Vikings are coming.'

Everybody is alert and scared. Does this mean that they have come to buy their honey? Certainly not; the village is too poor for the merchants to visit them. If Vikings have come to their settlement, it could mean only one thing. They have come to kill the weak, ill and old, and those not suitable for their intentions, to tear the children from their mothers' arms, and to take the healthy and fair to sell them into slavery.

Men run to get their swords and bows; women grab children and run for the forest. Yet they know, both men and women, that this heroic stand will be useless. They cannot defend themselves. But maybe they can hold off the raiders long enough for their family to hide so skilfully that the Vikings will not find them.

The Vikings come; they step out of their ships and fend off the first round of arrows. But they hold their ground and do not charge. The men hold their fire, waiting.

Then one of them comes, speaking the Slavic language, and says with a loud voice:

'We did not come to hurt you, do not fight us. It is useless anyway. No harm will come to your wives and children; we did not come to take your food or burn your houses. We came to talk. Listen to what we have to say.'

The men lower their bows. The women in flight turn around and watch a strange scene. The old men and women sitting in front of their houses watch and interest creeps into their frightened eyes. They had not even attempted to fly; they just sat there awaiting their death. But it seems as if some negotiations will take place. And then they will have their say as the elders of their village.

The man continues in their Slavic tongue:

'Our prince Rurik is a prince of Novgorod. He came to rule over your land as your prince. He came into your fair land and saw the abundance of honey, the fertile soil and saw you. You are people skilled in many crafts; you understand your land and can make it yield fruits and crops beyond measure. We have traded with you long enough to know. We do not wish to fight. We do not wish to make you slaves. However, we will if you resist. It is decided: you will be our people and Rurik will rule over you.'

All the village is bemused. Is this some kind of trick? They doubt it. Vikings do not need any ruse; they can simply come and take what they want. But if what they say is true, there is no danger; nobody needs to die today. They might continue with the harvest.

One of the elders stands up and speaks:

'Greetings, people from the North. It is a custom among us that we take decisions together. If your words are true, please let us gather and discuss what we heard.'

The herald does not frown; this is not the first Slavic village to which they have come to announce Rurik's conquest. He knows the Slavic customs; he is half-Slav himself.

'Very well, I hope your decision will be wise, old man.'

He sees the relief in the eyes watching him and does not doubt the outcome of the gathering.

'Thank you,' the old man says. 'In the meantime you can sit, and women will bring you something to eat and you can taste our famous mead.'

The herald allows himself a careful smile and nods. It is a good sign.

Novgorod and Kyiv

The Slavs did not have elites or noblemen of their own. If they had, these would indeed be conquered by the sword of the Vikings, bought or negotiated with. The villagers might have welcomed the Vikings who came to rule over them. At least this would mean that they could sleep at night without the threat of the Viking ships coming to enslave them. They could even hope for the protection of mighty warriors if someone attacked them. The Northmen would demand tribute for their protection, but that was a small price to pay.

So it was that Rurik established a ruling dynasty in Novgorod, though we know no more about his origin. We do know that he met some opposition from two men called Askold and Dir, their names implying that they were fellow Scandinavians rather than local elites. Rurik bequeathed the rule in Rus to Oleg and asked Oleg to serve as a custodian to Igor, Rurik's young son.

Oleg began an expansion that would turn Kyivan Rus into an empire. He ruled over Kyiv and moved the capital here. Kyiv was situated on the Dnieper; it was a wealthier city, a trading centre, more suitable for a future empire's capital. Then he set out south and turned against the mightiest power in the region, against Byzantium. Oleg defeated the Byzantine Empire and Constantinople had to pay tribute to the Rus. Yet a peace treaty was signed.

The Relationship Between the Slavs and the Scandinavians

What was the relationship between the ruling Scandinavians and the Slavs like? We have looked at this question before in discussing the Avar empire and the Bulgarians. In both of these cases, the settled Slavs were conquered by nomadic tribes. Yet each example was also different. The Avars definitely treated Slavs as lower people. They took Slavic women as concubines and did not acknowledge children born from this union as equals. They brutally demanded high tribute from the Slavs and kept them in separate units in the army. In the case of a military failure, they would punish the Slavs first.

The Bulgars treated the Slavs differently. They remained the ruling caste for some time and Bulgarian nobles ruled the Slavs. Yet in the sources we soon encounter noblemen with

Slavic names. We believe that the two ethnicities were equal in Bulgaria, at least by the time of the conversion to Christianity, for Christianity would not allow the old system to prevail. With the Bulgars, however, the emancipation of the Slavs must have come even sooner because the first Christian ruler used Old Church Slavonic to spread Christianity. If most of his court spoke the Bulgarian language, they would not accept Old Church Slavonic and the Cyrillic script as superior languages.

We are not sure about the case of the Varjags in Kyivan Rus. At least under the rule of the first three rulers, the Scandinavians and the Slavs seem to have kept their distance. When we read the names of the envoys Igor sent to Byzantium, for example, not a single Slavic name appears among them. Yet the relationship between the different peoples must have been better than in the case of the Avars.

Nestor informs us of the peace treaty that Oleg signed with the Greeks. Among other demands, he names the order of textiles for the sails.

Oleg gave orders that sails of brocade should be made for the Russes and silken ones for the Slavs, and his demand was satisfied.
The Primary Chronicle, Nestor, translated by Samuel Hazzard Cross; Olgerd P. Sherbowitz-Wetzor, 1953

This means that the different peoples were definitely kept apart, distinguishing Slavic and Scandinavian ships. Silk was costly, however, so if the Slavs were given such an expensive material, the Scandinavians regarded them as worthy military members.

The reign of Oleg (r. 957–977) is the last one in which the chronicle distinguishes between Slavs and Scandinavians. When Igor sat on the throne, he only spoke about the Russes as if no distinction mattered.

The Slavs soon earned their place in the prince's court and in higher places of society. The cohabitation of Slavs and Vikings must have been very peaceful, as shortly afterwards the Rurik ruler appointed Slavic stewards to rule over the regions of Rus. That means that the rulers had to trust the Slavs not to rebel. Both ethnicities probably saw the relationship as mutually beneficial, and soon there was no difference between the two. The Scandinavian element disappears. Rulers bear either Slavic names or Scandinavian names, but they turn them into their Slavic versions. The court's language probably changed to Slavic quickly, with Old Norse becoming just a memory.

KYIVAN RUS: AN INTRODUCTION

Kyivan Rus was a typical state of the early Middle Ages, yet its geography influenced the style of rule. The capital of Rus lay in Novgorod. In 882 the capital was moved to Kyiv as this wealthy trading centre suited the role of a princely capital much better. Despite this, the capital in the early Middle Ages was not what we are used to seeing today. It was more like the winter base for the court.

The ruler ruled from the saddle of his horse. His authority was there, wherever he currently was. Thus from April to

November the duke travelled the country with his family, company and entire court. They would stay in noble houses and fortresses or in wealthy cities. The moment the ruler came, he would set up his court there. The noble would host the whole court, expenditure that was considered an honour and the way to pay his taxes. Here the duke accepted petitioners, judged disputes among the people and executed his vision for the state if needed. His soldiers travelled the country and collected taxes from the villagers. The ruler would travel often to the countryside because his authority was only valid when the people could see him. There was no abstract notion of a state. Rather the ruler was respected when he did what a ruler should do: to judge justly, to accept petitions and to look magnificent.

The court of the ruler of the Kyivan Rus consisted of his family: his wives and their children, his concubines, his wider family and his most loyal company. The companions were the state's most influential people, a precursor of the aristocracy in feudal times. However, we do not talk about feudalism in the early Middle Ages. The lesser dukes who ruled the rest of Kyivan Rus were free to do as they wished. They respected the central power only when it suited them and the prince was strong enough to maintain his authority. These dukes were initially of Scandinavian origin; they were Varjags. From the end of the tenth century at the latest, however, we know of dukes with Slavic names. As the Varjags frequently took wives among the Slavs, it might be that the Slavic element got into the noble families; soon the Scandinavians had assimilated with their subjects.

The army too consisted of pure Scandinavians at first. However, by the time of Oleg, the second ruler, Slavs joined the military as independent units.

The Politics of the Kyivan Rus

As we saw in the previous chapters, Kyivan Rus had from the very beginning to gain the respect of the Byzantine Empire. There were also other dangers for the young state. Its people competed with the Khazars and later with the Bulgars, but it was the nomadic nations who posed the gravest dangers. Kyivan Rus lay dangerously close to the regions where the raiding tribes led their attacks. Thus, from the tenth century, the Pechenegs attacked Rus on the lower run of the Dnieper River. In 1008 a defensive fortification was built. Nevertheless, against the raiders, attack is always the best form of defence.

In 1036 Yaroslav the Wise (c. 978–1054) crossed the fortification and eradicated the Pechenegs. The threat prevailed, however, because the vacuum was filled by yet another belligerent tribe: the Cumans. These Turkic people, related to the Pechenegs, were better organized than their predecessors. In the eleventh century they conquered the whole area of the lower run of the Dnieper River. Not only did they attack the Rus, but also, more importantly, the Cumans restricted the trade on the Dnieper – a development that proved fatal to the Kyivan state. The dukes of Moscow set up a competing trade route on the Volga River, establishing competition to the central rule. The combination of dynastic crisis, economic problems and the Cumans meant Kyivan Rus was helpless against the Mongol invasion that destroyed the state in the thirteenth century. In fact, the whole of Europe was helpless against the Mongolian invasion. But for now let us return to the golden age of Kyivan Rus.

OLEG AND THE MAGICIAN

Oleg negotiated a peace treaty with Byzantium, thus giving Rus enough time to evolve and expand. As we read about the ninth century, it is important to remember that Kyivan Rus was still very pagan and that at this time the Central European powers did not negotiate with 'pagan dogs'. Rus's closest powerful neighbour was the Byzantine Empire, however, which had no problem in acting diplomatically with pagans, Jews or Muslims. Then there were the Bulgars, most of whom still bowed to some gods of the Steppes and the rest to the Slavic gods. Even if the Bulgar prince was a Christian, he had no scruples in dealing with his pagan neighbours. After all, the Arabian Empire lay close enough to spread the influence of Islam into the Rus, as we will see.

Kyivan Rus was not entirely pagan, however. Christianity spread naturally through the country, especially after the Old Church Slavonic reached Bulgaria and brought its influence to bear on the country. When the first ruler of Rus converted to Christianity, he found himself in an utterly different situation than the Bulgarian Khan. As Rus was already familiar with Christianity, some of the court members had already converted, and Christianization ran smoothly as a result.

Prince Oleg was a pagan, but he had an advantageous peace treaty with Byzantium. This was essential not only in a military sense but also, more importantly, for the trade with Byzantium. Such trade was crucial for the development of Rus in the future. Oleg died mysteriously, and we have no sources relating to his death apart from Nestor the Chronicler. It all started with Oleg asking some magician or a fortune-teller about the manner of his demise.

The magician promised that Oleg's favourite horse would cause his death. Thus, the prince sent the horse away, never to ride it again. He forgot about the animal entirely until one day, he remembered and asked how the horse was. The servant replied that the horse was dead, which pleased Oleg as that meant that the prophecy was wrong. To prove the tale's falsehood, he visited the horse's grave. There, he was bitten by a snake in the graveyard and died.

IGOR ASCENDS THE THRONE

Whatever the real cause of Oleg's death may have been, Igor was now able to start his independent rule. The young prince inherited a large empire – one too large to evolve in peace. First, the Pechenegs began creating trouble on the borders of the empire. Some tribes within refused to respect central rule and pay their taxes. Igor had to spend his time in the head of his army. In 944 he set out to punish Constantinople for their transgression of the peace treaty. The Byzantines knew what they were doing, however. They realized that Rus was not strong in a military sense, and that inner conflicts and outer enemies had weakened the empire further. They considered the moment to be ripe to carry outtheir intention of weakening Rus economically. Kyiv proved tough competition for Byzantine merchants, and the peace treaty negotiated by Oleg had given merchants from Russia too many rights in Constantinople.

Igor wanted to punish Byzantium and he attacked them. He was not as successful as his predecessor, however, and had to sign a disadvantageous peace treaty after a defeat. This treaty weakened Rus economically, placing Kyivan merchants were at a disadvantage. Even in the early Middle Ages trade meant more to the fate of empires and kingdoms than conflict did. But it was then expected that military victories and defeats defined the terms of the market.

Igor's worst adversary proved to be the Derevlians, who refused to pay the obligatory tribute. Nestor the Chronicler informs us that Igor was greedy and ordered them to pay twice as many fees as was customary. The Derevlians were angry that Igor returned asking for this second tribute. As he would not leave, they slew him with the whole company and buried him in Dereva.

It is perhaps unfair to blame the prince for greed; the state had economic problems and enemies threatened the borders. However, the Derevlians failed to understand the need and refused to pay the tribute. They rebelled and murdered Igor on the spot.

Igor had a son who was far too young to rule. But luckily for both Sviatoslav, his son, and for Kyivan Rus, his widow Olga (890–969) proved more than competent.

OLGA: THE MOTHER RULER

Olga was a wise woman, but to set herself firmly on the throne, she first had to settle the unpleasant business with the Derevlians. Not only had they murdered her husband, but they also wanted their own prince, named Mal, to marry her. In this way, they would obtain custody over young Sviatoslav. Olga had no intention of giving up her regency, especially not to the traitors to her late husband. But she agreed to accept their envoys and hear them out. When they arrived in Kyiv, she prepared a ruse for them. They ended up buried alive.

Olga is remembered as a cruel ruler, yet she was also a saint. Her actions served her well in the early Middle Ages when it was not customary for women to rule. Olga was certainly very clever. She subdued the Derevlians through a bloody revenge.

Before she murdered the first ambassadors, she listened carefully to their proposal and pretended to agree. She then cleverly sent the Derevlians a message asking worthy men to accompany her to Dereva where she could meet her future husband. That was smart because the Derevlians had no choice but to send the best warriors and most powerful nobles.

When they arrived in Kyiv, Olga welcomed them and offered them a hot bath after the long journey, which they accepted. They had no idea what happened to the first envoys, and it did not occur to them to ask.

Once they got in the bathhouse, Olga's men barred the doors and burned the Derevlians alive.

Now, Olga was ready to see the Derevlians herself, yet there would be no marriage, only revenge. Still, she did not let her intentions show and only asked to be allowed to weep over her husband's grave and prepare a funeral feast.

The Derevlians, still without any suspicions, agreed, and when the duchess came, they held a mighty feast for her husband. When the Derevlians got drunk enough to be helpless, Olga's men slaughtered them. Five thousand men died at the feast, and Olga went back to Kyiv, preparing an entire military campaign against her husband's murderers.

For days, her army lay at the walls of Dereva, and when the siege was prolonged, Olga used her wits and the Derevlians' naivety once more. She asked them to give up so she could take a small tribute and leave. They were not as naive as to open the gates to her army but were gullible enough to fulfil her seemingly innocent request. She asked for a pigeon from every family.

The city's inhabitants did not marvel at the request, or were hungry and devastated enough not to ask further questions. They sent the birds, and Olga's soldiers tied bags of sulphur to the birds' legs. As the pigeons were released, each returned to its house and set fire to every building in the city. Most of the population died in the slaughter that followed, and those who survived were made to pay a heavy tribute.

Thus Olga avenged her husband, but what is more, she strengthened her power and cut down one tribe who were confident enough to challenge the central power, making her son's position much easier once he came of age.

Olga later converted to Christianity and became a saint. So if Nestor, a devout Christian, describes her terrible revenge, we have no reason to doubt his words. There was a reason why Olga had to act relentlessly against her adversaries. Women rulers in the Middle Ages often proved to be crueller than men simply because they could not afford to be perceived as meek. Olga's successful revenge increased her authority; nobody dared to doubt her jurisdiction as a regent. But Sviatoslav was soon old enough to rule. He went on military campaigns while his mother ruled in Kyiv in his stead.

Olga Becomes a Christian

Nestor tells a romantic story about Olga's conversion: Supposedly, she went to Constantinople and met with the reigning Emperor Constantine. He fell in love with her, not only because of her beauty but also her remarkable intellect. They talked, and he implied that she could become the next empress if she married him.

Olga was not happy with this, as she had no intention of remarrying. Maybe because a saint does not remarry and we are reading a story of a saint. Or because she would not give up the freedom she enjoyed as a widow and the power she used as a regent when her son was on a military campaign. Anyway, she needed to get out of the situation and not insult the emperor.

She reminded him that she still was a pagan, but if he wished to marry her, she would accept baptism. But only if he would baptize her himself. The emperor agreed.

However, when all was done and she was to finally say yes, she told him:

'You have baptized me, so I am like a daughter to you. I cannot marry you now.'

The emperor immediately knew that she had outwitted him, but did not get angry. He valued her even more and sent her home with many gifts and called Kyiv an ally for her sake.

Nestor's story about Olga looks like a cliché. A cliché of a female saint who wished to avoid marriage so that she might remain chaste for God. Most noble saints in the Middle Ages suffered or had to refuse the noblest suitors cleverly (like Olga) and succeed (or die a martyr's death). However, the royal match with the emperor would have ensured an excellent situation for Olga's son. The union would be beneficial and if the emperor had asked Olga to marry him, it would not have been clever to refuse. We can probably refute this story of Nestor, therefore, however attractive it sounds. Olga probably came to Constantinople on a diplomatic mission, possibly also to be baptized. Perhaps her baptism had already been discussed with her son, who did not dare to convert due to the resistance of his company and nobles. According to Nestor he expressed fear they would laugh at him if he converted to Christianity.

SVIATOSLAV RULES INDEPENDENTLY

Olga's baptism may have been a political calculation. Perhaps Sviatoslav could not become a Christian himself, yet international policy demanded that at least someone from the ruling dynasty convert. Or Olga might have converted to make herself indispensable to her son, who now ruled alone and might not need her any more. Her baptism provided an excellent, suitable career for a noblewoman who ruled as a princess. The job of a future saint in a pagan country was attractive enough.

She took the name Elena after Saint Helena, he mother of Constantine the Great – a mother responsible for the emperor's conversion and thus for the victory of Christianity in the Roman Empire. That implies that Olga at least nominally proclaimed the desire to baptize her son. She definitely used her influence on her grandson, the future Vladimir the Great.

Whatever her motivation, Sviatoslav did not follow her advice. He declared that his company would laugh at him and treat him with derision. Christians in his court were considered weak. It was acceptable if a woman converted, but not a warrior. Not yet.

Sviatoslav's rule was marked by expansion. He fought the Khazars and the Bulgars and expanded the territories in the east. His campaign against the Khazars proved successful; the

Bulgarian campaign was a disaster. After his return home Sviatoslav was ambushed and killed by a group of Pechenegs. His sons went on to fight for power. His grandson Vladimir finally emerged victorious from this power struggle and became Vladimir the Great.

VLADIMIR THE GREAT: THE LAST PAGAN

Vladimir is a saint because he converted to Christianity, but he began his rule as a devout pagan. From the account of the gods he worshipped and the remains of their statues, we derive much of our knowledge about Slavic paganism.

He worshipped various Slavic deities in Kyiv, performed pagan rituals and encouraged the Slavic cult, including blood sacrifice. This refutes the claims about Olga's lasting influence over her grandson. At the beginning of his rule Vladimir did not consider adopting Christianity. He followed the customs of his people and probably tried to associate the Slavic pagan cult with his capital. Such actions imply that only after these failed did he adopt a monotheistic religion, which had proved to work better as a unifying idea in the neighbouring countries. For whatever reason, he remained a pagan for six years after he ascended the throne.

Saint Vladimir as a Young Ruler

Before we move to the defining moment in the history of Kyivan Rus, let us muse on the character of the greatest ruler of this East Slavic state. He is named Vladimir the Great, yet his early behaviour was a little disorderly.

As the account goes, Vladimir had intercourse with his brother's wife and his oldest son Sviatopolk came from this union. Not only was she Vladimir's sister-in-law, but she was also a nun and they never married – one can hardly imagine a more 'sinful' union.

But Vladimir's lust did not end with one woman: he had four sons and two daughters with his only legitimate wife Rogned. He he also had a son with a Czech concubine, two sons by another Czech concubine and twins by a Bulgarian woman. Supposedly, he had three hundred concubines at Vyshgorod, three hundred at Belgorod and another two hundred in Beresovoe. In addition, he seduced young women when travelling through the country. No wonder that in his youth Vladimir did not incline to Christianity, which would require him to be content with only one wife. And yet the needs of the time were against his earthly pleasures. Christianity was the future.

After his conversion to Christianity, Vladimir had just one lawful wife. Yet his numerous progeny proved helpful. Vladimir realized that Kyivan Rus had grown too large and he established his sons as his stewards, creating new administrative districts. He cleverly used his daughters to achieve political matches (after his conversion).

The Conversion of Vladimir the Great

Why Vladimir and why Christianity? At this moment Christianity had already spread among ordinary people and some of the nobility, although the court and the prince's company still remained pagan. Vladimir's future actions suggest that he intended to enter the field of international politics.

For that, as we have seen above, he had to be Christian. The legend about Vladimir refusing Islam only because he would not give up pork and alcohol is thus probably a myth. Rather, Islam would not help to place Kyivan Rus on the map. However, Vladimir still had a choice to make, one that confronted many of the Slavic rulers: East or West?

Let us first listen to the legend because it is very engaging. The story is engraved deep in the national memory of all Slavic lands and has entered popular culture. Sometimes all that people know about Vladimir is the famous courting of missionaries to the prince. Let us imagine a wise prince facing the pivotal moment of his rule:

Vladimir sat in the throne room on his high chair, watching the Khasar envoys. They came as emissaries from their Khan trying to convert him to Judaism.

'We believe in one God, the God of Abraham, Isaac, and Jacob,' said the envoy, slightly inclining his head.

Vladimir sighed. It seemed that they all believed in one God. Ever since he had started this religious competition, his suspicion grew, that this was hardly about the God for them. But that was okay; it was not about God for Vladimir either.

His personal beliefs had nothing to do with this public show. He was looking for a religion to replace paganism in Rus. Perun was no help, and the rituals were no help. All Vladimir did in favour of the pagan gods only turned all his mighty neighbours against him.

And the gods themselves did not intervene; perhaps they were just wooden idols, as all the wise men travelling to Kyiv these days proclaimed.

Vladimir himself was not sure what he believed in. He himself was of little importance because this decision was about the future of Rus, the future of his people.

But as he had been listening for days now to the speeches of educated philosophers and priests, he became genuinely intrigued. Once this competition was over, he promised himself, he would think about it; about his personal belief, about his…what did the German priest call it?

Yes, his soul.

Anyway, now the Jew stood before him and went on and on about his religion as Vladimir got lost in his thoughts.

'…and eating pork is forbidden, circumcision and observing Sabbath is mandatory.'

'I can do without pork,' replied Vladimir, waking up suddenly. The word 'pork' made him realize how hungry he was and wanted this thing over.

'Though,' continued Vladimir with distinct tiredness in his voice. 'I do not like the idea of a knife cutting my private member very much. Anyway, you live with the Khasar khan, but initially, where did the Jews come from?'

'Jerusalem, my lord,' replied the envoy.

'And how did you end up with the Khasars?'

'Our God was angry at our ancestors; so he scattered us among other nations.'

Vladimir was appalled: 'I do not wish to share this fate. Nor does anybody in Rus!'

He shook his head in disbelief. So, the Jews were out of the contest…

Yesterday, some Mohammedans were here. At least they promised something good: eternal pleasure after death with seventy women for every good man. But they are prohibited from drinking – no wine, no ale, no spirits. That would not do in Rus, and Vladimir doubted that they were telling the truth. He could not imagine the whole nation being sober all the time. So, the case was lost for the Mohammedans.

And then there were the Germans and the Greeks. Christianity looked fine so far: no drastic measures, no prohibition of pork or drinking, no cutting of sensitive body parts...

But there was a catch.

Unlike the Mohammedans, who lived far away, or the Jews, who were happy to live and let live, Christians would want to have their say in Russia.

That much was clear to Vladimir.

But, then, he had no choice but to choose one religion, and it seemed that it was the Germans or the Greeks. The Greeks were closer to his borders, so it had to be the Greeks.

He called his own ambassadors and ordered them to travel to Germany, Byzantium, Khasar Khaganate and Arabia. They would bring him reports from those lands. He made clear to them what the reports should look like. The report from Byzantium had to be magnificent and pleasing because Vladimir had already made his decision. Greek religion was his final choice.

Now, all that was left to decide was how to do it.

How to get baptized without supplications, and how to retain the upper hand.

He would wait.

All good things come to those who wait.

But there was yet another mighty incentive for Vladimir. It was a woman, which should not surprise us after what we have read about the only weakness of this prince. But this specific woman played a more significant political role. Basil II, the

Byzantine Emperor, struggled against a rebellion in 987 and asked Vladimir for help. Vladimir agreed, but he demanded the hand of the emperor's sister as a reward. The emperor was out of options, but Vladimir had to become Christian as an emperor's sister could not marry a pagan. Nor was that all: not just the prince himself, but his whole company was to be baptized.

Vladimir agreed and set on a military campaign to help his soon-to-be brother-in-law. After he conquered Kherson on the Crimean Peninsula, he and his company converted to Christianity. Nestor's version of the story presents Vladimir as an adventurous gambler who conquered the city. Only after he had done so did he ask for the princess as his prize.

After Vladimir converted to Christianity, he returned to Kyiv with his new duchess and started working hard. He would overthrow all the wooden idols, casting them into the Dnieper.

Vladimir the Great Enters the Family of European Rulers

Why is Vladimir called Vladimir the Great? With him the history of Kyivan Rus entered a new era. Now its rulers were not mere raiders; they earned respect throughout Europe. Vladimir supported education, established schools and built churches. The second period of his rule starkly contrasts with his earlier years, in which he had expanded the territory of Rus and waged many wars. Later he only started a war with White Croats on the borders, yet he had to stop it to protect Kyiv from Pecheneg raiders. Then he lived peacefully with his neighbours and spread his influence through marriage pacts.

Vladimir used his numerous progenies, many of whom had been born before his conversion and did not share noble origin with those born from the match with the Byzantine princess Anna. Vladimir's first prominent wife was of Polotsk origin. Her name was Rogneda and they married when he was a pagan. After the marriage with Anna, Vladimir divorced all of his pagan wives. Eventually Rogneda converted to Christianity, took the name of Anastasia and entered a convent. The children that she had with Vladimir, however, proved crucial for European history.

The eldest son, Yizyaslav of Polotzk, did not get his chance to rule Kyivan Rus because he died before his father in 1001. However, as was Scandinavian custom, he accompanied his mother to govern the land of her ancestors, Polotzk. Here he and his mother led a mutiny against Vladimir. Her second son, Yaroslav the Wise (983–1054), became Rus's greatest ruler after winning the dynastic battles against his brothers following Vladimir's death. Predstlava and Mstislava became concubines to the Polish king Boleslav I the Brave. The last daughter, Premislava, married Duke Laszlo (Vladislav), 'the Bald' of Arpadians, a Hungarian prince. These matches definitely served Vladimir's international relations because, as we read in the Primary Chronicle:

> *He lived at peace with the neighbouring princes Boleslav of Poland, Stephen of Hungary and Oldřich of Bohemia, and there was amity and friendship among them.*
> **The Primary Chronicle, Nestor, translated by Samuel Hazzard Cross; Olgerd P. Sherbowitz-Wetzor, 1953**

By the Bulgarian wife Adela, Vladimir sired Boris and Gleb. Boris became a prince of Rostov and Gleb became a prince of Murom. More importantly, however, these two brothers were so successful in spreading Christianity in Eastern Europe that they were later canonized and became Saint Boris and Saint Gleb.

The Byzantine princess Anna bore only one surviving daughter, Theofano, who married the Duke of Novgorod. Vladimir thus managed to strengthen his position within Kyivan Rus because Novgorod controlled trade on the Volga river and grew more powerful and bold.

After Anna's death Vladimir chose a wife again within the family of an emperor, thus proving how high Kyivan Rus had grown. He married a granddaughter of the Holy Roman Emperor Otto the Great (912–973). The daughter born of this union, Maria Dobroniega of Kyiv, later married Casimir the Restorer (1016–1058), a duke of Poland.

The marriage pacts of Vladimir himself and those of his children clearly demonstrate the growing influence of Kyivan Rus and the international interests of Rus.

Vladimir's Politics

First, we can see the constant clever balancing between the East and the West. Vladimir married into the families of both the Eastern and Western emperors. His children travelled both to the West (Poland and Hungary) and to the East (Boris and Gleb). The marriage pacts also illustrate that the time of expansion was over. Now Kyivan Rus set out to stabilize the central power and the authority of the state within its borders. As the territory was huge, this was not an easy task, but it would be achieved by one of Vladimir's sons, Yaroslav the Wise.

Vladimir was canonized, yet there is no wonder in that: most of the first Christian rulers in the early Middle Ages became saints. For the Church, converting a pagan country was enough to gain the reputation of a saint, as the defeat of paganism was the Church's main objective in this era. Vladimir definitely did much for the Christianization of his subjects. He also lived a virtuous Christian life, to which his confessors had little to object.

Vladimir built a dome for the Holy Virgin, invited architects and painters from abroad, and appointed priests from Kherson to serve in it. He also founded a new city in Belgorod and bestowed all kinds of privileges on its inhabitants, so the city flourished.

But he also lived a life of an exemplary royal saint, taking care of the poor and sick, importing delicious food to be given to beggars and ordering all poor in his cities to be fed and cared for. He even prepared feasts for his noblemen and invited beggars to take part. His companions loved him and he was smart enough to win their gratitude on every occasion.

Nestor tells a story of a feast when his retinue complained that they were to eat with wooden spoons.

'Very well,' replied Vladimir benignly. 'I will provide silver and golden spoons for you. Because gold and silver I can afford to miss. With you by my side I will win more gold and silver. You are more to me than my riches.'

His noblemen rewarded him with their loyalty in all things, and he surrounded himself with clever and wise men, always consulting with them on his decisions. That is truly a sign of a great monarch, one of the many reasons he won the name Vladimir the Great.

THE KYIVAN RUS

YAROSLAV THE WISE

Yaroslav became the eldest of Vladimir's children after the death of his brother Yizyaslav. First, he was sent to rule Rostov. According to the custom, after he acquired the title of the successor to the throne, he travelled to Novgorod. There the troubles began. Following the custom of young and ambitious princes in the early Middle Ages, he did not want to wait for the death of his ageing father. But luckily for both of them, Vladimir fell ill before the son could raise an army against his father and before the father could answer the challenge.

Vladimir died in the Orthodox faith before he could punish his son's insolence. After his father's death, Yaroslav had to fight for the throne because he was far away in Novgorod while his brothers lived closer to the capital. This applied especially to Svatopluk, who murdered most of the remaining brothers. The war was inevitable because Yaroslav decided to fight for his rights.

Svatopluk had a formidable force of Pechenegs, agile horse-riding warriors from the steppes. But Yaroslav the Wise was wise even in his military exploits and used the landscape to his advantage. As the final battle took place between two lakes, the Pechenegs could not come to aid his opponent. Yaroslav defeated his brother and set himself firmly in Kyiv.

This was not the end of the story, however. Yaroslav had to fight against the Polish king Boleslav I, who saw the dynastic crisis as an opportunity either to seize Kyiv for himself or to set the defeated Sviatopolk on the throne. The beginnings of Yaroslav's reign were marked by mutinies and rebellions that he had to suppress. It meant that the central rule in Kyivan Rus was not so stable as a result; local princes would rebel against the central authority at every opportunity. Such actions proved typical of Kyvian rulers for the whole of their history and would prove destructive in the end.

Yaroslav the Wise as a Ruler

Why is Yaroslav called the Wise? He certainly was wise and he inherited his father's diplomatic talent. In the struggles for succession, it is not usually the most belligerent or the fiercest contender who ultimately wins the throne: it is the cleverest. Yaroslav relied on diplomacy, unlike all his brothers who fell prey to Svatopluk's cruelty.

After his victory, Yaroslav did what was needed for Kyivan Rus to become a prosperous and stable state. He stabilized the central ruling power; he ascended to the throne and defended his right to succession. He suppressed all opposition to the central rule and destroyed the Pechenegs once and for all. He also continued his father's policy of marriage pacts that spread the influence of Rus within Europe. Yet the most important thing he did was none of these: he codified the law.

First, let us focus on the Pechenegs. In 1036 Yaroslav started a campaign to eliminate the Pechenegs' threat. The line of fortified defences proved useless. The Pechenegs had terrorized the south of Rus for centuries, mingled in its inner politics and once even laid siege to Kyiv. They controlled much of the Steppes in Eastern Europe as well as most of the Crimean Peninsula. In so doing the Pechenegs limited the trade on the Dnieper River and threatened the economy of Kyivan Rus as a result.

The Pechenegs overestimated their powers and, after continuously mingling in the inner politics of Rus, they attacked the capital. They never recovered from this defeat and were slowly overcome by other tribes. We have already explained how the nomadic nations rule; their leaders must go from victory to victory, and when defeat comes central authority is shredded to pieces. One significant military victory over a nomadic nation can mean its complete and utter destruction, unlike the cases of settled nations or a functioning state. Such was the case of the Pechenegs.

Yaroslav: the Perfect Christian Ruler

Yaroslav is revered in Rus for the lustre he gave to the cities, where he set up churches, castles and the Cathedral of Saint Sophia – the monument that tourists admire in Kyiv even today. Yaroslav also supported education and, under his rule, Kyivan Rus became a marvel among the Slavic states.

If Vladimir was a perfect Christian ruler, his son followed in his father's footsteps. He continued rebuilding the capital, erecting many churches, founding monasteries and above all else, building the Metropolitan Church of Saint Sophia, the marvel of today's Kyiv. He helped spread Christianity, invited monks and priests and discussed religious matters with them himself. He loved reading and supported education. Many books of prominent authors were copied and translated into Greek and Slavic. They filled the libraries of monasteries in Kyiv.

Books were a valuable gift, expensive and hard to get in the early Middle Ages. Vladimir gave many books to the churches he founded. But not only books he provided: gems, gold, silver and expensive works of arts flowed in the churches and monasteries.

Yaroslav did all he could to strengthen Christianity in the country. Still, Nestor complains that paganism was not fully uprooted even with Yaroslav and Vladimir devoting immense resources to spreading the faith. The chronicler may complain, but we understand. Two generations did not suffice to turn pagan Slavs into devote Christians.

Yaroslav the Law Giver

But the most renowned action of Yaroslav, the one for which he is undoubtedly called the wise, was the codification of law that entered history as *Russkaya Pravda*.

Written law marks the end of the full development of a state. Monarchs codify law when their reign is strong enough, when they are respected by all their nobles. Thus the act of creating legislation is what gave Yaroslav the right to call himself 'the Wise'.

But what laws did this code contain? It was fairly specific. In case of homicide, it provided clear instructions to the victim's relatives regarding who can avenge whom and how much to pay to the relatives for the corpse. We may find this rather brutal, but these rules were relatively mild compared to the blood feud that the common law allowed before Yaroslav's legislation forbade it.

Furthermore, punishment for violent crimes was rather pragmatic. If someone was beaten and provided eyewitnesses, he would be paid by the perpetrator of the deed. The law precisely defined how much was to be paid according to the severity of the offence or the injury. The legislation was quite elaborate and testifies to the high legal culture in Rus.

Yaroslav and the Byzantine Empire

Yaroslav also strove to weaken the influence of the Byzantine Empire in Kyivan Rus. First he started a military campaign against the mighty neighbour of Rus.

Open war with Constantinople did not go well. The great storm destroyed most of Yaroslav's boats, and no decisive battles were fought. Nevertheless, forces from Rus managed to plunder some Byzantine lands and do significant damage.

However, this campaign, although not as successful as Yaroslav might have hoped, helped to emancipate Kyivan Rus from Byzantine influence. Thus, in 1051, he dared to make an unprecedented move. Without consultation, he placed a Slavic monk, Hilarion of Kyiv, in the seat of Metropolitan of Kyiv (the equivalent of an archbishop in Eastern tradition). Hilarion served as a Metropolitan even though the patriarch in Constantinople did not appoint him. He was the first non-Greek in this position.

Yaroslav's Marriage Pacts and Legacy

Yaroslav the Wise continued his father's policy and negotiated interesting marriage pacts for his offspring. However, he did not have as many of them as his father, who had been a pagan and thus had more wives and concubines at one time.

His eldest daughter, Anastasia of Kyiv (1023–1074), married the Hungarian king, Andrew I of Hungary, one of the most significant figures in Hungarian Middle Ages history. His youngest daughter Agatha married into the English royal family, but the most notable marriage was arranged for Anne of Kyiv (1030–1075). She married the French king Henry I (r. 1031–1060) and ruled France after her husband's death as a regent for their son. At the beginning of her stay in France, Anne felt frustrated. In letters, she complained to her father that Paris was a barbarous provincial town compared to Kyiv. Neither her husband nor the majority of his court could read or write and she, being an educated woman, missed the intellectual wealth of her homeland. Such correspondence illustrates better than anything the cultural prime that Kyivan Rus had reached.

Yaroslav sought his sons to act in brotherhood, put aside their personal ambitions and always to put the interests of the empire first. Yet, as had happened so many times in the past, they did not listen.

THE FALL AND DECLINE OF KYIVAN RUS

It is sad that as soon as we reach the prime of an empire, its fall and decline lurk just around the corner. After Yaroslav's death conditions in Kyivan Rus became rapidly worse. His sons and grandsons were not strong enough to hold the state together. Nobles rebelled, the sons fought against each other and even ordinary people rebelled. At the worst point, the Cumans quickly conquered the regions once ruled by the Pechenegs. They limited trade on the Dnieper; even worse, the leading trading partner, the Byzantine Empire, was in a crisis. The last prince who ruled the whole territory of Kyivan Rus, at least for some time, was Mstislav the Great (1076–1132).

Mstislav had no time to defend the borders from the Cumans because he had to deal with another threat: a growing power centre around Novgorod.

Novgorod was an old city; it enjoyed autonomy within Rus, but had had to pay tribute to Kyiv since 1113. The Novgorod princes ruled the whole Rostol-Suzdal region and trade on the

Volga River was under their control. This trade route competed with the Dnieper, which suffered because the Cumans and the Novgorod princes grew wealthier and more powerful – they did not wish to respect the authority of a prince in Kyiv. In 1169 a prince of Novgorod sent an army to sack Kyiv. With the combination of succession crisis, economic troubles and the Cumans, Kyivan Rus quickly declined. Worse was to come, however. For a threat arose in the east against which the whole world seemed helpless.

Mongolian Invasion

In the 1220s Mongolian ponies first arrived on European land. Eastern Slavic nations were used to invading raiders from nomadic tribes, but the Mongolian invasion was different. Their army was efficiently organized and their skill with bows was deadly. They even excelled in state administration; their system of fast messengers, for instance, was renowned. The Mongolians established posts for their information service and their horsemen travelled across their large empire, so that the khan in the centre always knew what was happening.

After the death of the mightiest khan Genghis (c. 1162–1227), the army invaded Europe under the nominal leadership of Batu Khan (1212–1255). However, it was not Batu who the Europeans learned to dread. The horde had a military genius of common lineage at its head. General Subutai (1175–1248) had been raised by Genghis Khan himself and nobody could withstand his army. Kyivan princes fell one by one. Divided, they stood no chance against the advancing hosts. In 1240 the Mongols reached Kyiv and destroyed Kyivan Rus almost utterly.

The Continuity of Kyivan Rus

The Mongols destroyed the capital, shattered the unity of Kyivan princes (such as it was) and established the Golden Horde, a Mongolian state to which all the Slavic and non-Slavic nations in Eastern Europe were to be vassals. Under their influence Novgorod evolved, paying tribute to the Horde from the prosperous trade on the Volga River. More importantly, in the marches of Muscovy, a new power arose. The Muscovite princes paid tribute to the Horde. They would have to wait a hundred years before they could shake off the Mongolian yoke and unite the land into what would later be called Russia, with Moscow as its capital.

The remnants of Mongolian rule remained in the Crimean Peninsula for a long time; the Crimean Tartars were in fact the descendants of the Mongols. It would take the endeavour of the Russian tzarina Catherine the Great (1729–1796) and the terrible policy of Stalin (1878–1953) to uproot the Tartars from Crimea. That is a legacy of the Mongols in Eastern Europe that Stalin moved to far-off Siberian lands.

In the western part of late Kyivan Rus, some princes remained in Galicia and Volyhnia. They paid tribute to the Mongols; however, unlike Muscovy and Novgorod, the influence of the Golden Horde meant little here. The Mongols did not have enough power to reach the princes in the West and these used it to their advantage – manoeuvring between the East and the West, making alliances with the Poles and Lithuanians, balancing the scales of Orthodox and Roman Catholic influence. Their legacy was the Polish-Lithuanian commonwealth. The Lithuanian princes grew in power and influence, united what remained of Kyivan Rus and allied with

THE LEGACY OF KYIVAN RUS

What is the legacy of Kyivan Rus? We remained with Rus longer than the previous nations, perhaps because it is in Kyiv where the importance of ancient history is most prominent today.

When you enter Kyiv today, the cathedral of Saint Sophia, built by Yaroslav the Wise almost a thousand years ago, still stands, making you admire its magnificence and antiquity. Looking at it, you realize how old this city is. Yet even as you stand in front of the ancient building, you would be disturbed in your quiet sightseeing tour. For from time to time, a moment comes when panic strikes you, the sound of the siren tearing you from musing over history and beauty, for the bombs striking at the city after the Russian invasion in 2022 are also the legacy of Kyiv.

This is because the two nations both claim the Kyivan tradition. Two nations claim Vladimir, Yaroslav, Olga and Oleg, the victories at Constantinople's gates and the clever manoeuvring of Vladimir.

The Russian rouble's banknotes and the Ukrainian grivna both depict Yaroslav the Wise. The Ukrainian grivna banknote shows him dressed like a Cossack (a Ukrainian warrior of the sixteenth century) with the cathedral of Saint Sophia in Kyiv on the reverse of the note. The Russian rouble note depicts him as a Russian noble in the Middle Ages with a drawing of the magnificent dome in Russian Yaroslavl. Both images distort historical reality to illustrate the claims of present nations on the Kyivan legacy.

We have said enough about Kyivan Rus in the early Middle Ages for the reader to take sides in this argument. Nations have always battled for their heritage. Historians know this, yet even they must come clean with their opinions. This historian believes that these arguments should be solved by a civilized discussion, in which bombs and invasions have no place. However, disputes over heritage have always been a source of conflict. People are people, and people obviously love their wars.

Let us hope for a better future for the descendants of Kyivan Rus, wherever they live, and for the world.

Luckily, we can continue on a brighter note by and introducing two Slavic states that survived and succeeded: Bohemia and Poland.

In the next chapter, let us dive back into the Dark Ages of the ninth century and reveal what we know of Bohemian origins.

THE KYIVAN RUS

BOHEMIA: THE SLAVS IN THE HEART OF EUROPE

In the very heart of Europe lies the city of Prague, capital of a land protected by mountain ranges. These mountain ranges shielded the Slavic tribes who lived there in ancient times. While Great Moravia was devastated by the Magyars and Kyivan Rus by the Mongols, while their Polish neighbours waged constant wars and had to build heavy fortifications to save their domain, the Bohemians were allowed to live in peace.

Prague was not founded by the mythical Libuše, whom we know already from the Bohemian myth of origin. It was a power centre of the Přemyslid dynasty, who later established their rule over the country and remained on the throne until 1306. Their court historian Cosmas wrote a beautiful story about the house's founder, the wise ploughman called by Princess Libuše to rule the defiant men. Cosmas also endowed the lady with magical prophetic powers. In his chronicle, she prophesied a glorious future for the capital she and her husband built, Prague itself.

At the time of these early beginnings of the law, one day, the lady, being enthralled by the spirit of the oracle, before her husband Přemysl and in the presence of the elders of the people, thus prophesied:

> *'I see a great castle, which touches the glory of heaven, a place lying in a forest - it is thirty miles from this village, and the boundary is marked by the waves of the river Vltava.'*
>
> *This place is firmly protected on the northern side by the deep valley of the Brusnice stream. Still, on the southern side, a broad, very rocky mountain called Petřín overhangs its surroundings. The hill of this place twists like a dolphin, a sea-pig, towards the said river. And when you come thither, you will find a man amid the woods enjoying the threshold of a house. And because even great men bow down at the low threshold, you shall call the castle you built Prague after this incident. ['Práh' is a Czech word for a threshold.]*
>
> **The Chronicle of the Czechs, Cosmas of Prague, 1125; translated by the author**

Prague's position indeed is convenient. Unlike other countries, Bohemia has natural borders. We can thus determine where the centre and periphery are, unlike the Serbs, who moved their capital in response to political realities, and the Kyivan Rus, who established the capital on the river to favour trade. Prague lies in a natural centre that allowed the elites of the early Middle Ages to start the unification process.

THE DARK AGES IN BOHEMIA

In the eighth century the Slavic tribes, together with the remains of Germanic tribes (the Lombards), lived in peace in a tribal society that slowly began to lose its egalitarian characteristics. As Moravian elites in their immediate neighbourhood grew wealthier, the Bohemian tribes behind the mountain range of Palava prospered too. With the fall of the Avar khaganate at the end of the century, a new wave of Slavs came to Bohemia. Some settled here and others went further west.

From these times, the sources are scarce. The Czechs have their legends about these days, one of which is very beautiful. It includes maiden warriors and fits the chaotic image of the period:

> Then, the girls of our country grew up without a yoke, living like Amazons with weapons in their hands and choosing leaders. They served militarily in the same way as young men. Like men, they enjoyed hunting in the forests. They did not take husbands. Still, they themselves took men, whom and when they would, and like the Skythian tribe, they did not differ in dress, man and woman.
>
> This gave the women so much boldness that they built a strong castle on a rock not far from the castle previously mentioned, which was named Děvín from the name of the 'maiden'. When the young men saw this, they were indignant and jealous.
>
> They gathered together in greater numbers, and not much farther than within hearing of the trumpet, they built a castle on the other rock among the scabs, which is now called Vyšehrad, but at that time was named Chvrasten. And since often the girls were cleverer at tricking the youths, and often the youths were braver than the girls, soon there was war between them, soon peace.
>
> When the truce came, the two parties agreed to meet to eat and drink for three days to hold festive games at the appointed place. The first day was spent in merry feasting and drinking.
>
> When they sought to quench their thirst, a new thirst grew, and the youths could hardly stay until night.

> *The night was night, the moon was shining, and the sky was clear.*
>
> *And one of them blew a trumpet and gave the signal, saying:*
>
> *'Ye have played enough; ye have eaten and drunk enough.*
>
> *Wake up now, Venus of gold is waking you up with her trumpet.'*
>
> *They took away one girl each. When morning came, and peace was made, they removed the food and drink from their castle and gave the empty walls to Vulcan the Lemnian. Since then, after the death of Princess Libuše, our women have been under the power of men.*
>
> **The Chronicle of the Czechs, Cosmas of Prague, 1125; translated by the author**

This legend, together with the myth of Libuše, the prophet princess, illustrates well the position of women in Bohemia, which was exceptional compared to the rest of Europe. Even later, in the Middle Ages, Czech laws let women enjoy more rights than under the competing German legislation. In the religious battles of the late Middle Ages, women would enter theological disputation, leaving learned men of the Church to stand in awe. When civil war broke out in the fifteenth century, some chronicles even put weapons into women's hands.

THE EIGHTH CENTURY

The lives of the people of the eighth century differed very little from those of other Slavs we have already described in the book. When Great Moravia flourished, Bohemia fell under its influence as the periphery of the mighty empire. Bohemian elites looked up to Moravian nobility, traded with them and accepted their cultural and religious influence. In central Bohemia, around the future capital of Prague, one tribe became the most powerful of them all. The name that the sources reveal also gave a name to the whole country. The sources remember Bohemi, a Christian elite with knowledge of Roman warfare and Mediterranean culture. This elite began the unification process in the tenth century.

The eighth and ninth centuries hide in the same darkness regarding our sources as many other national beginnings in this book. Bohemia evolved more slowly regarding culture and religion than its neighbour Moravia; it also had fewer written records. We must rely almost solely on sources of German provenance, unreliable legends or archaeological findings. These findings reveal a deep crisis at the beginning of the ninth century. Many old castles declined and vanished and new ones were built, indicating a profound change in social structures, new elites and perhaps some political crisis. New society emerged from the situation, with the Přemyslid dynasty as the mightiest.

The Beginnings of Christianity in Bohemia

Archaeological sources reveal that Christianity significantly permeated the world of Bohemian elites in the ninth century. The nobles decorated their jewellery with the sign of the Cross and buried their dead instead of cremating them. That in itself is no surprise, as Bohemia was surrounded by Christian influence from all sides. Unlike the Balkan Slavs, who faced the nomadic nations with their animist religions, and the Muslims, the Bohemians had only Christians as their neighbours. Nothing but the domestic Slavic paganism competed with the Christian faith. Apart from a surprising religious tradition, which we will discuss later, Christianity had no serious competition here.

The sources do reveal one crucial date, however: that of 845. In that year, 14 'Bohemian leaders' converted to Christianity officially in Regensburg. One of them was found buried with significant pomp. The reason for this act was political, as between 846 and 856 the Holy Roman Emperor Louis the German came to Bohemia. A long war was fought between him and the local elites, who had to submit to his authority in the end. Some of them obviously used the crisis that followed, and the protracted conflict between the empire and Great Moravia, to establish their own political authority.

Other Religions in Bohemia

We have already described how Christianity served to stabilize the central power in the early Middle Ages. Unlike Slavic paganism, firmly bound to the traditional tribal society, it promoted the authority of one God-given ruler. However, we saw with the Bulgars how a different religious tradition could serve the same purpose. It seems that the Přemyslid dynasty in Prague had their own legitimization tradition. It even remained with them long after they converted to Christianity. Archaeological sources reveal the strange behaviour of the first builders of churches on the hill of Prague.

There was obviously a place named by the chroniclers 'Žíž'. This term implies some kind of place where sacrifice by fire was carried out. The first nobles used to be buried (or probably cremated) right here. However, after the rulers converted to Christianity, they built churches carefully around this place, which is unusual. We have seen how Vladimir, after his conversion, destroyed all pagan temples and statues, but the Christian rulers still feared the power of this pagan place. It was not the might of the pagan gods they worried about, but the authority that the place enjoyed. Here, as some historians believe, lay a stone chair, a kind of throne. The duke of the Přemyslid dynasty sat in it during the ritual at the start of his rule, and here the oldest living member of the family presented the new duke to the nobles. They would kneel, shout their acceptance and profess their loyalty.

This ritual preceded Christianity in Bohemia and had roots in older religious traditions. It seems that the deity that brought legitimacy to the first rulers in Prague was of Iranian origin. The the Iranian god Mithra was the Sun god, the god of fire; he was the keeper of contracts, pacts and peace itself. Every duke who ascended the throne made a deal with Mithra, the Sun god, and received the power and responsibility to bring peace to his subjects. The first rulers of Bohemia of the Přemyslid dynasty made Mithra's cult, Mithraism, the centre of their power. This unifying factor brought them authority to rule. Archaeological findings imply that Mithraism was strong among the inhabitants of Bohemia. In contrast to pagan tribal cults, this religion provided a sense of shared identity. This not only helped the rulers hold their prominent position, but also helped the people to feel safe during the ninth century's turbulent times.

And when the Přemyslid converted to Christianity, they did not dare break their pact with the Iranian deity. Instead they included the ritual in their new Christian set of beliefs. Wenceslaus (907–935) was the first ruler strong enough to defy Mithra, or Mihr, as he was sometimes called. He built a church right next to the ancient place, thus subduing Mihr under the power of the Christian God. After Wenceslaus died a martyr and became a saint, he was named the patron saint of Bohemia and said to hold the 'mihr' in his hands.

In subsequent centuries, every ruler who ascended the throne of Bohemia was proclaimed a keeper of the 'mihr' of Saint Wenceslaus. Later people forgot about the pagan deity but they still referred to the 'mihr' of Saint Wenceslaus, which legitimized the ruler's power. As the original deity was forgotten, people translated the word 'mihr' as 'mír', meaning 'peace' in Czech. Yet everybody knew the word described more than a simple 'peace'. This word, in the expression of 'mihr of Saint Wenceslaus', represented the primary idea of the ruler's authority in Bohemia. His contract was with the patron saint and the people. No ruler would be respected in the early Middle Ages if he did not ascend the stone chair and receive the 'mihr' in a carefully kept ritual held at that sacred place.

We have enough sources concerning the ritual of a new duke ascending the throne to describe it in vivid detail:

It was a fine morning of 1035, and autumn colours gave the whole place a magical atmosphere. It helped to set up the festive mood. Jaromir (935–1035) climbed the hill in Prague, panting. He was the eldest of the Přemyslid house; he had once sat on that stone chair. But now he was blind, and his groin was deprived of its fertility. He had lost the game to the intrigues of his brothers, would father no sons and was tired. The land needed a new duke, young and strong, to guide it. He felt it in the eyes of the noblemen climbing the hill with him. He saw hope as they watched the young prince. Hope for peace and a better future after years of civil wars, divisions and uncertainty.

Břetislav (1002–1055) was a wise, experienced and fierce prince. So unlike his drunkard father and cruel, stupid uncle. Jaromir was glad he could do the young man the honour of setting him on the throne of their ancestors. To put the 'mihr' in his hands. Jaromir stopped on the soil surrounding the stone chair atop the hill. This was an ancient place; he could feel it. He could not tell the source of the magic. Yet he did not ask. His forefathers made this place. They knew. That is all that mattered.

Břetislav and Jaromir stood alone. The crowd remained in the distance and dared not set foot on the sacred ground surrounding the stone chair. Only the members of the ruling family could do so. The ritual had no written rule, yet they all knew what to do. They heard their fathers and grandfathers describe it and would tell their children and grandchildren how they witnessed the glorious day. The young prince was not nervous at all as Jaromir took his hand and raised it for the crowd to see. They did not cheer, not yet. Only the rustling of dry leaves disturbed the silence as Jaromir led the prince to the chair. Břetislav sat down on the throne, and Jaromir held out his hand:

'Hail, here is your duke!'

And they shouted approvingly three times: 'Krlešu'.

Thus the first idea that helped the dynasty legitimize their claims in pagan times held on in Christian times. It still holds, as even modern Czechs look up to Saint Wenceslaus and know him as their keeper of 'peace'. They cannot gather by the stone chair that was lost over the centuries; so they gather under the statue of Saint Wenceslaus in his square every time they feel threatened (as happened many times in the turbulent twentieth century).

It all began with an Iranian god and an ingenious plan of the ruling dynasty that helped to connect the ancient and modern traditions and provide them with authority. It worked all through the Middle Ages; nobody dared doubt the claim of the

Přemyslid house until 1306, when the last male of the line died. Even after that, kings of other dynasties kept to the tradition and emphasized that they were related to Saint Wenceslaus. Every single one of them, until 1918, when the republic was born. That is a unique phenomenon; it took some time before Prof. Petr Charvát (1949–2023) worked this out – that the surprising reason for this continuity was an Iranian deity and the authority he held in Bohemia from the darkest of ages.

THE PŘEMYSLID DYNASTY EMERGES FROM THE DARKNESS

Bořivoj I (r. 852–889) may have been a relative of Moravian dukes. Svatopluk I recognized Bořivoj as an independent duke around 872 and the Bohemian duke supported Svatopluk in his campaign against the Franks. Bořivoj also accepted the religious authority of Great Moravia and, more importantly, the baptism from Methodius. However, we know little about him.

> *Gostivit begat Bořivoj, who was the first duke to be baptized. He was baptized by the venerable Bishop Methodius in Moravia at the time of Emperor Arnulf and Svatopluk, king of Moravia.*
> **The Chronicle of the Czechs, Cosmas of Prague, 1125; translated by the author**

Bořivoj's wife, Ludmila of Bohemia (c. 860–921) features more prominently in the sources. She came from Lusatia and may have been the descendant of a Serbian duke in Lusatia. She accepted the baptism from Methodius with her husband, devoting her whole body and soul to the new faith. At least, so the legends say. The ruling couple promoted Christianity and suppressed minor pagan revolts. In 889 Bořivoj died, leaving Ludmila with two sons, Spytihněv (c. 875–915) and Vratislaus (c. 888–921).

The two most important things that Bořivoj did were his conversion to Christianity and his marriage. Everything else is lost in the mists of time. His older son, however, managed to make his mark.

SPYTIHNĚV I: THE PROVIDER OF STABILITY AND PROSPERITY

Young Spytihněv started his successful rule with international political success. He made a treaty with Arnulf, Duke of Bavaria (?–937) – a peace treaty essential for Arnulf as he tried to gain as much independence as possible from the Roman Emperor. Peace with the Bohemian duke meant that his northern border was safe. Spytihněv, on the other hand, would not have to fear an invasion from the south. This treaty probably stated that Bohemia would be part of the diocese of Regensburg. We know that Regensburg (in Bavaria) was the place where the first Bohemian lords were baptized.

However, Bořivoj went to Moravia and accepted baptism from a Slavonic archbishop. We saw in the history of Great Moravia that Bavaria was the main competition for the Old Church Slavonic structures. Now the Bohemian duke bent his knee before the Bavarian bishop, and thus settled the country on a Western course. From then on the Czechs would orient their politics in the direction of the West, cooperating or competing with the German element for the rest of their history.

Spytihněv also reformed the tax system, and his tax legislation remained valid throughout the Middle Ages. The taxes in early medieval Bohemia would not be paid in coins, as few of them existed among the ordinary people. Only nobles paid in coins, and even then not always. The tax collectors moved across the land and took the ruler's share of the harvest, meat, milk, honey and other natural resources. Archaeologists have discovered ceramic containers of identical content bearing a specific mark. These were obviously tools for the tax collectors to measure the shares. In the early Middle Ages no scales could weigh the precise amount of goods. A united metric system that would be universally accepted belongs to modern history. In the tenth century people measured with practical tools, comparing the amounts to their body parts or commonly used objects.

Spytihněv's rule was marked by unseen prosperity. The first Mediterranean delicacies, such as figs, found their way to the tables of the nobles, and the clothes they wore implied Scandinavian or Byzantine origin. It seems that merchants travelled through Bohemia and the elites were wealthy enough to buy their luxury goods.

Bohemia and the Trade in the Tenth Century

The town of Praga is built of stone and lime and is the richest of towns in trade. There come to it Russians and Slavs from Cracow with merchandise, and from the lands of the Turks come Mohammedans, Jews and Turks, also with merchandise and with Byzantine money, and they export thence flour, tin and various furs. Their country is the best of the northern countries and the richest in food provision.

They sell for a kushar so much of wheat that it suffices a man for a month, and barley is sold for a kushar, enough to feed a horse forty days, and ten fowls are sold for one kushar. And in the town of Praga they make saddles and bridles and shields, which are applied and used in their countries. And they make in the lands of Bohemia light handkerchiefs of a very thin texture like a net, which is of no use. Their price is always one kushar for ten handkerchiefs. They trade with them and reckon in them. They have (whole) vessels of them and they reckon them to be wealth and most precious things. Wheat and flour, horses, gold, silver and all things are bought with them.

It is remarkable that the inhabitants of Bohemia are dark and have black hair, but (those) of reddish hair are rare amongst them.

'On the Early Slavs. The Narrative of Ibrahim-Ibn-Yakub', translated by Semen Rapoport, 1929

Although Ibrahin-Ibn-Yakub (?–962) travelled in Central Europe long after Spytihněv died, his vivid description also fits this period. This was a time of prosperity for Bohemia and the land seemed very fertile. We know from the coins discovered in the ground and the jewellery and clothes found in elite graves that Bohemia traded with Arabia, Byzantium, Scandinavia and, of course, Italian cities. We are unsure what the Slavs in Bohemia sold, but it was probably grain or slaves. The slave trade grew in the tenth century, yet there was tough competition for Bohemian slave traders. As Bohemia and neighbouring states provided limited numbers of pagans that could be sold on the market, they stood no chance against the competition of Italian slavers.

Bohemian merchants used rivers – the Oder and the Elbe – as their main trade routes. Their goods went in south-eastern and south-western directions to Baltic lands, the Black Sea and, of course, Byzantium. We are sure that Bohemians traded slaves because archaeologists found vast numbers of slave manacles on the lower stream of the Elbe River.

The text by Ibrahim quoted above mentions pieces of fabric that Bohemian people used as their currency. However, from the tenth century there was local currency. These coins would be made of silver, and the historians spent years desperately looking for the metal's source. Local mining technology was unable to extract silver naturally found in Bohemia until the fourteenth century. It thus seems that the coins minted in Bohemia in the tenth century were Arabian dirhams containing silver from Moroccan mines; these had been melted down and minted again.

VRATISLAV I AND DRAHOMÍRA

Spytihněv ruled for more than 10 years. But he did not have an heir, so his younger brother Vratislav I (r. 905–921) followed him on the stone chair and became a duke. Vratislav, like his father Bořivoj, is overshadowed by his wife. He chose to marry a foreigner, Drahomíra of Stodor (*c.* 877–*c.* 934). She was a noble lady from the Polabian region (close to Brandenburg), the daughter of a Stodoran prince, a Polabian Slav.

The legendists would have us believe that Drahomíra was a pagan. However, they would also have us believe in a black-and-white world, and we know from our experience that the world rarely is so clear cut, especially when real people are involved. Drahomíra married a Christian duke with high ambitions, and thus she had to be a Christian too. The legends are our primary sources, and in the legends she is the one who battled for power with a saint. Saint Ludmila was her mother-in-law, and the two women competed for the regency over, and influence on, the young Prince Wenceslaus. This conflict resulted in an assassination that made Ludmila a martyr and Drahomíra a villain, with a special place in the hell of Czech national memory. In fact we know very little about Drahomíra's character, but we do know that she was a skilled politician.

Ludmila and Drahomíra: Regency and Family Disputes

Vratislav died in 921, leaving Drahomíra a widow with at least four surviving children. The number of daughters is uncertain, but there were definitely two sons, both too young to rule.

So the pious Ludmila, widowed and having lost both sons, remained in her house and, remembering her former ignorance and error, mourned day by day. And as once she had given her members into the service of uncleanness and iniquity to sin, she now gave them into the service of righteousness to sanctify, saying the word of the apostle: What profit had I then that I am now ashamed of?

The poor testify to this, whom she immensely helped in their want and whose necessities she cared for as a mother, feeding the hungry, refreshing the thirsty, clothing the wayfaring and needy.

She was godly and gentle in all things and full of all the fruits of goodness. She was generous in alms, unwearied in watchfulness, devout in prayer, perfect in love, unmeasured in humility, so diligent in the care of God's servants that she was not able to satisfy them in the light of day, and, at night, with hidden hands, she sent to her household with zeal what they needed, fulfilling the word of the Gospel, which commands to do works of love, so that our left hand may not know what the right hand is doing. Rather than recount all her virtues' manifestations, we would rather have the light of day than writing paper. And indeed the doors of her house were open day and night to every passer-by, that she might have cried with blessed Job, my door was open to the stranger, I was an eye to the blind and a foot to the lame.

She was the mother of orphans, the comforter of widows, the tireless visitor of the captive or imprisoned and perfect in all good works.

When, therefore, the named Duke Vratislaus, as we have mentioned, took over the government from his deceased brother, he consolidated the empire, built a basilica in honour of the blessed George the Martyr, but, being caught in death, did not see its long-desired consecration. He sent his son Wenceslaus, a boy of fervent mind, to a castle called Budeč, where there was and is a church, dedicated by his predecessor and brother Spytihněv in honour of the prince of the apostles, blessed Peter, to be instructed there in the law of God and the Scriptures.

The boy of keen wit, being enlightened by the Holy Ghost, deeply imprinted in his memory all that he heard from his teacher, and when his father had departed from this world at the age of about thirty-three years, he was called to the castle of

Prague, and exalted to the father's seat by all the people. But because he had not yet fully grown to the age, all the nobles, agreeing on a wise plan, entrusted the inexperienced duke and his brother Boleslav to Ludmila of blessed memory, a servant of Christ to be brought up until they should, by the grace of God, grow in age and strength.

But when the mother of these boys saw that she was a widow and had taken the sceptre of her husband, she was enraged by the devil. With all the veils of her poisonous soul, she burned against Ludmila, the servant of God. And being consumed with evil conjectures, thinking that by entrusting the education of the young men to her mother-in-law, the whole nation was deprived of its government and possessions and that, on the contrary, Ludmila would seize all the dominion, she entered into the most perverse consultation with the men of Belial. She sought with all her might to destroy her mother-in-law.

But Ludmila, the worthy and devout servant of Christ, perceiving this, took up arms against the barbs of insolence with the weapons of humility and patience and, after listening, said to her daughter-in-law:

'Not a shadow of any desire for thy rule has taken hold of my heart; no such thing has taken root there and I least wish to command you in any way. And I do not want to have any wish for you, but I do not wish that you should rule over me. Give me the liberty to serve Christ Almighty in whatever place you will.'

For, as it is always the case that the more humility bows down to God, the more pride and haughtiness are turned off by the Devil's prodding, the most kind and benevolent request of the holy Duchess Ludmila was despised by her daughter-in-law.

This the handmaid of Christ saw, bearing in mind the apostolic word: If they persecute you in one place, flee to another. She moved with her family from the main castle to a castle called Tetin, adorning herself with the more pearls of virtue, the more confident she was that she would soon be caught by her persecutors and deserved the fuel of martyrdom. She insisted devoutly on her prayers, constantly tormented herself by fasting and gave alms with a generous hand.

Legenda Christiani, translated by the author

We have before us two women competing for power. Although the legendist would have us believe that the older woman, Ludmila, had no personal ambitions and that Drahomíra hated her out of pure spite, the reality was probably different. Ludmila enjoyed decisive influence over the young Prince Wenceslaus, as she was in charge of the education of both boys. She must also have had some allies in the court, as it was the nobles' idea to put the princes into her care. And as Drahomíra was to be regent, this posed a direct threat – for the regent remained in power only as long as the heir was in her custody.

Drahomíra: the First Assassination in the Přemyslid Family

This situation was unprecedented in Bohemia. A woman was to rule the land. In the chapters above we encountered only one similar example: Olga of Kyivan Rus. And we saw to what extent a woman regent had to go to retain authority in the early Middle Ages. Historians cannot tell how Drahomíra managed to consolidate power in Prague. In the early Middle Ages when the duke died and the heir was too young to rule, someone would usually defy the regent's rule, especially if the regent was a woman. However, we have no source mentioning the revolt against Drahomíra. The only reminder is the mention by legendists of some nobles wanting Ludmila to be in charge of the princes, which might appear to be a challenge. Yet Ludmila was a member of the ruling family and nobody dared to question the princes' claim.

It seems that Přemyslid authority was so firmly rooted in Bohemia at this time that nobody dared to threaten the claim of Prince Wenceslaus and the regency established by his father. The noble birth of the duchess would have brought her the respect she needed. However, the claim that she promoted pagan religion is probably just an invention of the legendists. Bohemian nobility was Christian; they would not at this point respect a pagan regent. Nor would the German neighbours.

However, the dispute between the two women did not end when Ludmila stood aside to spend the rest of her days on Tetin. She might have remained a hidden threat and retained some influence. But Drahomíra obviously feared her and the influence she had on her son. And so the sources describe the first political assassination in Czech history.

For when the handmaid of Christ, Ludmila, as we said before, has withdrawn from the eyes of the traitors, she was persecuted again by her enemies in the castle where she has taken refuge. The Duchess sent some of her great men, sons of iniquity named Tunnus and Gommon, with a solid band to Tetin to destroy her mother-in-law. But the handmaid of Christ, knowing beforehand the things to come, called her priest Paul, already mentioned, and asked him to celebrate Mass. And having already known the blessings of the Highest which she would receive, she poured out her confession in the presence of the searcher of hearts and armed herself with the weapons of faith.

Kneeling down in prayer, she begged God to accept her spirit, which He had created, in peace. When the Mass was ended, having been strengthened by the reception of the Lord's body and blood, she began to sing psalms with an unbroken mind. Then, in the evening, the usurpers broke into her house; the other companions, armed with spears and shields, stood outside; only the chief assassins Tunna and Gommon – with a few others – broke down the door, and with wild clamour rushed into the chamber in which the handmaid of God rested. Blessed Ludmila, in a humble voice, said to them:

'What sudden frenzy is this that is overwhelming you? Are you not ashamed, nor do you remember how I nurtured you as my sons and gave you gold, silver and splendid clothes? But if you have any grievance against me that I have committed, tell me, I pray you.'

But the fierce men, more steadfast than a stone, not willing to hear her and not daring to lay their hands on her, dragged her out of her bed and threw her to the ground. And she said to them:

'Let me pray a little.'

And when they suffered her to do so, she spread forth her hands and prayed unto the Lord. Then she said:

'If you come to destroy me, I pray you to cut off my head with the sword.'

For, after the example of the martyrs, she desired to bear witness to Christ by shedding her blood. Here she asked to receive with them the palm of martyrdom forever, which she also deserved, we doubt not.

So the cruel executioners, not heeding her pleas, threw a scarf around her throat. By strangling her, they deprived her of her earthly life so that she might live forever with Him whom she had always loved, Jesus Christ our Lord. Then Ludmila, the happy and devoted servant of Christ, suffered martyrdom on the seventh day of Saturday September 15, at the first vigil of the night.

When the shepherd was killed, all her clerics, of both sexes, scattered in all directions and hid in hiding places to preserve their earthly life. And when the cruel executioners had departed, they ran with great fear and lamentation to the funeral rite and, having most reverently performed all that was proper for her burial, they committed her consecrated remains to the earth. And the bloodthirsty murderers, having taken what they could, returned to their mistress, bringing her joyful tidings of the murder of the innocent. They thought they were enriched forever, though the terrible torments of hellfire would soon be upon them.

Then she, the traitorous lady of traitors, having seized all her mother-in-law's property with the usurpers named, set herself to rule, bestowing their relatives here the best goods of gold and silver and precious clothes of immense value. And they ruled over the whole land of Bohemia as great dukes, but not of God.

When they were living so splendidly, rejoicing immensely, the just punishment of God's vengeance came upon the wicked, who were not afraid to commit such a cruel crime and to stretch out their most shameful hands upon the most glorious servant of God without cause. For, provoked by their father, the prince of sedition, the devil, they began to despise all their contemporaries. And there arose a great dissension and hatred between the said great men Tunna and Gommon and their mistress until all the *thoughts and speeches of the mistress were day and night about how to destroy them. This when the said violent man Tunna, overwhelmed with terrible fear, beheld and fled with all his kindred from that land, here hated by all as a fugitive, an exile, wandering, here and there, none of his tribe having any more access to his home.*

And Gommon, when he and his brother sought refuge by flight, was caught here at the throat and punished here, and so forfeited his present and future life and that of his brother. And when their mistress saw that they fled, she poured out all the fury of her poisonous heart upon their descendants, from the eldest to the youngest, and put them to death in one day and with the same ordeal.

This was also the first sign of the holiness of the blessed Ludmila, that none of her murderers, by the control of divine providence, remained alive. Having left their dwellings and scattered to various places, others breathed out their souls from all the haters of God's vengeance. Their children were driven out of the world by an unholy death and too many were put to the sword.

In the same days, at the tomb of the martyr Ludmila, the venerable lady often mentioned here, the glorious miracles of her virtues came to light through God's grace. From her grave, such a strange and lovely fragrance emanated that the scent of all precious spices and flowers was overpowering; not a few people also noticed the candles burning three or four times with divine light in the silence of the dark night, all of which did not remain hidden from the ruler, namely her murderess.

And when she heard of it, she was in great fear and knew not what to do. Then she again made a poisonous proposal, and here

she sent her servants to the Tetin, where the venerable body lay buried, and ordered that a house in the form of a church should be built over the grave of the blessed Ludmila. Here she appointed a title in honour of the blessed Michael the Archangel so that if any other sign should appear there, it should be attributed not to the merits of the blessed martyr, but to those of the saints whose relics were buried here. When this was done, all who entered the basilica were in awe that they dared to enter it with nothing but the greatest reverence, and great miracles were performed there.
Legenda Christiani, translated by the author

SAINT WENCESLAUS AND THE BEGINNING OF HIS REIGN

When Wenceslaus reached adulthood, his mother probably did not want to give up power. Some historians dispute the claims of the legendists, which provide us with vivid details of their power struggle. This situation – mothers or uncles who did not want to relinquish power and tried to retain influence over their protégés even when they were old enough to rule – was not uncommon in the early Middle Ages, however. When we realize that the age at which a boy was deemed fit to rule was around 14 years, it seems logical that mothers would not let such a young boy rule independently. However, other forces, especially other nobles, also wanted their share of influence.

On many occasions in the Middle Ages, rulers began their reign with a power struggle against their former regents, even if the regent was their mother. This was the test of fire; either they managed to prove themselves or their authority would collapse. Let us listen to the legend once more:

For this reason, there was a great quarrel between the nobles who sided with the religious duke and the others who sided with the wicked mistress. And the counsellors and chief men of the land were divided, and the thorns of strife between them were stirred up to bloodshed. And the side of the righteous, though small, prevailed over the mighty side of the wicked, as it always does.

For the ever-remembered Duke Wenceslaus, anxious that peace should be established, by the inspiration of the Holy Ghost made a resolution in his heart to banish his mother, who was the cause of all iniquity, from his country: to expel her. All her adherents, men of wickedness, and the peace of the Church of Christ be raised up that all having one and the same lord may learn the true doctrine of Christ most perfectly, and when all that seems necessary for peace in the empire has been done the sons of strife shall be banished and driven out.

When peace shall be made, he desired to call his mother home again with honour. And all this, with the help of God the Creator, he did indeed accomplish, for he banished the mother from the empire with the greatest shame, whereby Almighty God repaid her with deserved punishment for the shedding of the blood of the innocent blessed Ludmila, whom she had put to death without cause.

But being full of chaste fear, which endures for ages, remembering the commandments of God, by which we are commanded to honour father and mother, he restored her to her country after a time. However, she remained deprived of her former dominion until death.

Legenda Christiani, translated by the author

Wenceslaus thus won the power struggle against his mother and her political party. He managed to stabilize power to the extent that he could call his mother back from exile. We hear no more about Drahomíra, who was obviously no threat to her son any more. They may have even returned to the loving relationship of mother and son. The legendists would not tell us about that, however, as they would have us believe that Drahomíra was the embodiment of the Devil. Be that as it may, both her sons proved competent enough and the young state survived the dynastic crisis with no significant unrest, a remarkable achievement.

Good King Wenceslas

Good King Wenceslas looked out, on the Feast of Stephen,
When the snow lay round about, deep and crisp and even;
Brightly shone the moon that night, tho' the frost was cruel,
When a poor man came in sight, gath'ring winter fuel.
'Bring me flesh, and bring me wine, bring me pine logs hither:
Thou and I shall see him dine, when we bear them thither.'
Page and monarch, forth they went, forth they went together;
Through the rude wind's wild lament and the bitter weather.
'Sire, the night is darker now, and the wind blows stronger;
Fails my heart, I know not how; I can go no longer.'
'Mark my footsteps, my good page. Tread thou in them boldly
Thou shalt find the winter's rage freeze thy blood less coldly.'

John Mason Neale, 'Good King Wenceslas'
(a Christmas carol), 1853

It may surprise you to learn that most Czechs have no idea that their beloved saint and patron of the Czech Republic features in an English carol that children and adults sing at Christmas. Still, they love Saint Wenceslaus. The anniversary of his death is a national holiday and people fly national flags; when they are anxious, they add the prayer: 'Saint Wenceslaus, do not let us perish today nor in the future.'

Here, the 'us' is referring to us, the Czechs. None of the rulers mentioned in this book earned such a significant place in the national memory, and it is a remarkable phenomenon worldwide. During the turbulent twentieth century, during German and Soviet occupation, the statue on Wenceslaus Square was a centre where people came together. They still gather on the same spot when they feel endangered, regardless of the source of the threat: be it the COVID-19 pandemic, economic problems or the climate crisis.

In a popular national myth, Saint Wenceslaus is the general of a mythical military force. These soldiers wait inside a mountain (Blaník) and will ride out to save the nation when the worst of times come. The real Wenceslaus lived in the tenth century and is irrelevant to this national myth. Still, there are moments in his life story that resonate with people.

He made a peace treaty with the Holy Roman Emperor, deciding to pay tribute to the empire instead of waging war. This historical fact was exploited by the Nazis during the German occupation of the Second World War, with Wenceslaus being pictured as the wise Czech – the one who understood that Germans are to be obeyed. Once again, as in the case of Kyivan Rus or earliest Bulgarian history, this signifies how crucial it is to understand the early history of the Slavs. It is still alive.

So let us learn more about the actual duke.

Wenceslaus and the Empire

Wenceslaus began his rule as a very young man. After he solved the issue with his mother and her remaining supporters, he faced the usual problem for a Bohemian ruler: the threat of German invasion.

In 929 the allied forces of the future Holy Roman Emperor (at that moment a king of Saxony) Henry the Fowler (c. 876–936) and Arnulf of Bavaria, who betrayed the peace treaty that he had signed with Wenceslaus's uncle, stood on Bohemian borders. Such betrayal was common in the early Middle Ages. The duke was young, and there had been uncertainty during the transfer of power from his mother; this was the chance to try how strong the new ruler was.

At the same time the Hungarians were causing trouble on the eastern borders, and Henry the Fowler proved a fierce enemy. His campaign against Bohemia was part of his long-term endeavours to strengthen the empire's hold over the Central European Slavs in Bohemia and Poland, and over Polabian Slavs within his empire. Wenceslaus faced war with a stronger enemy at a time when his land was not fully united. His power struggle with his mother, the regency period and his young age slowed the processes of unification and stabilization of power.

Wenceslaus negotiated a peace treaty with Henry that included paying a tribute. However, he did win a prize, a powerful relic, in the form of the arm of Saint Vitus, the national saint of Saxony. Wenceslaus brought the relic home and built a church of Saint Vitus on the Prague hill. He dared to set the church in the immediate neighbourhood of the old centre of the pagan cult. Thus the Christian saint finally subdued the Mihr, or Mithra.

Wenceslaus and Christianity

Wenceslaus continued with the Christianization of Bohemia, which in his times was far from complete. Powerful pagan nobles remained, and ordinary people needed time and teaching to accept the new faith. Wenceslaus was clever; he knew that more than force was required to persuade people to convert. He brought home a powerful relic, but wanted more. He desired to have a national saint, one of the ruling family, and duly found one in his grandmother, whose remains he transferred from her grave on Tetin.

In the early Middle Ages three steps were required to become a saint: a miracle, a martyr's death and the transfer of the remains. Wenceslaus's grandmother died a violent death and lived a pious life. Many witnesses would come to testify about miracles. The transfer of the saint's remains usually brought some miracles too, as the legend testifies:

Then, remembering his grandmother, how holy she had been in this life and what great merit and glory she had won with the Almighty, blessed Wenceslaus, sprinkled with a torrent of tears, made a holy intention with the priests and some religious men and sent them to the castle of Tetin, commanding them to carry the bones or the dust of the decayed body to him.

But by the inspiration of the Holy Spirit, he was assured and confided to several intimate friends that by the operation of God's grace, the appointed messengers would see some signs there. The men who had been sent, carrying out the orders of their master, entered the basilica and dug up the earth. On discovering the tomb, they found that the slab with which the venerable remains were covered was partly decayed. And they were afraid to lift it up.

And if the wood be stinking, how much more, they thought, had it grown old? And with the utmost caution, they would shut up the tomb again. But one of them, the priest Paul, whom we have also mentioned above, who was always associated with her by friendship while she was on earth and always supported her in all things by his services, resisted their purpose:

'If I find, as you say, but the dust of a decayed body, I will take it with me, according to the order of the prince.'

And the others, having given him the truth, with one accord, loosed the plate. And when they had lifted it, it broke, and the clay fell on the body. Paul rose up quickly and hastily raked away the clay, and there he and his companions found the body of the saint, preserved from all violation; only her face was covered with dust, which had fallen on it when the lid was broken as they were lifting it. Overjoyed beyond measure, they gave infinite thanks to the Almighty; they lifted her most holy remains from the earth, wrapped them in precious linen, as was fitting, and laid them before the altar, giving immeasurable praise and thanks to the grace of God.

And when all the rites had been duly performed, they laid her on a litter, which they tied to the backs of two horses. So that night they hastened steadily to the capital, namely, to Prague. For those who brought it, before they brought it into the castle, sent good tidings to the prince of the heralds. And when they came and heard that he had laid down his limbs to sleep, they woke him up with joy.

They told him the glad tidings that by the grace of God Almighty, they had found the body of the glorious lady, his grandmother, intact. And immediately he arose, and with great vigour hastened to the temple, giving thanks to Christ the Lord. And when the sun had lightened the earth, and with its splendour had quenched the darkness, he called together the priests and the *multitude of the faithful, and with a grand procession hastened to meet them. And they met those faithful bearers, bringing the oft-remembered relics of Saint Ludmila.*

The priests and deacons joyfully placed them on their shoulders, blessing God with psalms and praises, carrying them into the castle, entering the temple, setting them before the altar on the pavement and rejoicing with noisy cheers. Meanwhile, the general curiosity of believers and unbelievers alike sought to know what had happened, and they gathered together and flocked to the temple door. So the prince, consulting with the priests, had her body laid bare before all the people so that all might believe that Christ the Lord had preserved her intact. And when they saw it, they all proclaimed the miracles of Christ without ceasing, and no one could deny the truth, for the integrity of the body and the strength of the hair was evident to all. And her face shone as if she were alive, and her garments shone with such beauty and integrity as if they had been woven that day. At this, all the people cried aloud and rejoiced, declaring that she was worthy of all honour and praise.

And when they had dug the ground and prepared the grave, they prepared to bury her in the basilica. But suddenly, the grave that was dug was overflowed with water, whereby many concluded that the place was not pleasing to the handmaid of Christ. So they filled up the excavation again and set the coffin with the holy banner upon it, asking for help from God.

Then the prince, inflamed with the exceeding zeal of God, humbly begged the bishop to come to him himself and bury the body in the basilica, which had not yet received the episcopal consecration. But he excused himself that he could not come because of the weakness of old age and sent his fellow bishop

with several clerics to consecrate the church. This bishop came, first consecrating the church to the Lord. Then six days later he buried the body in the same place where the water had risen.
Legenda Christiani, translated by the author

The Words of the Legends

The legend is full of clichés, which help us to understand the mentality of people in the early Middle Ages. As we mentioned earlier, the freshly converted Christians had many difficulties in accepting Christian burial practices. Slavic pagans cremated their dead, and believing this practice to be the only proper way of dealing with death. Thus Christian legends usually emphasized miraculously preserved bodies of the saints and awe-inspiring stories about discovering their remains. The saint had to show his or her power after death to signify the primary message of Christianity: that faith conquers death. In the early Middle Ages, such abstract thinking as faith and the afterlife were insufficient. The Christian saint conquered the natural death and the processes of decay, retaining power even as a dead body: that was solid proof for the pagans. Tales of the transfer of Ludmila's body would spread.

Ludmila was a local saint whose canonization would raise the status of the dynasty and bring a unifying idea to Bohemia, one firmly rooted in the Christian religion. The legend also tells how the Bavarian bishop was initially reluctant to sanctify this act. He clearly understood its political significance and would refuse at first.

Wenceslaus and the Internal Politics

The legends would have us believe that Wenceslaus hated wars, so he bowed to the emperor. Yet that simply is not true. Within

Bohemia, he vigorously took the Přemyslid centre's direct influence in an Eastern direction. He also set out to subdue rebellious dukes from other dynasties. One of the legends provides evidence for these claims:

> *Having many people, a specific castle named Kourim exalted itself and plotted a rebellion against this holy one with its prince. But when enough blood had been shed on both sides, the counsel pleased all that the two dukes should fight together, and he that prevailed should reign. And when the princes went out to fight, the God of Heaven showed the Kourim a heavenly vision, namely, the holy Wenceslaus, with the image of the sacred Cross on his forehead. When he saw it far off, he threw his weapon and fell at his feet, declaring that no one could overcome him whom God was hastening to his aid by such signs.*
>
> *And when he had confessed this, the holy duke raised him to the kiss of peace. He comfortably established himself in his former power in the castle, giving him the government of the castle as long as he lived. Truly the Cross was seen, for he followed Christ and came to the kingdom, in which Christ reigns with the Father and the Holy Ghost forever.*
>
> **Legenda Christiani, translated by the author**

The legend emphasized the victory of a Christian saint over a pagan rebel. For us, however, it is proof that Wenceslaus was firm in his resolution to unify the Czech lands under the Přemyslid rule and that he helped spread Christianity.

Wenceslaus had one opponent, his younger brother Boleslav I (915–972). Boleslav was clever, competent and ambitious. However, we lack evidence of serious disputes preceding the events of one September morning, when assassins, supposedly hired by Boleslav, murdered Wenceslaus on his way to church. Some historians believe that only legends made Boleslav the murderer, precisely because no revolt of the younger brother was recorded in the written sources and because of the acts of reverence Boleslav showed to his brother immediately after his death. Some historians believe that Wenceslaus was murdered because of some personal grievance his lords had against him. Nevertheless, it happened in his brother's town on the morning after Boleslav invited his brother to a feast. This certainly sounds suspicious, although we will never know for sure.

The Famous Fratricide

In the year of our Lord's birth, 929, on 28 September, Saint Wenceslaus, Prince of Bohemia, was martyred by his brother's deceit in the castle of Boleslav.

He entered the eternal court of heaven with a happy destiny. For I think the legend of the same holy man sufficiently tells of how Boleslaus, unworthy to serve as the holy man's natural brother, insidiously invited his brother to a banquet when he was about to murder him to take possession of the country or how he hid the guilt of fratricide from the face of men but not from God.

And when Prince Wenceslaus had taken the reward of his life, Boleslaus, the second Cain, came to a princedom ill-gotten.
The Chronicle of the Czechs, Cosmas of Prague, 1125; translated by the author

This famous murder remains distinct in the national memory of Czechs. Let us picture it in vivid detail:

It is a muddy morning of 28 September. Prince Wenceslaus and a few companions are walking through the morning fog. Wenceslaus feels sorry for them; they squint their eyes at the road, visibly suffering. Last night's feast with brother Boleslav was merry. Wenceslaus drinks moderately, but does not deny others worldly pleasures. He is now heading to the Church of Saints Cosmas and Damian for the Mass. He knows that his companions would gladly remain in bed, but he made them follow him. He was their master and their souls were his responsibility. He might let them drink and whore all night, but would still make them honour God in the morning.

In the fog behind him, Wenceslaus hears footsteps. He shrugs. He's in his brother's place, nothing to worry about.

The footsteps are getting closer and faster. Could someone be in such a hurry for Mass? Hardly. Wenceslaus is usually among the first in church.

No need to worry; he has a large retinue with him. He looks around, judging the tired looks of his companions, who obviously haven't heard anything yet. They would be little help if anything happens. He sighs, puts his hand on the hilt of his sword and moves on. Whatever the heavy stamping of boots behind his back means, God will not wait; his will be done. It's time to go to Mass…

Guilty or not, Boleslav recognized the importance of a national saint. He created the cult of his brother, the cult of Saint Wenceslaus, that still lives in the minds of people in the twenty-first-century. However, he first had to set himself as a successful ruler.

BOLESLAV I: THE BUILDER OF THE CZECH STATE

Boleslav I was the first ruler of the Přemyslid dynasty who could say he really ruled a state. He retained the respect of all the nobles in Bohemia, spread the state religion and became a respected ally of the German emperor. Immediately after his brother's murder, he stopped paying the tribute, knowing that he would face an invasion of Henry the Fowler as a punishment. However, Boleslav won the decisive battle. He signed a peace treaty in which the Bohemian duke did not pay tribute and was fully respected as a European prince. As an ally of the emperor, Boleslav joined him on his campaigns. They helped to protect Europe from the Magyar invasion in the victorious Battle of Lechfeld in 955.

Boleslav also negotiated the ecclesiastic independence of Bohemia. With his competent daughter Mlada, who travelled to Rome in 965, they gained a papal licence to establish a bishop in Prague. Mlada also became an abbess to the first monastery built in Prague. Boleslav spread his influence further east, helping Moravians to free themselves from the Hungarian invaders and adding parts of Moravia to Bohemia. In doing so he clashed with the Polish dukes because his military exploits involved occupying the Polish city of Krakow, which disturbed Poland's trade with Kyiv. However, he diplomatically solved the conflict. Boleslav married one of his daughters, Doubravka (940–977), to the Polish ruler Mieszko I (c. 930–992), who had to convert to marry her. Doubravka remains a distinct figure in Polish history because she helped with the Christianization of the country. So it was that, for the first time in Central European history, Bohemia, not the empire, incentivized other rulers to enter the Christian family.

Boleslav stabilized the Czech state in political, military and ideological ways; founding the monastery also served to elevate Bohemia in cultural terms. At the end of his life, he transferred power peacefully to his oldest son, thus proving that the Czech state worked in every way.

Boleslav and the Cult of Saint Wenceslaus

Boleslav practically founded the Czech state in the early Middle Ages. However, he remains prominent in history as both the murderer of his brother and the keeper of his brother's legacy. It was Boleslav who recognized the potential of his brother's renown and began the process of making yet another saint of the ruling dynasty.

> *The blood of the blessed martyr, unholy shed by the wicked, which was splashed on the ground and on the walls, was carefully washed away with water. But the next day those who had washed it away the day before returned to find the walls and the ground soaked with blood, as if they had not touched them with water. And they hastened again to wipe away the blood. And when they had done this a third time, they went away again, seeing that they had done nothing.*
>
> *The body of the blessed martyr rested buried for three years in the Church of Saint Cosmas and Saint Damian. Later, however, it was revealed to some servants of God that they should transfer the servant of God from the place where he was buried to the Basilica of Saint Vitus the Martyr, which in the metropolis of Prague, by the will of God, he built from the ground up and decorated with temple ornaments exquisitely, and in which it is said that one day when it was being built, he was walking and uttered this verse of the Psalmist: 'This is my rest for ever and ever.'*
>
> *This was made known to the duke Boleslav. He could not resist the miracle of God, yet he was amazed, though too late. And he sent and commanded the saint's body to be transferred by night, with the condition that if the holy members were not brought to the place of reinterment by dawn, all those entrusted*

with it would no doubt be put to the sword. And they came by night, took the most holy body, loaded it into a cart and drove until they came to a brook called Rokytnice. And behold, the waters were so high that they overflowed all the meadows, and there was no hope for those who brought the holy body except death.

But when they were in such distress, it came into their minds to beg the blessed Wenceslaus himself to have mercy on them, for the martyr had already, by many apparitions, commanded that he should be carried away. And they said: 'O blessed martyr, we have heeded thy command; we are now all in danger of being cut down by the murderous sword.' But at the same time, they were working to build a bridge. As they are doing this, they look up and suddenly see themselves and the wagon with the body of the precious martyr on the bank of the river where they are heading.

When the servants see the holy martyr, they praise God and their saint with a loud voice and with all their hearts, who has delivered his servants from such a predicament with such mighty power. Thus was the goodness of the Lord miraculously shown, thus the merit of his servant, thus the glory of God, and thus the martyr was witnessed, when both his body was worthily carried.

And hastening on to the river Vltava and finding the bridge destroyed, they began to mourn. And they began to lose strength and could not lift it up. And they fled again to pray that he would help them by his known goodness, that they might not lose their early life, for the morning hail was just coming, which the prince had appointed for a time. Soon they saw that they were heard; they took him upon their shoulders and, as if they had borne no burden, they crossed the broken bridge with joy without difficulty.

> So they came without any hindrance or delay to the place the saint had once prepared for himself. And having kindled a light that they might see, they saw his body unbroken, and all his wounds healed, save the one which his cruel brother had inflicted on his head. For that, though, it was healed yet differed from the rest, as though it were covered with a white mantle. But when it was washed, it was found to be like the others.
>
> Gathering together as many priests and people as possible, with hymns and singing, they placed the holy body in a coffin. They buried it in the Basilica of Saint Vitus the Martyr where, by the grace of the Lord, many miracles are being performed for the merits of the holy martyr Wenceslaus, to the praise and glory of the name of Christ our Lord.
>
> **Legenda Christiani, translated by the author**

Thus we end the story of the complicated relations in the most famous family of early Czech history. Now we move on to consider the rulers who kept (or in some cases destroyed) their legacy.

BOLESLAV II THE PIOUS (c. 932–999)

The eldest son of Boleslav I is called the Pious primarily because of the endeavours of his father and his sister Mlada. Their diplomatic skills acquired the papal licence to build the diocese in Prague, but the first bishop in fact ascended the bishopric under Boleslav II's rule. Prague became a centre not only in a political way, but also in this spiritual and cultural sense of the word. It would be convenient for all the future rulers that the Czech Church and the Czech State looked up to the same city.

However, Boleslav II had also to deal with trouble on the international political field. First, there was the empire. After the death of Henry the Fowler, an ambitious dynasty of Ottonian rulers entered the scene. In 985 Otto II (955–985) died, leaving a baby and his mother, the Byzantine princess Theofano (955–991), as a regent. The mother managed to retain her rule and successfully suppressed the revolt of a Bavarian duke. However, Boleslav II failed to choose the right side, siding with the rebels. After they lost, the Bohemian duke was compromised in the eyes of Theophano.

The situation deteriorated. Bohemia was no longer the only Christian state the empire could look to; competition arose when the Polish state entered the Christian family under the first Piast ruler, then the Magyars settled down and began to build their own state.

Boleslav II had to fight against both new emerging states without the support of the empire. In the process he lost much of the territory in the east and north that his father had gained by his expansion. Boleslav II proved a skilled diplomat, however, entering into a very high-profile second marriage even in this complicated political situation. His second wife, the mysterious Emma (950–1006), was an Italian or French princess whose noble birth far exceeded that of her husband.

Then there was a dispute with the powerful houses of the Vršovci and Slavnik dynasty. This dispute was solved most brutally, as all the inhabitants in the seat of the house, Libice, were slaughtered, down to the last man and child. However, their blood probably did not lay on Boleslav's hands. It was a result of a blood feud between Adalbert of Prague and the second most powerful house in the country, Vršovci. Despite this, the duke in

Prague could and should have prevented it, yet he did not. The Přemyslid dynasty went on to profit by the eradication of their competition.

If the Přemyslid family was involved, Boleslav remains blameless. It was probably an act of one of his sons, as Boleslav himself suffered a stroke or some other illness that left him bereft of all strength in 995, the same year in which the massacre happened. He may have authorized the slaughter or been utterly unaware of it. Boleslav died in 999.

ADALBERT OF PRAGUE: THE THIRD BOHEMIAN SAINT

Bohemia's internal and external crisis under the rule of Boleslav II was exacerbated by a spiritual one. The second bishop of Prague, Adalbert (c. 959–997), was very ambitious and well educated. He also had connections in the highest places, being a personal friend of the Roman Emperor Otto III (980–1002). Adalbert set out to make Bohemia a Christian country, not only in name but also in actual fact. Adalbert desired to reform the social and moral norms of every soul in his diocese, whether common or noble. This was to prove difficult, however, because the nobility of Bohemia, although Christian in name, kept to many practices from pagan times, such as polygamy or the selling of Christian slaves. Some of them bowed to pagan idols and indulged in pagan rituals, or at least allowed their subjects to do so.

As Adalbert became the bishop of Prague in 982, he pressed his reforms and came into conflict with the nobles and the duke himself. The duke, no matter how virtuous a

Christian he may personally have been, did not enjoy a strong enough position to dictate the moral norms to his noble subjects – especially given the complicated situation in which Boleslav found himself.

Adalbert thus refused to serve as a bishop and left Bohemia. It did not assist the reconciliation of Bohemian lords with their bishop that he was of the Slavnik dynasty. After the slaughter at Libice, the breach became impossible to repair. Adalbert himself shared his guilt on the events. Before the slaughter, a married woman had sought Adalbert out. She committed adultery with a cleric, and her relatives (probably the members of the Vršovci, the second most powerful clan in the country) wanted to punish her cruelly, as the common law allowed them to do. Adalbert provided asylum in a monastery and refused to give her to her family for punishment. In return they swore an oath that put a blood feud on his house.

Some historians believe in the direct involvement of the Přemyslid dynasty in the slaughter. Whether this is true or not, they could have prevented it and did not. Adalbert had thus no inclination to act favourably to the duke and his family in the future. From his point of view, he never crossed any line. He only kept to the canonical law that allowed him to provide asylum to a sinner in a monastery, yet did not allow a blood feud.

Let us listen to our chronicler who, like historians after him, dedicated many pages to Saint Adalbert – one of the first Czechs to play such a prominent role in European politics.

In the meantime, a distinguished hero named Adalbert, who had only just been ordained, had returned to Prague from the camp of philosophy, where he had served for ten years or more, bringing many books. Like a little lamb among the sheep mourning the death of his shepherd, he diligently performed the funeral rites and, persevering day and night in prayer, praised God with them and provided generous alms for the soul of the spiritual father (Bishop Thietmar).

Prince Boleslaus and his nobles, seeing how pious he was in his good works and hoping that he would be even more righteous in the future, by the inspiration of the grace of the Holy Spirit, took hold of the youth. However, he was very reluctant and brought him into the assembly, saying:

'Willingly or unwillingly, you shall be our bishop, and though unwillingly, you shall serve as Bishop of Prague. Thy nobility, manners and deeds are best suited to the dignity of a high priest.

You are known to us from the top of your head to the bottom of your heels. Thou knowest well how to open the way to the heavenly country for us. Thy commands are indispensable to us, that we may be able and willing to obey them. All the clergy pronounce thee worthy, all the people pronounce thee fit for the episcopate.'

This election took place near Prague at Leve Hradec on 19 February of the same year that Bishop Dětmar died.

I must not even omit what I see others have omitted. For Bishop Vojtěch, seeing that the flock entrusted to him was still falling into ruin and that he could not turn them to a right course, feared lest he himself also should perish with the perishing people. And he had no courage to remain with them any longer, and he could not bear to see his preaching work continue to be frustrated. And when he was about to start on his journey to Rome, it was by a happy chance that Strachkvas, of whom we have mentioned above, came with the permission of his abbot from Reims to visit his dear country, his relatives and his brother, the Prince of Bohemia, after many years.

With him, the man of God, Bishop Vojtěch, taking him aside, had a conversation and lamented much about the infidelity and wickedness of the people, about the sinful marriages and illicit divorces of unstable marriages, about the disobedience and negligence of the clergy, about the impudence and intolerable power of the peasants. At last, he fully revealed to him the intention of his heart that he wished to go to Rome to the Apostolic Father for counsel and never to return to the rebellious nation.

And to this, he added:

'And it is well that thou art known as the brother of a prince, and art of the lords of our country; whom these people would rather have for a lord and obey than me. Thou shalt be able, with thy brother's counsel and help, to restrain the proud, to reprove the careless, to punish the disobedient, and to rebuke the unbelieving. By thy dignity, learning and the holiness of thy conduct, thou art well suited to the office of bishop. And so that this may be done, I, with the will of God and my power, grant thee, and with all kinds of entreaties, will intercede with the Apostolic Father that thou mayest be bishop here during my lifetime.'

And he put the bishop's sceptre, which he had just held in his hand, into his lap. But the latter threw it on the ground as if he were mad and said:

'I do not wish to have any rank in the world; I shun dignity; I despise worldly splendour. I consider myself unworthy of episcopal dignity and cannot bear so heavy a burden of pastoral care. I am a monk, I am dead, and I cannot bury the dead.'

To this the bishop replied:

'Know, brother, know that what you do not want to do now for your own good you will do later, but to your great harm.'

Then, as he had intended, the bishop set out on his journey to Rome, leaving the people who would not obey his commands. Since, at that time, the prince could not rule himself but was ruled by his lords, these, turning into haters of God, the worst sons of wicked fathers, did an evil and sinful deed.

For one feast day, they stealthily entered the castle of Libice, where the brothers of St. Adalbert and the warriors of the castle all stood like innocent sheep at the solemn mass, celebrating the feast. But the noblemen, like ravenous wolves, ran down the castle walls, and slaughtered men and women alike, and, having beheaded the four brothers of St. Adalber and all their offspring before the very altar, set fire to the castle, and sprinkled the streets with blood, and, weighed down with bloody plunder and cruel booty, returned home merrily. And five brothers of St. Adalbert were killed in the castle of Libice in the year 995, in the year of the Lord's birth; their names are Soběbor, Spytimír, Dobroslav, Pořej and Čáslav.

After this event, Prince Boleslav, in consultation with the clergy, entreated the Archbishop of Mainz in these words:

'Either call our shepherd Adalbert back to us, which we desire more or ordain another in his place, which we do not like to ask. For the sheepfolds of Christ in our nation are still new to the faith, and unless the watchful guard of the shepherd is with them, they will indeed become fodder for bloody wolves.'

Then the metropolitan of Mainz, fearing lest the nation, recently won to Christ, should perish into the old ungodly orders, sent messengers to the apostolic father, beseeching him either to restore her husband to the widowed church of Prague or to permit another to be ordained in his place.

And since the servant of God, Adalbert, by order of the Apostolic Father, was exempted from keeping the Lord's flock, he lived in the monastery of St. Alexius; the Pope called to him:

'Dearest son and dearest brother! For the reverence of God, we beseech thee, and for love of thy neighbour, we beseech thee, that thou wilt be pleased to return to thy diocese, and willingly to take up the charge of thy flock again. If they obey thee, thanks be to God; but if not, flee from those who flee from thee, lest thou perish with them that perish, and have permission to preach to foreign nations.'

The bishop, being greatly pleased with this statement, for he had been given permission to teach the Gentiles, left the pleasant communion with them to the great sorrow of the brethren.

Then Strachkvas, the brother of the prince we mentioned above, saw that the bishop had been banished from his people by a sort of just order and burned for the bishopric in a haughty pride. And because it is easy to force the willing, the wicked people immediately raised this ignorant and scheming man to the episcopal chair. For so often does God in his providence permit the power of evil men to increase, as in this defective election, the plans of the son-in-law of Ceres prevailed. For this bishop, Strachkvas was vain in dress, puffed up in mind, dissipated in deeds, volatile in eyes, vain in speech, a hypocrite in morals, and a shepherd in all error, and in all evil deeds an archpriest of the wicked.

I am ashamed to write more of Strachkvas, the odd bishop.

The Chronicle of the Czechs, Cosmas of Prague, 1125; translated by the author

St. Adalbert did not remain long in Prague, as stubbornness reigned on both sides, and the blood of his relatives on Czech noblemen's hands could not be so easily washed away.

He left again, this time for Prussia, where he died a martyr's death at the hands of pagan savages. Nevertheless, we will meet Adalbert again in our story because he travelled through Poland and left his mark there.

THE FIRST DYNASTIC CRISIS

When Boleslav II died in 999, nothing indicated that a dynastic crisis would follow. He had three full-grown sons; the oldest, Boleslav III, could succeed him on the throne in peace (c. 965–1037). Yet, none of the sons inherited the character of their father; all proved utterly incompetent to navigate the complicated sea of European politics. Boleslav, the eldest, was incompetent and paranoid, a fatal combination in a ruler. After becoming engaged in a conflict with the Bishop of Prague, he suspected his family members were plotting against him and made his move. First his brother Jaromir suffered his rage, whom he imprisoned and castrated. Oldřich, the youngest brother, was smarter and escaped the assassins, fleeing with the rest of the princely family to Germany to seek the protection of Henry II (973–1024).

Boleslav's actions provoked a revolt of Bohemian nobles. The Polish king, Boleslav the Brave (c. 967–1025), became involved in the chaos and occupied Bohemia and Moravia. He put a certain Vladivoj (c. 981–1003) on the ducal throne. Vladivoj's only significant act before he drank himself to death was to allow the emperor Henry II to give him the Bohemian duchy as an enfeoffment, thus becoming his feudatory. When Jaromir returned, he repeated the act and this resulted in Bohemia's partial dependence on the empire. The national historians placed this act in the context of everlasting Czech-German conflict and saw it in a negative light. However, the truth is that Bohemia was truly independent. Bohemian dukes and later kings would be equal to German princes of the empire and would play major role in the Holy Roman Empire's politics in the Middle Ages.

Chaos followed the death of Vladivoj, and Jaromir returned with the support of the empire. However, he could not retain power. A man who had lost the ability to produce an heir would not gain the respect of nobility in the early Middle Ages. The youngest of the three brothers, Oldřich, had proved fertile enough in the past; he imprisoned Jaromir, blinded him and became a duke.

Oldřich was a drunkard and a brute, the worst of the three brothers. Some historians believe that it was Oldřich who stood behind the terrible slaughter of the whole population of Libice in 995. Yet Boleslav III was rotting in a Polish dungeon after losing all diplomatic battles; Jaromir had no testicles and no eyes; in the dynasty, only Oldřich could rule. He also had a powerful ally, his illegitimate son, who would become an essential figure of the early Middle Ages. It would be this son who would transform Bohemia into an actual Czech state.

OLDŘICH AND BŘETISLAV: THE FATHER AND SON

Prince Oldřich had no offspring from a proper marriage because of his wife's barrenness. Still, by a woman named Bozena, who belonged to Křesina, he had an extraordinarily handsome son named Břetislav.

> *One day, returning through a village from hunting, he saw the woman washing her robes at a well, and, looking at her from head to toe, he burst into an immense glow of love. She was exquisite in appearance, whiter in complexion than snow, finer than a swan, shinier than an old ivory, more beautiful than a sapphire. The prince, sending for her immediately, took her in marriage. Still, he did not dissolve the old marriage, for at that time, every man was permitted to have two or three wives as he pleased. It was no sin for a man to take his neighbour's wife nor for a wife to marry a married man. And as for morality, it was then a great disgrace if a man lived with one wife or a woman with one man, for they lived like foolish brutes, having marriages together.*
> **The Chronicle of the Czechs, Cosmas of Prague, 1125; translated by the author**

The chronicler is wrong. It indeed was forbidden by the Church to take another man's wife. For a duke to marry a (married) common woman without dissolving his marriage with a noblewoman would be considered a scandal even in the tenth century. He would need to ask the pope for a dispensation or the children from the matrimony would be illegitimate. Yet, when Oldřich met the slender Božena, he was a nobody. The third son had a minimal chance of becoming a duke, his father was too busy to care and the princeling did as he pleased.

And when Oldřich ascended the throne, his son's illegitimate birth would be pardoned. Because that boy would be the only male in the dynasty and would prove far more competent than his father or uncles. Bohemian nobles had lived through the tumult of the dynastic crisis; if a boy born out of wedlock was to save them, so be it.

So it was that Břetislav (1002–1055) helped his father to retrieve Moravia, chased away the remains of the Polish army and started his rule here. He had to leave the studies of political craft in his Moravian realm at least once to save his father from German invasion. Still, he remained mostly in Moravia, evading his father, who was as unpredictable as he was paranoid. In 1029 Oldřich died in the middle of a feast, probably due to a stroke or a heart attack. Břetislav could begin his rule that would mark the end of this chapter.

Břetislav and Judith: The Romantic Story

Břetislav aimed high from the beginning, and thus chose a suitable wife for his ambitions. However, his illegitimate birth hindered him in this choice. So he had to do the only possible thing: he abducted his bride from a convent.

> *Meanwhile, Břetislav, the prince's son, having passed from childhood to youth, went from virtue to virtue. He was more successful in his actions than any other. He had a strong body and a beautiful figure, great strength and wisdom, courage in adversity, and prudent meekness in happiness.*
>
> *At that time, a mighty count named Ota the White lived in the German region. He was descended by paternal succession from royal blood. He had only one daughter, Jitka, who surpassed all other maidens under the sun in beauty.*
>
> *Her excellent father and good mother allowed her to learn the Psalter in a monastery called Svinibrod, which was very strong in position and walls. But what towers, though higher, or what walls stronger, can withstand love and separate lovers?*

Love triumphs over all things; even the prince and the king shall yield to it.

Then Břetislav, the fairest of the youths and the most valiant of heroes, having heard from many accounts of the extraordinary beauty, nobility, and noble birth of the said maiden, could not control his spirit and began to think in his heart whether he should attempt to take her by force or to make a proper bid for her.

But he resolved to act manfully rather than to stoop to supplication. For he thought of the innate pride of the Germans and how they always looked down upon the Slavs and their language with haughty conceit. But the harder the approach to love, the fiercer the fire the son of Venus always breathes into his lover. The mind of the youth, inflamed by the fire of Venus, boils like the fire of Etna. And with a clear voice, he cries out to himself:

'Either a marriage of honour be my lot, or I shall sink into everlasting ridicule. Jitka may be mine, a daughter noble by birth, a maiden fair, charming, brighter than the sun's light, dearer than life to me; that she may live long, praise be to God permanently.'

He immediately ordered those of his people whom he knew to be incredibly agile and devoted to him to prepare proven and hardened horses and make it as if he would go quickly to the emperor and return even more quickly. The men obeyed the order, but what their master intended, they knew not. They wondered among themselves that they were in such a hurry. After a ride of about seven days, they entered the sub-hall of the monastery as guests. Before, the prince's son had ordered all his men not to let anyone know who he was or where he was from but to treat him as if he were one of their own.

As the wolf, when he prowls round the fold, seeking to break into it to snatch the white lamb, so the hero Břetislav, when he has been permitted to lodge in the monastery, scouts it with piercing eye and keen spirit; he would fain have broken into the cloister with might, but dare not, not having so many warriors with him. But by a happy chance, it was a holiday, and behold, Jitka, the virgin a thousand times desired, comes out of the convent with her companions, for it was customary for the gentle maidens to ring the vespers bells within the church. As the bold captor, joyfully unaware of himself, saw her, like a wolf that breaks out of his hiding place and seizes a lamb, and then, conscious of his deed, runs away with his tail drooping to a distant hiding place, so he, too, grabbing the virgin, flees, and, rushing to the gate, finds that a chain thicker than a mill-rope is stretched across it, and the way out thus barred.

Immediately drawing his sharp sword, he cuts the chain like a straw, and the broken link is still seen as proof of the violent blow. But the rest of his companions, who knew nothing of it and still remained in their tents, were taken by the enemies when they struck at them, and some had their eyes plucked out and their noses cut off; others had their hands and feet cut off, and only the prince, with a few men and the kidnapped maiden, barely escaped in the darkness of the night. The virgin Jitka was taken in the year of the Lord's birth, 1021.

And so that the Germans might not be given a reasonable excuse to blame Bohemia for some injustice, the hero Břetislav, saluting his father, Prince Oldřich, immediately rode with the bride directly to Moravia.

The Chronicle of the Czechs, Cosmas of Prague, 1125; translated by the author

Unwillingly, we have to diminish the 'romantic' elements of the story. The marriage was probably negotiated long before and all that happened was for show. No severe punishment from the bride's family or the emperor followed, nor did anybody dispute the legitimacy of the marriage.

Břetislav the Legislator

Břetislav expanded Bohemian territory and further stabilized power. However, the legislation was the defining act that could mark the transition between a state-like formation and an authentic medieval state. Břetislav gave the Czech nobility their first written laws and the story is worth mentioning. It was part of a Polish campaign when the Czech duke used the crisis of the Polish state that followed after the death of Boleslav the Brave and raided Polish Gniezno, a centre with a Polish church and the grave of Saint Adalbert.

Břetislav watched the faces of his warriors. They looked confused and tired after yesterday's feast. That was good: clear minds were the last thing the duke needed. He stood here over the grave of Saint Adalbert with Bishop Severus and prepared for the show.

Břetislav was ready. Before the campaign to Gniezno, he made it clear to the company that Saint Adalbert was their goal. He let them take booty rich enough to make them happy, but never let them forget the primary objective, which was the saint. The Czech saint, their countryman, who had been stolen from them by the Polish. The Polish would make Adalbert their saint and their patron.

'Was there a better way to show our superiority than to take back such a prize? To claim what was ours and unlawfully taken? Our saint, our patron, our Adalbert.'

He made sure they accepted this goal enthusiastically; he provoked their rage with his speech, especially last night at the feast. Now it was time to take it a little further. Everybody knew why Adalbert left Prague. He was repelled by the unvirtuous, immoral and impious behaviour of the Czechs, especially of the nobles who would not respect Christian laws.

What if the saint still remained angry with them? What if he refused to return to Prague unless they promised to change their ways? Everything depended on the context. If he did it right, they would promise anything. And Břetislav would be the lawgiver once and for all times.

Thus, Břetislav, with Bishop Severus, carefully established the scene. Over the body of Saint Adalbert, he made the nobles swear to uphold the laws that he would write down as soon as they returned. Once they returned victorious and recovered from their righteous anger, they would have no choice but to respect their promises. Let us listen to what they promised, and let us listen to the powerful tale of the saint told by the chronicler. Because, for once, we do not doubt that this is how it happened, or how the nobles kneeling at the grave believed it happened.

On the third night, the holy Bishop Adalbert appeared to Bishop Severus, as he was resting after the morning hours, in a vision and said:

'Tell the prince and his peasants this: The Heavenly Father will not give what you ask unless you give up again the sins you have renounced in the water of baptism.'

In the morning, the bishop told the prince and his company this, and they immediately entered the church of the Virgin

Mary, which was full of joy. They fell down before the tomb of St. Adalbert and prayed together for a long time. Then the prince arose and, standing in the pulpit, broke the silence:

'Do you wish to make amends for your iniquities and to become wise after your evil deeds?'

And they cried with tears in their eyes:

'We are willing to make amends for all that our fathers or ourselves have sinned against the saint of God and to cease evil deeds altogether.'

Then the prince, lifting up his hand over the holy sepulchre, began to speak thus to the assembly of the people, saying:

'Brethren, lift up your right hands together to the Lord, and heed my words; I would have you confirm them by the oath of your faith. Let this then be my chief and first commandment, that your marriages, which hitherto ye have had as with loose women, and disorderly after the manner of foolish beasts, be henceforth lawful, private and indissoluble, according to the ordinances of the Church, the man living in possession of one wife, and the woman in possession of one man.

If, however, the wife should despise her husband, or the husband the wife, and the quarrel between them should flare up to the point of rupture, I desire that the disturber of the marriage, who should not wish to return to the previous union legally contracted, should not be brought into bondage according to the order of our country, but rather, as our immutable decision firmly preaches, let him be taken, whatever person he may be, to Hungary, and he shall not be ransomed with any money, or be allowed to return to our country, lest the whole fold of Christ is infected with the sins of one sheep.'

Bishop Severus said:

'Whoever would do otherwise, let him be accursed! The same punishment shall be inflicted on virgins, widows and adulteresses who are known to have lost their good name to have committed fornication. For if they can marry of their own free will, why do they commit adultery and expel their foetus, which is the worst of crimes?'

Then the prince argued:

'But if the woman should declare that her husband does not repay her with equal love but beats and torments her mercilessly, it shall be decided between them by the judgment of God, and he who is found guilty shall suffer the punishment of the guilty. Likewise also as to those who are accused of murder: let the archpriest report their names to the governor of his castle, and let the governor summon them to the court, and if they resist, let him cast them into prison until they either repent or, if they deny, let them be tried with hot iron or purgative water, whether there is guilt upon them.

But the murderers of brothers, fathers or priests, and persons accused of similar capital crimes, let the archpriest mark them to the castle governor or to the prince. He shall banish them from the land, bound hand and waist, that, being wanderers and fugitives, they may wander about like Cain in the world.'

Bishop Severus said:

'This ordinance of the prince has just been confirmed by a curse! To this end, you princes have the sword hanging by your side, that you may wash your hands more often in the sinner's blood.'

Again, the prince says:

'He who would set up a tavern, which is the root of all evil, whence come thefts, murders, fornication and other iniquities, *and he who would buy it.' Bishop Severus added: 'Let there be a curse!'*

And the prince: 'Any innkeeper that is a violator of this ordinance shall be punished. Let him be tied to a stake amid the marketplace, beaten till the bailiff is exhausted, and shaved on the head; but his goods shall not be confiscated, but only his drink poured out on the ground, lest any man be defiled by a cursed draught. But the drunkards, if caught, shall not be released from prison until they have each deposited three hundred money in the prince's pension.

Bishop Severus said: 'What the prince has decreed, our power confirms.'

To this, the prince added: 'We forbid that there should be markets on Sundays, which in our regions the people attend so mainly for this reason, that they may have time for their work on other days. But suppose any man be found at the church on a Sunday or on a day publicly ordered to be celebrated, doing some work. In that case, the archpriest shall take away the work itself and the covering found in the work and pay three hundred pence to the prince's pension.

Likewise, let those bold men who bury their dead in the fields or woods pay the archdeacon's ox and three hundred money to the prince's pension, but let them bury the dead again in the cemetery of the faithful. These are the things which God does not like to see; for these, St. Adalbert was displeased and, leaving us, his sheep, went instead to teach foreign nations. We swear by our faith and yours that we will do no more of this.'

So said the prince. And the bishop, invoking the name of the Holy Trinity and taking up his hammer while the other priests were chanting the seven psalms and other prayers appropriate to this holy work, began slowly to tear down the top of the tomb and to bring it down to the holy treasure. When they opened the coffin, all in the church were enveloped in such a penetrating and sweet odour that for three days, as if they had eaten the most nourishing food, they thought not of refreshment with food. Very many of the sick were healed that day. The prince, the bishop, and a few peasants looking on saw the saint of God, how his face and form were glorious, and how his body was perfectly intact, as if he had celebrated a glorious Mass that day. The priests sang the Te Deum Laudamus, and the laity the Kyrieleison, and their voices went up to heaven.

Then the prince, whose face was drowned in tears of joy, prayed thus:

'O martyr of Christ, St. Adalbert, who has everywhere had mercy on us, look upon us now with your usual kindness, be gracious to us sinners, and grant that you may be graciously delivered from us, though unworthy, to your seat in the Church of Prague.'

The Chronicle of the Czechs, Cosmas of Prague, 1125; translated by the author

THE LEGACY OF BOHEMIAN STATE

We end this chapter with Břetislav codifying the law and finishing the structure of the first Czech state. Unlike in the previous chapters, there is no need to look for the legacy of the actors of the previous lines. The early Middle Ages Bohemian state that included Moravia and became a Czech state, founded by the mythical figures of the Přemyslid dynasty, still stands.

Its legacy lies in the heart of Europe, surrounded by the mountains that helped protect it and guarded by the statue of Saint Wenceslaus that decorates the capital's very centre.

All the rulers, all their wives and children, the good and the bad, live in Czech national memory and fill schoolchildren's textbooks. There will be more battles that the Czechs fought, won or lost during the following centuries. However, nobody doubts the importance of their early history and ancient Slavic origins.

THE SHOOTING STAR OF POLAND

The Poles emerged like a shooting star in the tenth century; in the eleventh century the state became a kingdom. This miraculously fast development is even more surprising if we realize that the Polish kingdom has survived to the present day. There were periods of division in Poland, but one thing typifies its history: even though the land was far from united, and there were times when the Polish state ceased to exist entirely, the Poles would always stand up tall in the end. They never gave up and they survived – part of their pride is reflected in the honour they show to the country's founding dynasty, the Piasts.

THE FOUNDING MYTH OF THE POLISH DYNASTY

The beginning of the Piast rule in Poland is very similar to the myth of the Přemyslid dynasty in Bohemia. In Gniezno there lived a man named Piast who, according to the legend, died around 841. Notice how late is the date for the mythical origins of Poland. This was a time when Moravia was already struggling against the empire, Bulgarian khans were already established and the Přemyslid dynasty had started the unification process in Prague. However, Poland had to put its mythical origin into the ninth century because its first recorded duke, the one who united Poland, the first ruler of the Piast dynasty, died as late as 992. First, however, let us listen to the story of the mythical Piast the ploughman; the chroniclers usually tell the story this way:

There was a duke named Popiel who had two sons. Among pagans, there was a custom to hold a feast when the sons grew to a certain age, and the time came to cut their hair. So, the duke had a feast. Two strangers arrived at the city during the feast but were not allowed to enter. Disgusted, they looked for a place to stay and found a humble dwelling of a poor man who also prepared a feast for his son.

This man's name was Piast. He and his wife Rzepka were happy to invite strangers to dinner, even though they had little for themselves. But they would not refuse refuge to travellers.

But the strangers were God's messengers, and seeing poor Piast's goodwill, they multiplied ale and food. This was a sign to Piast and everybody around that their son, whose hair was to be cut during the feast, was blessed amongst men.

The boy's name was Siemowit, and he grew in virtue and wit, yet still in blindness, for in those days, faith in Christ was scarce in the duchy.

Can we believe the words of the chroniclers? Probably not. Apart from the Piast dynasty coming from Gniezno, the story contains little historical truth. The critical moment in the story is the humble origin of the dynasty. Like the ploughman Přemysl, Piast was a poor, humble and good craftsman. It is a Christian legend. The pagan legend written by nomadic Bulgarians would sound different, but a Christian legend made the founder poor and humble. The two visitors who prophesy the future of Piast's son are a literary cliché from the Bible. The duke who did not invite these angelic prophets to his court and was thus proved unfit to rule is also of biblical origin. It is also essential that although Piast was a pagan (just like Libuše and her husband), he still lived a godly life.

But what about the reality of Poland in the ninth century before the first duke united the lands? Various tribes were living in the area of future Poland: the Lechitis, the Pomerians and the Masovians, to name just a few. These tribes would retain their identity during the Middle Ages. This case differs significantly from their neighbours, who took Bohemian identity completely. The Polish still remembered their tribal ancestry.

Under the first rulers, they accepted a higher authority, the identity of Poles, above their regional tribal allegiance. The unification process was probably started by the Lechitic. However, the historians are not sure because the sources speak of the Polans, yet it seems as though Polans never existed as a tribe. The central rulers from the Lechitis tribe invented the Polish identity to shelter all tribes under one authority.

MIESZKO I: POLAND EMERGES

Siemomysl had a son named Mieszko, but this began as a sad tale, for the boy was blind. When his seventh birthday arrived, his father invited a large company for a feast. Siemomysl could hardly hide his sadness because having a blind child was a shameful fate for the whole family.

But then a miracle came, and nobody could believe it before they saw it with their own eyes. Mieszko's eyes opened, and he could see.

Everybody was happy and started to look for a sign in these events. Poland was pagan then, and nobody saw the miracle as a work of God. But the chroniclers who recorded the fable afterwards were clear.

Poland had been blind, living in sin and worshipping pagan idols. Mieszko's eyes were opened by God; he would open the eyes of the whole of Poland and bring them salvation.

The story of a blind boy who magically recovered his sight after the pagan rite of passage is a clear allegory. Mieszko converted Poles to Christianity and he entered the family of Christian rulers; we have seen this pattern before. Accepting Christianity is often considered the beginning of Slavic history, a point at which the superpowers start to take the new state seriously, even to make political marriage pacts. Turning to Christianity is thus the starting point from which the chroniclers begin. With regions as fragmented as Poland, Christianity offered the desired unifying factor that pagan religions did not. We have seen above attempts to use the Iranian god Mithra in Bohemia or the tengrist deity in Bulgaria. However, in the end, all these rulers converted to Christianity as it provided them with the most advantages.

Mieszko I Unifies Poland

Before the ambitious duke converted, however, he began the unification process and expanded the territory under his direct rule. We lack sources to determine where precisely this territory lay. Still, we can say that Mieszko's expansion did not start in a vacuum. It must have resulted from the continuous endeavours of his father and grandfather before him. And, of course, the nobles saw the rapid growth of their Bohemian and Kyivan neighbours, the wealth the central state brought and the rich booty that expansion under one leader offered. Remember, too, that we are still in the period of slavery. For ordinary people, the choice is between paying taxes or being enslaved. In the tenth century Europe saw enough examples of when the process of building a state paid off for everybody involved.

The Polish nobles retained more autonomy under the central rule. The opposition to the Piast unification process was diminished. Thus Mieszko's position was easier; he could continue very quickly with his father's work as he sat on the ducal throne in Gniezno between 950 and 960.

We know that under the rule of Mieszko, Polish society thrived economically and culturally on a level equal to that of their Bohemian neighbours. Ibrahim-ibn-Yakub, the Jewish traveller, whom we already met in this book, describes Mieszko's Poland thus:

> *The country of Mieszko is the greatest of the Slavs' countries. It is rich in bread and meat and honey and fish. The taxes collected by Mieszko are paid in Byzantine money. They also form the salary of his men. Every month, each of them receives a fixed number of mitkals. And he has 3,000 men in armour, warriors of whom a hundred is equal to ten hundreds of others.*
>
> *And he gives these men dresses, horses, armament and everything they need. And when a child is born to one of them, he (Mieszko) orders at once after the child's birth to appoint him a salary, whether male or female. And when the child reaches full age, he makes him take a wife, if it is a man, and pays for him to the father of the girl the marriage present, and if it is a female, he makes her take a husband and pays to her father the marriage*

present. The marriage among the Slavs is very considerable, and their customs about it are like the customs of the Berbers. And when one has born to him two or three daughters they become the cause of his growing rich, but when two sons are born they are the cause of his becoming poor.

On the Early Slavs. The Narrative of Ibrahim-Ibn-Yakub, translated by Semen Rapoport, 1929

This description fits a fully evolved state: a society that knows how to trade, where elites wear luxurious gowns and protect their subjects from slavery. Thus we start with Mieszko because, before him, we know little. Still, we admit that before the first well-recorded ruler Poland already flourished, preparing for its star to shine high on the European political sky.

Doubrava: A Bohemian Princess on the Polish Throne

Mieszko lived with seven wives. But later he decided to marry a highborn lady, Doubravka, daughter of Bohemian duke. She refused to marry him, unless he accepted Christ. She was charming, fair and Mieszko valued her above every other woman. He agreed.

She came to Poland and brought Christian priest with her and told her husband: 'Promises are fine, yet only deeds count, my lord. I shall not lie with thee unless you give up your idols.'

Mieszko did as she asked, received the grace of baptism, and from that day God's grace shone on Poland.

We have read a legend of how Poland became Christian. However, legends are legends, and politics is politics. Doubrava was the daughter of Boleslav I, the one who supposedly murdered his brother and practically set the foundations for a medieval Czech state. It is an enchanting romantic story, the duke converting to please his beloved Christian lady. And it is a story we have seen before. The Bulgarian khan converted because of his sister's pleas. Vladimir the Wise chose Byzantine Christianity in order to marry the beautiful sister of the emperor. Probably the marriage did provide an incentive for conversion; unless Mieszko became Christian, Boleslav would not send his daughter to a marriage in pagan lands. That would threaten his new orientation, his politics and his reputation. Conversion must have been part of the pre-marital negotiations.

However, there is another reason why the chronicler describes the intercessions of a beautiful lady in favour of Christianity. Among the pagan warriors in the early Middle Ages, Christians, with their compassion and mercy, were considered weak. The Kyivan duke, Sviatoslav, said in response to his mother's pleas that his comrades would laugh at him if he accepted Christ. Women, on the other hand, could afford to be seen as weak, humble and meek. Thus they often converted before their husbands, brothers and sons, then used their influence to spread their faith.

Be it as it may, Mieszko entered the European family of Christian rulers and started his expansion. Because Poland lacked the protection of mountains that Bohemia had, he had first to build strong fortifications around the centre of the future state and start his expansion from there. Mieszko conquered Pomerania, where he clashed with the empire. He led wars with Kyivan Rus in the east and Denmark in the north. He tactfully navigated the central European political arena and gained a most profitable second marriage. His second wife, Oda, was a Saxon princess. Mieszko thus became part of the family of German princes, being their equal. He bequeathed his son with a unified territory of immense size. Before he died, however, he accomplished a political masterpiece.

Dagome Iudex

The act entered Polish history under the name of Dagome Iudex in 991 or 992. In this mysterious text Mieszko (under the name Dagome) and Oda, his wife, place all their lands under the direct rule of the pope. This was an unprecedented act. Some Polish historians consider it to be an act that protected Poland from German influence – and the reason why, unlike Bohemia, Poland never became part of the Holy Roman Empire.

In order to understand the reasons for this, we must look deeper into the process of Christianization in Poland.

The Christianization of Poland under Mieszko I

Regardless of the reasons for Mieszko's conversion, the task that awaited him was not easy. Most nobles were then Christians, yet most of the ordinary people were not. We do not know where the baptism of Mieszko took place, but it could not have been in Prague. We accept that the first Christian vocabulary in Polish was borrowed from the Czech language; it probably arrived with the influence of Duchess Doubrava and her court. However at that time the Czechs were negotiating their own diocese. For baptism, Mieszko had to go somewhere else, probably to Regensburg.

However, in 968 the sources testify of a Polish bishop, Jordan, who probably resided in Poznan and was responsible for the missions in Poland. Here comes the catch: Jordan was not sent to Poland by an archbishop, but by the pope himself. How he got to Poland, and how it happened that a pagan land acquired a bishop, we cannot tell. It seems probable that the diplomacy of Boleslav I and his daughter Mlada, who obtained a papal licence to set up a diocese in Prague, may have contributed to Poland's ecclesiastical independence. Here, however, the interests of mighty rulers clashed. The first emperor of the Ottonian dynasty, Otto I, established an archbishopric of Magdeburg as a starting point for missions to the Slavs in Central Europe. These Slavs, the Polish and the Czechs went directly to Rome and evaded Magdeburg's influence.

We do not know if this was the motivation of Mieszko when he wrote the supplication to Rome. There might have been other reasons. In this text he mentions all his children apart from the eldest son from his first marriage, Boleslav I the Brave – who, as an adult, had already obtained his heritage, the rule in Krakow. Mieszko may have only wanted to protect his other children from the ambition of his oldest son and to place them under the pope's protection. If that was his intention, it did not help. However, later, the document really did help Poland to keep its independence in a political sense. The rulers had to pay taxes to the pope, but the papal seat nevertheless defended their claims and freedom during the Middle Ages. We will also see how a similar act helped the kingdom of Croatia to protect their integrity. Clearly the pope was a mighty ally.

BOLESLAV I THE BRAVE

Boleslav I started his reign as a typical duke of the Middle Ages. He knew about his father's will. Mieszko did not believe anyone could hold the large territory he created and divided it among his sons. Boleslav not only managed to hold it; he even expanded it. First, however, he got rid of all competition. He expelled his stepmother and half-brothers, blinded or imprisoned their supporters, set up in Gniezno instead of Krakow, minted the coins as dux of Gniezno (995) and reigned alone. His reign would be the apex of Polish power in the early Middle Ages, and he would set up the state and get a royal title in the end.

Boleslav I the Brave and His Connections

Boleslav was a skilled military leader and an outstanding diplomat who used every tool his father gave him. But he also made himself influential friends. Boleslav would be a personal friend of the two most influential men of Central Europe in the eleventh century – Saint Adalbert and the young Emperor Otto III.

Never underestimate personal connections and human emotions such as love and friendship. Historians tend to emphasize structures, politics and the need of time. But sometimes people, even in history, really loved their spouses and remained loyal to their friends. They were human, after all, with human virtues as well as vices.

Boleslav I met young Otto when he personally joined the German campaigns against the Polabian Slavs. Here he also met with the head of the Slavnik family, whom the Přemyslid dukes in Bohemia slaughtered. This Soběslav, the Slavnik, and his brother Adalbert found shelter on Boleslav's court in Poland, and both men befriended the young duke. Especially Adalbert, whose conflict with Prague was evident at the moment. At this time the idea of setting things right in Bohemia might have settled in Boleslav's mind. 'Přemyslid dukes murdered a family of his friends and opposed the holiest man on earth, Saint Adalbert. Did they not deserve to be governed by someone more worthy?'

Saint Adalbert Again

We have already entered Gniezno in this book with Břetislav and his army, who came to retrieve the remains of Saint Adalbert. However, we did not pause to wonder why exactly was Gniezno the resting place of the second bishop of Prague. It was not that the Polish duke would steal the bishop from Prague; he retrieved his friend's body from the Prussian pagans and paid for it heavily in gold.

And when we told the story of Bohemian nobles resisting Adalbert as he tried to reform their morals, we might have overlooked the true significance of this remarkable man. Adalbert was a member of the court of Emperor Otto III. And Otto was a charismatic character; he dreamt of a united, universal Christian empire. He sought to renew the church and state, and desired to rule it from the very heart of Western Christianity, from Rome. Adalbert was close to the young emperor, so they might have dreamt this dream together. It is probable because immediately after the martyr's death suffered by Adalbert, Otto swore to continue in his effort, proclaiming that the death of Adalbert only made his resolution stronger.

In this context, we must tell the story of Boleslav I, his expansion and his success. Because he had the best of friends a duke could have: an ambitious visionary emperor and the most educated man in Europe, whose influence was accepted everywhere he went (apart from the pagan Prussians).

Before starting his mission to Prussia, Adalbert stopped at Boleslav's court in 996. The duke provided armed company for the future saint.

Congress of Gniezno

This was the most glorious moment in Polish medieval history. Emperor Otto travelled to Gniezno with one intent: to say farewell to his old friend Adalbert and pray by his grave. However, Otto was not a simple man; he was the Holy Roman Emperor. Although the chroniclers love to tell this story as a spontaneous spark of friendship, the young emperor undoubtedly knew what he was doing. He came to visit the Polish duke, Boleslav.

Boleslav did all he could to exceed expectations, showcase his wealth, provide the utmost hospitality and show loyalty to the Roman emperor. He lined up his warriors splendidly dressed, gathered the most beautiful women in Poland, and ordered them to wear expensive robes with silk and fur. Gold was everywhere, and even the forks at feasts were made of gold.

The emperor did not fail to notice and supposedly proclaimed:

> *'Such a great man does not deserve to be styled duke or count like any princes, but to be raised to a royal throne and adorned with a diadem in glory.'*
> ***The Deeds of the Princes of the Poles**, translated by Paul W. Knoll and Frank Schaer, 2003*

After these words, he placed the diadem on Boleslav's head and made him royal. The feast continued for days, and Otto was always on the newly crowned king's side. When his departure grew closer, he declared that Poland would always be the Holy Roman Empire's friend and that the Polish king was the mightiest among his peers.

Polish historians take this narration very seriously; however, some scholars from abroad doubt it. The Congress of Gniezno mentioned in the story was probably planned long before, resulting from long-term diplomatic endeavours. However, let us not underestimate the personal friendships of the three protagonists: Boleslav, Otto and Saint Adalbert. Of course, when the chronicler mentions the imperial diadem, he really means a royal crown to the future Poland. However, even that was an elevation far beyond anything a Slavic noble, a European noble, could have hoped for. There were not many kings in Europe then and there were no Slavic kings, not one whose title would be accepted and even granted by the emperor.

Otto III was a visionary. He aimed at reforming the world and creating a universal empire, and he would not look back. The act of crowning Boleslav meant that in the future Poland would play a prominent part in the world he dreamt about. Furthermore, it was not just about the coronation. Gniezno was given complete independence; it would become an archbishop's seat, an honour previously given only to Methodius in the Slavic lands. It was a direct challenge to the bishops and archbishops in the empire, a sign that the emperor and the pope (who acted in complete accord with Otto) counted on Poland to be a fully independent state, one of the leading players on the political scene.

With justification, Polish historians consider the Congress of Gniezno to be a founding moment. It represented the moment that Poland became a kingdom, when it indeed became great. They do not agree on the precise date; whether the coronation and founding of the archdiocese really happened in 1000 or later is the subject of debate. But it did happen under Boleslav I the Brave, with Otto III playing the crucial role.

Boleslav I and His Expansion

At this point in our story, Poland is a fully established state. Thus it is a great moment to leave it, as the story of Polish ancient origins is complete. However, it seems unfair to leave the story of Boleslav I the Brave untold – or to spare the reader the next 200 years of the Polish kingdom's history, which were far from glorious.

The expansion of Boleslav belongs in this book because under his rule everything clicks together. In his expansion, we meet the Bohemian dukes, Yaroslav the Wise and the remains of Great Moravia's administration. We have seen above how Boleslav intervened in the Bohemian dynastic crisis and occupied Moravia, and to what ends he went.

Let us now move to the east and again meet our long-lost friend Yaroslav the Wise. As many times in this story, it all begins with a woman.

Boleslav intended to marry a Russian princess, a sister to Yaroslav the Wise. But Yaroslav would not send his sister to Poland. Women in his family married into French royalty; who was this Polish savage who called himself king to claim his sister? Thus, Yaroslav refused the offer. Boleslav would not stand the insult and planned revenge. At first, he was successful in his campaign.

The Polish king entered Kyiv without meeting significant resistance. He took the said Russian princess and her sister as concubines to humiliate the duke's family and plundered and took many riches. Nobody came to take Kyiv from him.

Thus, he left for home, supposedly feeling homesick. An unsuspected attack came only when Boleslav's army was nearing his borders. Yaroslav managed to gather forces of his own warriors and added Pechenegs to his troops. The situation looked hopeless for the Polish king.

The chronicles then tell a tale of a heroic king and his motivational speech igniting the soldiers' fervour and being victorious. These are Polish chroniclers; thus, we will never know the truth. However, let us not dismiss stories of old just because they sound too heroic and fairy-tale-like. Sometimes, the motivating speech makes the difference and unexpected victors emerge in worldwide battles, even today.

Yet, sadly, we must admit that the Russian campaign was probably not about a woman or hurt pride but rather about politics.

The real reason for Boleslav's attack on Kyiv was the same as in the Bohemian case. He intervened in the dynastic crisis and came in support of Sviatopolk against Yaroslav the Wise. Although he achieved a victory celebrated by Polish historians, his support still did not help Sviatopolk, who lost the throne to his brother, as we know. Whether a marriage was refused to Boleslav or not, he indeed took Vladmir's sister (and Sviatopolk's half-sister) Predslava and her sister Mstislava as concubines. In the same year Boleslav married Oda, the daughter of a high-ranking German noble, which was a more convenient political match. No children who could add to the chaos following the Polish king's death were born out of the illegitimate matches with the Russian princesses, at least not as far as we know.

The Death of Boleslav I

The chronicler celebrated Boleslav in his work; he wrote the book to honour him. It is thus only fitting to end the life of the great ruler with his verses:

> *Come, men, women of all ages, of all stations, run to me;*
> *Lo! King Boleslav is dead and passed from us;*
> *come grieve with me.*
> *Come and join with me and mourn,*
> *so great a man has passed away.*
> *Ah Boleslav, ah Boleslav, where is all your glory gone?*
> *All your valour, splendour and the treasures you had won?*
> *Woe to me, O Poland, there is much too much for us to mourn.*
> **The Deeds of the Princes of the Poles, translated**
> **by Paul W. Knoll and Frank Schaer, 2003**

THE LEGACY OF THE FIRST KINGDOM OF POLAND

Boleslav I the Brave died, leaving three adult sons. He named the second born Mieszko II (c. 990–1034) the heir to the crown, but failed to ensure the support of the remaining brothers and their acceptance on an international field. One of Mieszko's brothers gained the support of Kyiv, the other of the empire. As the Czech duke, Břetislav, exploited the chaos and Hungary also stirred the boiling cauldron, the royal title of Polish king was disputed by European rulers. The successors of Boleslav fought among themselves. A period of fragmentation followed until King Casimir III the Great (r. 1333–70) managed to unify Poland again. But that is a chapter for another story.

This part of our story studied the ancient origins of the Polish state, set up by the first Piast rulers. Although we end on a sad note, with the disintegration of the kingdom after the death of its greatest ruler, we can at least talk about a kingdom. There is an archbishop in Gniezno and every ruler, however successful, would only take up what the Piast rulers established.

Nor did Polish history end here. In the late Middle Ages a great empire would rise, the Polish-Lithuanian commonwealth, which went on to rule most of Eastern Europe, including present-day Poland, Ukraine, Belarus and Lithuania. This Poland would struggle for its place on the map in the early modern ages; it would lose its independence and even cease to exist for a time, only to emerge strong after the First World War that transformed the map of Europe. Today Poland is an essential player in European politics, confident and proud. And all Poles look with warm remembrance back to the first Piast rulers, who established their identity in ancient times.

THE KINGDOM OF CROATIA

If we said about Poland that their neighbours had paved the road well for the first Piast rulers, the same applies to Croatia. The centre of the future Duchy of Croatia lay on the wealthy Dalmatian coasts in the former Roman province of Dalmatia. Here the so-called White Croats settled and began their story.

According to ancient sources, the Croats expelled the Avars from Dalmatia and won the favour of Emperor Heraclius. Their first recorded, but perhaps mythical, prince was named Porgas. Croats accepted Christianity very early, under their mythical ancestor Porgas and during Heraclius's rule (575 – 645). They lived on friendly terms with the Byzantine Empire, and very early on, they focused their policy westwards and turned to Rome. Italy was just over a narrow stretch of sea from Dalmatia. Their main competitor, Venice, had to maintain a good connection with Italian cities. Their alliance with Rome paid off, as we can see.

Croatia was then divided between two independent regions. The Pannonian part of the country was subject to conquest from the West. The future unified Croatian state originated in the Duchy of Croatia.

THE DUCHY OF CROATIA

This is where the friendly Christian Croats lived, with the blessing of the Byzantines. They followed the local tradition and grew rich through trade in the Dalmatian cities. Split used to be a centre of administration of the great Diocletian (242–312); it was a trading town with rare architectural beauty and history. As we saw with the Serbian Dalmatian cities, merchants in these lands cared not for politics but rather for the profits they could make. The Dalmatian cities on the coast were colourful, cosmopolitan and culturally developed beyond anything those living further inland in the Balkans, troubled by generations of Slavic and Avar raiders, knew. Here the Croats learned the Byzantine culture, and time seemed to stand still. The old Roman province of Dalmatia did not appear to have changed from when the Romans ruled it. Only when walking through the cities, listening to the many tongues of the international population, was the Slavic language heard more often than before.

In the eighth century an attack came from the West. Charlemagne subdued a part of Istria, making the Dalmatian duke a vassal to the Carolingian Empire in 810. In 821, however, Vladislav (r. 821–c. 835) ascended the throne and things started to change for Croatia.

VLADISLAV AND MISLAV

Vladislav succeeded his uncle after the Croatian nobles elected him. It seems that he must have had the blessing of Louis the Pious, the Carolingian emperor, because no adverse reaction to his ascension was recorded. However, the sovereignty of Francia over Dalmatia was certainly a mere formality. Not even Charlemagne could press his will in Croatia. The Frankish conquest was successful, more or less, because the Dalmatian merchants did not care where their taxes went; they could afford to pay them. New political ties meant new commercial opportunities. But they could not afford an expensive war.

Despite this, Vladislav's successor Mislav (r. 835–845) was belligerent enough to stand up for the Duchy of Croatia's independence. He did not fight against Francia, which fell into dynastic crisis after Louis's death. Mislav focused on diminishing the influence of the Byzantine Empire. He first turned against the leading representative of Byzantine interests in Dalmatia, Venice. This proved a critical moment. Venice would become the archenemy of Croatia and everybody who wished to rule it. The competition started here, with Mislav. He was victorious and for a time stopped the spread of Venetian influence to Dalmatia. The apex of Croatian history came with his successors of the Tripimirovic dynasty.

THE TRIPIMIROVIC DYNASTY

Vislav's successor Tripimir (r. 845–864) was the first to bear the official title 'the duke of the Croats'. It was he who started the usual diplomatic dance that we know from all Balkan states, balancing Western and Eastern influence. First, Tripimir made a treaty with the emperor of the West. He helped him on a campaign in Italy to free the city of Bari from

Arabian rule. However, Byzantium did not like the growing influence of a new Balkan state. Under the pretext of an attack on the papal envoys, the Byzantine emperor Basileios I invaded Croatia. The struggle between Croatian rulers and Byzantium continued under Tripimir's successors.

Under the rule of the Tripimirovic dynasty, the Croatian inland was Christianized and grew in culture and wealth. Politically, the influence of Byzantium was strong. However, because of turbulent relations with Venice and the formal alliance with East Francia, in terms of religion Croats mainly looked to Rome.

Tomislav I: the First King of Croatia

Tomislav I (r. 910–930) is an essential figure of Croatian history. He used the mayhem of the Bulgarian-Hungarian-Byzantine wars to free and unify the land under the central power, relying entirely on the pope to guarantee Croatia's independence. It was the pope who confirmed Tomislav's royal title in 924. Under his rule both Venice and Byzantium paid tribute to Rome, and the Bulgars left Croatia in peace.

In 925 a Church council was held in Split under the supervision of Pope John X (r. 917–928). Some dogmatic issues were resolved there. In addition, most importantly, this council guaranteed the Croatian kingdom's political and ecclesiastical integrity. The Croatian king hosted the council and other Slavic Balkan rulers were commanded to attend by papal authority.

The greatest challenge to Tomislav's rule was his war with Bulgaria. When the Bulgarian emperor Simeon I occupied Serbia, the Serbian duke and part of the population that resisted the occupation fled to Croatia. Here Tomislav provided them with shelter. He allied with Byzantium against Bulgaria, although in fact Byzantine power was too weak at that time to make any significant difference. More critical was the intervention of the pope. The pope was ready to step in for his Croatian protégé and he negotiated favourable peace terms. Tomislav died of unknown causes before the negotiations brought a result and was succeeded by his younger brother, Tripimir II. He did not manage to retain power, however, leading to a dynastic crisis that weakened the state.

Stephen Držislav: the Checkerboard King

The rulers of the Tripimirovic dynasty changed very often. Nobody seemed to be able to remain in power in such a complicated political environment. Nevertheless, these short-lived rulers managed to retain the independence of the Croatian state. Their borders shifted, the location of the power centre changed and names in the chronicles emerged and disappeared. Yet Croatia remained independent, next to Bulgaria and Serbia, which fell under direct Byzantine rule. After the Byzantines destroyed their empire's fiercest enemy, Bulgaria, they focused entirely on Croatia. Its rulers fought for power, fell under Constantinople's influence and lost islands on the Dalmatian coast to Venice. Still, a state remained that was independent enough to rise to its full power in the twelfth century.

One legend is worth mentioning. Probably dating from the nineteenth century, it concerns Stephen Držislav (r. 969–997). According to the legend, Stephen was captured by the

Venetians. His freedom and dominion over Dalmatian cities rested on his ability to play chess: he defeated his opponent, the Venetian doge, in a match. Stephen then recovered his freedom and the rule of Dalmatian towns. To commemorate the event, he put the checkerboard on the Croatian coat of arms. If you ever wondered why Croatian football players wear checkered outfits, now you know.

Peter Krešimir IV: Croatia Rises from the Ashes

Peter Krešimir IV (r. 1058–1074) ruled in a different political reality. New enemies were arriving from the north. Vikings raided all coasts within their reach and settled in Sicily, which proved a significant threat to the Croatian coast. The beach had to be protected, as the coast with the prosperous Dalmatian cities was where the source of Croatian wealth lay. The Normans conquered Bari in Italy in 1071 and Drač, on the west coast of the Adriatic Sea, a decade later. Meanwhile the Byzantine Empire was helpless. It had to protect itself from the Turks in the east and could not also protect the Adriatic Sea from the Normans.

So it was that the Croatian king once again gained Byzantine friendship. Byzantium entrusted Peter with government of the Dalmatian cities, enabling Croatia to grow rich on their trade. During the Croatian administration, many ethnic Croats came to Dalmatia and spread their influence and language there.

In the eleventh century, another player enters the Croatian political arena: Hungary. It seems incredible that Croatia remained independent for so long, with many powerful candidates seeking to grow rich in the Dalmatian cities under their rule.

Demetrius Zvonimir: the Apex and the Decline

The reign of Demetrius Zvonimir (r. 1075/76–1089) marks the beginning of the decline of Croatian power. He was crowned in October 1075 (or 1076) in the Basilica of Saint Peter and Moses at Salona (today's Solin in Croatia) by a representative of Pope Gregory VII (r. 1073–1085), following a successful battle with the Normans. However, Hungary was on the march, under the rule of Bela I (c. 1015–1063), and Bela was hungry.

Demetrius continued with the politics of relying on papal support. He paid taxes to the pope and supported the Church. This earned him a place in the pantheon of saints, and he is today a national saint of Croatia. However, the council of Split 1060 marked the final decline of the Slavonic Church in Croatia.

Demetrius and the Pope

As in all the Balkan countries, Old Church Slavonic was widespread in Croatia, and laymen and clerics used the Glagolitic alphabet. Unlike Bulgaria and Serbia, however, which remained under the influence of the Byzantine Greek Church, Croatia paid a price for Roman support. In 1060 the council proclaimed use of the Glagolitic alphabet and Slavonic language to be a heresy and banned Slavic liturgy. The council took place after the final division of the Eastern and Western Church in 1054, so no compromise was possible. Croatia is thus one of the few Balkan nations to use the Latin alphabet today, and the Croats are mostly Catholics.

Demetrius employed papal support to full advantage and, with the help of the Croatian Church, sought to stabilize power. Many rebellious nobles were sent into exile, and he managed to grasp the reins of power firmly in his hands. The papal support paid off when the Holy Roman Empire desired to invade parts of Croatia but had to withdraw under a papal threat of excommunication for all involved.

Demetrius Zvonimir died of natural causes in 1089, but left no male heir. Anarchy followed. After a few years the Hungarian king Ladislaus I of Hungary (c. 1040–1095) conquered Croatia. Some sources imply that he came to Croatia after receiving a direct invitation from Croatian nobles, weary of the chaos and total collapse of central rule.

THE LEGACY OF THE TRIPIMIC DYNASTY: CROATIA UNDER HUNGARIAN RULE

The **Croatian nobles** who cooperated with the Hungarian king knew what they were doing. These Hungarian rulers saved the country from complete disintegration. From then on Croatia formed a close bond with Hungary, and the Hungarian king bore the title of Croatian king as well. The government retained a certain amount of autonomy that would be doubted only in the nineteenth century with the nationalist actions of the Hungarians.

The legacy of the Croatian Middle Ages state is a fitting conclusion to our story of Slavic origins. In a similar way to the Russian and Ukrainian battles over the legacy of the Kyivan Rus, the Croatian story reaches far into the present. It illustrates the complicated Balkan reality that came to a tragic end in the Balkan Wars of the 1990s. In this book we have described how the Balkan nations went their separate ways very early on.

The Serbians embraced Orthodoxy and the Byzantine cultural heritage. At the same time the Croats turned to the west, became Catholics and allied with the Hungarians. Ethnicity played relatively little role. In ancient times, Serbians and Croats were indistinguishable from one another. They spoke the same language and mingled together freely. However, historical developments in later centuries estranged them completely. Although they would form one kingdom, together with Slovenia and Bosnia, after the First World War and remained under the communist regime's firm grip for much of the twentieth century, their differences were to surface again after the collapse of communism.

The whole world stood in awe and terror as it witnessed the atrocities that occurred during the Balkan Wars in the 1990s. Many of those watching were bewildered:

Are they not Slavs? Do they not speak nearly identical languages?

However, those who aware of their ancient history know better. Here lies the key to understanding the recent past of the Balkan nations. Memory of the massacres of the Balkan Wars continues to highlight the importance of the ancient origins of Slavic countries.

… SLAVIC ANCIENT ORIGINS

ANCIENT SLAVIC ORIGINS: THE STORY GOES ON

We have travelled far with the Slavs, from their homeland in Eastern Europe to the Dalmatian coasts and on to the heart of Europe. They have changed on the journey. The tribes of wild pagans who lived in perfect harmony with nature with their rituals became settled people in established societies, building cities, frequenting churches and bowing to their elites.

These elites helped to shape the world of their time: the Kyivan duke married the sister of the emperor, the Bulgarian khan acquired the title of an emperor himself, the Croatian king hosted a council of the Western Church and the Polish king entertained the Holy Roman Emperor in Gniezno. Some of the Slavic states lived through their moments of glory within the scope of our book; others were still to celebrate their most glorious moments in later centuries.

THE STORY OF SLAVIC STATES

The Czech kings of the Přemyslid dynasty would grow very powerful throughout the Middle Ages. Přemysl Otakar II (1233–1278) shifted the borders of the Czech kingdom to the

Baltic Sea and reached for the crown of the Holy Roman Emperor. His son would unite Poland and Hungary under one rule. When the last male of the Přemyslid dynasty fell under the assassin's knife in 1306, his sister married into the dynasty of emperors – the Luxembourg. Her son Charles, an heir to the Přemyslid kings, loved his Czech and Slavic heritage. He became the most powerful man in Europe, the Holy Roman Emperor, who set out to reform the empire. So did his son Sigismund, who once again united the Hungarian and Czech crowns. Invested with the title of Roman Emperor, he set out to reform the Church and solved the papal schism in 1416.

The Polish state would rise from the ashes of anarchy where this narrative left it. After uniting with the Jagiellonian dynasty from Lithuania, it built a state surpassing in glory anything the Slavs had made in the early Middle Ages. The Polish-Lithuanian commonwealth lay on the territory of today's Poland, Ukraine, Lithuania and Belarus. It connected Eastern Europe with the Renaissance culture and Humanist literacy coming from the West.

Nor let us forget the heritage of Kyivan Rus. The western part of its territory would join the Polish in building the commonwealth, a true Renaissance marvel. However, in the east, on the Volga River, a new Slavic power arose during the years of Mongolian occupation. Daniel of Moscow (1261–1303) founded the Duchy of Moscow and defeated the remains of the Mongol overlords in the region. Slowly Moscow grew into a Russian superpower.

Ivan III the Great (1404–1505) became a tzar and, when Constantinople finally fell into the hands of the Turks in 1453, claimed the heritage of the Orthodox Eastern Church. It is a complicated matter for Slavic nations in Europe to admire the rise of Russia, although it certainly deserves our respect.

ANCIENT SLAVIC ORIGINS: THE STORY GOES ON

However, ever since Moscow became a superpower, danger for Slavs in Europe grew. Friends had to obey and enemies had to fall; there was never a middle line with Russia regarding other Slavic nations. Both the western part of the former Kyivan Rus (future Ukraine) and Belarus had to choose between Polish and Russian forces. Only in the nineteenth century would they remember their past and decide to be themselves.

The Balkan Slavs mostly fell under the dominion of the Ottoman Empire as the Turks advanced to Europe. Nobody seemed to be able to stop them, although Croatians fought bravely as a part of the Hungarian kingdom under the rule of the multinational Habsburg Empire. The Balkan history is complicated. Ottomans, Russians, Hungarians: all fought for the Balkans and the Balkan nations had to choose, if given a choice at all. However, they were accustomed to that. We have shown here how the Balkan Slavs have always struggled for independence; even the first rulers faced difficult diplomatic choices.

THE SPECTRE OF NATIONALISM

We began our narrative by discussing a nationalist historian working on his version of the Slavic origins. It seems only fitting to end on the same note.

Nationalism emerged in the nineteenth century, a time when the Slavic, Germanic and Romanic nations all re-engaged with their past. Their historians invented their own versions of the past and the emerging nations accepted their historical story.

The Czechs portrayed their history as a constant struggle with the German element. The Poles looked back to Boleslav I the

Brave, portraying their story as a battle against the rest of the world. The Ukrainians discovered they were neither Russians nor Poles; they began to dream instead about their own state. So did the Slavs in the Balkans: Bulgars, Serbians and Croats. Nations seldom spoken of then also remembered their Slavic origins. The Slavs in the old Roman province of Carinthia, living peacefully within Austrian lands, learned the Slavic language and aspired to become independent for the first time. They realized their dream after the First World War, when they became part of the Balkan Kingdom under a new name – Slovenia.

Yet the building of nations was difficult for the Slavs. They spoke Slavic languages and were drawn to other Slavs in Europe. Most supported their Slavic brothers in their national aspirations, but there was always the shadow cast by the Big Brother in the East: the Slavic superpower to whom some looked with hope, others with terror. In the nineteenth century the idea of pan-Slavism emerged. A number of nations sought to find protection under the great wings of Russia; the Russians were Slavs, after all. And Russia was swift to answer these calls. We have not discussed Russia in this narrative because the Russian story does not belong to the early Slavic origins. Only after the Mongols left did Russia come into being.

Moscow grew out of blood and fire. From the beginning, the dukes in the Duchy of Moscow had to fight the terrifying Mongols; their fate was either to succeed in battle or to be trampled under the hooves of Mongolian ponies. Mongols knew only power; they engaged in no diplomacy, nor formed alliances. For the Mongols, everybody else was either a slave to be exploited or an enemy to be destroyed. This was the environment in which Russia evolved. Other Slavic nations, such as the Czechs,

Poles, Ukrainians and the Balkan nations, learned how to use diplomacy to build their states. The Russians built their state with fire and blood.

However, in the nineteenth century, when nationalism emerged as a romantic notion, some countries chose to overlook the differences. They felt like brothers of shared Slavic blood.

But family is a complicated matter, no doubt – and we have seen many brothers killing each other in our story.

THE SLAVS OF TODAY AND THEIR ORIGINS

Today the Slavs look back to their past – but they also remember their much more recent history. The romantic notions of Slavic brotherhood have vanished, destroyed by the horrors of the Balkan Wars, the Polish-Czech War in the 1920s, the Polish-Ukrainian ethnic cleansing and the horrors of the Stalinist regime felt by Poles, Ukrainians and Belarussians – not to mention the years of communist rule in Eastern Europe. Recent history has shattered the romantic visions of Slavic unity, focusing our attention instead on the colourful and varied history of the early Slavs. The world has realized the need to appreciate the Slavs' multifaceted history, far from uniform or easy to understand. We thus believe that this book on the Slavic ancient origins, and the stories that make up their turbulent past, powerfully serves the needs of our time.

Because whatever the outcome, stories will always survive.

ANCIENT KINGS & LEADERS

Ancient cultures often traded with and influenced each other, while others grew independently. This section provides the key leaders from a number of regions, to offer comparative insights into developments across the ancient world.

SLAVIC NATIONS TIMELINE & KEY LEADERS

This list is not exhaustive and dates are approximate. The legitimacy of some kings is also open to interpretation. Where dates of rule overlap, kings either ruled jointly or ruled in opposition to one another. There may also be differences in name spellings between different sources.

ORIGINS AND MIGRATIONS

Thought by many to have originated in Polesia, a region encompassing parts of Central and Eastern Europe and southwestern Russia, the Slavic people were made up of tribal societies. Many of these societies migrated across Europe integrating with Czech, Russia, Bulgaria, Croatia, Bosnia, Poland, Hungary and other countries and cultures.

While their beliefs and myths diverge, some believe the legend of three brothers who founded three of the main Slavic peoples. The three brothers, Lech, Czech and Rus', were on a hunting trip when they took different directions to hunt their own prey. Lech travelled to the north, where he would eventually found Poland; Czech travelled west to found Czech;

and Rus' travelled east to found Russia, Ukraine and Belarus.

The timelines that follow chart the main migrations, key events and major rulers of several branches of the Slavic people.

WESTERN STEM

Czech

?	Czech founds what is now the Czech Republic (mythological)
623 CE	Samo, the first King of the Slavs, founds Samo's Empire which includes the kingdom of Moravia
626 CE	Samo leads the Slavs against the Avars
631	Samo leads his realm in the Battle of Wogastisburg, defeating the Franks
658	Samo dies. His sons do not inherit and the Slavic kingdom dissolves
?	Little is known about this period but it might have fallen under Avar rule
820s	Mojmir I founds the House of Mojmir and converts to Christianity
833	Mojmir unifies Moravia and Nitra (Slovakia) as the state of Great Moravia
846	Mojmir I is deposed. Ratislav becomes the second prince of Moravia
862	Prince Ratislav of Moravia converts to Christianity
872	Ratislav is dethroned by his nephew, Svatopluk I, who succeeds him as prince of Moravia
870/874	Borivoj I becomes prince of Bohemia, founding the House of Premysl

880	Svatopluk I 'the Great' is crowned king of Great Moravia
882	The Moravians invade Bohemia and Pannonia
895	The dukes of Bohemia under Spytihnev I separate from the Moravian kingdom
902/907	The Moravian kingdom collapses
912	Vratislav I becomes duke of Bohemia
921	Wenceslas I (posthumously declared patron saint of Czech) becomes duke of Bohemia
929	Boleslav I 'the Cruel' becomes duke of Bohemia after murdering Wenceslas I Bohemia conquers Moravia (Slovakia)
972	Boleslav II 'the Pious' becomes duke of Bohemia
999	Boleslav III 'the Red' becomes duke of Bohemia (first reign)
1003	After a brief revolt, Boleslav III is restored to the dukedom (second reign)
1003	Poland conquers Moravia and Boleslaw I (also duke of Poland) becomes duke of Bohemia
1013	Bohemia reconquers Moravia from Poland under Ulrich, duke of Bohemia
1038	Bohemia under Bretislav I invades Poland conquers Silesia and Wroclaw
1061	Vratislav II becomes duke of Bohemia
1085	Henry IV (Holy Roman Emperor) makes Vratislav II the first king of Bohemia (non-hereditary title) The House of Premysl continues to rule Bohemia
1158	German Emperor Friedrich I Barbarossa makes Duke Vladislav II of Bohemia the second king of Bohemia (non-hereditary title)

1198	The duchy of Bohemia officially becomes a kingdom
1253	Ottakar II becomes king of Bohemia and the kingdom grows
1278	Wenceslas II becomes king of Bohemia
1300	Wenceslas II of Bohemia becomes king of Poland
1305	Wenceslas III becomes king of Bohemia and Poland
1306	Wenceslas III of Bohemia is murdered, ending the House of Premysl

Poland

?	Lech founds what is now Poland (mythological)
c. 8thC CE	Krak I or Krok founds Kracow (mythological)
c. 8thC	Krak II founds Kracow (mythological)
c. 9thC	Piast 'the Wheelwright' founds the Piast dynasty and names his state Polska (semi-mythological)
960?	Mieszko I founds the duchy of Poland
966	Mieszko I converts to Christianity
992	Boleslaw I 'the Brave' succeeds his father Mieszko I on his death
999	Poland becomes a Christian kingdom
1000	Poland becomes part of the German Empire under Emperor Otto III
1025	Boleslaw I is crowned first Polish king by the Pope
1025	Mieszko II becomes king of Poland
1034/1040	Casimir 'the Restorer' becomes king of Poland
1058	Boleslaw II 'the Generous' becomes duke, then king of Poland
1079	Wladyslaw I becomes duke of Poland
1102	Boleslaw III 'the Wry-mouthed' becomes duke, then king of Poland

1138	Boleslaw III dies. The kingdom is divided among his sons, which begins the fragmentation of Poland
1226	Konrad I of Masovia asks the Teutonic Order (crusading knights based in Germany) to help subdue the pagan tribes of Prussia
1240/1241	The Mongols invade Poland, defeating a joint army of Henry I of Silesia and the Teutonic Order at the Battle of Legnica
1290	The Teutonic Order conquer all of Prussia
1295	Premysl II returns Poland to a kingdom with a hereditary title. Vytenis become grand duke of Lithuania and unites the country
1300	Wenceslas II of the house of Premysl, Bohemia, becomes king of Poland
1315/1316	Vytenis' brother Gediminas expands Lithuania to span from the Baltic Sea to the Black Sea
1320	Wladyslaw I Lokietek (known as Wladyslaw the Short) reunites the kingdom of Poland

EASTERN STEM

Russia and Former Soviet Republics

?	Rus' founded the Rus' people (mythological)
c. 800 CE	The Varangian Rus' found the state of Kyiv (Kiev)
c. 862/870	The Varangian Rus' prince Rurik begins the Rurik dynasty by founding Novgorod
879	Rurik's son, Oleg 'the Wise', becomes ruler of Novgorod

ANCIENT KINGS & LEADERS

882	Oleg of Novgorod conquers Kyiv and later unifies it with Novgorod to form what would become Kyivan-Rus'
912	Oleg dies and Igor 'the Old', Rurik's younger son, becomes the ruler of Kyiv-Novgorod
921	Igor moves the capital of the duchy to Kyiv
941 & 944	Igor besieges Constantinople
945	Igor is assassinated and his widow, Olga, succeeds him
962	Olga of Kyiv is succeeded by Sviatoslav I, her son
964–968	Sviatoslav launches a military campaign to the east and south, conquering first the Volga Bulgars and then the Khazar Empire
972	Sviatoslav dies. His son Yaropolk I is given Kyiv, but civil war soon breaks out
980	Vladimir I 'the Great' of Novgorod conquers Kyiv and creates a unified Rus. He soon begins a campaign to conquer the Baltic people
988	Vladimir, previously a pagan, converts to Greek-Orthodox Christianity. His kingdom now extends from Ukraine to the Baltic Sea
1015	Vladimir dies and civil war erupts again under the dubious claim of Sviatopolk I
1019	Yaroslav I 'the Wise' becomes the new ruler of Kyiv
1054	Yaroslav dies, splitting the kingdom among his sons and leaving it weakened. He leaves Kyiv and Novgorod to Iziaslav I
11–12thC	The kingdom remains divided. The Crusades further weaken the Baltic states and Constantinople
1237	The Mongols invade Kyivan Rus'

1237–1239　Mongol leader Batu Khan raids Kyiv before sacking Vladimir, Moscow, and many other Kyivan Rus' cities
1253　Danylo Halitski of Galicia is crowned king by the Pope
1283　Daniil Alexsandrovich becomes the first prince of Moscow and establishes the grand duchy of Moscow

Illyrico-Servian branch

South Slavs migrate and begin to settle in countries including what are known today as Bosnia, Montenegro, Serbia and Croatia.

up to the late 500s　South Slavic tribes remain fragmented. Invasions on territories take place, including the Balkans, Dalmatia and Greece
558 CE　Several South Slavic tribes are defeated by the Avars. Many of the Slavs move east from the Russian Steppes
600s–700s　South Slavs begin to settle along the Danube, in the Balkans, Bulgaria, Montenegro and Serbia. There is some assimilation of the cultures; South Slavs invade Greece, reaching Macedonia and Thessalonica; States or kingdoms are formed but many are threatened by invasion
870　The Serbs begin to convert to Christianity
925　The kingdom of Croatia is formed under Tomislav, its first king
1042　Duklja in Montenegro gains independence from the Roman Empire
1168　Stefan Nemanja founds the Nemanjic dynasty in Serbia

1217	Stefan Nemanjic 'the First-Crowned', son of Stefan Nemanja, is crowned by the Pope as first king of Serbia. The kingdom of Serbia is formed
Mid-12thC	The Banate of Bosnia is formed
Mid-14thC	Principality of Zeta is formed, covering parts of what is today Montenegro

Magyars/Hungary

14 BCE	Pannonia which includes parts of Hungary is classed as part of the Roman Empire
5 CE	The Romans found Aquincum (now Budapest)
370–469	The Hunnic Empire invades much of Central and Eastern Europe, including Hung
c. 5thC	The Magyars migrate from the Ural Mountains in Russia. Some settle along the Don River in the Khazar Khanate
862	The Magyars raid the Frankish Empire and parts of Bulgaria and the Balaton principality
895/896	Arpad, head of the seven Magyar tribes and thought to be a descendant of Attila, founds the kingdom of Hungary with three Khazar tribes
906	The Hungarians defeat the Moravian kingdom and annex Slovakia
907	The Hungarians defeat the Bavarian army in the Battle of Pressburg
917–934	The Hungarians raid parts of France, Switzerland, Saxony, Italia and Constantinople
948	Bulcsu, a descendant of Arpad, signs a peace treaty with the Roman Empire and converts to Christianity

955	Bulcsu and his troops meet the German army led by Otto I 'the Great' and are defeated in the Battle of Lechfeld, resulting in an end to further Hungarian invasions
1001	Stephen I (Saint Stephen) is crowned king of Hungary and sets out to consolidate and extend his rule
1030	Stephen I repels an invasion led by the Holy Roman Emperor, Conrad II
1038	Stephen I of Hungary dies. There follows a series of civil wars
1077	King Ladislaus I becomes king of Hungary (he also becomes king of Croatia in 1091)
1095	Coloman 'the Learned' becomes king of Hungary. Over the next few years, he annexes Croatia (becoming its king in 1097), Slavonia and Dalmatia
1116	Stephen II becomes king of Hungary and Croatia,
1141	Geza II becomes king of Hungary and Croatia and seeks to expand his borders. For the next century, the country faces both expansion and revolt
1241	Bela IV (who became king in 1235) refuses to surrender to the Mongols under Batu Khan, but the Hungarian army is defeated. However, the Mongols retreat in 1242
1242	With the country weakened, Bela IV concentrates on rebuilding, including the castle of Buda
1272	Ladislaus IV becomes king of Hungary and Croatia
1290	Ladislaus IV is murdered and his throne is taken by Andrew III, a descendant of the Arpads

1301	Andrew II dies, causing the Arpad dynasty to become extinct in the male line. Charles Robert I of Anjou, a 13-year-old Catholic, inherits the throne of Hungary

Bulgaria

6th century–479 BCE	The Achaemenid Empire controls parts of what is now Bulgaria
341 CE	Philip II of Macedon makes Bulgaria part of his empire
3rd century	Bulgaria is attacked by the Celts
45 CE	Bulgaria becomes part of the Roman Empire
c. 381	The Gothic (Wulfila) Bible is created in what is now northern Bulgaria
482	Following migration, the Turkic-speaking tribes of the Bulgars mainly reside northeast of the Danube River. The tribes are fragmented and remain so for the next century. Some are under the control of the Avars
584	Kubrat of the Dulo dynasty unifies the main Bulgarian tribes
619	Kubrat converts to Christianity
632	Kubrat unites all Bulgarian tribes and founds the state known as Old Great Bulgaria
650/665	Kubrat dies. Old Great Bulgaria largely disintegrates
680	Under Kubrat's sons, the Bulgars migrate across parts of Europe. Asparukh, one of Kubrat's sons and thought to be a descendant of Attila, travel west towards the Danube
680/681	Asparukh establishes the First Bulgarian Empire

700	Tervel becomes king of Bulgaria following Asparukh's death in battle. Terval is also given the title of Caesar in 705
753	Sevar, king of Bulgaria, dies, ending the reign of the Dulo dynasty
753/756	Vinekh begins the Ukil dynasty. The period is marked by the short reigns and murders of many of its kings, and by a series of attacks on Bulgaria by the Byzantine Empire
777	Kardam becomes king of Bulgaria and restores order and power
c. 803	Krum 'the Fearsome' becomes king of the Bulgars, beginning the rule of the Krum dynasty
810	The Bulgars under Krum expand their empire and destroy the Avars
807–811	Krum's Bulgars are attacked by the Byzantine army, but defeat them in the Battle of Pliska, killing the Byzantine Emperor, Nikephoros I
814/815	Krum dies while preparing to attack Constantinople. He is succeeded by his son Omurtag, who signs a 30-year peace treaty with the Byzantine Empire. This marks a period of peace and expansion in Bulgaria
852	Boris I becomes king of Bulgaria, marking a ten-year period of instability
864	Boris converts Bulgaria to Christianity and is regarded as a saint by the Eastern Orthodox Church
893	Boris' son, Simeon I 'the Great', becomes Bulgaria's first tsar. Under him, the state becomes among the most powerful in Eastern and Southeastern Europe

927	Simeon dies and is succeeded by his son, Peter I. This ushers in a golden age of peace and prosperity
934–965	A series of raids by Hungarians, coupled by political insecurity, causes the start of decline in Bulgaria
969	Boris II, Peter's son, becomes tsar when Peter abdicates. He spends most of his reign in captivity of the Byzantine Emperor, Nikephoras II
997	Samuel becomes tsar. His reign is hindered by constant war with the Byzantines
1015	Ivan Vladislav becomes tsar
1018	Ivan dies, and the Byzantine Empire under Basil II annexes the kingdom of Bulgaria
1185	The Second Bulgarian Empire is established by Peter II. It remains a dominant power until the mid-1200s when the Mongols invade

CELTIC & BRITISH LEADERS

This list is not exhaustive and dates are approximate. Where dates of rule overlap, emperors either ruled jointly or ruled in opposition to one another. There may also be differences in name spellings between different sources.

BEGINNINGS

The Celts were thought to have originated in central Europe at around 1400 BCE. Migrations across Europe began around 900 BCE and saw the Celts migrate west to parts of France, Spain, Italia, Greece, and into Scotland, England, Ireland and Wales. Broadly speaking, a Celt can be defined as someone speaking a Celtic language and being from a Celtic culture. The Celts that settled in Britain in around 300 BCE became the island's dominant ethnic group.

GAUL, IBERIA AND THE EUROPEAN CONTINENT

Ambicatus, Bituriges	c. 600 BCE
Bellovesus, Bituriges	c. 600 BCE
Segovesus, Bituriges	c. 600 BCE
Brennus, Senones	c. 390 BCE
Onomaris	c. 400–300 BCE

ANCIENT KINGS & LEADERS

Britomaris, Senones	c. 283 BCE
Acichorius/Brennus	c. 279 BCE
Bolgios	c. 279 BCE
Cambuales	c. 279 BCE
Cerethrius	c. 277 BCE
Autaritus	d. 238 BCE
Aneroëstes, Gaesatae	d. 225 BCE
Concolitanus, Gaesatae	d. 225 BCE
Viridomarus	d. 222 BCE
Ducarius, Insubres	c. 217 BCE
Olyndicus, Celtiberians	d. c. 170 BCE
Punicus, Lusitani	c. 155 BCE
Caesarius, Lusitani	c. 155 BCE
Caucenus, Lusitani	c. 153 BCE
Tanginus, Celtiberians	c. 140 BCE
Tautalus, Celtiberians	c. 139 BCE
Virathius, Celtiberians	d. 139 BCE
Divico, Helvetii	c. 109 BCE
Orgetorix, Helvetii	c. 60 BCE
Casticus, Sequani	c. 60 BCE
Dumnoix, Haedui	c. 60 BCE
Viridovix, Unelli	c. 56 BCE
Acco, Senones	c. 54 BCE
Ambiorix, Eburones	c. 54 BCE
Cativolcus, Eburones	c. 54 BCE
Cingetorix, Treveri	c. 54 BCE
Tasgetius, Carnutes	d. 54 BCE
Indutiomeris, Treveri	d. 53 BCE
Camulogene, Aulerci	d. 52 BCE
Convictolitavis, Haedui	c. 52 BCE

Aegus, Allobroges	c. 50 BCE
Regus, Allobroges	c. 50 BCE
Vercingetorix, Averni	c. 80–46 BCE
Commius, Atrebates	c. 57-c. 20 BCE
Tincomarus, Atrebates	c. 30 BCE–c. 8 BCE
Eppillius, Atrebates	c. 20-7 BCE
Biatex, Boii	1st century BCE
Diviciacus, Suessiones	c. 70 BCE?
Verica, Atrebates	c. 15–c. 42 CE
Julius Indus, Treveri	d. c. 65 CE
Julius Sabinus, Lingones	c. 69 CE

KINGS OF BRITONS/BRYTHONS

Legendary Kings

This includes a selection of mythological rulers. There is much diversity of opinion over who the kings actually consisted of and the dates they ruled.

Brutus   c. 1115 BCE (23 years)

Founder and first King of the Britons, Brutus is thought to be a descendant of Troy. He divided the land between his three sons: Albanactus who gained Albany (Scotland); Kamber who gained Cambria (Wales); and Locrinus who gained Lloegr (roughly England), and was also high king of Britain

Pwyll Pen Annwn	King of Dyfed
Pryderi fab Pywll	Son of Pwyll, succeeded his father as king of Dyfed

Leir/Llyr	c. 950 BCE, possible inspiration for Shakespeare's King Lear
Beli ap Rhun	c. 500s, king of Gwenydd
King Arthur	5th–6th century, king of Britain, led the Knights of the Round Table

Historical Kings of Briton (c. 54 BCE–50 CE)

This section mainly covers people of England, Wales and southern Scotland.

Cassivellaunus	54 BCE; led the defence against Julius Caesar's second invasion
Carvilius (one of the four kings of Kent)	c. 54 BCE
Cingetorix (one of the four kings of Kent)	c. 54 BCE
Segovax (one of the four kings of Kent)	c. 54 BCE
Taximagulus (one of the four kings of Kent)	c. 54 BCE
Imanuentius, Trinovantes	c. 54 BCE
Lugotorix	c. 54 BCE
Mandubracius, Trinovantes	c. 54 BCE
Tasciovanus	20 BCE–9 CE
Cunobeline	9–40 CE
Tiberius Claudius	40–43 CE
Caractacus, Catuvellauni	43–50 CE
Togodumnus, Catuvellauni	d. 43 CE

Roman Era Onwards

This section mainly covers people of England, Wales and southern Scotland. These rulers may have only governed part of Briton, with many being based in and ruler of Wales, which itself was split into several kingdoms. Some are disputed.

Prasutagus, Iceni	d. 60 CE
Boudicca, Iceni	d. 60 CE
Cartimandua, Brigantes	c. 69 CE
Vellocatus, Brigantes	c. 69 CE
Venutius, Brigantes	c. 70 CE
Vortigern	mid-5th century
Riothamus	c. 469 CE
Ambrosius Aurelianus	late 5th century
Maelgwn Gwynedd	mid- to late-5th century
Selyf ap Cynan	c. 613 CE
Ceretic of Elmet	c. 614–617 CE
Cadwallon ap Cadfan	c. 634 CE
Idris ap Gwyddno	c. 635 CE
Eugein I of Alt Clut	c. 642 CE
Cadwaladr	c. 654–664 CE
Ifor	683–698 CE
Rhodri Molwynog	c. 712–754 CE
Cynan Dindaethwy	798–816 CE
Merfyn Frych	825–844 CE
Rhodri ap Merfyn 'the Great'	844–878 CE
Anarawd ap Rhodri	878–916 CE
Idwal Foel ap Anarawd	916–942 CE
Hwyel Dda 'the Good'	942–950 CE
Dyfnwal ab Owain	930s–970s CE
Maredudd ab Owain	986–999 CE
Llywelyn ap Seisyll	1018–1023 CE
Iago ab Idwal	1023–1039 CE
Gruffyd ap Llywelyn	1039/1055–1063 CE

MONARCHS OF ENGLAND (886-1066 CE)

House of Wessex (c. 886-924 CE)

The House of Wessex was founded when Alfred became King of the Anglo-Saxons.

Alfred 'the Great'	c. 886–899 CE
Edward 'the Elder'	899–924 CE
Aethelstan 'the Glorious'	924–939 CE
Edmund I 'the Magnificent'	939–946 CE
Eadred	946–955 CE
Eadwig	955–959 CE
Edgar 'the Peaceful'	959–975 CE
Edward 'the Martyr'	975–978 CE
Aethelred II 'the Unready'	978–1013 CE

House of Denmark (c. 1013-1014 CE)

England was invaded by the Danes in 1013. Aethelred abandoned the throne to Sweyn Forkbeard.

Sweyn Forkbeard	1013–1014 CE

House of Wessex (restored, 1014-1016 CE)

Aethelred II was restored to the English throne after the death of Sweyn Forkbeard.

Aethelred II 'the Unready'	1014–1016 CE
Edmund Ironside	1016–1016 CE

House of Denmark (restored, 1016–1042 CE)

Cnut became king of all England apart from Wessex after signing a treaty with Edmund Ironside. He became king of all England following Edmund's death just over a month later.

Cnut 'the Great' (Canute)	1016–1035 CE
Harold Harefoot	1035–1040 CE
Harthacnut	1040–1042 CE

House of Wessex (restored, second time, 1042–1066 CE)

Edward 'the Confessor'	1042–1066 CE

House of Goodwin (1066 CE)

Harold II Godwinson	1066–1066 CE

Following Harold II's death in the Battle of Hastings, several claimants emerged to fight over the English throne. William the Conqueror of the House of Normandy was crowned king on 25 December 1066.

HIGH KINGS OF IRELAND

Mythological High Kings of Ireland

Dates and rulers are different depending on the source.

Nuada	?–1897 BCE; first reign
Bres	1897–1890 BCE
Nuada	1890–1870 BCE; second reign

Lug	1870–1830 BCE
Eochaid Ollathair (the Dadga)	1830–1750 BCE
Delbaeth	1750–1740 BCE
Fiacha	1740–1730 BCE
Mac Cuill	1730–1700 BCE

Ireland was split into several kingdoms until the national title of High King began, despite mythological stories of unbroken lines of High Kings.

Semi-historical High Kings (*c.* 459–831 CE)

Most of these kings are thought to be historical figures, but it is disputed whether they were all High Kings.

Ailill Molt	459–478 CE
Lugaid mac Loegairi	479–503 CE
Muirchertach mac Ercae	504–527 CE
Tuathal Maelgarb	528–538 CE
Diarmait mac Cerbaill	539–558 CE
Domhnall mac Muirchertaig	559–561 CE; joint ruler
Fearghus mac Muirchertaig	559–561 CE; joint ruler
Baedan mac Muirchertaig	562–563 CE; joint ruler
Eochaidh mac Domnaill	562–563 CE; joint ruler
Ainmuire mac Setnai	564–566 CE
Baetan mac Ninnedo	567 CE
Aed mac Ainmuirech	568–594 CE
Aed Slaine	595–600 CE; joint ruler
Colman Rimid	595–600 CE; joint ruler
Aed Uaridnach	601–607 CE
Mael Coba mac Aedo	608–610 CE

Suibne Menn	611–623 CE
Domnall mac Aedo	624–639 CE
Cellach mac Maele Coba	640–656 CE; joint ruler
Conall mac Maele Coba	640–656 CE; joint ruler
Diarmait	657–664 CE; joint ruler
Blathmac	657–664 CE; joint ruler
Sechnassach	665–669 CE
Cenn Faelad	670–673 CE
Finsnechta Fledach	674–693 CE
Loingsech mac Oengusso	694–701 CE
Congal Cennmagair	702–708 CE
Fergal mac Maele Duin	709–718 CE
Fogartach mac Neill	719 CE
Cinaed mac Irgalaig	720–722 CE
Flaithbertach mac Loingsig	723–729 CE
Aed Allan	730–738 CE
Domnall Midi	739–758 CE
Niall Frossach	759–765 CE
Donnchad Midi	766–792 CE
Aed Oirdnide	793–819 CE
Conchobar mac Donnchada	819–833 CE
Feidlimid mac Crimthainn	832–846 CE

Historical High Kings of Ireland (c. 846–1198 CE)

It is disputed whether these were all High Kings.

Mael Sechnaill mac Maele-Ruanaid	846–860 CE
Aed Findliath	861–876 CE
Fiann Sinna	877–914 CE
Niall Glundub	915–917 CE

Donnchad Donn	918–942 CE
Congalach Cnogba	943–954 CE
Domnall ua Neill	955–978 CE
Mael Sechnaill mac Domnaill	979–1002 CE; first reign
Brian Boruma	1002–1014 CE
Mael Sechnaill mac Domnaill	1014–1022 CE; second reign
Donnchad mac Brian	d. 1064
Diarmait mac Mail na mBo	d. 1072 CE
Toiredelbach Ua Briain	d. 1086 CE
Domnall Ua Lochlainn	d. 1121 CE
Muirchertach Ua Briain	d. 1119 CE
Toirdelbach Ua Conchobair	1119–1156 CE
Muirchertach Mac Lochlainn	1156–1166 CE
Ruaidri Ua Conchobair	1166–1198 CE

RULERS OF SCOTLAND

Legendary kings

Fergus I	c. 330 BCE
Feritharis	305 BCE
Mainus	290 BCE
Dornadilla	262 BCE
Nothatus	232 BCE

Some of the significant rulers between 200 BCE and 800 CE are listed here.

Caractacus (King of the Britons, he was also considered king of Scotland in legend)   1st century CE, to c. 50 CE

Donaldus I (Some consider him to be the
first Christian king of Scotland)
Calgacus, Caledones												c. 85 CE
Argentocoxos, Caledones										c. 210 CE
Fergus Mor							c. 500 CE; possible king of Dál Riata

The list ends around the time of Kenneth MacAlpin, who founded the House of Alpin. Following the Roman departure from Britain, Scotland split into four main groups: the Picts, the people of Dál Riata, the Kingdom of Strathclyde and the Kingdom of Bernicia. The Picts would eventually merge with Dál Riata to form the Kingdom of Scotland.

Monarchs of Scotland (c. 848–1286 CE)

House of Alpin (848–1034 CE)

Kenneth I was the son of Alpin, king of Dál Riata, a Gaelic kingdom located in Scotland and Ireland.

Kenneth I MacAlpin								843/848–13 February 858
			CE; first King of Alba thought to be of Gaelic origin
Donald I													858–13 April 862 CE
Causantin mac Cinaeda (Constantine I)					862–877 CE
Aed mac Cinaeda											877–878 CE
Giric 'mac Rath'											878–889 CE
Donald II													889–900 CE
Causantin mac Aeda (Constantine II)						900–943 CE
Malcolm I													943–954 CE
Indulf														954–962 CE
Dub mac Mail Coluim										962–967 CE

ANCIENT KINGS & LEADERS

Cuilen	967–971 CE
Amlaib	973–977 CE
Constantine III	995–997 CE
Kenneth III	997–25 March 1005 CE
Malcolm II	1005–1034 CE

House of Dunkeld (1034-1286)

Duncan was the grandson of Malcolm II. He founded the House of Dunkeld.

Duncan I	1034–1040 CE
Macbeth	1040–1057 CE
Lulach	1057–1058 CE
Malcolm III	1058–1093 CE
Donald III	1093–1097 CE
Duncan II	1094 CE
Edgar	1097–1107 CE
Alexander I	1107–1124 CE
David I	1124–1153 CE
Malcolm IV	1153–1165 CE
William I	1165–1214 CE
Alexander II	1219–1249 CE
Alexander III	1249–1286 CE

NORSE MONARCHS

This list is not exhaustive and dates are approximate. The legitimacy of some kings is also open to interpretation. Where dates of rule overlap, kings either ruled jointly or ruled in opposition to one another. There may also be differences in name spellings between different sources.

BEGINNINGS

The Norse people or Vikings migrated from Norway, Denmark and Sweden during the Middle Ages to many places including Britain, Ireland, Scotland, Normandy, Iceland, Greenland and even as far as North America. They brought their religious beliefs and mythology with them. The first two humans were created by three Norse gods, including Odin. Ask, a man created from an ash tree, and Embla, a woman created from an elm tree, went on to create the whole human race who dwelled at Midgard.

HOUSE OF YNGLING

Descendants of the family, whose name means children of the god Frey, became the first semi-mythological rulers of Sweden,

ANCIENT KINGS & LEADERS

then Norway. There are several versions of this dynasty showing different names or orders descending from Fiolner, son of Frey, son of Njord, who was part of the Vanir tribe. The family is also known as the Sclyfings.

Fiolner (son of the god Frey)
Sveigoir (son of Fiolner, mythological king of Sweden)
Vanlandi (son of Sveigoir)
Visbur (son of Vanlandi)
Domaldi (son of Visbur)
Domar (son of Domaldi)
Dyggvi (son of Domar)
Dag 'the Wise' spaki (son of Dyggvi)
Agni (son of Dag)
Alrekr and Eirikr (sons of Agni)
Yngvi and Alfr (sons of Alrekr)
Jorundr (son of Yngvi)
Aunn (son of Jorundr)
Egill/Ongentheow (father of Ohthere and Onela)
Ottarr/Ohthere and Onela (son of Egill)
Aoils/Eadgils and Eanmund (son of Ohthere)
Eysteinn (son of Eadgils)
Yngvarr (son of Eysteinn)
Onundr (son of Yngvarr)
Ingjaldr (?)

From the Yngling family came these semi-mythological kings.

Olaf the Tree-feller	approx. 700s CE
Halfdan Whiteleg	approx. 800s CE

Gudrod the Hunter approx. 850s CE
Halfdan the Swarthy (Halfdan the Black) 821–860 CE

The following list runs from 872 which is when King Harald Fairhair was victorious in the Battle of Hafrsfjord, after which he merged the petty kingdoms of Norway into a unified kingdom.

FAIRHAIR DYNASTY (872-970 CE)

Dates for the Fairhair dynasty are estimated.

Harald I Halfdansson (Harald Fairhair)	872–928/932 CE
Eirik I Haraldsson (Eric Bloodaxe)	928/932–934 CE
Haakon I Haraldsson (Haakon the Good)	934–960 CE
Harald II Ericsson (Harald Greycloak)	961–970 CE

HOUSE OF GORM/EARL OF LADE (961-995 CE)

Harald Gormsson (Harald Bluetooth; ruled with
  Harald Greycloak) 961–980 CE
Earl Hakkon Sigurdsson (Hakkon Jarl, Eric
  the Victorious) 965/970–995 CE

FAIRHAIR DYNASTY (RESTORED) (995-1000 CE)

Olav I Tryggvason 995–1000 CE

ANCIENT KINGS & LEADERS

HOUSE OF GORM/EARL OF LADE (RESTORED) (1000-1015 CE)

Sweyn Forkbeard; joint ruler	1000–1013 CE
Earl Eirik Haakonsson; joint ruler	1000–1015 CE
Earl Sweyn Haakonsson; joint ruler	1000–1015 CE

ST OLAV DYNASTY (1015-1028 CE)

Olav II Haraldsson (Saint Olav)	1015–1028 CE

HOUSE OF GORM/EARL OF LADE (SECOND RESTORATION) (1028-1035 CE)

Cnut the Great (Canute)	1028–1035 CE
Earl Haakon Ericsson; joint ruler	1028–1029 CE
Sweyn Knutsson; joint ruler	1030–1035 CE

ST OLAV DYNASTY (RESTORED) (1035-1047 CE)

Magnus I Olafsson (Magnus the Good)	1015–1028 CE

HARDRADA DYNASTY (1046-1135 CE)

Harald III Sigurdsson (Harald Hardrada)	1046–1066 CE
Magnus II Haralldsson	1066–1069 CE
Olaf III Haralldsson (Olaf the Peaceful)	1067–1093 CE

Hakkon (II) Magnusson (Haakon Toresfostre)	1093–1095 CE
Magnus III Olafsson (Magnus Barefoot)	1093–1103 CE
Olaf (IV) Magnusson; joint ruler	1103–1115 CE
Eystein I Magnusson; joint ruler	1103–1123 CE
Sigurd I Magnusson (Sigurd the Crusader)	1103–1130 CE
Magnus IV Sigurdsson (Magnus the Blind)	1130–1135 CE

GILLE DYNASTY (1130–1162 CE)

Harald IV Magnusson (Harald Gille)	1130–1136 CE
Sigurd II Haraldsson; joint ruler (Sigurd Munn)	1136–1155 CE
Inge I Haraldsson; joint ruler (Inge the Hunchback)	1136–1161 CE
Eystein II Haraldsson; joint ruler	1142–1157 CE
Magnus (V) Haraldsson; joint ruler	1142–1145 CE
Haakon II Sigurdsson (Hakkon the Broadshouldered)	1157–1162 CE

HARDRADA DYNASTY (RESTORED, COGNATIC BRANCH) (1161–1184 CE)

Magnus V Erlingsson	1161–1184 CE

SVERRE DYNASTY (1184–1204 CE)

Sverre Sigurdsson	1184–1202 CE
Haakon III Sverresson	1202–1204 CE
Guttorm Sigurdsson	January to August 1204 CE

GILLE DYNASTY (COGNATIC BRANCH) (1204-1217 CE)

Inge II Bardsson   1204–1217 CE

SVERRE DYNASTY (RESTORED) (1217-1319 CE)

Haakon IV Hakkonsson (Hakkon the Old)   1217–1263 CE
Haakon (V) Haakonsson (Hakkon the Young)   1240–1257 CE
Magnus VI Haakonsson (Magnus the
  Law-mender)   1257–1280 CE
Eric II Magnusson   1273–1299 CE
Hakkon V Magnusson   1299–1319 CE

HOUSE OF BJELBO (1319-1387)

Magnus VII Eriksson   1319–1343 CE
Hakkon VI Magnusson   1343–1380 CE
Olaf IV Hakkonsson   1380–1387 CE

HOUSE OF ESTRIDEN (1380-1412)

Margaret I   1380–1412 CE

HOUSE OF GRIFFIN (1389-1387)

Eric III   1389–1442 CE

HOUSE OF PALANTINATE-NEUMARKT (1442-1448)

Christopher   1442–1448 CE

HOUSE OF BONDE (1449-1450)

Charles I   1449–1450 CE

HOUSE OF OLDENBURG (1450-1814)

Christian I   1450–1481 CE

Interregnum (1481–1483) in which Jon Svaleson Smor served as regent

John	1483–1513 CE
Christian II	1513–1523 CE
Fredrick I	1524–1533 CE

Interregnum (1533–1537) in which Olaf Engelbrektsson served as regent

Christian III	1537–1559 CE
Fredrick II	1559–1588 CE
Christian IV	1588–1648 CE
Fredrick III	1648–1670 CE
Christian V	1670–1699 CE
Fredrick IV	1699–1730 CE

Christian VI	1730–1746 CE
Fredrick V	1746–1766 CE
Christian VII	1766–1808 CE
Fredrick VI	1808–1814 CE

Interregnum (1814–1814) in which Christian Frederick served as regent

Christian Frederick	1814–1814 CE

Interregnum (1814–1814) in which Marcus Gjoe Rosenkrantz served as prime minister

HOUSE OF HOLSTEIN-GOTTORP (1814-1818)

Charles II	1814–1818 CE

HOUSE OF BERNADOTTE (1818-1905)

Charles III John	1818–1944 CE
Oscar I	1844–1859 CE
Charles IV	1859–1872 CE
Oscar II	1872–1905 CE

ANCIENT NEAR EAST LEADER LIST

This list concentrates on leaders with at least some proven legitimate claim. Dates are based on archaeological evidence as far as possible but are approximate. Where dates of rule overlap, rulers either ruled jointly or ruled in opposition to one another. There may also be differences in name spellings between different sources.

SUMER

The Sumerian list that follows is based on the *Sumerian King List* or *Chronicle of the One Monarchy*. The lists were often originally carved into clay tablets and several versions have been found, mainly in southern Mesopotamia. Some of these are incomplete and others contradict one another. Nevertheless, the lists remain an invaluable source of information.

After the kingship descended from heaven, the kingship was in Eridug.

Alulim	28,800 years (8 *sars**)
Alalngar	36,000 years (10 *sars*)

Then Eridug fell and the kingship was taken to Bad-tibira.

En-men-lu-ana	43,200 years (12 *sars*)
En-mel-gal-ana	28,800 years (8 *sars*)
Dumuzid the Shepherd (or Tammuz)	36,000 years (10 *sars*)

Then Bad-tibira fell and the kingship was taken to Larag.

En-sipad-zid-ana   28,800 years (8 *sars*)

Then Larag fell and the kingship was taken to Zimbir.

En-men-dur-ana   21,000 years (5 *sars* and 5 *ners*)

Then Zimbir fell and the kingship was taken to Shuruppag.

Ubara-Tutu   18,600 years (5 *sars* and 1 *ner**)

Then the flood swept over.

*A *sar* is a numerical unit of 3,600; a *ner* is a numerical unit of 600.

FIRST DYNASTY OF KISH

After the flood had swept over, and the kingship had descended from heaven, the kingship was in Kish.

Jushur	1,200 years	Nangishlisma	1,200 years
Kullassina-bel	960 years	En-tarah-ana	420 years

Babum	300 years	Enme-nuna)	1,200 years
Puannum	840 years	Zamug (son of	
Kalibum	960 years	Barsal-nuna)	140 years
Kalumum	840 years	Tizqar (son of Zamug)	
Zuqaqip	900 years	305 years	
Atab (or A-ba)	600 years	Ilku	900 years
Mashda (son of Atab)	840 years	Iltasadum	1,200 years
		Enmebaragesi	900 years
Arwium (son of Mashda)	720 years	(earliest proven ruler based on archaeological sources; Early Dynastic Period, 2900–2350 BCE)	
Etana the Shepherd	1,500 years		
Balih (son of Etana)	400 years		
En-me-nuna	660 years	Aga of Kish (son of Enmebaragesi)	625 years
Melem-Kish (son of Enme-nuna)	900 years	(Early Dynastic Period, 2900–2350 BCE)	
Barsal-nuna (son of			

Then Kish was defeated and the kingship was taken to E-anna.

FIRST RULERS OF URUK

Mesh-ki-ang-gasher (son of Utu)	324 years (Late Uruk Period, 4000–3100 BCE)
Enmerkar (son of Mesh-ki-ang-gasher)	420 years (Late Uruk Period, 4000–3100 BCE)
Lugal-banda the shepherd	1200 years (Late Uruk Period, 4000–3100 BCE)
Dumuzid the fisherman	100 years (Jemdet Nasr Period, 3100–2900 BCE)

Gilgamesh	126 years (Early Dynastic Period, 2900–2350 BCE)
Ur-Nungal (son of Gilgamesh)	30 years
Udul-kalama (son of Ur-Nungal)	15 years
La-ba'shum	9 years
En-nun-tarah-ana	8 years
Mesh-he	36 years
Melem-ana	6 years
Lugal-kitun	36 years

Then Unug was defeated and the kingship was taken to Urim (Ur).

FIRST DYNASTY OF UR

Mesh-Ane-pada	80 years
Mesh-ki-ang-Nuna (son of Mesh-Ane-pada)	36 years
Elulu	25 years
Balulu	36 years

Then Urim was defeated and the kingship was taken to Awan.

DYNASTY OF AWAN

Three kings of Awan	356 years

Then Awan was defeated and the kingship was taken to Kish.

SECOND DYNASTY OF KISH

Susuda the fuller	201 years
Dadasig	81 years
Mamagal the boatman	360 years
Kalbum (son of Mamagal)	195 years
Tuge	360 years
Men-nuna (son of Tuge)	180 years
Enbi-Ishtar	290 years
Lugalngu	360 years

Then Kish was defeated and the kingship was taken to Hamazi.

DYNASTY OF HAMAZI

Hadanish — 360 years

Then Hamazi was defeated and the kingship was taken to Unug (Uruk).

SECOND DYNASTY OF URUK

En-shag-kush-ana	60 years (*c.* 25th century BCE)
Lugal-kinishe-dudu	120 years
Argandea	7 years

Then Unug was defeated and the kingship was taken to Urim (Ur).

SECOND DYNASTY OF UR

Nanni	120 years
Mesh-ki-ang-Nanna II (son of Nanni)	48 years

Then Urim was defeated and the kingship was taken to Adab.

DYNASTY OF ADAB

Lugal-Ane-mundu   90 years (*c.* 25th century BCE)

Then Adab was defeated and the kingship was taken to Mari.

DYNASTY OF MARI

Anbu	30 years	Zizi of Mari, the fuller	20 years
Anba (son of Anbu)	17 years	Limer the 'gudug' priest	30 years
Bazi the leatherworker	30 years	Sharrum-iter	9 years

Then Mari was defeated and the kingship was taken to Kish.

THIRD DYNASTY OF KISH

Kug-Bau (Kubaba)   100 years (*c.* 25th century BCE)

Then Kish was defeated and the kingship was taken to Akshak.

DYNASTY OF AKSHAK

Unzi	30 years	Ishu-Il	24 years
Undalulu	6 years	Shu-Suen (son of	
Urur	6 years	Ishu-Il)	7 years
Puzur-Nirah	20 years		

Then Akshak was defeated and the kingship was taken to Kish.

FOURTH DYNASTY OF KISH

Puzur-Suen (son of Kug-bau)	25 years (c. 2350 BCE)
Ur-Zababa (son of Puzur-Suen)	400 years (c. 2300 BCE)
Zimudar	30 years
Usi-watar (son of Zimudar)	7 years
Eshtar-muti	11 years
Ishme-Shamash	11 years
Shu-ilishu	15 years
Nanniya the jeweller	7 years

Then Kish was defeated and the kingship was taken to Unug (Uruk).

THIRD DYNASTY OF URUK

Lugal-zage-si	25 years (c. 2296–2271 BCE)

Then Unug was defeated and the kingship was taken to Agade (Akkad).

DYNASTY OF AKKAD

Sargon of Akkad	56 years (c. 2270–2215 BCE)
Rimush of Akkad (son of Sargon)	9 years (c. 2214–2206 BCE)
Manishtushu (son of Sargon)	15 years (c. 2205–2191 BCE)
Naram-Sin of Akkad (son of Manishtushu)	56 years (c. 2190–2154 BCE)
Shar-kali-sharri (son of Naram-Sin)	24 years (c. 2153–2129 BCE)

Then who was king? Who was not the king?

Irgigi, Nanum, Imi and Ilulu	3 years (four rivals who fought to be king during a three-year period; c. 2128–2125 BCE)
Dudu of Akkad	21 years (c. 2125–2104 BCE)
Shu-Durul (son of Duu)	15 years (c. 2104–2083 BCE)

Then Agade was defeated and the kingship was taken to Unug (Uruk).

FOURTH DYNASTY OF URUK

Ur-ningin	7 years (c. 2091?–2061? BCE)
Ur-gigir (son of Ur-ningin)	6 years
Kuda	6 years
Puzur-ili	5 years
Ur-Utu (or Lugal-melem; son of Ur-gigir)	6 years

Unug was defeated and the kingship was taken to the army of Gutium.

GUTIAN RULE

Inkišuš	6 years (c. 2147–2050 BCE)
Sarlagab (or Zarlagab)	6 years
Shulme (or Yarlagash)	6 years
Elulmeš (or Silulumeš or Silulu)	6 years
Inimabakeš (or Duga)	5 years
Igešauš (or Ilu-An)	6 years
Yarlagab	3 years
Ibate of Gutium	3 years
Yarla (or Yarlangab)	3 years
Kurum	1 year
Apilkin	3 years
La-erabum	2 years
Irarum	2 years
Ibranum	1 year
Hablum	2 years
Puzur-Suen (son of Hablum)	7 years
Yarlaganda	7 years
Si'um (or Si-u)	7 years
Tirigan	40 days

Then the army of Gutium was defeated and the kingship taken to Unug (Uruk).

FIFTH DYNASTY OF URUK

Utu-hengal	427 years / 26 years / 7 years (conflicting dates; c. 2055–2048 BCE)

ANCIENT KINGS & LEADERS

THIRD DYNASTY OF UR

Ur-Namma (or Ur-Nammu)	18 years (*c.* 2047–2030 BCE)
Shulgi (son of Ur-Namma)	48 years (*c.* 2029–1982 BCE)
Amar-Suena (son of Shulgi)	9 years (*c.* 1981–1973 BCE)
Shu-Suen (son of Amar-Suena)	9 years (*c.* 1972–1964 BCE)
Ibbi-Suen (son of Shu-Suen)	24 years (*c.* 1963–1940 BCE)

Then Urim was defeated. The very foundation of Sumer was torn out. The kingship was taken to Isin.

DYNASTY OF ISIN

Ishbi-Erra	33 years (*c.* 1953–1920 BCE)
Shu-Ilishu (son of Ishbi-Erra)	20 years
Iddin-Dagan (son of Shu-Ilishu)	20 years
Ishme-Dagan (son of Iddin-Dagan)	20 years
Lipit-Eshtar (son of Ishme-Dagan or Iddin Dagan)	11 years
Ur-Ninurta (son of Ishkur)	28 years
Bur-Suen (son of Ur-Ninurta)	21 years
Lipit-Enlil (son of Bur-Suen)	5 years
Erra-imitti	8 years
Enlil-bani	24 years
Zambiya	3 years
Iter-pisha	4 years
Ur-du-kuga	4 years
Suen-magir	11 years
Damiq-ilishu (son of Suen-magir)	23 years

BABYLON

FIRST DYNASTY OF BABYLON (AMORITE, *C.* 1894–1595 BCE)

Sumu-abum	1894–1881 BCE
Sumulael	1880–1845 BCE
Sabium	1844–1831 BCE
Apil-Sin	1830–1813 BCE
Sin-muballit	1812–1793 BCE
Hammurapi	1792–1750 BCE
Samsu-iluna	1749–1712 BCE
Abi-eshuh	1711–1684 BCE
Ammi-ditana	1683–1647 BCE
Ammi-saduqa	1646–1626 BCE
Samsu-ditana	1625–1595 BCE

KASSITE DYNASTY (*C.* 1729–1155 BCE)

Gandash	1729–1704 BCE
Agum I	1703–1682 BCE
Kashtiliashu I	1681–1660 BCE
Abi-Rattash?	
Kashtiliash II?	
Urzigurumash	
Harba-Shipak?	
Shipta'ulzi?	
Burna-Buriash I	
Ulamburiash?	

ANCIENT KINGS & LEADERS

Kashtiliash III?	
Agum III?	
Kara-indash	
Kadashman-Harbe I	
Kurigalzu I	
Kadashman-Enlil I	1374–1360 BCE
Burna-Buriash II	1359–1333 BCE
Kara-hardash	1333 BCE
Nazi-Bugash	1333 BCE
Kurigalzu II	1332–1308 BCE
Nazi-Maruttash	1307–1282 BCE
Kadashman-Turgu	1281–1264 BCE
Kadashman-Enlil II	1263–1255 BCE
Kudur-Enlil	1254–1246 BCE
Shagarakti-Shuriash	1245–1233 BCE
Kashtiliashu IV	1232–1225 BCE
Tukulti-Ninurta I of Assyria	1225 BCE
Enlin-nadin-shumi	1224 BCE
Kadashman-Harbe II	1223 BCE
Adad-shuma-iddina	1222–1217 BCE
Adad-shuma-usur	1216–1187 BCE
Meli-Shipak	1186–1172 BCE
Merodach-Baladan I	1171–1159 BCE
Zababa-shuma-iddina	1158 BCE
Enlil-nadin-ahi	1157–1155 BCE

DYNASTY OF ISIN (C.1157–1026 BCE)

Marduk-kabit-ahheshu	1157–1140 BCE

Itti-Marduk-balatu	1139–1132 BCE
Ninurta-nadin-shumi	1131–1126 BCE
Nebuchadrezzar I	1125–1104 BCE
Enlil-nadin-apli	1103–1100 BCE
Marduk-nadin-ahhe	1099–1082 BCE
Marduk-shapik-zeri	1081–1069 BCE
Adad-apla-iddina	1068–1047 BCE
Marduk-ahhe-eriba	1046 BCE
Marduk-zer-X?	1045–1034 BCE
Nabu-shumu-libur	1033–1026 BCE

SECOND DYNASTY OF THE SEALAND (C. 1025–1005 BCE)

Simbar-Shipak	1025–1008 BCE
Ea-mukin-zeri	1008 BCE
Kashshu-nadin-ahhe	1007–1005 BCE

DYNASTY OF BAZI (C. 1004–985 BCE)

Eulmash-shakin-shumi	1004–988 BCE
Ninurta-kudurri-usur I	987–985 BCE
Shirikti-Shuqamuna	985 BCE

DYNASTY OF ELAM (C. 984–979 BCE)

Mar-biti-apla-usur	984–979 BCE

PERIOD OF MIXED DYNASTIES (C. 978–732 BCE)

Nabu-mukin-apli	978–943 BCE
Ninurta-kudurri-usur II	943 BCE
Mar-biti-ahhe-iddina	942–? BCE
Shamash-mudammiq	
Nabu-shuma-ukin I	
Nabu-apla-iddina	(33+ years)
Marduk-zakir-shumi I	(27+ years)
Marduk-balassu-iqbi	?–813 BCE
Baha-aha-iddina	812–? BCE
(*interregnum*)	
Ninruta-apl-X?	
Marduk-apla-usur	
Eriba-Marduk	(9+ years)
Nabu-shuma-ishkun	?–748 BCE (13+ years)
Nabonassar	747–734 BCE
Nabu-nadin-zeri	733–732 BCE
Nabu-shuma-ukin	732 BCE

NINTH DYNASTY OF BABYLON (C. 731–626 BCE)

Nabu-mukin-zeri	731–729 BCE
Tiglath-Pileser III of Assyria	728–727 BCE
Shalmaneser V of Assyria	726–722 BCE
Merodach-Baladan II	721–710 BCE
Sargon II of Assyria	709–705 BCE
Sennacherib of Assyria (first reign)	704–703 BCE
Marduk-zakir-shumi II	703 BCE

Merodach-Baladan II	703 BCE
Bel-ibni	702–700 BCE
Ashur-nadin-shumi	699–694 BCE
Nergal-ushezib	693 BCE
Mushezib-Marduk	692–689 BCE
Sennecherib of Assyria (second reign)	688–681 BCE
Esarhaddon of Assyria	680–669 BCE
Ashurbanipal of Assyria	668 BCE
Shamash-shuma-ukin	667–648 BCE
Kandalanu	647–627 BCE
(*interregnum*)	626 BCE

NEO-BABYLONIAN DYNASTY (C. 625–539 BCE)

Nabopolassar	625–605 BCE
Nebuchadrezzar II	604–562 BCE
Amel-Marduk	561–560 BCE
Neriglissar	559–556 BCE
Labashi-Marduk	556 BCE
Nabonius (co-ruler)	555–539 BCE
Belshazzar (co-ruler/regent)	555–539 BCE

ASSYRIA

PUZUR-ASHUR DYNASTY (2025–1809 BCE)

Puzur-Ashur I

Shalim-ahum
Ilu-shuma
Erishum I   1974–1935 BCE
Ikunum   1934–1921 BCE
Sargon I   1920–1881 BCE
Puzur-Ashur II   1880–1873 BCE
Naram-Sim   1872–1829 or 1819 BCE
Erishum II   1828 or 1818–1809 BCE

SHAMSHI-ADAD DYNASTY (1808–1736 BCE)

Shamshi-Adad I   1808–1776 BCE
Ishme-Dagan I   1775–1765 BCE
Mut-Ashkur
Rimush
Asinum

NON-DYNASTIC USURPERS (1735–1701 BCE)

Puzur-Sin
Ashur-dugul
Ashur-apla-idi
Nasir-Sin
Sin-namir
Ipqi-Ishtar
Adad-salulu
Adasi

ADASIDE DYNASTY (1700–722 BCE)

Belu-bani	1700–1689 BCE
Libaya	1688–1672 BCE
Sharma-Adad I	1671–1660 BCE
Iptar-Sin	1659–1648 BCE
Bazaya	1647–1620 BCE
Lullaya	1619–1614 BCE
Shu-Ninua	1613–1600 BCE
Sharma-Adad II	1599–1597 BCE
Erishum III	1596–1584 BCE
Shamshi-Adad II	1583–1578 BCE
Ishme-Dagan II	1577–1562 BCE
Sharmshi-Adad III	1561–1546 BCE
Ashur-nirari I	1545–1520 BCE
Puzur-Ashur III	1519–1496 BCE
Enlil-nasir I	1495–1483 BCE
Nur-ili	1482–1471 BCE
Ashur-shaduni	1471 BCE
Ashur-rabi I	1470–1451 BCE
Ashur-nadin-ahhe I	1450–1431 BCE
Enlil-nasir II	1430–1425 BCE
Ashur-nirari II	1424–1418 BCE
Ashur-bel-nisheshu	1417–1409 BCE
Ashur-ra'im-nisheshu	1408–1401 BCE
Ashur-nadin-ahhe II	1400–1391 BCE
Eriba-Adid I	1390–1364 BCE

MIDDLE ASSYRIAN EMPIRE (1363–912 BCE)

Ashur-uballit I	1363–1328 BCE
Enlil-nirari	1327–1318 BCE
Arik-den-ili	1317–1306 BCE
Adad-nirari I	1305–1274 BCE
Shalmaneser I	1273–1244 BCE
Tukulti-Ninurta I	1243–1207 BCE
Ashur-nadin-apli	1206–1203 BCE
Ashur-nirari III	1202–1197 BCE
Enlil-kudurri-usur	1196–1192 BCE
Ninurta-apil-Ekur	1191–1179 BCE
Ashur-dan I	1178–1133 BCE
Ninurta-tukulti-Ashur	1132 BCE
Mutakkil-Nusku	1132 BCE
Ashur-resh-ishi I	1132–1115 BCE
Tiglath-Pileser I	1114–1076 BCE
Ashared-apil-Ekur	1075–1074 BCE
Ashur-bel-kala	1073–1056 BCE
Eriba-Adad II	1055–1054 BCE
Shamshi-Adad IV	1053–1050 BCE
Ashurnasirpal I	1049–1031 BCE
Shalmaneser II	1030–1019 BCE
Ashur-nirari IV	1018–1013 BCE
Ashur-rabi II	1012–972 BCE
Ashur-resh-ishi	971–967 BCE
Tiglath-Pileser II	966–935 BCE
Ashur-dan II	934–912 BCE

NEO-ASSYRIAN EMPIRE (911–609 BCE)

Adad-nirari II	911–891 BCE
Tukulti-Ninurta II	890–884 BCE
Ashurnasirpal II	883–859 BCE
Shalmaneser III	858–824 BCE
Shamshi-Adad V	823–811 BCE
Adad-nirari III	810–783 BCE
Shalmaneser IV	782–773 BCE
Ashur-dan III	772–755 BCE
Ashur-nirari V	754–745 BCE
Tiglath-Pileser III	744–727 BCE
Shalmaneser V	726–722 BCE

SARGONID DYNASTY (722–609 BCE)

Sargon II	721–705 BCE
Sennacherib	704–681 BCE
Esarhaddon	680–669 BCE
Ashurbanipal	668–627 BCE
Ashur-etil-ilani	626–623 BCE
Sin-shumu-lishir	623 BCE
Sin-shar-ishkun	622–612 BCE
Ashur-uballit II	611–609 BCE

(fall of Assyrian Empire 609 BCE)

ANCIENT KINGS & LEADERS

PERSIA

ACHAEMENID DYNASTY (559–330 BCE)

Cyrus the Great	559–530 BCE
Cambyses	529–522 BCE
Smerdis	522 BCE
Darius I the Great	521–486 BCE
Xerxes I	485–465 BCE
Ataxerxes I (Longimanus)	464–424 BCE
Xerxes II	424 BCE
Sogdianus	424 BCE
Darius II (Nothus)	423–405 BCE
Ataxerxes II (Mnemon)	404–359 BCE
Ataxerxes III (Ochus)	358–338 BCE
Arses	337–336 BCE
Darius III (Codomannus)	335–330 BCE

(The Persian Empire ended when Alexander the Great invaded in 330 BCE)

PHOENICIA

ANCIENT TYRIAN LEADERS (MYTHOLOGICAL), (2050–1450 BCE)

Agenor (son of Posiedon or Belus)	c.2050–1450 BCE
Phoenix (son of Agenor, gave his name to Phoenicia)	?

375

SLAVIC ANCIENT ORIGINS

LATE BRONZE AGE (1350–1335 BCE)

Abi-Milku	c.1350–1335 BCE

KINGS OF TYRE AND SIDON (990–785 BCE)

Abibaal	c.993–981 BCE
Hiram I	980–947 BCE
Baal-Eser I	946–930 BCE
Abdastartus	929–921 BCE
Astartus	920–901 BCE
Deleastartus	900–889 BCE
Astarymus	888–880 BCE
Phelles	879 BCE
Ithobaal I	878–847 BCE
Baal-Eser II	846–841 BCE
Mattan I	840–832 BCE
Pygmalion (Dido's brother, who formed Carthage in 814 BCE)	831–785 BCE

UNDER ASSYRIAN CONTROL (C. 750–660 BCE)

Ithobaal II	750–739 BCE
Hiram II	739–730 BCE
Mattan II	730–729 BCE
Elulaios	729–694 BCE
Abd Melqart	694–680 BCE
Baal I	680–660 BCE

ANCIENT KINGS & LEADERS

AFTER ASSYRIAN CONTROL (C. 592–573 BCE)

Ithobaal III   591–573 BCE

(Overthrow of monarchy in favour of oligarchic government)

RESTORATION OF MONARCHY (551–532 BCE)

Hiram III   551–532 BCE

UNDER PERSIAN CONTROL (539–411 BCE)

Mattan IV   c.490–480 BCE
Boulomenus   c.450 BCE
Abdemon   c.420–411 BCE

UNDER CYPRIOT CONTROL (SALAMIS, 411–374 BCE)

Evagoras of Salamis   411–374 BCE

UNDER PERSIAN CONTROL (374–332 BCE)

Eugoras   c.340s
Azemilcus   c.340–332 BCE

(The Phoenician Empire ended when Alexander the Great invaded in 332 BCE)

ANCIENT EGYPTIAN PHARAOHS

There is dispute about the dates and position of pharaohs within dynasties due to several historical sources being incomplete or inconsistent. This list aims to provide an overview of the ancient Egyptian dynasties, but is not exhaustive and dates are approximate. There may also be differences in name spellings between different sources. Also please note that the throne name is given first, followed by the personal name – more commonly they are known by the latter.

ANCIENT EGYPTIAN DEITIES

Ancient Egyptian gods and goddesses were worshipped as deities. They were responsible for maat (divine order or stability), and different deities represented different natural forces, such as Ra the Sun God. After the Egyptian state was first founded in around 3100 BCE, pharaohs claimed to be divine representatives of these gods and were thought to be successors of the gods.

While there are many conflicting Egyptian myths, some of the significant gods and goddesses and their significant responsibilities are listed here.

Amun/Amen/Amen-Ra	Creation
Atem/Tem	Creation, the sun

ANCIENT KINGS & LEADERS

Ra	The sun
Isis	The afterlife, fertility, magic
Osiris	Death and resurrection, agriculture
Hathor	The sky, the sun, motherhood
Horus	Kingship, the sky
Set	Storms, violence, deserts
Maat	Truth and justice, she personifies *maat*
Anubis	The dead, the underworld

PREDYNASTIC AND EARLY DYNASTIC PERIODS (*c.* 3000–2686 BCE)

First Dynasty (*c.* 3150–2890 BCE)

The first dynasty begins at the unification of Upper and Lower Egypt.

Narmer (Menes/M'na?)	*c.* 3150 BCE
Aha (Teti)	*c.* 3125 BCE
Djer (Itej)	54 years
Djet (Ita)	10 years
Merneith (possibly the first female Egyptian pharaoh)	*c.* 2950 BCE
Khasti (Den)	42 years
Merybiap (Adjib)	10 years
Semerkhet (Iry)	8.5 years
Qa'a (Qebeh)	34 years
Sneferka	*c.* 2900 BCE
Horus-Ba (Horus Bird)	*c.* 2900 BCE

Second Dynasty (*c.* 2890–2686 BCE)

Little is known about the second dynasty of Egypt.

Hetepsekhemwy (Nebtyhotep)	15 years
Nebra	14 years
Nynetjer (Banetjer)	43–45 years
Ba	unknown
Weneg-Nebty	c. 2740 BCE
Wadjenes (Wadj-sen)	c. 2740 BCE
Nubnefer	unknown
Senedj	c. 47 years
Peribsen (Seth-Peribsen)	unknown
Sekhemib (Sekhemib-Perenmaat)	c. 2720 BCE
Neferkara I	25 years
Neferkasokkar	8 years
Horus Sa	unknown
Hudejefa (real name missing)	11 years
Khasekhemwy (Bebty)	18 years

OLD KINGDOM (c. 2686–2181 BCE)

Third Dynasty (c. 2686–2613 BCE)

The third dynasty was the first dynasty of the Old Kingdom. Its capital was at Memphis.

Djoser (Netjerikhet)	c. 2650 BCE
Sekhemkhet (Djoser-Teti)	2649–2643 BCE
Nebka? (Sanakht)	c. 2650 BCE
Qahedjet (Huni?)	unknown
Khaba (Huni?)	2643–2637 BCE
Huni	2637–2613 BCE

Fourth Dynasty (*c.* 2613–2498 BCE)

The fourth dynasty is sometimes known as the 'golden age' of Egypt's Old Kingdom.

Snefru (Nebmaat)	2613–2589 BCE
Khufu, or Cheops (Medjedu)	2589–2566 BCE
Djedefre (Kheper)	2566–2558 BCE
Khafre (Userib)	2558–2532 BCE
Menkaure (Kakhet)	2532–2503 BCE
Shepseskaf (Shepeskhet)	2503–2498 BCE

Fifth Dynasty (*c.* 2498–2345 BCE)

There is some doubt over the succession of pharaohs in the fifth dynasty, especially Shepseskare.

Userkaf	2496/8–2491 BCE
Sahure	2490–2477 BCE
Neferirkare-Kakai	2477–2467 BCE
Neferefre (Izi)	2460–2458 BCE
Shepseskare (Netjeruser)	few months between 2458 and 2445 BCE
Niuserre (Ini)	2445–2422 BCE
Menkauhor (Kaiu)	2422–2414 BCE
Djedkare (Isesi)	2414–2375 BCE
Unis (Wenis)	2375–2345 BCE

Sixth Dynasty (*c.* 2345–2181 BCE)

Teti	2345–2333 BCE
Userkare	2333–2332 BCE
Meryre (Pepi I)	2332–2283 BCE

Merenre I (Nemtyemsaf I)	2283–2278 BCE
Neferkare (Pepi II)	2278–2183 BCE
Merenre II (Nemtyemsaf II)	2183 or 2184 BCE
Netjerkare (Siptah I) or Nitocris	2182–2179 BCE

FIRST INTERMEDIATE PERIOD (c. 2181–2040 BCE)

Seventh and Eighth Dynasties (c. 2181–2160 BCE)

There is little evidence on this period in ancient Egyptian history, which is why many of the periods of rule are unknown.

Menkare	c. 2181 BCE
Neferkare II	unknown
Neferkare III (Neby)	unknown
Djedkare (Shemai)	unknown
Neferkare IV (Khendu)	unknown
Merenhor	unknown
Sneferka (Neferkamin I)	unknown
Nikare	unknown
Neferkare V (Tereru)	unknown
Neferkahor	unknown
Neferkare VI (Peiseneb)	unknown to 2171 BCE
Neferkamin (Anu)	c. 2170 BCE
Qakare (Ibi)	2175–2171 BCE
Neferkaure	2167–2163 BCE
Neferkauhor (Khuwihapi)	2163–2161 BCE
Neferiirkkare (Pepi)	2161–2160 BCE

Ninth Dynasty (*c.* 2160–2130 BCE)

There is little evidence on this period in ancient Egyptian history which is why many of the periods of rule are unknown.

Maryibre (Khety I)	2160 BCE to unknown
Name unknown	unknown
Naferkare VII	unknown
Seneh (Setut)	unknown

The following pharaohs and their dates of rule are unknown or widely unconfirmed.

Tenth Dynasty (*c.* 2130–2040 BCE)

Rulers in the Tenth dynasty were based in Lower Egypt.

Meryhathor	2130 BCE to unknown
Neferkare VIII	2130–2040 BCE
Wahkare (Khety III)	unknown
Merykare	unknown to 2040 BCE
Name unknown	unknown

Eleventh Dynasty (*c.* 2134–1991 BCE)

Rulers in the eleventh dynasty were based in Upper Egypt.

Intef the Elder	unknown
Tepia (Mentuhotep I)	unknown to 2133 BCE
Sehertawy (Intef I)	2133–2117 BCE
Wahankh (Intef II)	2117–2068 BCE
Nakhtnebtepefer (Intef III)	2068–2060/40 BCE

MIDDLE KINGDOM (c. 2040-1802 BCE)

Eleventh Dynasty Continued (c. 2134-1991 BCE)
This period is usually known as the beginning of the Middle Kingdom.

Nebhepetre (Mentuhotep II)   2060–2040 BCE as king of Upper Egypt, 2040–2009 BCE as King of Upper and Lower Egypt
Sankhkare (Mentuhotep III)   2009–1997 BCE
Nebtawyre (Mentuhotep IV)   1997–1991 BCE

Twelfth Dynasty (c. 1991-1802 BCE)
The twelfth dynasty was one of the most stable prior to the New Kingdom, and is often thought to be the peak of the Middle Kingdom.

Sehetepibre (Amenemhat I)	1991–1962 BCE
Kheperkare (Senusret I / Sesostris I)	1971–1926 BCE
Nubkaure (Amenemhat II)	1929–1895 BCE
Khakheperre (Senusret II / Sesostris II)	1898–1878 BCE
Khakaure (Senusret III / Sesostris III)	1878–1839 BCE
Nimaatre (Amenemhat III)	1860–1815 BCE
Maakherure (Amenemhat IV)	1815–1807 BCE
Sobekkare (Sobekneferu/Nefrusobek)	1807–1802 BCE

SECOND INTERMEDIATE PERIOD (c. 1802-1550 BCE)

Thirteenth Dynasty (c. 1802-c. 1649 BCE)
There is some ambiguity on the periods of rule of the thirteenth dynasty, but it is marked by a period of several short rules. This

ANCIENT KINGS & LEADERS

dynasty is often combined with the eleventh, twelfth and fourteenth dynasties under the Middle Kingdom.

Sekhemre Khutawy (Sobekhotep I)	1802–1800 BCE
Mehibtawy Sekhemkare (Amenemhat Sonbef)	1800–1796 BCE
Nerikare (Sobek)	1796 BCE
Sekhemkare (Amenemhat V)	1796–1793 BCE
Ameny Qemau	1795–1792 BCE
Hotepibre (Qemau Siharnedjheritef)	1792–1790 BCE
Lufni	1790–1788 BCE
Seankhibre (Amenemhat VI)	1788–1785 BCE
Semenkare (Nebnuni)	1785–1783 BCE
Sehetepibre (Sewesekhtawy)	1783–1781 BCE
Sewadjkare I	1781 BCE
Nedjemibre (Amenemhat V)	1780 BCE
Khaankhre (Sobekhotep)	1780–1777 BCE
Renseneb	1777 BCE
Awybre (Hor)	1777–1775 BCE
Sekhemrekhutawy Khabaw	1775–1772 BCE
Djedkheperew	1772–1770 BCE
Sebkay	unknown
Sedjefakare (Kay Amenemhat)	1769–1766 BCE
Khutawyre (Wegaf)	c. 1767 BCE
Userkare (Khendjer)	c. 1765 BCE
Smenkhkare (Imyremeshaw)	started in 1759 BCE
Sehetepkare (Intef IV)	c. 10 years
Meribre (Seth)	ended in 1749 BCE
Sekhemresewadjtawy (Sobekhotep III)	1755–1751 BCE
Khasekhemre (Neferhotep I)	1751–1740 BCE
Menwadjre (Sihathor)	1739 BCE

Khaneferre (Sobekhotep IV)	1740–1730 BCE
Merhotepre (Sobekhotep V)	1730 BCE
Knahotepre (Sobekhotep VI)	c. 1725 BCE
Wahibre (Ibiau)	1725–1714 BCE
Merneferre (Ay I)	1714–1691 BCE
Merhotepre (Ini)	1691–1689 BCE
Sankhenre (Sewadjtu)	1675–1672 BCE
Mersekhemre (Ined)	1672–1669 BCE
Sewadjkare II (Hori)	c. 5 years
Merkawre (Sobekhotep VII)	1664–1663 BCE
Seven kings (names unknown)	1663–? BCE

Note: the remaining pharaohs of the thirteenth dynasty are not listed here as they are either unknown or there is a lot of ambiguity about when they ruled.

Fourteenth Dynasty (c. 1805/1710–1650 BCE)

Rulers in the fourteenth dynasty were based at Avaris, the capital of this dynasty.

Sekhaenre (Yakbim)	1805–1780 BCE
Nubwoserre (Ya'ammu)	1780–1770 BCE
Khawoserre (Qareh)	1770–1745 BCE
Aahotepre ('Ammu)	1760–1745 BCE
Maaibre (Sheshi)	1745–1705 BCE
Aasehre (Nehesy)	c. 1705 BCE
Khakherewre	unknown
Nebefawre	c. 1704 BCE
Sehebre	1704–1699 BCE
Merdjefare	c. 1699 BCE

Note: the remaining pharaohs of the fourteenth dynasty are not listed here as they are either unknown or there is a lot of ambiguity about when they ruled.

Fifteenth Dynasty (c. 1650–1544 BCE)

The fifteenth dynasty was founded by Salitas and covered a large part of the Nile region.

Salitas	c. 1650 BCE
Semqen	1649 BCE to unknown
'Aper-'Anat	unknown
Sakir-Har	unknown
Seuserenre (Khyan)	c. 30 to 35 years
Nebkhepeshre (Apepi)	1590 BCE?
Nakhtyre (Khamudi)	1555–1544 BCE

Sixteenth Dynasty (c. 1650–1580 BCE)

Rulers in the sixteenth dynasty were based at Thebes, the capital of this dynasty. The name and date of rule of the first pharaoh is unknown.

Sekhemresementawy (Djehuti)	3 years
Sekhemresemeusertawy (Sobekhotep VIII)	16 years
Sekhemresankhtawy (Neferhotep III)	1 year
Seankhenre (Mentuhotepi)	less than a year
Sewadjenre (Nebiryraw)	26 years
Neferkare (?) (Nebiryraw II)	c. 1600 BCE
Semenre	c. 1600 BCE
Seuserenre (Bebiankh)	12 years
Djedhotepre (Dedumose I)	c. 1588–1582 BCE

Djedneferre (Dedumose II)	c. 1588–1582 BCE
Djedankhre (Montensaf)	c. 1590 BCE
Merankhre (Mentuhotep VI)	c. 1585 BCE
Seneferibre (Senusret IV)	unknown
Sekhemre (Shedwast)	unknown

Seventeenth Dynasty (c. 1650–1550 BCE)

Rulers in the seventeenth dynasty ruled Upper Egypt.

Sekhemrewahkhaw (Rahotep)	c. 1620 BCE
Sekhemre Wadjkhaw (Sobekemsaf I)	c. 7 years
Sekhemre Shedtawy (Sobekemsaf II)	unknown to c. 1573 BCE
Sekhemre-Wepmaat (Intef V)	c. 1573–1571 BCE
Nubkheperre (Intef VI)	c. 1571–1565 BCE
Sekhemre-Heruhirmaat (Intef VII)	late 1560s BCE
Senakhtenre (Ahmose)	c. 1558 BCE
Seqenenre (Tao I)	1558–1554 BCE
Wadkheperre (Kamose)	1554–1549 BCE

NEW KINGDOM (c. 1550–1077 BCE)

Eighteenth Dynasty (c. 1550–1292 BCE)

The first dynasty of Egypt's New Kingdom marked the beginning of ancient Egypt's highest power and expansion.

Nebpehtire (Ahmose I)	c. 1550–1525 BCE
Djeserkare (Amenhotep I)	1541–1520 BCE
Aakheperkare (Thutmose I)	1520–1492 BCE
Aakheperenre (Thutmose II)	1492–1479 BCE

ANCIENT KINGS & LEADERS

Maatkare (Hatshepsut)	1479–1458 BCE
Menkheperre (Thutmose III)	1458–1425 BCE
Aakheperrure (Amenhotep II)	1425–1400 BCE
Menkheperure (Thutmose IV)	1400–1390 BCE
Nebmaatre 'the Magnificent' (Amehotep III)	1390–1352 BCE
Neferkheperure Waenre (Amenhotep IV)	1352–1336 BCE
Ankhkheperure (Smenkhkare)	1335–1334 BCE
Ankhkheperure mery Neferkheperure (Neferneferuaten III)	1334–1332 BCE
Nebkheperure (Tutankhamun)	1332–1324 BCE
Kheperkheperure (Aya II)	1324–1320 BCE
Djeserkheperure Setpenre (Haremheb)	1320–1292 BCE

Nineteenth Dynasty (c. 1550–1292 BCE)

The nineteenth dynasty is also known as the Ramessid dynasty as it includes Ramesses II, one of the most famous and influential Egyptian pharaohs.

Menpehtire (Ramesses I)	1292–1290 BCE
Menmaatre (Seti I)	1290–1279 BCE
Usermaatre Setpenre 'the Great', 'Ozymandias' (Ramesses II)	1279–1213 BCE
Banenre (Merneptah)	1213–1203 BCE
Menmire Setpenre (Amenmesse)	1203–1200 BCE
Userkheperure (Seti II)	1203–1197 BCE
Sekhaenre (Merenptah Siptah)	1197–1191 BCE
Satre Merenamun (Tawosret)	1191–1190 BCE

Twentieth Dynasty (c. 1190–1077 BCE)

This, the third dynasty of the New Kingdom, is generally thought to mark the start of the decline of ancient Egypt.

Userkhaure (Setnakht)	1190–1186 BCE
Usermaatre Meryamun (Ramesses III)	1186–1155 BCE
Heqamaatre Setpenamun (Ramesses IV)	1155–1149 BCE
Heqamaatre Setpenamun (Ramesses IV)	1155–1149 BCE
Usermaatre Sekheperenre (Ramesses V)	1149–1145 BCE
Nebmaatre Meryamun (Ramesses VI)	1145–1137 BCE
Usermaatre Setpenre Meryamun (Ramesses VII)	1137–1130 BCE
Usermaatre Akhenamun (Ramesses VIII)	1130–1129 BCE
Neferkare Setpenre (Ramesses IX)	1128–1111 BCE
Khepermaatre Setpenptah (Ramesses X)	1111–1107 BCE
Menmaatre Setpenptah (Ramesses XI)	1107–1077 BCE

Twenty-first Dynasty (c. 1077–943 BCE)

Rulers in the twenty-first dynasty were based at Tanis and mainly governed Lower Egypt.

Hedjkheperre-Setpenre (Nesbanadjed I)	1077–1051 BCE
Neferkare (Amenemnisu)	1051–1047 BCE
Aakkheperre (Pasebakhenniut I)	1047–1001 BCE
Usermaatre (Amenemope)	1001–992 BCE
Aakheperre Setepenre (Osorkon the Elder)	992–986 BCE
Netjerikheperre-Setpenamun (Siamun)	986–967 BCE
Titkheperure (Pasebakhenniut II)	967–943 BCE

Twenty-second Dynasty (c. 943–728 BCE)

Sometimes called the Bubastite dynasty. Its pharaohs came from Libya.

Hedjkheneperre Setpenre (Sheshonq I)	943–922 BCE
Sekhemkheperre Setepenre (Osorkon I)	922–887 BCE
Heqakheperre Setepenre (Sheshonq II)	887–885 BCE
Tutkheperre (Sheshonq LIb)	c. the 880s BCE
Hedjkheperre Setepenre (Takelot I Meriamun)	885–872 BCE
Usermaatre Setpenre (Sheshonq III)	837–798 BCE
Hedjkheperre Setepenre (Sheshonq IV)	798–785 BCE
Usermaatre Setpenre (Pami Meriamun)	785–778 BCE
Aakheperre (Sheshonq V)	778–740 BCE
Usermaatre (Osorkon IV)	740–720 BCE

Twenty-third and Twenty-fourth Dynasties (c. 837–720 BCE)

These dynasties were led mainly by Libyans and mainly ruled Upper Egypt.

Hedjkheperre Setpenre (Takelot II)	837–813 BCE
Usermaatre Setpenamun (Meriamun Pedubaste I)	826–801 BCE
Usermaatre Meryamun (Sheshonq VI)	801–795 BCE
Usermaatre Setpenamun (Osorkon III)	795–767 BCE
Usermaatre-Setpenamun (Takelot III)	773–765 BCE
Usermaatre-Setpenamun (Meriamun Rudamun)	765–762 BCE
Shepsesre (Tefnakhte)	732–725 BCE
Wahkare (Bakenrenef)	725–720 BCE

Twenty-fifth Dynasty (c. 744–656 BCE)

Also known as the Kushite period, the twenty-fifth dynasty follows the Nubian invasions.

Piankhy (Piye)	744–714 BCE
Djedkaure (Shebitkku)	714–705 BCE
Neferkare (Shabaka)	705–690 BCE
Khuinefertemre (Taharqa)	690–664 BCE

LATE PERIOD (c. 664–332 BCE)

Twenty-sixth Dynasty (c. 664 – 525 BCE)

Also known as the Saite period, the twenty-sixth dynasty was the last native period before the Persian invasion in 525 BCE.

Wahibre (Psamtik I)	664–610 BCE
Wehemibre (Necho II)	610–595 BCE
Neferibre (Psamtik II)	595–589 BCE
Haaibre (Apreis)	589–570 BCE
Khemibre (Amasis II)	570–526 BCE
Ankhkaenre (Psamtik III)	526–525 BCE

Twenty-seventh Dynasty (c. 525–404 BCE)

The twenty-seventh dynasty is also known as the First Egyptian Satrapy and was ruled by the Persian Achaemenids.

Mesutre (Cambyses II)	525–1 July 522 BCE
Seteture (Darius I)	522–November 486 BCE
Kheshayarusha (Xerxes I)	November 486–December 465 BCE
Artabanus of Persia	465–464 BCE
Arutakhshashas (Artaxerxes I)	464–424 BCE
Ochus (Darius II)	July 423–March 404 BCE

Twenty-eighth Dynasty (c. 404–398 BCE)

The twenty-eighth dynasty consisted of a single pharaoh.

Amunirdisu (Amyrtaeus)	404–398 BCE

Twenty-ninth Dynasty (c. 398–380 BCE)

The twenty-ninth dynasty was founded following the overthrow of Amyrtaeus.

Baenre Merynatjeru (Nepherites I)	398–393 BCE
Khnemmaatre Setepenkhnemu (Hakor)	c. 392–391 BCE
Userre Setepenptah (Psammuthis)	c. 391 BCE
Khnemmaatre Setepenkhnemu (Hakor)	c. 390–379 BCE
Nepherites II	c. 379 BCE

Thirtieth Dynasty (c. 379–340 BCE)

The thirtieth dynasty is thought to be the final native dynasty of ancient Egypt.

Kheperkare (Nectanebo I)	c. 379–361 BCE
Irimaatenre (Teos)	c. 361–359 BCE
Snedjemibre Setepenanhur (Nectanebo II)	c. 359–340 BCE

Thirty-first Dynasty (c. 340–332 BCE)

The thirty-first dynasty is also known as the Second Egyptian Satrapy and was ruled by the Persian Achaemenids.

Ochus (Artaxerxes III)	c. 340–338 BCE
Arses (Artaxerxes IV)	338–336 BCE
Darius III	336–332 BCE

MACEDONIAN/ARGEAD DYNASTY (c. 332–309 BCE)

Alexander the Great conquered Persia and Egypt in 332 BCE.

Setpenre Meryamun (Alexander III of Macedon 'the Great')	332–323 BCE
Setpenre Meryamun (Philip Arrhidaeus)	323–317 BCE
Khaibre Setepenamun (Alexander IV)	317–309 BCE

PTOLEMAIC DYNASTY (c. 305–30 BCE)

The Ptolemaic dynasty in Egypt was the last dynasty of ancient Egypt before it became a province of Rome.

Ptolemy I Soter	305–282 BCE
Ptolemy II Philadelphos	284–246 BCE
Arsinoe II	c. 277–270 BCE
Ptolemy III Euergetes	246–222 BCE
Berenice II	244/243–222 BCE
Ptolemy IV Philopater	222–204 BCE
Arsinoe III	220–204 BCE
Ptolemy V Epiphanes	204–180 BCE
Cleopatra I	193–176 BCE
Ptolemy VI Philometor	180–164, 163–145 BCE
Cleopatra II	175–164 BCE, 163–127 BCE and 124–116 BCE
Ptolemy VIII Physcon	171–163 BCE, 144–131 BCE and 127–116 BCE
Ptolemy VII Neos Philopator	145–144 BCE

Cleopatra III	142–131 BCE, 127–107 BCE
Ptolemy Memphites	113 BCE
Ptolemy IX Soter	116–110 BCE
Cleopatra IV	116–115 BCE
Ptolemy X Alexander	110–109 BCE
Berenice III	81–80 BCE
Ptolemy XI Alexander	80 BCE
Ptolemy XII Auletes	80–58 BCE, 55–51 BCE
Cleopatra V Tryphaena	79–68 BCE
Cleopatra VI	58–57 BCE
Berenice IV	58–55 BCE
Cleopatra VII	52–30 BCE
Ptolemy XIII Theos Philopator	51–47 BCE
Arsinoe IV	48–47 BCE
Ptolemy XIV Philopator	47–44 BCE
Ptolemy XV Caesar	44–30 BCE

In 30 BCE, Egypt became a province of the Roman Empire.

ANCIENT GREEK MONARCHS

This list is not exhaustive and dates are approximate. Where dates of rule overlap, emperors either ruled jointly or ruled in opposition to one another. There may also be differences in name spellings between different sources.

Because of the fragmented nature of Greece prior to its unification by Philip II of Macedon, this list includes mythological and existing rulers of Thebes, Athens and Sparta as some of the leading ancient Greek city-states. These different city-states had some common belief in the mythological gods and goddesses of ancient Greece, although their accounts may differ.

KINGS OF THEBES (c. 753-509 BCE)

These rulers are mythological. There is much diversity over who the kings actually were, and the dates they ruled.

Calydnus (son of Uranus)
Ogyges (son of Poseidon, thought to be king of Boeotia or Attica)
Cadmus (Greek mythological hero known as the founder of Thebes, known as Cadmeia until the reign of Amphion and Zethus)
Pentheus (son of Echion, one of the mythological Spartoi, and Agave, daughter of Cadmus)

Polydorus (son of Cadmus and Harmonia, goddess of harmony)

Nycteus (like his brother Lycus, thought to be the son of a Spartoi and a nymph, or a son of Poseidon)

Lycus (brother of Nyceteus)

Labdacus (grandson of Cadmus)

Lycus (second reign as regent for Laius)

Amphion and Zethus (joint rulers and twin sons of Zeus, constructed the city walls of Thebes)

Laius (son of Labdacus, married to Jocasta)

Oedipus (son of Laius, killed his father and married his mother, Jocasta)

Creon (regent after the death of Laius)

Eteocles and Polynices (brothers/sons of Oedipus; killed each other in battle)

Creon (regent for Laodamas)

Laodamas (son of Eteocles)

Thersander (son of Polynices)

Peneleos (regent for Tisamenus)

Tisamenus (son of Thersander)

Autesion (son of Tisamenes)

Damasichthon (son of Peneleos)

Ptolemy (son of Damasichton, 12 century BCE)

Xanthos (son of Ptolemy)

KINGS OF ATHENS

Early legendary kings who ruled before the mythological flood caused by Zeus, which only Deucalion (son of Prometheus) and a few others survived (date unknown).

Periphas (king of Attica, turned into an eagle by Zeus)
Ogyges (son of Poseidon, thought to be king of either Boeotia or Attica)
Actaeus (king of Attica, father-in-law to Cecrops I)

Erechtheid Dynasty (1556–1127 BCE)

Cecrops I (founder and first king of Athens; half-man, half-serpent who married Actaeus' daughter)	1556–1506 BCE
Cranaus	1506–1497 BCE
Amphictyon (son of Deucalion)	1497–1487 BCE
Erichthonius (adopted by Athena)	1487–1437 BCE
Pandion I (son of Erichthonius)	1437–1397 BCE
Erechtheus (son of Pandion I)	1397–1347 BCE
Cecrops II (son of Erechtheus)	1347–1307 BCE
Pandion II (son of Cecrops II)	1307–1282 BCE
Aegeus (adopted by Pandion II, gave his name to the Aegean Sea)	1282–1234 BCE
Theseus (son of Aegeus, killed the minotaur)	1234–1205 BCE
Menestheus (made king by Castor and Pollux when Theseus was in the underworld)	1205–1183 BCE
Demophon (son of Theseus)	1183–1150 BCE
Oxyntes (son of Demophon)	1150–1136 BCE
Apheidas (son of Oxyntes)	1136–1135 BCE
Thymoetes (son of Oxyntes)	1135–1127 BCE

Melanthid Dynasty (1126–1068 BCE)

Melanthus (king of Messenia, fled to Athens when expelled)	1126–1089 BCE
Codrus (last of the semi-mythological Athenian kings)	1089–1068 BCE

LIFE ARCHONS OF ATHENS (1068–753 BCE)

These rulers held public office up until their deaths.

Medon	1068–1048 BCE	Pherecles	864–845 BCE
Acastus	1048–1012 BCE	Ariphon	845–825 BCE
Archippus	1012–993 BCE	Thespieus	824–797 BCE
Thersippus	993–952 BCE	Agamestor	796–778 BCE
Phorbas	952–922 BCE	Aeschylus	778–755 BCE
Megacles	922–892 BCE	Alcmaeon	755–753 BCE
Diognetus	892–864 BCE		

From this point, archons led for a period of 10 years up to 683 BCE, then a period of one year up to 485 CE. Selected important leaders – including archons and tyrants – in this later period are as follows:

SELECTED LATER LEADERS OF ATHENS

Peisistratos 'the Tyrant of Athens'	561, 559–556, 546–527 BCE
Cleisthenes (archon)	525–524 BCE
Themistocles (archon)	493–492 BCE
Pericles	c. 461–429 BCE

KINGS OF SPARTA

These rulers are mythological and are thought to be descendants of the ancient tribe of Leleges. There is much diversity over who the kings actually were, and the dates they ruled.

Lelex (son of Poseidon or Helios, ruled Laconia)   c. 1600 BCE
Myles (son of Lelex, ruled Laconia)   c. 1575 BCE
Eurotas (son of Myles, father of Sparta)   c. 1550 BCE

From the Lelegids, rule passed to the Lacedaemonids when Lacedaemon married Sparta.

Lacedaemon (son of Zeus, husband of Sparta)
Amyklas (son of Lacedaemon)
Argalus (son of Amyklas)
Kynortas (son of Amyklas)
Perieres (son of Kynortas)
Oibalos (son of Kynortas)
Tyndareos (first reign; son of Oibalos, father of Helen of Troy)
Hippocoon (son of Oibalos)
Tyndareos (second reign; son of Oibaos, father of Helen of Troy)

From the Lacedaemons, rule passed to the Atreids when Menelaus married Helen of Troy.

Menelaus (son of Atreus, king of Mycenae, and husband of Helen)   c. 1250 BCE
Orestes (son of Agamemnon, Menelaus' brother)   c. 1150 BCE
Tisamenos (son of Orestes)
Dion   c. 1100 BCE

From the Atreids, rule passed to the Heraclids following war.

Aristodemos (son of Aristomachus, great-great-grandson of Heracles)

Theras (served as regent for Aristodemes' sons, Eurysthenes and Procles)
Eurysthenes   c. 930 BCE

From the Heraclids, rule passed to the Agiads, founded by Agis I. Only major kings during this period are listed here.

Agis I (conceivably the first historical Spartan king)   c. 930–900 BCE
Alcamenes   c. 740–700 BCE, during First Messenian War
Cleomenes I (important leader in the Greek resistance against the Persians)   524 – 490 BCE
Leonidas I (died while leading the Greeks – the 300 Spartans – against the Persians in the Battle of Thermopylae, 480 BCE)   490–480 BCE
Cleomenes III (exiled following the Battle of Sellasia)   c. 235–222 BCE

KINGS OF MACEDON

Argead Dynasty (808–309 BCE)

Karanos	c. 808–778 BCE	Alcetas I	c. 576–547 BCE
Koinos	c. 778–750 BCE	Amyntas I	c. 547–498 BCE
Tyrimmas	c. 750–700 BCE	Alexander I	c. 498–454 BCE
Perdiccas I	c. 700–678 BCE	Alcetas II	c. 454–448 BCE
Argaeus I	c. 678–640 BCE	Perdiccas II	c. 448–413 BCE
Philip I	c. 640–602 BCE	Archelaus I	c. 413–339 BCE
Aeropus I	c. 602–576 BCE	Craterus	c. 399 BCE

Orestes	c. 399–396 BCE	Perdiccas III	c. 368–359 BCE
Aeropus II	c. 399–394/93 BCE	Amyntas IV	c. 359 BCE
Archelaus II	c. 394–393 BCE	Philip II	c. 359–336 BCE
Amyntas II	c. 393 BCE	Alexander III 'the Great' (also King of Persia and Pharaoh of Egypt by end of reign)	c. 336–323 BCE
Pausanias	c. 393 BCE		
Amyntas III	c. 393 BCE; first reign		
Argeus II	c. 393–392 BCE	Philip III	c. 323–317 BCE
Amyntas III	c. 392–370 BCE	Alexander IV	c. 323/317–309 BCE
Alexander II	c. 370–368 BCE		

Note: the Corinthian League or Hellenic League was created by Philip II and was the first time that the divided Greek city-states were unified under a single government.

Post-Argead Dynasty (309–168 BCE, 149–148 BCE)

Cassander	c. 305–297 BCE
Philip IV	c. 297 BCE
Antipater II	c. 297–294 BCE
Alexpander V	c. 297–294 BCE

Antigonid, Alkimachid and Aeacid Dynasties (294–281 BCE)

Demetrius	c. 294–288 BCE
Lysimachus	c. 288–281 BCE
Pyrrhus	c. 288–285 BCE; first reign

Ptolemaic Dynasty (281–279 BCE)

Ptolemy Ceraunus (son of Ptolemy I of Egypt)	c. 281–279 BCE
Meleager	279 BCE

Antipatrid, Antigonid, Aeacid Dynasties, Restored (279–167 BCE)

Antipater	c. 279 BCE
Sosthenes	c. 279–277 BCE
Antigonus II	c. 277–274 BCE; first reign
Pyrrhus	c. 274–272 BCE; second reign
Antigonus II	c. 272–239 BCE; second reign
Demetrius II	c. 239–229 BCE
Antigonus III	c. 229–221 BCE
Philip V	c. 221–179 BCE
Perseus (deposed by Romans)	c. 179–168 BCE
Revolt by Philip VI (Andriskos)	c. 149–148 BCE

SELEUCID DYNASTY (c. 320 BCE–63 CE)

Seleucus I Nicator	c. 320–315, 312–305, 305–281 BCE
Antiochus I Soter	c. 291, 281–261 BCE
Antiochus II Theos	c. 261–246 BCE
Seleucus II Callinicus	c. 246–225 BCE
Seleucus III Ceraunus	c. 225–223 BCE
Antiochus III 'the Great'	c. 223–187 BCE
Seleucus IV Philopator	c. 187–175 BCE
Antiochus (son of Seleucus IV)	c. 175–170 BCE
Antiochus IV Epiphanes	c. 175–163 BCE
Antiochus V Eupater	c. 163–161 BCE
Demetrius I Soter	c. 161–150 BCE
Alexander I Balas	c. 150–145 BCE
Demetrius II Nicator	c. 145–138 BCE; first reign
Antiochus VI Dionysus	c. 145–140 BCE

Diodotus Tryphon	c. 140–138 BCE
Antiochus VII Sidetes	c. 138–129 BCE
Demetrius II Nicator	c. 129–126 BCE; second reign
Alexander II Zabinas	c. 129–123 BCE
Cleopatra Thea	c. 126–121 BCE
Seleucus V Philometor	c. 126/125 BCE
Antiochus VIII Grypus	c. 125–96 BCE
Antiochus IX Cyzicenus	c. 114–96 BCE
Seleucus VI Epiphanes	c. 96–95 BCE
Antiochus X Eusebes	c. 95–92/83 BCE
Demetrius III Eucaerus	c. 95–87 BCE
Antiochus XI Epiphanes	c. 95–92 BCE
Philip I Philadelphus	c. 95–84/83 BCE
Antiochus XII Dionysus	c. 87–84 BCE
Seleucus VII	c. 83–69 BCE
Antiochus XIII Asiaticus	c. 69–64 BCE
Philip II Philoromaeus	c. 65–63 BCE

Ptolemaic Dynasty (305–30 BCE)

The Ptolemaic dynasty in Greece was the last dynasty of Ancient Egypt before it became a province of Rome.

Ptolemy I Soter	305–282 BCE
Ptolemy II Philadelphos	284–246 BCE
Arsinoe II	c. 277–270 BCE
Ptolemy III Euergetes	246–222 BCE
Berenice II	244/243–222 BCE
Ptolemy IV Philopater	222–204 BCE
Arsinoe III	220–204 BCE
Ptolemy V Epiphanes	204–180 BCE

Cleopatra I	193–176 BCE
Ptolemy VI Philometor	180–164, 163–145 BCE
Cleopatra II	175–164 BCE, 163–127 BCE and 124–116 BCE
Ptolemy VIII Physcon	171–163 BCE, 144–131 BCE and 127–116 BCE
Ptolemy VII Neos Philopator	145–144 BCE
Cleopatra III	142–131 BCE, 127–107 BCE
Ptolemy Memphites	113 BCE
Ptolemy IX Soter	116–110 BCE
Cleopatra IV	116–115 BCE
Ptolemy X Alexander	110–109 BCE
Berenice III	81–80 BCE
Ptolemy XI Alexander	80 BCE
Ptolemy XII Auletes	80–58 BCE, 55–51 BCE
Cleopatra V Tryphaena	79–68 BCE
Cleopatra VI	58–57 BCE
Berenice IV	58–55 BCE

In 27 BCE, Caesar Augustus annexed Greece and it became integrated into the Roman Empire.

ANCIENT ROMAN LEADERS

This list is not exhaustive and some dates are approximate. The legitimacy of some rulers is also open to interpretation. Where dates of rule overlap, emperors either ruled jointly or ruled in opposition to one another. There may also be differences in name spellings between different sources.

KINGS OF ROME (753–509 BCE)

Romulus (mythological founder and first ruler of Rome)	753–716 BCE
Numa Pompilius (mythological)	715–672 BCE
Tullus Hostilius (mythological)	672–640 BCE
Ancus Marcius (mythological)	640–616 BCE
Lucius Tarquinius Priscus (mythological)	616–578 BCE
Servius Tullius (mythological)	578–534 BCE
Lucius Tarquinius Superbus (Tarquin the Proud; mythological)	534–509 BCE

ROMAN REPUBLIC (509-27 BCE)

During this period, two consuls were elected to serve a joint one-year term. Therefore, only a selection of significant consuls are included here.

Lucius Junius Brutus (semi-mythological)	509 BCE
Marcus Porcius Cato (Cato the Elder)	195 BCE
Scipio Africanus	194 BCE
Cnaeus Pompeius Magnus (Pompey the Great)	70, 55 and 52 BCE
Marcus Linius Crassus	70 and 55 BCE
Marcus Tullius Cicero	63 BCE
Caius Julius Caesar	59 BCE
Marcus Aemilius Lepidus	46 and 42 BCE
Marcus Antonius (Mark Anthony)	44 and 34 BCE
Marcus Agrippa	37 and 28 BCE

PRINCIPATE (27 BCE-284 CE)

Julio-Claudian Dynasty (27 BCE-68 CE)

Augustus (Caius Octavius Thurinus, Caius Julius Caesar, Imperator Caesar Divi filius)	27 BCE–14 CE
Tiberius (Tiberius Julius Caesar Augustus)	14–37 CE
Caligula (Caius Caesar Augustus Germanicus)	37–41 CE
Claudius (Tiberius Claudius Caesar Augustus Germanicus)	41–54 CE
Nero (Nero Claudius Caesar Augustus Germanicus)	54–68 CE

Year of the Four Emperors (68–69 CE)

Galba (Servius Sulpicius Galba Caesar Augustus)	68–69 CE
Otho (Marcus Salvio Otho Caesar Augustus)	Jan–Apr 69 CE
Vitellius (Aulus Vitellius Germanicus Augustus)	Apr–Dec 69 CE

Note: the fourth Emperor, Vespasian, is listed below.

Flavian Dynasty (66–96 CE)

Vespasian (Caesar Vespasianus Augustus)	69–79 CE
Titus (Titus Caesar Vespasianus Augustus)	79–81 CE
Domitian (Caesar Domitianus Augustus)	81–96 CE

Nerva-Antonine Dynasty (69–192 CE)

Nerva (Nerva Caesar Augustus)	96–98 CE
Trajan (Caesar Nerva Traianus Augustus)	98–117 CE
Hadrian (Caesar Traianus Hadrianus Augustus)	138–161 CE
Antonius Pius (Caesar Titus Aelius Hadrianus Antoninus Augustus Pius)	138–161 CE
Marcus Aurelius (Caesar Marcus Aurelius Antoninus Augustus)	161–180 CE
Lucius Verus (Lucius Aurelius Verus Augustus)	161–169 CE
Commodus (Caesar Marcus Aurelius Commodus Antoninus Augustus)	180–192 CE

Year of the Five Emperors (193 CE)

Pertinax (Publius Helvius Pertinax)	Jan–Mar 193 CE
Didius Julianus (Marcus Didius Severus Julianus)	Mar–Jun 193 CE

Note: Pescennius Niger and Clodius Albinus are generally regarded as usurpers, while the fifth, Septimius Severus, is listed below

ANCIENT KINGS & LEADERS

Severan Dynasty (193–235 CE)

Septimius Severus (Lucius Septimus Severus Pertinax)	193–211 CE
Caracalla (Marcus Aurelius Antonius)	211–217 CE
Geta (Publius Septimius Geta)	Feb–Dec 211 CE
Macrinus (Caesar Marcus Opellius Severus Macrinus Augustus)	217–218 CE
Diadumenian (Marcus Opellius Antonius Diadumenianus)	May–Jun 218 CE
Elagabalus (Caesar Marcus Aurelius Antoninus Augustus)	218–222 CE
Severus Alexander (Marcus Aurelius Severus Alexander)	222–235 CE

Crisis of the Third Century (235–285 CE)

Maximinus 'Thrax' (Caius Julius Verus Maximus)	235–238 CE
Gordian I (Marcus Antonius Gordianus Sempronianus Romanus)	Apr–May 238 CE
Gordian II (Marcus Antonius Gordianus Sempronianus Romanus)	Apr–May 238 CE
Pupienus Maximus (Marcus Clodius Pupienus Maximus)	May–Aug 238 CE
Balbinus (Decimus Caelius Calvinus Balbinus)	May–Aug 238 CE
Gordian III (Marcus Antonius Gordianus)	Aug 238–Feb 244 CE
Philip I 'the Arab' (Marcus Julius Philippus)	244–249 CE
Philip II 'the Younger' (Marcus Julius Severus Philippus)	247–249 CE
Decius (Caius Messius Quintus Traianus Decius)	249–251 CE
Herennius Etruscus (Quintus Herennius Etruscus Messius Decius)	May/Jun 251 CE

Trebonianus Gallus (Caius Vibius Trebonianus Gallus) 251–253 CE
Hostilian (Caius Valens Hostilianus Messius
   Quintus) Jun–Jul 251 CE
Volusianus (Caius Vibius Afinius Gallus
   Veldumnianus Volusianus) 251–253 CE
Aemilian (Marcus Aemilius Aemilianus) Jul–Sep 253 CE
Silbannacus (Marcus Silbannacus) Sep/Oct 253 CE
Valerian (Publius Licinius Valerianus) 253–260 CE
Gallienus (Publius Licinius Egnatius Gallienus) 253–268 CE
Saloninus (Publius Licinius Cornelius
   Saloninus Valerianus) Autumn 260 CE
Claudius II Gothicus (Marcus Aurelius Claudius) 268–270 CE
Quintilus (Marcus Aurelius Claudias
   Quintillus) Apr–May/Jun 270 CE
Aurelian (Luciua Domitius Aurelianus) 270–275 CE
Tacitus (Marcus Claudius Tacitus) 275–276 CE
Florianus (Marcus Annius Florianus) 276–282 CE
Probus (Marcus Aurelius Probus Romanus;
   in opposition to Florianus) 276–282 CE
Carus (Marcus Aurelias Carus) 282–283 CE
Carinus (Marcus Aurelius Carinus) 283–285 CE
Numerian (Marcus Aurelius Numerianus) 283–284 CE

DOMINATE (284-610)

Tetrarchy (284–324)

Diocletian 'Iovius' (Caius Aurelius Valerius Diocletianus) 284–305
Maximian 'Herculius' (Marcus Aurelius Valerius
   Maximianus; ruled the western provinces) 286–305/late 306–308

ANCIENT KINGS & LEADERS

Galerius (Caius Galerius Valerius Maximianus; ruled the eastern provinces)	305–311
Constantius I 'Chlorus' (Marcus Flavius Valerius Constantius; ruled the western provinces)	305–306
Severus II (Flavius Valerius Severus; ruled the western provinces)	306–307
Maxentius (Marcus Aurelius Valerius Maxentius)	306–312
Licinius (Valerius Licinanus Licinius; ruled the western, then the eastern provinces)	308–324
Maximinus II 'Daza' (Aurelius Valerius Valens; ruled the western provinces)	316–317
Martinian (Marcus Martinianus; ruled the western provinces)	Jul–Sep 324

Constantinian Dynasty (306–363)

Constantine I 'the Great' (Flavius Valerius Constantinus; ruled the western provinces then whole)	306–337
Constantine II (Flavius Claudius Constantinus)	337–340
Constans I (Flavius Julius Constans)	337–350
Constantius II (Flavius Julius Constantius)	337–361
Magnentius (Magnus Magnentius)	360–353
Nepotianus (Julius Nepotianus)	Jun 350
Vetranio	Mar–Dec 350
Julian 'the Apostate' (Flavius Claudius Julianus)	361–363
Jovian (Jovianus)	363–364

Valentinianic Dynasty (364–392)

Valentinian I 'the Great' (Valentinianus)	364–375
Valens (ruled the eastern provinces)	364–378

Procopius (revolted against Valens)	365–366
Gratian (Flavius Gratianus Augustus; ruled the western provinces then whole)	375–383
Magnus Maximus	383–388
Valentinian II (Flavius Valentinianus)	388–392
Eugenius	392–394

Theodosian Dynasty (379–457)

Theodosius I 'the Great' (Flavius Theodosius)	Jan 395
Arcadius	383–408
Honorius (Flavius Honorius)	395–432
Constantine III	407–411
Theodosius II	408–450
Priscus Attalus; usurper	409–410
Constantius III	Feb–Sep 421
Johannes	423–425
Valentinian III	425–455
Marcian	450–457

Last Emperors in the West (455–476)

Petronius Maximus	Mar–May 455
Avitus	455–456
Majorian	457–461
Libius Severus (Severus III)	461–465
Anthemius	467–472
Olybrius	Apr–Nov 472
Glycerius	473–474
Julius Nepos	474–475
Romulus Augustulus (Flavius Momyllus Romulus Augustulus)	475–476

Leonid Dynasty (East, 457–518)

Leo I (Leo Thrax Magnus)	457–474
Leo II	Jan–Nov 474
Zeno	474–475
Basiliscus	475–476
Zeno (second reign)	476–491
Anastasius I 'Dicorus'	491–518

Justinian Dynasty (East, 518–602)

Justin I	518–527
Justinian I 'the Great' (Flavius Justinianus, Petrus Sabbatius)	527–565
Justin II	565–578
Tiberius II Constantine	578–582
Maurice (Mauricius Flavius Tiberius)	582–602
Phocas	602–610

LATER EASTERN EMPERORS (610–1059)

Heraclian Dynasty (610–695)

Heraclius	610–641
Heraclius Constantine (Constantine III)	Feb–May 641
Heraclonas	Feb–Nov 641
Constans II Pogonatus ('the Bearded')	641–668
Constantine IV	668–685
Justinian II	685–695

Twenty Years' Anarchy (695–717)

Leontius	695–698
Tiberius III	698–705

Justinian II 'Rhinometus' (second reign)	705–711
Philippicus	711–713
Anastasius II	713–715
Theodosius III	715–717

Isaurian Dynasty (717–803)

Leo III 'the Isaurian'	717–741
Constantine V	741–775
Artabasdos	741/2–743
Leo V 'the Khazar'	775–780
Constantine VI	780–797
Irene	797–802

Nikephorian Dynasty (802–813)

Nikephoros I 'the Logothete'	802–811
Staurakios	July–Oct 811
Michael I Rangabé	813–820

Amorian Dynasty (820–867)

Michael II 'the Amorian'	820–829
Theophilos	829–842
Theodora	842–856
Michael III 'the Drunkard'	842–867

Macedonian Dynasty (867–1056)

Basil I 'the Macedonian'	867–886
Leo VI 'the Wise'	886–912
Alexander	912–913
Constantine VII Porphyrogenitus	913–959
Romanos I Lecapenus	920–944

ANCIENT KINGS & LEADERS

Romanos II	959–963
Nikephoros II Phocas	963–969
John I Tzimiskes	969–976
Basil II 'the Bulgar-Slayer'	976–1025
Constantine VIII	1025–1028
Romanus III Argyros	1028–1034
Michael IV 'the Paphlagonian'	1034–1041
Michael V Kalaphates	1041–1042
Zoë Porphyrogenita	Apr–Jun 1042
Theodora Porphyrogenita	Apr–Jun 1042
Constantine IX Monomachos	1042–1055
Theodora Porphyrogenita (second reign)	1055–1056
Michael VI Bringas 'Stratioticus'	1056–1057
Isaab I Komnenos	1057–1059

COLLECTOR'S EDITIONS

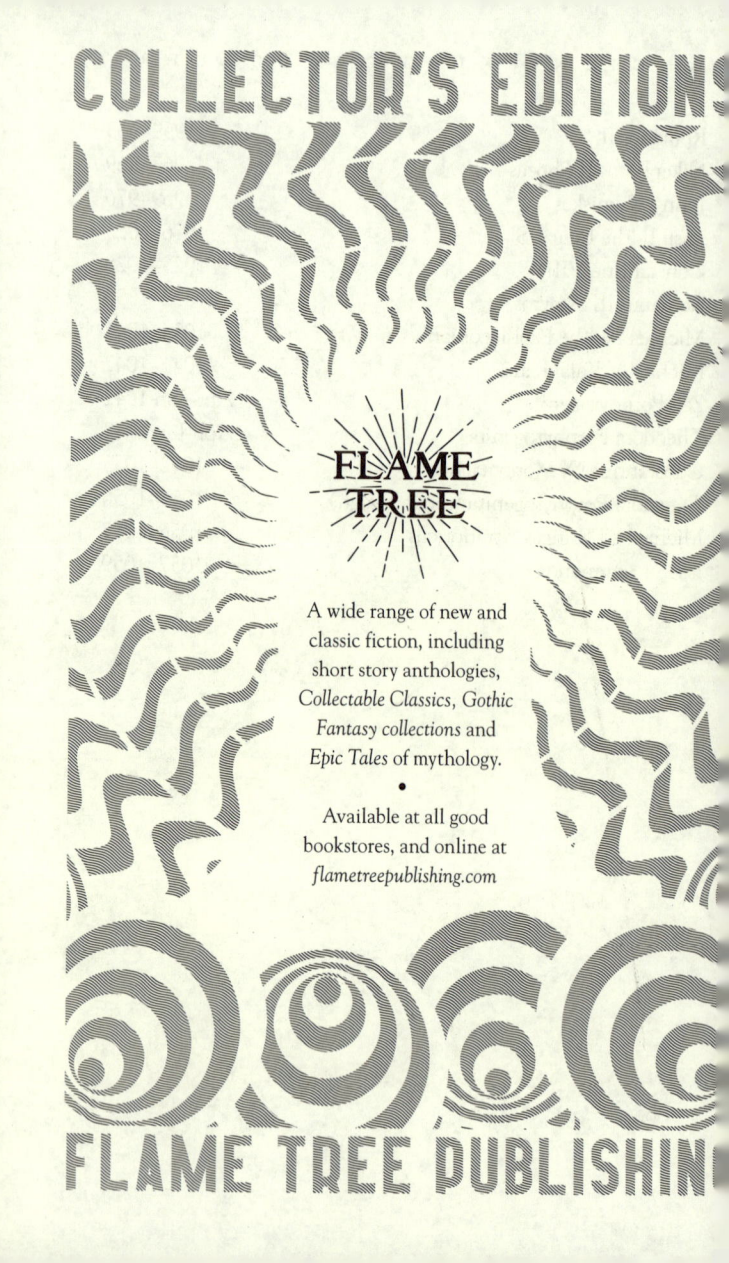

FLAME TREE

A wide range of new and classic fiction, including short story anthologies, *Collectable Classics*, *Gothic Fantasy* collections and *Epic Tales* of mythology.

•

Available at all good bookstores, and online at
flametreepublishing.com

FLAME TREE PUBLISHING